CW01645578

Robert Sterling's

THE LOVE CHRONICLES OF A VERY FUSSY MAN

Michael Terence Publishing

First published in paperback by
Michael Terence Publishing in 2019
www.mtp.agency

Copyright © 2019 Robert Sterling

Robert Sterling has asserted his right to be identified
as the author of this work in accordance with the
Copyright, Designs and Patents Act 1988

ISBN 9781913289225

All rights reserved. No part of this publication may be reproduced,
stored in a retrieval system, or transmitted,
in any form or by any means, electronic, mechanical,
photocopying, recording or otherwise,
without the prior permission of the publisher

Cover images
Copyright © Валерий Качаев

Cover design
Copyright © 2019 Michael Terence Publishing

Although not entirely a work of fiction; names, characters, businesses, places, events and incidents are either the products of the author's imagination or used in a fictitious manner. Any resemblance to actual persons, living or dead, or actual events is purely coincidental. Any opinions expressed are the author's alone. This includes dating websites, films, places and any other content herein.
All film ratings quoted from the International Movie Database (IMDb) were accurate as of August 11, 2019.

This book is dedicated to Eric's mum and dad and friends for their love and unyielding support and for having had to put up with Eric along his rather turbulent path.

This book is also dedicated to all those who are too shy or lacking the confidence to meet a potential love-interest in their lives. Everyone is in the same boat so stop worrying about shit and just go for it!

About Robert Sterling

Robert Hannibal Sterling was the middle child born to (Big) Ted and Jemima in Ouagadougou, Burkina Faso, during their lifelong crusade caring for sick animals. Stationed at the country's Chimpanzee and Ungulate National Treatment Sanctuary for almost two decades, Robert became tired of mucking out stables and having monkey-shit thrown at him so migrated to his parents' native homeland of England aged 19.

After setting up in Chipping Sodbury, Robert found work as the kit-man for the local women's football team; The Sodbury Sirens, where he met his future wife, Floella, who played centre-back (and one of only two players who weren't lesbian). As Robert was impressed with her as he watched her dribbling out of her own box, he got down on bended knee in front of the hotdog van and 14 home supporters and Floella said yes.

Expecting their first child, Robert was forced to get himself a part-time job in the week spray painting pubic hair on blow-up dolls, in order to make ends meet.

However, Robert's real passion was for writing; having kept a diary throughout his earlier years and he was therefore keen to make something of his literary talents.

Robert received his lucky break one day, when the head of a publishing company came across his scribblings, whilst picking up some nipple-clamps from the sex shop where he worked.

That chance meeting sprouted a professional partnership and Robert went on to write his first book; 'Shit on the Villa' in 2017; telling the story of a twitcher on a year-long sabbatical in Marbella where the avifaunal population seemed to have contracted a bad case of diarrhoea. Set against the backdrop of Aston Villa's first relegation for almost thirty years, the book was an instant success with birdwatchers and football fans alike and won Robert the prestigious 'Golden Inkpot' award for best literary newcomer.

Other works were soon forthcoming and included 'There's Only One Djamolidine Mirgarifanovich Abdoujaparov', paying homage to the Uzbekistani sprint cyclist and 'He Had No Right To Score From There'; a look at some of the most ridiculous and nonsensical clichés uttered by commentators since football began in 1992.

Nowadays, Robert lives in Hemel Hempstead with Floella and their three children; Humpty, Hamble and (Little) Ted.

Introduction

When I first met Eric back in 2018, I thought there'd been a mix-up and Tom Hardy had appeared instead. As I watched him holding the door to the Costa Coffee, for a woman trying to exit with a child's buggy, he tipped his head and smiled at her to acknowledge her gratitude and then proceeded to stare back at her arse as she left. His accentuated smile was now replaced with a facial expression not dissimilar to that of a wine taster; having gargled with a mouthful before deciding it was definitely a good vintage. That's how much alike Eric was aesthetically with Mr Hardy... well more the incarnation of Tom in his Peaky Blinders role than of anything more palatable and desirable within the female fraternity.

Having shaken hands and joined me at my table, it was clear to see that Eric was also very particular; wiping the already clean-looking surface with a serviette before resting his forearms. He then began to give me his in-depth account of the veritable catalogue of women that had shaped his personal life.

Throughout the conversation; the thing about him that stood out was his demeanour; not big-headed or pretentious and despite what came over at times as him being rather fussy (bordering on shallow) with his staunch list of prerequisites that he looked for in a woman; he never came across as a twat. Eric was self-deprecating and humble; a genuinely down-to-earth guy who knew he wasn't perfect by the longest piece of chalk in the box but that's what made him more interesting and likeable as a result. I was always guaranteed an entertaining time whenever we met up.

As I was ultimately going to chart Eric's love story in print; it soon became apparent that I would need to record our conversations as there was so much detail to take in; and that my shorthand was just not able to keep up with. After meeting Eric frequently over a six-month period and having gotten to know him pretty well over that time, gaining an understanding of his opinions and style and deciphering his complex history timeline; I set out writing 'The Love Chronicles'. I hope you enjoy.

Robert Sterling

Chapter One

El Leggo Grande

Growing up, Eric had suffered from a profound lack of confidence with the fairer sex. A large reason (and I use the word large purposefully) was his right leg, or 'el leggo grande' as one young foreign brat felt the need to spout out to his extensive family who were all lounging around the hotel swimming pool in Kos or at least that's what it sounded like to Eric. The curly-haired olive-skinned little chubster gesticulated in Eric's direction and his fog-horn voice echoed off every cement-built apartment block within a 100-mile radius. Eric realised that later pushing him into the pool <u>was</u> infantile but felt it warranted such recompense on this occasion and besides; with nobody else looking, it was a textbook manoeuvre.

Despite Eric having been put through every conceivable test and scanner known to man, the so-called leading specialists in the field of vascular surgery had found it difficult at first to pinpoint why his right leg was vastly greater in size than his other. A number of theories had been put forward over the years; mostly by Eric himself. At first, he remembered a serious dead leg he'd suffered whilst playing 5-a-side football in his youth, wondering whether this had caused internal damage to his vascular circuitry. Another idea he had was perhaps the sweat glands in his leg were not working under his body's thermo-regulation and therefore unable to release any fluid.

The medics finally conceded that the most reasonable cause of the gargantuan leg was that the lymph channels, situated in Eric's groinal area, whose primary purpose was to transport lymphatic fluids containing immune cells, were damaged and not functioning properly. The liquids that his body was trying to pump back up his leg without his conscious effort were being restricted and as a result, there was a greater volume of fluid retained which appeared as swelling. There was no reason as to why Eric's lymphatic system was not operating normally, other than to accept his body wasn't perfect.

Specialists had mentioned there was a 5% chance of fixing the problem using surgery, fitting a conduit to help bypass the damaged vessel, thereby helping to correct the natural flow. As 5% didn't seem like very good odds to Eric (like Burnley beating Liverpool in the Premier League) and given the condition hadn't prevented him from doing anything up to that point, then Eric chose to decline. He accepted his aesthetic peculiarity, hoping the problem would either correct itself or the odds on a successful surgery would rise dramatically in the future.

Eric realised that the one thing that had remained a constant throughout the twenty years of his adulthood was his big leg. Extremely conscious of his abnormality, Eric had been amazed that not one of the girls he'd slept with had ever noticed it; or if they had, never mentioned it, which Eric found hard to believe. He did, however, concede that when <u>he</u> got naked with a girl, especially for the first (and in most cases last) time, then there were other parts of the anatomy more keenly anticipated than the legs. On that basis, it was probably correct to hypothesise that the same applied to her.

It was only on the rare occasions that a relationship ensued and progressed long enough to warrant it, that Eric would finally point out his asymmetrical lower half. By then he would feel confident enough to know that unless he had gotten her all wrong, then she wouldn't make a hasty dash for the exit on hearing the news. Prior to this, Eric had been military-like with his disrobing; turning off the lights first, changing in another room or learning to remove his full-length compression stocking in tandem with his trousers if denied the first two options.

Looking at family photographs from holidays gone by, it was noticeable that his leg seemed to be a little larger than its neighbour for the first time in May 1992, a fifteen-year-old Eric sat atop a railing at a Cape Canaveral Space Port lookout in his then (apparently) fashionable Bermuda shorts, the shuttle launch site purposely captured over his shoulder in the distance.

Yes, every day for around 20 years, putting on a compression stocking had been as normal to Eric as donning his undercrackers and socks. He was now wearing the next generation stocking no-less; black in colour and with a nifty rubber-ribbed opening which meant, theoretically, it would cling to his gigantic right thigh and prevent it from slipping during the rigours of his day.

Eric had laughed his ball bags off when he was first introduced to vascular hosiery, the nurse not only deathly serious that nobody would tell he was wearing it because it was skin-coloured but also saying, 'you don't wear shorts that often anyway'. Eric found this a slightly strange assumption for her to be making, having only met him about twenty minutes earlier.

The fact of the matter was, the stocking was a kind of sandy beige so if anybody had skin that colour, let alone no markings, hairs or any superficial detail whatsoever, then they were inflicted with a far worse medical condition than he. Eric's conclusion was both decisive and swift; from that day forth he would not be wearing shorts in public ever again.

Chapter Two

Eric's Complex Brain

Eric was a self-confessed mid-level obsessive-compulsive and pretty hung up about having things in a particular order; like Hercule Poirot they had to be symmetrical or even wherever possible, otherwise it just annoyed the shit out of him. For example, he could never have the digital temperature control readout in his car set to an odd number or including half a degree.

It was extremely ironic; therefore, that the one thing Eric could do nothing about was his own unsymmetrical lower half. It had been suggested that perhaps his passion for symmetry had been due to him being a twin but then Eric was non-identical (fraternal) and looked nothing like his brother. It was, however, clear that symmetry was a characteristic and basic requirement that most people subconsciously assessed when finding a partner and well documented that the trait was linked to what many defined as beauty.

Eric was also OCD about things he read or saw, unable to let things ride if there was a continuity error or a glaring factual inaccuracy. The biggest example of this was the film Gremlins (7.2/10 IMDb). It annoyed him that the third and final rule of looking after Gizmo had been to 'never feed him after midnight' but with no stipulation given as to what time the eating curfew ended. With this vitally important piece of information missing, then as far as Eric was concerned then any time in the day would surely contravene this.

Another popular gripe he had was with panellists or judges on talent-shows, the uber-popular format having diluted TV schedules for many a year. Eric was only really interested in the auditions (you too?) as it was here that you would witness both the very best and worst exhibits of talent on offer. However, it annoyed the shinola out of him, when after someone had raised the roof following a meteoric performance; the judges, left with hard-ons and smiling like raging mentalists and having given a standing ovation, would still utter the words, 'but we still need to vote'.

'Oh fuck off!' Eric would holler at the tellybox and roll his eyes so far that he could actually check-out the inside of his own cranium.

One of the drawbacks to a logical and methodical brain was that he found it almost impossible to suspend his disbelief and with the advent of next-generation CGI, then as far as he was concerned, modern films were far too incredulous and puerile.

Eric was meticulous when it came to planning things; anything, from a trip away or to buying new home furnishings; he left nothing to chance. Yes, he realised that others could see this as him perhaps living too much of a rigid life, not just letting things take their natural course but Eric could not rest easy to have things up in the air and jeopardising his control over his surroundings. It was in his genes and that was the way it was. Organisation was key. I suppose you could say he was the biggest control freak imaginable and woe betide anybody leaving a used teaspoon on the chopping board!

Yes, it was fair to say that Eric was a little bit weird in this regard and also had rather an eclectic taste too, probably the only person that fancied Jonny Briggs' sister for a start (you don't remember Jonny Briggs?) and would listen to the Best Of Julio Iglesias through choice.

In a world of ever-increasing variety and personal opportunity, Eric noted that there was an abundance of initiatives to champion diversity; their aim to promote awareness and inclusion for all. To him, this was akin to a menu at a restaurant becoming larger and larger as people's preferences evolved.

However, despite the increasingly extensive and varied choice to be found on the menu nowadays, Eric definitely remained an option underneath the section entitled 'traditional fayre', like eggs on toast or toad in the hole. He wasn't boring by any means; far from it; but in respect of his demographic pigeon-hole in society, he was certainly rather vanilla in essence; a single, white, cisgender, heterosexual, non-religious, able-bodied, middle-aged male. He was the definitive definition of a pair of camouflage pantaloons of the demographic world; nothing about Eric was mildly different or stood out (with his clothes on) making him potentially the least employable person in his mind, his box-ticking in the 'about you' section on application forms looking like the default settings after he'd completed the task.

Chapter Three

The Early Years

Eric was a sociable sort but didn't mind admitting that when he was out, he didn't really want to make it look like he was interested in a girl for fear of looking desperate. There was also his confidence issue; not just his big leg but having worn glasses throughout his youth, he'd always felt it was the reason why girls had simply not been interested in him. Ironically, Eric could tell that there was a definite stigma attached to his own stigmatism and wearing glasses was definitely looked upon (by those not requiring them) with an almost air of disapproval. In addition to this, it didn't help that Eric was thinner than Olive Oyl after a low-carb diet and a sponsored 24-hour fast.

As a result, Eric managed nothing in the way of experience with the opposite sex throughout his schooling years, discounting a couple of snogs with girls from his class at occasional birthday parties as a result of the perennial game of spin the bottle.

Contact lenses had been by far the greatest thing to happen to Eric and sparked the biggest single turning point in his life at the age of seventeen, even more important than online dating would turn out to be later. This was not least because it allowed him to participate in sports without disadvantage (previously having to wear an elasticated tricolour band that fastened to his specs and fitted tightly around the back of his head and basically made him look like a twat) but now his confidence soared to new uncharted levels.

Still, given Eric's tussle with an inherent lack of confidence from his early years, he was never big-headed or indeed vain about his newfound appearance, having also seemingly filled out enormously overnight after finishing sixth form and embarking on life at University. He still felt the idea of being knocked back by a girl (on the very rare occasion he did make the effort to chat one up) was a feeling he could really do without, being a sensitive soul and taking things very personally, especially as this was the girl in effect criticising what he looked like.

Having grown up with his twin brother, Ernie, you'd have to surmise that given the available clues on offer, Eric had certainly not shown any natural acumen for a role as a detective or a contestant on Through the Keyhole. 'Let's take a look at the evidence' said in my best Loyd Grossman Bostonian tones. There were the Sindy Dolls, My Little Ponies, Care Bears, Wuzzles, a propensity for playing with the Ram Man figurine in He-Man and the Masters of the Universe, staying up after midnight to watch Eastern European films on C4 in the late 80s (which were partial to a bit of full-frontal nudity of both sexes), a stash of male-oriented porn mags under the wardrobe and a dildo wrapped in a sock inside their shared underwear drawer. 'Hmmm; I wonder if he could be gay?' To be fair, the last two only came to light after his brother had come out.

Yes, despite having shared a room and bunk bed for nigh on 15 years, it only seemed tres obvious about his twin's sexual preference <u>after</u> his announcement, which came at their nan and granddad's Golden wedding anniversary celebration in the 'big room' of a local social club. Not that he got up on stage and asked for everybody's attention; no, the news began percolating its way through the ranks of family and friends who were dispersing into the foyer and out into the car park at the end of the evening.

It seemed Eric was the last person to find out on account of his twin worrying how his 'closest' brother would take the news, believing him to be staunchly homophobic and likely to disown him. Ernie was pleasantly surprised and relieved that there were no such ramifications and it was a lot different anyway now as the pair had taken their own paths for the first time; Eric to read mathematics at Leeds and Ernie to study fashion and design in Nottingham… well I did say the clues were obvious!

Ernie's sexual orientation had also given Eric pause for thought regarding the possible cause of his big leg. Eric's favourite suggestion, which had been greeted with great jollity on all sides, was that perhaps his levels of testosterone had and continued to cause the abnormal swelling of the appendage. Eric thought it scientifically plausible that he may have conversely absorbed more than a normal foetus's fill of the hormone whilst in the womb, if his twin was harbouring a distinct lack of it.

After Ernie had harnessed the courage to proclaim who he really was to everyone, Eric remembered how ridiculous a lot of guys, who knew both him and Ernie through school, had reacted when he saw them in a social setting not long afterwards. 'I know he's gay but I still think your brother's ace' some of them exclaimed. This angered Eric as Ernie was Ernie and the fact he was gay was not something he felt they needed to highlight as part of their critique.

Eric was beginning to worry that others may think he too was travelling on the other bus if he wasn't seen with a girl on his arm soon; especially as they were twins (although fraternal, the only thing it seemed they hadn't had to share in their lives was an ovary). Eric remembered being asked by a good looking girl, whose father was the landlord of a pub he used to frequent, if he had a girlfriend. On confirming he didn't then imagine Eric's surprise when the next thing that came from her mouth was 'are you gay?'

Eric was about to put the record straight; well a lot more to do with wanting a girlfriend for sexual reasons than to prove to others he wasn't a sausage jockey (or Scottish jockey as his late brother used to say, his obvious misinterpretation having stuck with him for years. Eric still found it amusing to think that any Scottish male who chose to ride horses was notably a raging homosexual in his brother's mind).

Despite feeling more confident physically, Eric's lack of experience was still holding him back and he took this continued lack of confidence to uni with him (packed in his suitcase). He didn't manage to have sex whilst there either, despite chances presenting themselves on a couple of occasions. The first time, with Eric having made some progress and ended up semi-clad in bed with a girl from the darts club (she was not as manly as that sounds apparently) he'd resorted to tying the strings on his cerise Liverpool away shorts so tight that she couldn't slip her hand down to Eric's trouser snake as try as she might and so gave up trying.

The other occasion took place when one of the other lads in Eric's shared flat had invited his girlfriend up to stay and she brought along her friend for the ride. As everyone had gone out together that evening and the other girl having taken a shine to Eric, she managed to infiltrate his room and end up in his bed when they returned, aware that she didn't want to play the gooseberry with her friend and boyfriend.

The girl was a veritable tigress, oozing confidence and very much at the opposite end of the sex experience scale to Eric. It was a relief, therefore, that he shared a room with his best mate, Ant, whose presence at the other side of the room, tucked up in bed 'asleep', provided Eric with an excuse not to participate in any slap and tickle under the auspices of respect for him; although had Eric been a smidge more confident then he perhaps may have signed up for a bit of ninja sex.

No, the sex education video he remembered vividly in the physics lab at school aged 12, watching a naked family enjoying a game of beach ball between the dunes, had somehow been wasted on Eric. Apart from the few incidents of heavy petting (not in the deep end) as mentioned, Eric hadn't exactly accomplished much with the opposite sex and certainly not enough to write home about. It was whilst readapting to home-life post-uni with a much more confident demeanour, however, that Eric was champing at the bit to do something about it and had a burning desire to finally play catch-up.

Chapter Four

Practice Makes Perfect

Equipped with his newfound confidence, Eric was now ready to go out into the big wide world and sew his wild oats… well, within a three-mile radius of his home anyway. He lived with his parents and his eldest brother and not going on to pass his driving test until he was 27 (on his second attempt) he was not keen to start shimmying up alongside musty smelling octogenarians on the bus so ideally any romantic escapades needed to be within walking distance.

Eric and his mates began frequenting the Blue Parrot pub for three reasons; one, it was kind of equidistant for all parties concerned (a two-mile walk for Eric or a hell for leather sprint come the end of a night to ensure he made it home for Private Dancer, a rather cheesy striptease show on an even cheesier cable channel, which he had come across when searching for nudity late one evening). Two, it had four fantastic league standard pool tables and three, the clientele, although a little primitive in nature, were a lot younger than could be found at alternative venues, with a healthy spattering of females to boot.

It was whilst ensconced in a game of pool with his mates that Eric's love radar picked up its first target. She was a very shy thirty-something, hanging back in the shadows away from the glare of the lamps, which shone down over the green baize, illuminating the field of play and periphery. It was obvious that she had no confidence whatsoever, reticent and standing well away from her three friends, who could not have been more different, making conversation easily and readily interacting with those around them. In fact, one of her so-called friends was the complete apotheosis of Eric's worst nightmare of the female form; short-haired, multiple ear piercings resembling a fork prong packed with spaghetti hoops, tattooed arms and with all the femininity of Pat Butcher.

She'd introduced herself to Eric by reaching between his legs whilst he was bent over cueing for his next shot and grabbed his meat 'n' two with a certain voracity that caused him to react immediately, standing bolt upright, alarmed at what had just happened. There was nothing he could do about it after the event as she was technically a 'woman' and she and her friends found the whole thing hilarious.

Eric was pretty angry, although did his best not to show it. I mean it was tantamount to sexual assault and Eric knew if he'd been caught slipping his hand between a girl's legs and feeling her undercarriage in the pub then the ramifications would be far different and probably include a swift trip outside and end with a search for his teeth in the car park.

Most people thought it was funny, except that was for the quiet girl, who Eric had learnt was called Abbie. Her vulnerability was a great turn on to Eric, who knew he did not want to end up with a self-assured gobshite who had obviously handled more cock than a French butcher for his first foray into Sexsville. This girl seemed like the perfect choice to help hone his skills, Eric a wannabe fighter pilot getting to grips with manoeuvres in a highly realistic simulator before having the confidence to handle the real thing.

Eric knew he could be the worst shag this girl had ever had without fear of reprisal or being ridiculed by the wider fraternity as she was just too soft, too shy and too far removed from the social hub for any bad review to spread like wildfire. This was a massive stroke of luck for Eric, whose last bit of luck involved him picking out his mother's raffle ticket at a school summer fete when he was nine years old. He was genuinely excited at his prospects with Abbie but realised he was getting way ahead of himself… there was still plenty that could scupper his plan… Eric would have to be patient and wait to see her a few more times.

A couple more weeks passed and a couple more sightings later and it was noticeable that Abbie was becoming more relaxed in her surroundings and certainly less shy. 'Abbie fancies you Eric!' one of her friends exclaimed from across the pool table. 'Bingo bango bongo!' he thought, realising he was now firmly in the driving seat. It was time for him to make his move.

As the evening wore on, Eric gradually made his way over towards Abbie and started conversing, having had the occasional word with her over the last few weeks. She didn't drink and it had become obvious to Eric that her so-called friends were just using her for a free lift more than for her entertainment value.

It just so happened that Abbie was leaving before closing time on that particular evening and not tasked with dropping anyone off as her friends were all moving on to a nightclub. Eric saw his chance and running after Abbie, he caught up with her as she sat in her car outside, just about to set off. Although she had come out of her shell somewhat since Eric had first noticed her, the idea of Eric coming back to hers was still a big step. However, Eric could charm the birds down from the trees when he wanted and it wasn't long before he was sat in the shotgun seat and heading home with her.

Chapter Five

Chopped Liver

On arrival, Eric noticed that Abbie appeared to live in a council house, the area not the most salubrious but ultimately as he wasn't looking for anything long-term then it wasn't such a biggie. On entering the house it soon became apparent that Abbie also had a dog and not just any old dog; no, a fourteen stone Rottweiler and strangely still with its whole tail intact. This wasn't panning out quite as Eric had daydreamt.

On asking to use her facilities, Eric's trip upstairs then revealed a further oddity in the shape of a Stannah stair-lift, having to squeeze passed it before ascending to the bog. Eric assumed that the lift may have already been in situ previous to Abbie's tenure so imagine his surprise when she confirmed it was for her and had followed an accident she'd had falling off a horse, having been registered disabled as a result. 'Fucking great' Eric thought knowing that the fellas would have a field day when they heard about that; the girl he was seeing disabled and having a stair-lift to carry her to bed, giving them the impression she was a great deal older than he. This was before the Phoenix Nights comedy series so Eric couldn't even replicate 'the things I'm gonna do to you' gag sat in the chair holding Abbie's hand as they slowly ascended to the bedroom.

It wasn't long before Eric was lying on top of Abbie on her two-seater couch, the lights purposely turned off by her and the massive pooch with the big pointy teeth and phlegm dripping from its mouth housed in the kitchen behind a baby gate some six feet away. It wasn't the best set-up in the world but it appeared Abbie's bedroom must have been a mess as she was reluctant to offer Eric a more comfortable option for the night.

The more he discovered about her the more he realised that she was certainly not what he was looking for at all. However, it was now or never he thought and as the situation wasn't conducive to stripping off completely, he pulled his pants to his knees, one benefit of the darkness at least shrouding his big leg from Abbie's gaze. He pulled her knickers down in a gentle fashion, which felt like big cotton efforts and not anything fancy. It was time… Eric jockeyed for position and then 'hello' he was in.

The first thing he thought, apart from how enjoyable it felt, was how he now appreciated why soldiers had put their cock in a jam-jar of chopped liver to recreate the experience, although Eric stressed he'd not gone to quite such measures previously. Yes, it was short and sweet and yes there was little in the way of foreplay but given the surroundings and circumstances it was a simple case of job done and Eric had finally done it.

Eric did see Abbie a couple more times after that and got to test out her bed. However, during those further occasions, Eric had naturally learnt a little more about her and some of it was just a little too disconcerting; not least the fact that Abbie had admitted to stabbing her ex-boyfriend with a screwdriver after he'd told her he wanted to split up.

It seemed that rather than press charges, he'd allowed her to take him to A&E, telling the medical staff that he'd slipped in the garage and fallen on a tool. 'What, 13 times?' Eric had said jokingly, although slightly perturbed at the idea that Abbie was obviously not all there and that he could be next. Yep, it was definitely time for Eric to bail out but before he did so he made a mental note; 'ensure to wear my trainers when giving her the bad news.'

Abbie took it pretty well, which Eric could see was due to her not being confident enough for a relationship and happier to be on her own at that stage. She even dropped Eric off and sat there in her car crying as she watched him follow the bend in the street and disappear out of sight.

One thing that Eric had done during their brief interlude was to instil some confidence in Abbie, which was quite ironic given Eric's own lack of it for many a year. It turned out that she kept two horses on someone's land a couple of miles away and she'd recently noticed that one of her old school friends appeared to live at one of the adjoining properties. She'd asked Eric what she should do as she was unsure as to whether the girl would a) remember her and b) want anything to do with her even if she did.

Eric's advice had been instant, recommending to Abbie that she should just knock on her door and find out, rather than have doubts or regrets running through her head in the future. Eric could see that Abbie did not have many friends and this seemed like a perfect opportunity for her to be repatriated with someone who she notably thought a lot of.

The last thing Abbie had said to Eric before he got out of her car and walked out of her life, was that she'd followed his advice and approached her old school friend. It turned out that she was also pleased to see Abbie and they were planning to meet for a catch-up, especially as she too had her own horses. This was great news for Eric, now feeling slightly less guilty about the whole break-up situation. This wasn't the only time that Eric made like the Littlest Hobo though, playing a cameo role in a girl's life and moving on after helping her out in some way as there would be further examples along his relationship path.

Chapter Six

Thick as Pig Shit

Now with Abbie a distant memory, Eric continued frequenting 'the Blue' and given him and his chums were all likeable, savoury types, then they soon became part of the rubric of the pub; the landlord and his wife (landlady) even permitting them to remain there after hours for the occasional lock-in (although Eric and his friends weren't always that arsed to stay out for too long and get hammered).

As part of being accepted into the class of 1999, that meant Eric got to know the 'crew' including the young fillies, who would spend most of their free-time there also. The majority of the girls seemed a little too uncouth for Eric's liking it had to be said and the longer he continued to drink there, he noticed the nucleus of the 'locals' seemed to be swapping partners from one week to the next, like some cheap soap opera (think channel 4 or 5).

This whole carry-on put Eric off even more, although to be fair it wasn't like he had to bat them off with his pool cue. Eric never made it look like he was interested; that was just Eric. He had heard that girls preferred fellas who didn't look arsed with them at all; the mysterious and aloof types apparently, which was just as well as Eric was not confident enough to chat them up in any case. Then one evening Eric's hopes were finally realised.

Becky was a naturally big girl, quite broad and almost as tall as him in heels (Becky that was and not Eric wearing the heels). She had long auburn hair and definitely fell under the banner of curvy, although you could never describe her as fat; perhaps fuller figure. Basically, she had massive boobs, Eric's favourite part of the female anatomy. The bigger the better was Eric's opinion of the matter (think Gary and Wyatt creating their dream woman in Weird Science – 6.6/10 IMDb) which was probably due to the fact that size was the most obvious physical indicator to tell the sexes apart. Eric was very aware that he shared this opinion with all of mankind, unable to recall a time when he'd overheard another fella saying

'I love a small pair of tits me'.

One of the other girls, also called Becky (who was much better looking in Eric's opinion although waaay too far up her own arse) had come over and mentioned that her friend was keen on him. Despite not having wished to join the 'swingers' club that seemed to be in operation, Eric couldn't help but think back to the advice his elder brother had given him a few years earlier; namely that 'every hole's a goal'. Taking this on board and remembering that he was still very much playing catch- up, Eric decided to give it a go… I mean what did he have to lose?… and besides he thought, 'just look at those tits'.

I guess you could say that Becky was Eric's first real girlfriend, the 'relationship' lasting a few months, either side of a lads holiday to Lloret de Mar. Looking back at it, however, the experience definitely did more harm than good, damaging Eric's future opinion of women and cementing a deep mental marker that prevented him from really trusting any of them ever again. In fact, he pretty much became paranoid and suspicious of all his future partners no matter the circumstances.

Still not the <u>most</u> confident person in the world, Becky was possibly thee worst type of girl Eric could have shacked up with at that early stage of his relationship career, very much at the opposite end of the spectrum to Abbie. She was extremely gregarious and loved attention and once under the influence of alcohol was bordering on being a common or garden tart.

An example of this was when she had her nipples pierced (yes, exactly). Not content with having them pierced for her own sake, she'd felt the need to show all of her friends in the pub, including Eric's, simply pulling up her top to reveal her sizable boobs to whoever was interested and in the case of Eric's friends, even those who were trying desperately not to be. Yes, such actions merely reminded Eric why he had previously felt the clientele at the Blue were rather uncouth and definitely not the type you'd want to take home and introduce to the parentals.

Apart from her ample bosoms that Eric enjoyed immensely, there was nothing else that really attracted him to Becky, soon discovering that her intellect was rather basic or even sub-basic in truth. Her heart was in the right place though (just a little to the left under the sternum) but Eric needed a partner who would stimulate his brain and not just his loins if there was to be any mileage in it.

Early on in the relationship, Eric and Becky had gone out for a drink together at Eric's local pub, which wasn't the Blue Parrot for a change, opting instead for a break from the running soap opera and usual suspects. Unwittingly, it happened to be quiz night (this was before the proliferation of mobile phones and the demise of the traditional question and answer based pub quiz) and therefore the pair decided to partake for a bit of fun. However, it soon became apparent to Eric that he was on his own if he really wanted to compete for the prize of 8 pints of beer as Becky was as useful as 'a truckload of hedgehogs in a tampon factory' (Top Secret! – 7.2/10 IMDb).

One of the questions related to the period drama (hate that expression… historical drama) Poldark, which first appeared back in the mid to late 70s prior to the drama's rebirth in 2015. The quizmaster asked 'in which century was the TV series Poldark first set?' As neither Eric nor Becky had seen it, then Eric guessed a century as the quiz continued.

Later on, when the quizmaster regaled the questions before supplying the corresponding answers, he confirmed that Poldark had first been set in the 18th Century.
'I didn't realise TVs were around in the 18th Century' Becky exclaimed.
'Jeezaloo' Eric thought, too polite to respond as he sat eyes glazed over and realising conversation wasn't the way forward and perhaps he should take up smoking again.

This wasn't a one-off as Becky had gone on to show her complete lack of knowledge and common sense on many an occasion.

Chapter Seven

It's Who You Know

So imagine Eric's sheer amazement when, some ten years later and completely out of the blue, he received a round-robin email from the Deputy Head at the bank where he worked, to say 'Please note that we have a new member of staff starting with us on Monday. She is called Becky Blackbeard and will be joining the marketing team…' or words to that effect.

'Fuck me', Eric thought, almost falling off his swivel chair remembering how thick she was and that there surely couldn't be too many Becky Blackbeards to the pound.

It was indeed the same girl Eric had enjoyed a trip to Blackpool with back in the day, having booked a bed and breakfast near to the idyllic promenade and long line of boarded-up shop windows interspersed with tacky amusement arcades (you picked up on the sarcasm). It was the first real chance to spend some 'quality' time together in the bedroom, both having lived with their parents and the only chances they'd had to dabble in carnal activity up to that point some contortionist sex in Becky's small Peugeot down lover's lane and the dark and brambly field adjacent to her mum and dad's house before Eric dropped her off one night; both easily forgettable and not what Eric would count as enjoyable.

Despite an old man seemingly dying in the next bedroom, his coughing-fit not quite the ambience Eric was looking for when finally getting down to brass tacks with Becky, he discovered that she was a rather big girl downstairs too, with a fanny as voluminous as the Royal Albert Hall. He'd regaled to his mates that it was like rattling a stick in a bucket and expecting to see potholers exiting donned in helmets complete with head torches ('this ain't blinkin' Calais, this is blinkin' Catford').

Eric was confident that his size wasn't in question, realising this admission could be interpreted that way to the layperson. This was just another reason to add to the growing list as to why Becky was just not the girl for him.

Gaining employment at Eric's place of work was proof to him that sometimes, it was definitely who you knew that could get you places in life. Despite the intervening years having helped to eradicate any fear of real awkwardness in the office between them, Eric couldn't help but have flashbacks, remembering sex with her when he passed her in the corridor or saw her in weekly meetings; I guess that was only natural. She'd matured a great deal since then though, had at least two children and was even married, before the bank had made all staff redundant some four or five years later. It was still a rather big coincidence that someone Eric had courted in the past was now technically a colleague, especially as, given her intellect; she was certainly the last person he'd have expected to see given a job there.

It wasn't long till Eric discovered that one of the line managers, who was nearing 60 at the time and was the personification of a letch had put her name forward for the job after having befriended her when seeing her regularly in her position as a bank cashier in town. It seemed he too had been hypnotised by her pendulous pair of baubles.

One thing Eric regretted most about his time working with Becky was not taking the opportunity to ask her something that had taken up far too much of his thought processes at the time he was seeing her; had she been playing around with his mate behind his back? Despite the curiosity, he'd decided that perhaps some things were best left in the past, especially as their lives had moved on a long way since then.

It had all started not long after getting together, Becky having met Eric's friends, including Robert, or Rob as he was better known by everyone. Becky loved playing up to a crowd and Eric got the impression that she wasn't the type of girl who could settle with just one fella and it seemed she was always flirting and hunting in new fishing grounds.

At the time, only a few of Eric's mates had girlfriends as such and so it was a chance for the others to socialise with the opposite sex too, whenever she was in tow. As Eric spent quite a bit of time knocking around with Rob, then it meant that he and Becky came into contact quite often also. Eric wasn't stupid and he could tell innocent flirting and flirting with more serious connotations and he soon became convinced that Rob and Becky had a mutual interest in one another. Perhaps it was the fact that Rob had his own wheels and was renowned for his erratic behaviour and what others would refer to as continual showing off.

Whatever the reason, Eric just had a hunch that something was happening behind the scenes and as he was notably not wishing to be made a fool out of (who is?) he became very suspicious, bordering on paranoid. What made no sense looking back at the whole situation was that Eric wasn't even that loved up with Becky, knowing their relationship was dead in the water since Poldarkgate and with more chance of someone inducing resonance in a bath full of honey (as one of his maths lecturers used to say when studying in Leeds) than it leading anywhere.

However, he allowed his own pride to become the principle and therefore continued to allow the series of events to eat away at him, rather than just put it all down to experience and walk away. He couldn't get on with his work normally, imagining Becky spending time with Rob whilst he did, finding it easy to pick holes in any of her messages; things just didn't add up.

Eric knew he'd had enough when he confided in his workmate and asked if he could have a lift to Becky's house one lunchtime, to satisfy himself that she was there and not out and about with <u>someone</u> else. It was like an old cop show, where the two detectives were staking out the suspect's house although in this case sat in a shitty brown coloured Ford Fiesta and with no snack food on the dashboard at all. Eric had to keep a low profile as he was the one who Becky would recognise if she saw them.

Despite the covert operation achieving absolutely nothing, it did make Eric aware that he was best to walk away and shortly after he hand wrote a John Deere letter (Dumb and Dumber – 7.3/10 IMDb). Then, after Becky dropped him off at his parent's house after their final outing (as it turned out) Eric nonchalantly left the envelope on the passenger seat as he alighted and walked up the drive to the front door. Becky, clearly upset after the penny had dropped (it took some time obviously) then sped off like the proverbial bat out of hell.

This final chapter (don't worry, I mean in their relationship) had come about after Eric's mates had finally come around to his thinking, at first assuring him that he was just being paranoid. However, after meeting one time at his local pub to embark on a night out, Eric's friends including Rob were in attendance. As Eric wasn't feeling too great and not really in the mood for an all-nighter, he made his excuses and bailed out, returning home. He didn't feel too bad as there were half a dozen others there and knew his omission would not be too detrimental to their plans. The idea had been to walk the half a mile or so to the station and catch a train into town.

It wasn't until Eric next saw his mates that they told him how, after walking to the station, Rob had been constantly on his phone and before the train had arrived, he'd also made off back down the lane, providing no real reason for his change of heart. 'Perhaps you're not being paranoid after all' they said, which came as welcome news to Eric; 'well how can you be paranoid if you're in fact correct as to your assertions?' he thought.

Eric saw Becky in passing a few times at the Blue Parrot following their split; of course, it was still going to happen given they'd both frequented the pub in the first place. Perhaps this was partly the reason as to why Eric and his mates eventually stopped going or perhaps it was just a coincidence, as Eric's and his mate's love lives had taken new turns following a night out in town. I guess you could say it was a little from column A and a little from column B. Eric never saw Becky again until her arrival at the bank a decade later and like his other friends, never saw Rob ever again.

Chapter Eight

Trouble at Mill

Eric was now back on Single Street, somewhere he would become only too familiar with throughout adulthood. Fortunately, Eric already had his feelers out and had been keen to get to know a certain girl from work a lot better.

The average age of men in the open-plan finance office at the paper mill, where Eric got his first real job, was somewhere in the mid-forties and Eric knew that he was definitely one of the only options that Claire would consider if at all. He'd spent the best part of a year there and by now Claire had admired both his comedic charms and of course his chiselled looks, having picked up the nickname Dolph after bearing a slight resemblance to the Swedish all-action beefcake, Dolph Lundgren. In fact, the full nickname had actually been 'Dolph Lundgren after a car crash and six-months muscle-wastage' but, thankfully for Eric, Dolph seemed to roll off the tongue a lot easier.

Working at close quarters with Claire, Eric had got to know her a lot better and he'd become more and more attracted to her. However, he was still lacking in the 'balls out chatting a girl up' department and so tried to remain as calm and unflustered as possible whenever their paths crossed ('I don't know Chewie; fly casual').

It was the one time in the year that happily married good-looking women dread the most; having to negotiate the gauntlet of alcohol-infused male colleagues chancing their arm at the work's Christmas do. Eric had already considered the prospect with Claire; a bit of Dutch courage in her company and voila; he would be turned into a confident studmuffin and his problems would be temporarily erased. Well, that was the plan anyway. Eric realised though that there was a very fine margin between being suitably inebriated to carry out a charm offensive with Claire and risking hurling-up due to too much intoxication. It was something that blighted Eric throughout his earlier dating escapades.

The evening seemed to have raced by following the devouring of

Christmas fayre and drunken dancing and Eric realised that if he was going to act, he'd have to do it now. The nerves he had for stepping across the line and making his feelings known to Claire were only slightly beaten by knowing the sense of deflation and disappointment at arriving home without having pushed himself to make the effort would be worse. It was now or never. Eric walked up to Claire on the dancefloor and whispered in her ear 'I really like you Claire'. Not exactly an award-winning chat up line Eric realised but he was just taken aback that he'd said anything to her at all.

Due to the decibellage of the disco churning out the usual Christmas ditties, Claire and Eric exited the main room and found a two-seater couch just outside in the foyer of the hotel. It was there that they were able to have a more coherent chat and Eric could turn on his Nigel Havers routine.

He hadn't considered trying to charm his way back to Claire's before the evening got underway but now aided by the booze it seemed to be a cracking idea to end the night. To his literal astonishment, Claire agreed that Eric could go back to hers. He was happier than a puppy with two penises but tried to contain his remarkable accomplishment, reacting as though it was the usual response he was used to. However, this was Eric and as you'll already have learnt and will continue to learn, things never tended to run smoothly at the best of times and here was yet another exhibit.

Had Eric thought about making his move with Claire ten minutes earlier then he would have been able to share a cab home with her. However, it was just after midnight and unfortunately for Eric, Claire had already telephoned her dad, who was picking her up; ensuring that his daughter returned home safely. They were both agreed that the timing was atrocious but Claire was quick to write her address down for Eric and suggested he grabbed a taxi after giving her a head start so to speak. After she received word that her dad was outside, Claire said 'see you in a bit' and left the hotel.

It was the first time Eric had chance to release the pent up happiness that he'd been suppressing in front of Claire for fear of looking like a raging mentalist and turning to the couple sat next to him on an identical two-seater sofa he exclaimed 'she said yes!' Their smiles encapsulated both the surprise at Eric's crass announcement and a certain amount of empathy at seeing Eric's sheer adulation.

Although not the best situation, Eric was still buoyed by the turn of events and knew it was still easily within his grasp to ensure he got to Claire's and to a nailed-on shag. Surely she was up for it and wasn't thinking of just playing dominos when he got there. He then realised one slight set-back with the plan. After counting the money in his pockets, Eric knew that he didn't have enough money to cover the likely cost of a cab to Claire's who lived some 15 miles away.

Eric had a sudden brainwave. Coincidentally, his older brother was under the same roof of the hotel, also enjoying his work's Christmas do and was, in fact, sat only a few tables away. A result if ever there was one, Eric thought, feeling relieved that he had found a way around his cash-flow problem.

However, this was Eric as I said and it seemed his brother had also spent up, only able to offer him a Lady Godiva. As Eric realised that wouldn't get him very far, then he declined, especially as he also didn't want to leave his brother penniless. Eric would need to come up with another plan.

A week after Eric had started his job, another lad called Steve had started the following week and coincidentally, he'd also studied at Leeds University and actually played football against him, although not having known one another at the time. They had subsequently bonded through having similar interests, a shared sense of humour as well as being of similar age. Eric, therefore, turned to Steve, cap in hand to ask if he could borrow a few notes and explained the position.

It was bad news once again as Steve was pretty skint too. Eric was just a smidge frustrated at how things seemed to be conspiring against him; he was on a promise and it appeared he was slowly losing the battle.

Realising Eric's predicament, Steve suggested they both walked into town and he could take some money out of a hole in the wall and lend him the dough. Eric, with little other choice having left his bank cards at home, had to take him up on his offer but was unable to coax Steve into making haste.

As the time ebbed away, the more Eric knew he'd blown his chance and there was a certain inevitability about it; like a black man winning the

Olympic 100-metres or the Germans being dumped out of the World Cup in the group stage having finished bottom (how Eric laughed). He did not want to give up hope though as was still very much champing at the bit and desperate to get to Claire's.

Chapter Nine

Full Marks for Effort

After finally arriving in the town-centre and Steve taking out some cash as promised, he was then reluctant to hand it over, realising that as he would be travelling in that direction too, then the pair could share the same cab home. However, Steve was in no mood to head home just yet and put it to Eric that they should enjoy some more drinks in a club before calling it a night.

Eric was beside himself with frustration as technically he couldn't force Steve to go home or to give him some money to enable his onward journey. He could do nothing but chaperone his mate and the pair ended up in the biggest dive Eric had ever witnessed in his life. He didn't even want to text Claire about the situation as he knew that she would not be particularly overwhelmed to hear he had waltzed off into town for some more drinks when he'd told her he'd catch a cab to hers not long after she'd set off with her dad.

By the time Steve finally called it a day, now technically arseholed, the pair jumped a cab. Eric couldn't believe how late it was. It was now around 3:30 a.m. and by the time he was dropped off outside Claire's, it was nearer to four hours since she'd left the Christmas party. Looking back at it, Eric knew he should probably have just bitten the bullet and returned straight home to his parent's house with his tail between his legs. However, Eric had endeavoured to get to Claire's come what may and even allowing for the massive delay, he still believed there would be the chance of a happy outcome.

It was pitch black outside her house, Eric having ensured he had the right address before knocking on the door. There were no lights on in the house whatsoever. With no response, Eric then carried out something that he'd only ever seen on old American TV programmes and films, where (predominantly) teenage lads tried to gain their mates' attention (without being caught by their parents) by throwing dried earth or small stones at their bedroom window. The difference here was that Eric was not wishing to place his hands in the soil as with little visibility then he couldn't really see anything that would suffice.

Instead, he decided to use some pound coins that he had leftover in his pocket. He didn't know which was Claire's bedroom but believed it was worth a punt (or a pound). Had he been seen or heard by the neighbours then it was likely that his Romeo and Juliet carry on would have ended with his collar being felt and answering some questions whilst sat in the back of a panda-car.

This was back in the day when Eric had his first mobile phone but he was unable to contact Claire due to the battery having died at some point in the nightclub, hence he'd taken to lobbing pound coins at her upstairs windows. As things were becoming altogether more ridiculous Eric realised that the coins he'd thrown were now lost forever, having no way of seeing where they'd landed, especially given the shrubbery that lined the path between the house and garden.

Eric had a final brainwave. He'd noticed a traditional red phone box around a hundred-yards or so from her house and noting he had a couple of pound coins still left in his pocket, decided to try and call Claire from there.

Now for those not old enough to remember using a phone box, then you would lift the handset and then insert the coinage before dialling the number. Usually, if there was no answer, you would have your money refunded once placing the handset back down. On this occasion, however, Eric lost both his final pound coins as although Claire hadn't answered, it switched to her answerphone after a number of rings, the second time even quicker to do so and catching Eric out who was poised with his fingers ready to pull down on the receiver-cradle. Too late and the phone, having read that as getting through, kept hold of his final sovereign. 'Fan-fucking-tastic!' Eric thought to himself, now sobering up somewhat, stood in the dark, the last of his money now either somewhere in Claire's herbaceous borders or robbed off him by BT.

The worst thing about it was that what had started out as a dead-cert for a shag with a girl he really fancied had well and truly gone tits-up. Eric was not amused. To rub insult into injury, Eric had no way of contacting anyone as his phone was dead and he no longer had any money to pay for a cab even if he'd been able to call one. It was 4:30 a.m. in the morning and there was no way he was reversing the charges to call his mum or dad at that ungodly hour. He didn't have a choice; he'd have to use shanks' pony and walk the five miles home in his new shoes which had already been causing him mild discomfort all evening.

The only thing Eric could be thankful for was that it remained dry, although he'd had such a great end to his evening that it wouldn't have surprised him if a small black cloud had suddenly appeared over his head and followed him all the way home à la Charlie Brown. It had well and truly been a night to forget.

Eric was expectedly nervous going into work on the Monday for obvious reasons. He saw Claire and rather embarrassingly explained what had happened again, having texted her later on the Saturday after finally reaching home and charging his mobile. The damage it seemed was irreversible though and there would be no second chance for Eric. It seemed his over-enthusiasm after arriving at 04:00 a.m. had not been taken lightly by Claire, the idea that anyone would rock-up three-and-a-half hours after they'd been expected having been the nail through Eric's inflated plums.

Eric was sure to remind his mate Steve of the squandered opportunity to empty his sacks that night at every possible opportunity afterwards, although it soon became a funny anecdote that the two shared. Eric was left thinking what may have been had he arrived without delay and how weird it was how things could turn out. One thing was for sure and that was that Eric would not be celebrating the turn of the new Millennium with a special someone.

Chapter Ten

Whose Wife is it Anyway?

The opening of a brand new nightclub in town called Randy's had given Eric and his mates a different option in the going out stakes and had become a popular haunt, especially as the other clubs in the locale were limited and old hat; Randy's somewhat futuristic in comparison. There was a smaller club within the club catering for older clientele or those who preferred 'old skool' music from the 70s and 80s to that of rifts stolen from 70s and 80s tracks and made into dance music with a whole cacophony of over the top bass ('it's got a good beat' said in the stylee of 'Embarrassing Dad' from Punt and Dennis); or so Eric thought.

It was in this smaller club where Eric met Diane or Di as she was better known and began his first proper 'relationship', Becky, although seeing her for a few months didn't count as they'd never lived together.

There was a spattering of good fortune (some would say fate) that brought the pair together. It all started with a defunct television set that Eric had received for Christmas 2000. It wasn't defunct when he first received it but had noticed problems with it not long afterwards. As Eric's mum and dad had bought him the TV, they suggested taking it back early in the New Year to replace it.

The TV was fooking heavy, a cathode ray tube effort, which was the standard for televisions back then (look them up if you were born after 1995). After lugging it 200-yards into the Argos store, it soon became apparent that they were out of stock, receiving a full refund instead. Eric wanted a TV though so clutching the reddies they made their way to Comet (which for all you younger types was an electronic hardware store back in the day). As there was nothing there that took Eric's fancy he left empty-handed but it did mean that he was now feeling a little flush.

The brother of Eric's mate, who Eric had socialised with over the last few years, especially pre-university was hankering to go out that very evening and so given Eric's finances had taken an unexpected boost; he decided to join him, inviting another mate along. The three of them, therefore, enjoyed a night out at Randy's, spending their time exclusively in the smaller club, given it was more befitting of their personal musical tastes. Eric enjoyed dancing but always needed alcoholic lubrication before doing so… he was no Billy Elliot (7.7/10 IMDb). Having consumed enough whisky and cokes to remove any self-consciousness, Eric couldn't resist the toe-tapping 80s classics any longer and made his way onto the dance-floor.

Eric was renowned for his energetic performances when it came to dancing, akin to a workout without his Kellogg's Start sweatbands and jogging bottoms. In fact, it was usual for Eric to get so swept up by certain iconic tracks that he usually ended up pulling off his famous swan-dive; a break dancing move, where he would place his hands out in front of him on the floor as though carrying out a handstand, only to let his body then fall systematically in a wave-like motion, culminating in an instantaneous return to his feet within the one single routine.

Just as night followed day, Eric did indeed pull off his swan-dive, although unbeknown to him, Di was busy admiring his moves as she danced nearby. One unexpected result of Eric's energetic showpiece had been his Ericsson flip-phone coming free from his breast-pocket and shooting across the dancefloor. Slightly embarrassed, Eric had gone searching for it on his hands and knees hoping nobody had obliterated it (with their overzealous reactions to 'Come On Eileen') having noticed it jettisoning off mid-dive. The phone mishap had either not been spotted by Di or hadn't bothered her in the slightest as she walked over to Eric in any case as everyone began a mass exodus once the music stopped and the lights came on.

The music was still very much on in Randy's though and was very loud, conversation only possible by shouting at each other from closer than six inches. Di was keen on Eric and Eric, having had the chance to give her the once over, was now just as keen. She was older than he; eight years older as he later found out (in fact the security guard at Eric's work had asked him whose wife he was messing with given the noticeable age gap which Eric found hilarious).

Diane was blonde, around medium height for a girl and medium build too, blessed with an ample chest that made Eric smile from ear to ear. They tried to converse, the noise really not helping with their intentions and so Eric had taken to speaking to Di directly into her ear in order to be heard, their heads now as close as you could get. Eric spoke for a few seconds, telling Di that she looked amazing, being the Nigel Havers silver-tongued bastard that he could be.

After finishing his initial chat-up volley, imagine Eric's embarrassment cum awkwardness, when Di then said 'I'm profoundly deaf in that ear, can you say that again in my good ear?' It seemed that despite being blissfully unaware of having had a 50/50 chance ('Never go for a 50/50 ball unless you're 80/20 sure' Ian Darke) of choosing the right (or was it left) ear, he'd failed; and therefore had to regurgitate what he'd just said, with slightly less enthusiasm and gusto the second-time it must be said.

The thing that Eric couldn't understand looking back at it was if Di knew she was deaf in that ear, then why the dickens had she not immediately intervened, letting Eric ramble on for so long? They both saw the funny side of meeting for the first time; Di only too used to her deafness by this stage in her life.

Chapter Eleven

I Wouldn't Piss on You if You Were on Fire

Eric fell for Di in a big way. He fancied her rotten and her age was also a plus-factor, Eric preferring a girl who was more mature, especially after the problems he'd faced with Becky previously. Di was the complete opposite; career-minded, intelligent and classy. Despite this, she wasn't in any way prudish; to the contrary and Di had one or two fetishes that Eric hadn't yet come across before.

Firstly, she had a penchant for dressing up provocatively. There was nothing peculiar about that. However, she then found it a turn-on to walk over his bare back in stilettos; leaving Eric looking like he'd received a thousand lashes for committing a crime back in biblical times. He did concede that it was perhaps unwise for him to have worn a white shirt to work the next day after first experiencing the ritual, his scars still very much visible through the semi-transparent cloth as he discovered to his horror after arriving home.

Another altogether more 'quirky' sexual preference of hers was for Eric to evacuate his bladder over her, commonly known as a golden shower. Eric found the whole notion went very much against his OCD and clean-freak mentality (already contemplating which washing machine setting was best to use on the urine-stained bedsheets afterwards) but he was happy to do anything to please her at that stage; 'Of course I'll piss on you angel-face'.

The concept seemed all kinds of wrong after starting, Eric not happy if he missed the toilet pan with a few stray jets in his usual day-to-day life. This was very different and the other thing he was keenly aware of was that when he started, there was just no way he could stop (like Harry in Dumb and Dumber when filling empty beer bottles in transit). Having a bladder like a camel also meant Eric couldn't help but saturate the entire bed, akin to an arsonist liberally pouring-out gasoline from a canister and not just a few forced dribbles in key areas. Yes, Di was indeed kinkier (deranged) than he when it came to sex but Eric was happy to play along.

Fortunately, Di only lived a short walk from his mum and dad's, which was very handy indeed. There was a slight catch though; there always was Eric found; she was still technically married.

Di was going through divorce proceedings with her husband and Eric soon learnt that it had been Di who had committed adultery with someone she worked with or had got to know through work. Despite convincing Eric that her husband was moving on and had a new girlfriend of his own and that they would never get back together, the whole admission from Di had worked only to sew some seeds of doubt right from the start, Eric hoping that he could see through the past for what it was and not allow himself to become bogged down with thoughts of Di being the untrustworthy type.

This was the first time Eric had felt smitten, probably bordering on infatuation rather than a healthier alternative. Unfortunately, Eric could not overturn the deep-rooted trust issues that blighted him and this would ultimately put paid to his relationship with her. It certainly appeared that the whole debacle with Becky had only served to make him very suspicious from that day forth, having had his fingers burnt at the first fence and the worst possible stage.

I guess what wrangled most with Eric was the perception that somebody else's deviousness in potentially trying to cheat on him was them believing they could get one over on him without him knowing; a somewhat lack of respect to his intellect. Maybe he wouldn't be able to trust another girl in a relationship ever again and that's how it would be.

Chapter Twelve

Mad Cows and Caravans

They were together for around ten months or so in all, although having been through quite a bit together over that time, with quite a few trips to Eric's mum and dad's caravan in Anglesey, getting away from it all and enjoying the tranquillity that the island could offer. They certainly tested the caravan's foundations and it was the first time Eric had given a girl a pearl necklace.

He'd bought the pearls from a second-hand jeweller in town as he'd overheard her say how she'd always wanted one (what were you thinking I meant?) Coincidentally, Di had mentioned them again in passing whilst at the caravan after Eric had already stashed them in their presentation case under her pillow in the bedroom. Imagine her surprise later that evening when she found them. Eric was besotted with Di and despite not earning a great deal, would often buy her things to surprise her.

Eric had a very original mind and often played practical jokes or did things a little bit differently. Like the time he was due to pay her his monthly contribution to the household bills and food with his wages, having drawn out the cash and placed each of the 25 £20 notes (that's £500 if you were struggling to do the maths) in a Hansel and Gretel style trail from the front door to the bedroom where he lay naked in wait for Di to return, including one note on each of the stairs.

The best practical joke he played, however, was his textbook April fool's prank. Realising he and Di would be away at the caravan on that day, Eric's brain sprung into gear and he had a conniving plan that he knew would be quite funny and relatively easy to pull off. It was around the time of a widespread foot and mouth outbreak, which had led to the isolation and in some cases extermination of cattle to prevent the further possibility of it spreading.

As the caravan was in an orchard on a farm, then Eric had devised a very authoritative looking notice from Anglesey Council, complete with their coat of arms and some fictitious telephone numbers at the base. It told occupants of the caravan that they were in effect quarantined and were not permitted to leave the farm until a local foot and mouth outbreak had been dealt with. As it was a Sunday and with Eric and Di planning to return that day before starting back at work on the Monday, then Eric felt it would make for quite an amusing reaction from Di.

Waking up on Sunday morning, Eric had already attached the notice to the outside of the caravan door before going to bed (he'd laminated it, of course, to make it look even more official and besides which; he didn't want it potentially ruined by the changeable weather). Conscious that he couldn't depend on Di seeing the notice through the frosted glass, Eric opened the door and made it look obvious he'd retrieved it from outside.

'Have a read of that' Eric said passing Di the notice, remembering to play the role as the confused and slightly alarmed boyfriend in the process, his award-winning performance unfortunately not captured on celluloid for him to be in the reckoning for the film and TV awards later that year. Di was in obvious shock, not long been up and about and now looking perplexed. 'What are we going to do?' she exclaimed.
'Well I guess we have to stay put and wait for further communication… it says on there that they'll bring food and drink'.

Di was a very intuitive and sharp woman but Eric had her hook, line and sinker and just had to keep it going for as long as he could. Half-an-hour later and Di suggested they go and speak with the couple who lived in the farmhouse and get further clarification from them. Eric had no other choice but to go along with her as otherwise he wouldn't have seemed believable and his cover would be blown.

The pair, therefore, donned their jackets and shoes and made the short walk from the van across the lawned area to the front and towards the house, Eric hanging back slightly knowing that it was, of course, a load of hooey. Just before Di reached the front door, Eric shouted from behind her; 'Why are you asking the farmer about it?'

Turning to see Eric, with a broad grin on his face and starting to laugh, the penny suddenly dropped and Di, beginning to laugh also, ran after him for a couple of minutes, a Benny Hill-style chase having ensued around the caravans and gardens with Di desperate to enact some form of physical harm on him. Eric had pulled it off and had enjoyed seeing Di being taken in by his elaborate April Fools' Day prank.

Chapter Thirteen

Every Infected Leg has a Silver Lining

Although things were going great-guns between the couple, Di met Eric's mum and dad a lot sooner than they planned and not under normal circumstances by any means.

Eric had been out with his friends and Di in a pub next to the hospital, which was the first time they had frequented it. The weekly quiz was on, which may have been the reason for the choice of venue.

Despite the relative toastiness of the pub's interior, Eric still felt cold and was shivering, like a fever had taken over his entire body. The others, who were literally stripping layers off due to the heat, could not believe Eric was doing the complete opposite and zipping up his outdoor coat.

There was something not altogether right with Eric. Having been dropped off by Di at the end of the evening and getting into bed, Eric noticed that his right leg (big leg) had swollen considerably and was red and hot to the touch but as it was late and he didn't want to wake his parents, he thought if he could just get a good night's sleep then he'd hopefully feel much better in the morning.

Eric was wrong. He woke feeling worse than before and was now a little worried, to say the least. Making his mum aware of the situation, she mentioned calling for an ambulance but Eric was not the type for a lot of fuss so after dressing, she took him to the A&E at the hospital, just next to the previous night's venue where the fever had begun. It was cellulitis, a bacterial skin infection that had taken over much of Eric's leg and it was hot enough 'to melt a cheese sandwich from across the room' (Naked Gun 2 1/2 – 6.9/10 IMDb).

Eric was laid up in a hospital bed for a week, having to have strong inflammatory antibiotics administered intravenously through a cannula. Eric did not have a fear of needles, especially when required to help him recover but the number of times the nurses tried to puncture him in order to connect to a 'good vein' was just a little frustrating; telling him that despite having a good blood supply, his skin was seemingly thicker than that of a rhinoceros.

Once finally fitted, it was then time for Eric's first dose of antibiotics, the nurse using a large hypodermic needle (or hypodeemic nerdle as Eric preferred to call them). Just as she was about to flush the anti-serum into his arm, an old scouse fella ('Ay… calm down calm down' The Scousers on Harry Enfield) who occupied the bed next to Eric's suddenly piped up. "as he got room in 'is body for all dat?' he announced, noticing the size of the needle and realising that it was a great deal bigger than he'd seen previously. Eric's initial alarm at hearing him reduced somewhat after his laugh came afterwards and Eric realising that it was just the typical scouse humour for you.

As Eric was now tied up in hospital (not literally) that meant he couldn't see Di as much as he was used to, texting her to let her know where he was. She was concerned to hear the news and was naturally wishing to see him. As the visiting times were pretty rigid and not overly accommodating, however, it meant that she was likely to bump into his mum and dad, given that they too would be keen to visit their son during his hospitalisation.

So as it turned out, Di met Eric's mum and dad for the first time outside the ward, the unusual situation helping to make this coming together a lot easier, a lot more practical and a great deal less formal for all interested parties.

Chapter Fourteen

End Transmission

What Eric was still more than a little uncomfortable with was Di's marriage misdemeanour coming with someone she had met through work and as Di hadn't been completely transparent as to whether this person still worked at her office, then it was difficult for Eric to feel completely at ease in the relationship, especially still scarred by his last outing with Becky.

Something else that didn't sit well with Eric was of Di's continued relationship with her ex-husband's sister and mother, choosing to see them both from time to time, although the frequency had reduced somewhat given their honeymoon period. In fact, Di had been out with her sister-in-law on the night that the two had met at the nightclub. In Eric's mind, this all came back to his previous ethos, which was regarding baggage. A relationship could only work if both components were happy to accept previous events and would not let them interfere. This is why Eric had never kept in touch with any of his exes as he knew that they would just cause more problems for him in the future and although maybe slightly archaic and immature to some, was something that made life a lot easier for him.

It wasn't long after Eric and Di had gotten together that Eric had moved in with her, Di having previously spent a few weeks actually living with Eric at his parents' house as she felt vulnerable living with her ex or so she had said. Despite his parents getting on with Di relatively well, it was still a little awkward with her living at the family home but it showed how kind and generous Eric's parents were to agree to it in the first place.

It was quite a funny set-up as Eric and Di not only shared Eric's old bedroom that he'd previously shared with his twin brother, Ernie (who now lived in Nottingham following his studies at the university there) but meant that they also had to share a bunk bed, Eric taking his usual position on top. Eric and Ernie had outgrown their bunk bed by the age of 15 or so, having to slip their feet through the slats at the end in order to lie flat out.

Despite everyone's best intentions, however, the arrangement soon became a little too much for everyone and it was much better when Eric moved into Di's. It meant not only did they have their own privacy and a normal bed but Eric's parents could relax, not being constantly on 'guest reception' mode whenever Di was about.

After moving into Di's house and getting used to calling it home, Eric was not particularly enamoured with then being asked to vacate it one evening to enable her to host her ex-husband in order to 'discuss the divorce'. Eric was aware of their age-gap but this made him feel like a ten-year-old boy being given a pound and told to go and buy some sweets. Eric couldn't really fathom out the truth about Di's feelings for her ex and believed that Di regretted her affair massively and would have liked nothing more than to have made amends with her ex and stayed together.

Eric could see their wedding video (VHS) sat with other videos underneath the television and it made him realise that in the case of meeting someone older, who had already been married or in previous relationships, then he was never going to see that girl in her prime, when she was younger and more beautiful and having already discovered all those occasions in life that Eric had not yet experienced for himself.

Eric reluctantly made way with little fuss but his curiosity and paranoia were such that he had made a purposeful trip to Argos earlier that day to purchase a voice-activated Dictaphone in time for the planned rendezvous. Eric left the device in the kitchen on top of a cupboard, assuming that's where they were likely to be sat. He needed to satisfy himself as to the real relationship between the pair. In Eric's mind, it seemed rather unusual for a couple to have a convivial chat about their divorce, expecting the exchange of letters between solicitors was usually the case. No matter what he thought, Eric's plan hadn't worked and the Dictaphone hadn't picked anything up. He was frustratingly none the wiser. Still, with a 14-day no-quibble refund policy, then at least he wasn't out of pocket.

Chapter Fifteen

Does my Cock Look Big in This?

During their relationship, Di contacted Eric at work one day to give him the alarming news that she had Chlamydia and that the doctor who had diagnosed it had thought it a good idea for him to be tested also. It could be treated quite easily with antibiotics but in order to ascertain if Eric was also infected, then there was nothing he could do to avoid a trip to the STD clinic in town, although it went by the name of 'Family Health Clinic' or the like to make it sound less repulsive. 'Swell' Eric thought, 'I could really do without this… what happens if I see someone I know?'

Although not knowing exactly what Chlamydia was, he knew it wasn't something you'd want to brag about or announce to the world. Eric felt embarrassed to high-heaven and a little nervous sat in the very quiet waiting lounge at the clinic, trying to keep a low profile and not catch anybody else's gaze. Doing his level-best to blend into the background as though on an MI6 covert operation, a nurse then ruined everything by calling out his name, which pissed Eric off no-end… 'like keep your fucking voice down won't you?'

Eric was taken into a small room with a hospital bed, on which he was asked to sit, the pillow end raised almost vertically so he was sat up rather than lying down. Eric had a horrible feeling about it and what the procedure entailed and so imagine his reaction when one of the two nurses explained that she would indeed be inserting a needle up his jap's eye. 'Fucking great' Eric thought to himself, not only having two nurses handling his penis but the eye-watering prospect of having them plow a needle up his pisser was an experience he could happily pass on.

Having removed his trousers and undercrackers in preparation, his first thoughts had been that perhaps he should have slapped it around a bit prior to entering the room, the rather cold temperature having done nothing for his apparent size. 'It's cold in here isn't it?' Eric exclaimed, trying desperately to break the awkward silence, whilst at the same time putting forward an excuse as to why his penis may not have looked altogether impressive. The nurses laughed.

Eric was now literally in their hands, one of them having placed his cock on the palm of her hand like she was holding a pet hamster. She then straightened it out as best she could and held it in place, to ensure the needle could negotiate his Aretha Franklin with less chance of it getting snagged on any kinks.

He'd momentarily considered closing his eyes and not watching the process but then it suddenly dawned on Eric that if he didn't look, the fact that someone else was handling his spam-javelin may have unwittingly turned him on and he didn't want any potential complications to arise.

He then came out with another classic line, still feeling more than a little awkward about the whole situation. 'Does it look normal to you?' he enquired whilst his member had both of their attentions.

'Yes, it looks normal' one of them replied laughing now preparing for the important insertion part. Eric was hoping she'd said something a little more complimentary but hey ho, at least it seemed normal. The procedure hadn't been as painful as Eric was expecting, perhaps some mild discomfort but it didn't smart like vinegar being poured onto an open sore as he'd anticipated.

With the results back a few days later, Eric was given the all-clear, which came as a great relief to him. As they also tested for other more serious conditions, it was indeed peace of mind to know he was as clean as a whistle and you could probably eat your dinner off it.

Filled with the happy news that he wasn't infected in any way, Eric failed to realise or question how Di had, therefore, contracted the disease in the first place. He'd assumed, naively, that it could just occur and didn't have to be the result of intercourse with someone else already carrying the strain. Perhaps it was a good thing that he hadn't thought along those lines as otherwise, he may have had an even shorter relationship with her.

Chapter Sixteen

Strip to the Waist

Despite the whole process regarding the STD clinic not being one that Eric looked back on with much fondness, it was a mishap the previous year that had led to an altogether more embarrassing situation.

After Eric's right leg had become the most famous appendage this side of Skelmersdale, he'd had to go on a long and medical mystery tour as mentioned, seeing specialists and having a plethora of tests done to aid them with their search for a prognosis. Eric and his parents had spent more than their fill of time in hospital waiting rooms over the years. One of the more painful methods of checking Eric's circulation within the rogue leg was to inject a nuclear trace-element into him to enable its path to be charted. That meant injecting Eric between the toes on his right foot, which was possibly one of the last places you'd choose to be injected he thought, not having been squeamish about needles until that point.

As they wished to keep an eye on developments, Eric saw a number of different doctors and specialists and would have check-ups every few months or so. For one particular appointment, he was asked to attend his local cottage hospital. This was all water off a crocodile's eye-socket for Eric at this stage of his life, which had become very much the norm for him.

On this occasion he sat in the waiting-room wondering whether he would be seen anywhere near the time of his scheduled appointment, staring at the token fish tank for any signs of life and the covers of the 1980s gardening magazines on the table in front of him.

Eventually, his name was then called out by a nurse and Eric, surprised at the apparent punctuality, stood up and followed her. Eric soon realised that his surprise had been misplaced as he wasn't seeing the specialist just yet and was merely being taken to a holding room, which was annexed to the specialist's office, part of the process to make it seem like something was happening. The room was small, the hospital bed taking up half of it and the other half the walkway from the corridor to the specialist's quarters, no fish tank nor ancient horticultural magazines to thumb through.

The nurse was flanked by a much younger student nurse or intern and asked Eric if it was okay if she was in attendance throughout his consultation. Eric had no problem whatsoever as he had been only too used to medical students gathered around his hospital bed carrying clipboards and scrutinising his leg like some sort of circus freakazoid act… 'Come and see the Elephant Boy' he'd thought to himself, looking at them all peering at him and wishing he had a hat to shove under their noses in an attempt at some sarcastic humour and to collect their spare change.

At that time Eric had been a little more self-conscious about his condition and didn't particularly like the fact that he wasn't normal in that regard. It reminded him of The Elephant Man film (8.2/10 IMDb), which first aired on terrestrial television back in the mid-eighties and how after hearing it was grotesque and a little scary, Eric had simply envisaged the main character looking like Babar the elephant from the cartoons, a man's body but his head complete with big flappy ears and a trunk. 'What could be so bad about that?' he'd thought. He was only around eight-years-old at the time though so could be forgiven for not having been au fait with the whole backstory of Joseph (John) Merrick.

Back in the holding-room and the nurse told Eric that the specialist shouldn't be too long and with that, she and the intern made their way into his room. Before she disappeared, though, she turned her head and exclaimed 'Can you strip to the waist' and the dividing door closed behind her.

'Hmm' Eric thought unsure as to her last instruction. 'Strip to the waist?' He repeated it several times to himself before removing his clothing in preparation.

A couple of minutes later and the door to the specialist's office opened and the nurse and the young intern stood staring at Eric from the doorway, the surprise evident in their eyes.

'I meant your top half' the nurse exclaimed smiling at his faux pas, Eric stood calm as you like with his cock and plums for all to see.

Eric was just a smidge embarrassed at the outcome, especially as there was a young intern but as he was there to see the specialist about his leg, then he thought it reasonable that she meant strip to the waist from the bottom-up and not top-down. It was safe to say that the two females had rather an unexpected bonus (Eric thought) putting his pants back on before making his way through to see the specialist, mortified at the misunderstanding.

That wasn't the end of the story; no, this is Eric remember. After returning to work the next morning and into the office, Eric could see a small group of colleagues chatting in the next pod. There was nothing unusual about that. However, as he honed in on the conversation, he heard one of the fellas regaling a story and the situation sounded eerily familiar. 'And this guy took his trousers and pants off' he exclaimed to the select few around him, to which they all laughed.

Yes, Eric's colleague who he'd worked with for several months, had a wife who unbeknown to Eric was a nurse working at a local cottage hospital. It appeared her highlight from the previous day had been Eric and had told her husband about the 'nutter' who exposed his meat and two to her and a young intern after being asked to strip to the waist. You couldn't make it up. Eric was just a little embarrassed but not wishing to draw any suspicion on himself, effected a smile as though agreeing with the others that this fella must have indeed been a complete retard.

Chapter Seventeen

Greek Tragedy – Part One

It was after returning from the Greek island of Kos in September (2001) that Eric had decided that he'd had enough with Di. The time spent together on holiday had been up and down but the bottom line was that Eric just couldn't feel like he could trust her and couldn't see that changing anytime soon. Eric had witnessed a fella by the pool where Di was sunbathing asking her if she needed some lotion rubbing into her back as she lay topless on her front and it was obvious that Di was being waay too friendly, Eric having witnessed the scene from afar.

She'd also confirmed that she had a male friend back home who she would occasionally meet with for lunch and who wasn't linked to her work. There was just a little too much mystery and given her previous misdemeanours, Eric felt he would be better off alone than to live in a situation where he was constantly questioning things about her. He realised he was still only starting out in terms of relationships and had much to learn ('much to learn, you still have'… Master Yoda) but something just didn't feel right. Eric, therefore, split from Di and moved the short distance back to his parents' house, his mate Terry playing the role of removal man and in so doing helping to have the least impact or inconvenience to them.

After the final split, Di had actually had a private chat with Eric's mum and told her that she would never have done anything to hurt Eric and as far as she was concerned wanted to spend the rest of her life with him. 'Big claims' Eric thought after learning of this but looking back at it, as difficult as it was adjusting to life back on Single Street, it was probably for the best.

Eric spent weeks doing very little, moping around his bedroom and questioning himself about his own actions. He felt the world had pretty much ended and learnt how emotions could seriously affect someone, not having experienced something like this before. Looking back at it weeks later and even today, he realised how ridiculous he'd been to feel that way and could even laugh at himself about it; but at the time, when things were raw, it had almost felt like grieving for a loved one, the difference being they were very much alive and well.

That wasn't the last time that Eric saw Di, as Eric started his new job in the October of that year (2001) approximately three weeks after 911 and coincidentally, of all the places he could start a new job, approximately 150-200 yards from Di's place of work, directly opposite the main thoroughfare that bisected the business park. 'Great', Eric thought, as the last thing he wanted was being continually reminded of her or worse, distracted by any potential sightings.

More coincidences were afoot mind, as Steve, the reason why he hadn't had sex with Claire at his last workplace, had a friend who worked for her. Life was certainly full of them it seemed. However, thoughts of Di took a back-seat for Eric, not long having crossed the welcome mat at the bank and getting his feet under his new desk, when he spotted a new target on his love radar and that girl, Eric could tell, was also interested in him.

Chapter Eighteen

Professor Plums in the Bedroom with his Lead Piping

Emma was an attractive girl, despite Eric's best mate suggesting she looked like Michael Jackson, which was notably on account of her ashen complexion and raven-hair more so than her razor-sharp nose or affinity to moonwalk out of a room. Eric was positive he wasn't attracted to Wacko Jacko and so conceded that his friend had been just a little harsh with his comparison.

Emma was 5'7" and was quite a broad-shouldered girl and not a stick insect catwalk type by any means, perhaps best described as bonny; although Eric had always believed the word bonny was just a kind way of referring to a girl who perhaps needed to shed a few pounds.

The best thing about Emma's slight plumpness was her boobs, which as mentioned previously, were like Eric's kryptonite, rendering him powerless when confronted by a pendulous pair, especially those seemingly defying gravity ('Don't stop me now'). Emma was also a very shy girl, their initial exchanges brief and with her blushes being obvious to see, given the contrast against her usual porcelain hue.

Eric had little to do with Emma on a work-front, himself working in a different department, with her on a separate floor of the building. However, there would be the weekly office meeting where everyone was present, the occasional chance that he saw her walking between the two floors or when arriving/leaving for the day.

There was a fly in the ointment though as Eric soon discovered that Emma was already engaged and despite being rather disappointed to hear the news, decided to cast his net in another direction, not the kind of guy who would try to muscle-in on any other girl who was already taken. There was still an obvious attraction between the two but Eric realised he would have to pursue other girls outside the four walls of the office.

Christmas came and went and not long into the New Year (2002) with Eric still reasonably new to his job, Eric received some very interesting news along the grapevine. Emma had broken off her engagement. Eric's own section, headed up by Patsy, an attractive woman in her own right and some 11 years older than he, was quite a gossiper and Eric had overheard her mentioning that she'd met Emma's now ex-fiancé at works dos and the like and her impression of him was that he was a bit of a twat.

As the weeks rolled by, Eric remained interested in Emma but appreciated the fact that if Emma had only just recently split-up, then she was unlikely to want to jump into another relationship quite so soon. He bided his time and hoped that perhaps Mohammed would come to the mountain so to speak.

Eventually, the news he had been waiting for was delivered to Eric by one of her friends on her section, an older woman who was on Eric's four-weekly post rota. 'I think Emma likes you Eric' she exclaimed. 'Jack-a-nack-a-nory!!' (Alan Partridge) Eric thought to himself and privy to this insider knowledge and with a work's night out on the horizon, then he could start to devise a plan of attack.

It was the second week in May; the venue a quaint hotel and a murder mystery night that Eric and his fellow colleagues had been invited to as part of a 'getting to know one another' initiative. This followed the takeover of the bank by a larger one and as a result, there were a few new faces in the office. Eric wasn't really that bothered with the theme of the evening or socialising with the others but it gave him the opportunity to speak to Emma and see if his charms would work in sealing a first date with her.

The practical aspect of meeting someone at work (as was the case with Claire previously) was that you got to know someone without any pressure or a need to impress, probably the reason why there were a few couples across the two departments already. On hearing the news that she was interested then it was obviously less of a gamble for Eric; less probability of rejection which was great news. He was still very nervous mind, not allowing himself to believe it was like shooting fish in a barrel and it was in no way a done deal just yet.

Noticing Emma and her friends had made their way to the dancefloor;

Eric joined them and soon he had a chance to put his plan into operation. Moving over to Emma, whilst continuing to impress with his rhythmic choreographic routine (although no swan-dive) he bent down and spoke into her ear, confirming he was attracted to her and would really like to see her at some point in the near future. Emma was notably blushing through interest and once back in work she sent Eric an email to confirm she would like to go on a date with him. Eric later found out that Emma's dad had commented on Eric when dropping off his daughter and friend, who also worked at the bank, suggesting he looked like a big-time Charlie in his sunglasses. Little was he to know that they would soon be getting to know one another a lot better also.

Eric and Emma got on very well and both were happy in their new relationship together, although it was still a little bit awkward with Eric still living at home with his parents and older brother. Perhaps guilty of not learning his lesson from having moved in with Di far too soon, Eric was soon moving in with Emma at her house, in a rather insalubrious part of North Wales. Not driving also meant Eric was rather isolated, unable to meet up with his friends quite as readily as he had previously.

The end of August 2002 saw Eric fly out to New York with his family to attend a wedding, which had been in the pipeline for some time. Despite how well things had gone between Emma and Eric, he'd thought it best for her not to tag along, what with the cost of flights at short notice and the logistics involved making it just a little too impractical. Emma was very upset at seeing Eric leave, crying as she dropped him off at his parents' house the night before his flight out across the pond. Eric had been a little bemused at her reaction to him departing and it left a rather uncomfortable feeling in the pit of his stomach.

The longer that Eric had been with Emma, the more he could tell that she had been rather badly mistreated and affected by her ex. He had caused her a lot of mental anguish and this was clear to see with her general nervousness, especially noticeable in the bedroom. She had no libido whatsoever, not turned on by the thought of sex and certainly not the one to instigate any bedroom gymnastics whatsoever. It was disappointing to Eric as here he was as horny as a herd of stags at a stag do in Hornsville Arizona, with a girl he was very attracted to and yet sex in her mind was lying perfectly still on her back impersonating roadkill.

Eric knew it wasn't her fault and was extremely patient, trying his best to coax her into a more mutually beneficial relationship but it soon appeared to be a rather futile task, the situation culminating in an angry tirade by Emma, when she threw some expensive lingerie back at him that he'd bought her when sharing their first Christmas together. Perhaps he had been just a little misguided with his purchase taking into account all that had gone before.

Given that Eric was feeling a little short-changed when it came to carnal instincts, this may have accounted for his rather shameful pursuits of sex with other girls whilst still in a relationship with Emma. He was only human at the end of the day and perhaps he should have been more focussed on ending things with her before looking for someone more compatible. Nevertheless, it happened and Eric, although not proud of his extra-curricular activities, had managed to increase his experience somewhat.

Chapter Nineteen

American Pie

The first occurrence of this had actually taken place whilst over at the wedding in the U.S. of Stateside, him and his family staying in a friend's apartment or condo as our American cousins prefer to call it. She was called Fiona. Funnily enough, others had mentioned how they thought Eric and Fiona would get on and their instincts were proven correct.

Eric first clapped his mince pies on her after disembarking the Wagon Queen Family Truckster (National Lampoon's Vacation – 7.4/10 IMDb) which they'd hired and picked up at Newark airport on touching down. Fiona was at least ten years older than Eric, a rather gregarious (typical American exuding confidence) red-head who appeared very classy and despite not being big up top, Eric was attracted to her. Conscious that his girlfriend Emma was waiting patiently back home, however, Eric was not interested in breaking her trust and with the reason for the trip solely based on the wedding arrangements, then his mind was very much occupied on that in any case.

That was until Eric's phone call with Emma, which he made from the condo a few days in. The phone call didn't last long as Eric was conscious that he wasn't paying the bill but the call left him feeling rather less than content once it had come to an end.

Instead of asking questions about Eric, Emma had instead used the call predominantly to put in requests from her workmates regarding certain items that could only be bought over in the States. Eric was rather annoyed at the idea that she was seemingly more interested in them than of him and her. With a somewhat perplexed feeling and questioning the genuine validity of their relationship even more, Eric's thoughts soon turned to Fiona and to making the most of his time with her.

Fiona was obviously interested in Eric, choosing to drive him around and show him off to people she knew, although in Eric's mind acting rather pretentiously as she introduced him to others as Frederick from London, Eric living approximately 200-miles from the Big Smoke (those crazy

Americans). However, Eric was happy to look past this matter and continue to enjoy himself.

The highlight of the trip, apart from the wedding celebrations, was Fiona driving them to the Atlantic coast after dark, parking up and taking a blanket with them to sit on and experience the sound of the waves crashing onto the beach, the only light being cast by the moon in the night sky.

As things progressed on a romantic front, it wasn't long until Eric was lying on top of Fiona, kissing and generally getting it on (said in my finest American twang). As things progressed even further, they'd started removing items of clothing or more accurately hitching Fiona's dress up and both their pants down to their ankles. Again, here was another situation where Eric didn't have to worry about his big leg as they fumbled around in the pitch black trying to locate one another's erogenous zones.

Then things got a little more steamy but no sooner had it started then they were both rudely interrupted, the very faint outline of a man with his dog passing not ten feet away from them and the pair stopping, waiting patiently for him to walk out of range before returning to it.

Seconds later they were again interrupted. However, this time by something that would put the nail in the coffin as far as any sexual gratification was concerned. Eric couldn't believe it; a huge great beachcomber vehicle complete with tank tracks came over the brow of a nearby dune, an array of lights which ran across its front blinding Eric and Fiona as they lay in flagrante, Eric's naked bum cheeks now in the spotlight as he remained motionless and highly embarrassed. 'Ha-ha' I hear you all cry and perhaps 'that's just what he deserved'.

With the beachcomber having passed, the moment had well and truly past also; there was no coming back from that one and Eric was as limp as an earthworm. The pair got dressed and made their way back to the car, feeling a little awkward and Eric more than just a little frustrated.

Arriving back home in Blighty and being repatriated with Emma, Eric was still very much preoccupied with thoughts of his shenanigans over in the States. Fiona had brought to light how Eric was evidently not happy in his relationship as why else would he carry on like he had? He really needed to tell Emma and move on; especially as she had noticed Eric was acting more than a little strange.

Eric had not been brave enough to admit that he'd had physical relations with another woman and merely put his change in persona down to the result of realising that she and he may not be as compatible as he'd hoped. Emma, who was notably still keen to stay together, accepted what Eric had to say and that they would see how things progressed, Emma fully aware that she had some mental baggage that she needed to address also.

Chapter Twenty

Eric the Agony Aunt

A couple of months later and it was the turn of one of Eric's best mates, Jim, to get wed, the venue down in Northamptonshire, where his bride-to-be was originally from. Given Eric's somewhat chequered dating past and the fact that they had been sent out long in advance, Eric's invite was for him and no plus-one. Eric was selfishly happy about this as it meant he could really let his hair down and given his position as one of the ushers, meant he also didn't have to worry about Emma's wellbeing throughout and could enjoy himself even more.

Eric and his mate Reg stopped off first in the Midlands to pick up their whistles at a house which the bride rented out to two student friends, both girls. Eric didn't think much of the felines and they weren't exactly the friendliest he'd ever come across. After a hysterical mix-up with their suits, Eric trying desperately to squeeze into his in one corner of the room, whilst Reg stood there in the other looking like Coco the Clown with oversized pantaloons, they swapped garments and made their way to a Travelodge to check-in and ready themselves for the church service later that day.

The church was very quaint, a typical English looking affair in a setting fit for an Agatha Christie murder mystery. Eric and Reg, both ushers, stood at the main doors welcoming guests and after asking the bride's mum and dad if they were with the bride or groom, then Eric realised they should possibly have done a little homework prior to their starring roles.

It was a beautiful day despite the time of the year and the women looked resplendent in their floral dresses and hats. This included a pair of girls who Eric and Reg had almost not recognised; the same girls they'd seen earlier that morning. 'Blimey' Eric thought noticing a rather significant difference in their appearance, which had notably followed several hours of preparation and the application of make-up.

Following the service, there was then the task of getting to a local golf club, which was the venue for the reception, its remote location not entirely appreciated until later when the celebrations had ended.

Eric had a great time at the reception, loving his position as an usher in that he got to dress up and feel the part, without the real stress of having to write a speech. Standing by the bar mostly, he chatted to old school teachers who were the groom's godparents amongst other guests, drinking a fair bit and making merry.

Then, with the introduction of the jazz band, playing one of Eric's favourite pieces 'When You're Smiling', Eric felt compelled to dance and he danced like there was no tomorrow, the band members telling him that they'd never seen dancing like it before. Eric was conscious that they meant it in a positive way and weren't suggesting that he looked like a new-born giraffe-calf failing miserably to get to its feet.

Another person who seemed impressed was one of the two girls, who we shall call Susan for the sake of convenience. Now, Eric had learnt that Susan was the ex-girlfriend of Adam, the best man and who had known Jim since starting uni together. It was true that Jim had mentioned to Eric that he had two people in mind to be his best man when out having a quiet drink some several months before the big day. However, despite Eric having known Jim since they fought over Lego roof tile pieces in playgroup, he was happy to relinquish the responsibility in favour of his newfound university chum. This was despite also knowing that the speech would fail to compete with his own efforts but he remembered the recent best man role he carried out, conceding that it was quite possibly thee most nerve-wracking experience of his life bar none.

Where was I? Yes. Adam had split up with Susan and during the evening, after flagons of ale had been consumed and everyone was feeling more confident and forthright, Adam approached Eric to ask him for his advice.
'I still really like Susan and am thinking of telling her that and seeing if we can get back together' he exclaimed. 'What dya reckon?'
'Just go for it' Eric replied, feeling on top of the world having taken a breather from the dancefloor. 'You've got nothing to lose and I guess you'll find out how she feels without having regrets later' he added.
Plied with Eric's positive recommendations, Adam disappeared and Eric did not notice him for the remainder of the evening.

Then, not half-an-hour later, Adam's best friend, who Eric had only met that day, approached him; he too in a quandary and in search of some advice (at this point Eric was feeling quite the old sage, being called on by his peers to prescribe them advice on the matters pertaining to women and relationships. Eric had certainly come a long way it seemed).

'I really like Susan' he exclaimed 'but I'm obviously conscious that Adam went out with her for some time and the last thing I want to do is to tread on his toes; what do you think I should do?'

Well, Eric was taken aback to think that both he and Adam were after the same girl and yet neither had obviously said anything to each other, despite being close friends. Party to all of the information and yet still pretty much sozzled lest we forget, Eric decided to offer him some advice. 'Just go for it. You've got nothing to lose and I guess you'll find out how she feels without having regrets later' came the rather familiar-sounding reply, Eric not really wishing to get dragged into the whole affair. Plied with Eric's positive recommendations, he too disappeared and again Eric didn't notice him for the remainder of the night.

As the evening progressed, Eric found himself back on the dancefloor more often than not and whilst making like an epileptic at a Jean-Michel Jarre concert, was joined by a girl who looked very tasty in her blue and white floral dress; it was Susan. She was also a bit tipsy and enjoying herself and it appeared, despite having at least two keen admirers, she was only interested in one fella that night. Yes, despite having acted as the neutral agony aunt and advising the two others on how they should go about their desire to be with Susan, it was he who she wanted. To this day, Eric never learnt whether either or both of the fellas had actually followed up his advice and spoke with her.

Chapter Twenty-One

The Cat That Got the Cream

After the music finally stopped and the lights came on (and people bent down picking up party popper covers believing them to be coinage… Peter Kay) it was apparent that Susan wanted to be escorted back to the Travelodge by Eric. As mentioned earlier, the remoteness of the golf course had backfired somewhat as nobody was able to hire a taxi, leaving the mass ranks of guests having no other option than to walk a few miles to the nearest built-up area in order to increase their chances. It was absolutely freezing, the women, including Susan, having not considered the possibility when picking out their outfits.

Eric and Susan found themselves very much at the tail end of the crocodile of drunk guests that were heading down the country lanes, like some scene from a post-apocalyptic film (Threads – 8.1/10 IMDb) where survivors were migrating in search of civilisation. Eric, ever the gentleman, had given Susan his suit jacket, which given their size differential acted as a significant addition to her attire.

When finally making it back to the Travelodge some hours later, Eric rushed to his room trying to avoid any propositions from Susan, Eric starting to sober up by now and his thoughts turning to both Emma (remember her?) and the pressure to perform had Susan got him back to her room. What Eric hadn't reckoned on or realised was that he was supposed to be sharing a room with two others; yes you've guessed it none other than Adam and his friend, aka Susan's biggest fans.

Opening the door to the room, there they were, both sat fully-clothed next to one another on a bed with their backs against the wall and both staring menacingly at Eric. It was just a smidge awkward but before the awkwardness could be remedied, Susan came in through the door behind him and exclaimed 'get your bag… you're staying with me tonight'. Cue an even greater feeling of awkwardness. Before Eric could say anything, Susan had grabbed his bag and he was following her to her room. A lucky escape you might say for Eric and a far more entertaining and enjoyable end to his evening lay in store.

The next morning and having heard nothing from Eric all evening, Emma called him on his mobile. Eric hated speaking on the phone but answered realising that he hadn't exactly been the best boyfriend material in the ways of communication, although lying in bed with another girl having just had sex with her and watching her get up and walk to the bathroom naked as he spoke to his girlfriend was possibly not the best advert for boyfriend material either.

Given that the golf course was remoter than the sea of tranquillity, there was no mobile phone reception (this was 2002 and before 4G or even 3G) and therefore Emma was to some degree satisfied as to his lack of text messages.

After dressing and meeting everyone in the car park, having missed out on breakfast due to a much-needed lie-in, Eric watched as Susan got into the back of a car with both of her admirers, which was heading back to their hometown. She smiled at Eric enthusiastically through the rear passenger window as the car pulled away flanked by two rather less smiley individuals it had to be said. Eric could finally relax and summed the night up as a job well done and another very happy customer.

Less than a fortnight later, Eric and Emma lay in bed together trying to get some shuteye. Eric's phone, which was purposely situated away from the bed charging (to ensure that Eric got up out of bed once his alarm went off and therefore less chance of simply knocking it off and falling back asleep) started to ring, although not in the traditional sense; it was probably the theme to Knightrider or Airwolf at that stage. It was after midnight, which was considered late by Emma, Eric having had to readapt to earlier bedtimes to assist with relationship harmonics.

Eric did not leap out of bed to answer it, instead allowing it to ring out, himself not sure who it could be, the pair now wide awake. A minute or so later and the phone rang again, prompting a multitude of tuttage and Eric's reluctant dismount from the bed and nervous walk over to his phone to check. He noticed that the unrecognised number had left a voice message.

'Who is it?' Emma asked inquisitively witnessing Eric's illuminated face from across the darkroom. Eric, having started listening to the message, realised instantly it was Susan and acting aloof, made out it was just a wrong number, remembering to curse and sound pissed off for added effect.

Eric was unhappy at the occurrence, which could have proved rather costly, especially having intentionally kept his number from Susan, having no real desire to see her again. It appeared someone else had furnished her with his number and as Jim confirmed it hadn't been him, then who else could it have been? Who else would not have been that bothered if Eric's own relationship had been jeopardised by giving Susan the opportunity to make contact with him?

Given things weren't exactly great between Eric and Emma for all of the above reasons; it was no surprise when they split-up. Their relationship seemed unsolvable in Eric's eyes; Eric, not for the first time, returning to live with his mum and dad like some perennial boomerang. The good news was that Eric felt like he was back in the land of the living, not isolated anymore and given Emma no longer worked at the same bank, there was no real awkwardness for him to endure.

Chapter Twenty-Two

Chorley Not

After Eric had parted company with Emma, he was desperate to get out there and mingle, not wanting to be stuck indoors staring at the four walls of his bedroom, his independence thwarted once more after moving back with his parents. So, when his mate Terry invited him to join him and his brother on a trip to Chorley to visit a friend, Eric leapt at the chance.

It was winter so already dark by the time they set off early evening and travelled up in Terry's brother's car, the 50-mile journey taking approximately an hour up the motorway. They drove to Terry's brother's mate's house first and after the pleasantries were out of the way, the four of them carried on into town for a few beers. It seemed Eric was on a mission that night, putting quite a bit away and not looking like he was slowing up anytime soon. Come closing time in the pub, Eric was panicked to see that Terry, his brother and their mate Martin were packing up and heading home. 'Whaaaaat?' Eric exclaimed expecting that they'd be out clubbing till the wee hours.

With the three remaining staunchly set in their ways and heading back to Martin's, Eric decided to stay out on his own as it was just far too early to retire for the evening in his eyes. However, as Eric didn't have a Scooby-doo where Martin lived, he managed to commandeer an eyeliner pencil from a girl to use as a writing utensil and wrote Martin's address down on a napkin, before putting it in his pocket for safekeeping. He could then use this to give to the taxi driver (8.3/10 IMDb) when he'd finished for the night and be able to find his way back.

Eric said adios to the others and headed from the pub towards the bright lights of the Chorley nightlife (coming in your ears… Phoenix Nights). Noticing a nightclub called Applejacks, Eric entered and made his way to the bar. The place was only sparsely populated considering it was a Saturday, which was rather a disappointment to Eric, who was hoping for wall to wall fanny. Instead, the clientele was akin to that of Mos Eisley, lots of weirdos and flasher mac types stood on their own overlooking the black and white chessboard design dancefloor, which was emptier than John Wayne Bobbit's underpants. Despite the place oozing cheese and tackiness, Eric had paid to get in and not knowing what his other options were in Chorley, then he decided to stay put.

By now Eric had begun to drink whisky and cokes, having drunk pints at the pub previously and for whatever reason, he suddenly came over all sick. He tried unsuccessfully to overcome the feeling as eventually his brain had been passed some rather decisive information; he'd have to run for the ablutions if he wanted to preserve his dignity. He'd had the same feeling a few times in his life, usually after falling into bed after arriving home from a heavy session, his attempt to sleep rudely interrupted when realising he was going to hurl chunks, vaulting out of bed and rushing to the toilet, sometimes making it and other times sadly not.

After Eric flew across the empty chequered dancefloor and made it to the men's, he was mortified to find that the single cubicle at the far end was taken and each of the urinals was also occupied. As the sick had begun to come up into his mouth, then Eric had no time to acknowledge queuing etiquette and noticing one of the fellas moving away from one of the pissers, he dived in towards it, reaching the basin just in the nick of time.

It was a great feeling of relief but Eric felt rather embarrassed as after throwing up he'd rendered it useless, the urinal completely caked in whatever Eric had eaten earlier that day. As there were still fellas waiting to evacuate their bladders and who witnessed his involuntary act, Eric was not hanging around, wiping his mouth on the back of his hand before exiting the toilets and club with great haste; still tasked with finding his way back to Martin's.

Chapter Twenty-Three

No Room at the Inn

It was around 2:00 a.m. by now and it was absolutely freezing outside as Eric tried to locate a taxi, only donned in a going out shirt (and trousers of course). After finding a rank, he queued up behind a rabble of drunken youths, one girl offering him a slice of her pizza and flashing her boobs to heckling passersby, who obviously knew she was a classy bird.

Eventually making it into the warmth of a cab, Eric took out the napkin he'd kept safe in his pocket and despite a bit of smudging was luckily still able to decipher Martin's address. Arriving at the house, Eric recognised Terry's brother's car and was therefore confident he had the right place. It must have been at least minus three degrees, a white frost present on lawns and car windows of the built-up housing estate.

Eric paid the driver and then made his way to the front door and began knocking. No answer. Eric knocked again, this time slightly harder. Still nothing. Eric was conscious that he didn't want to make too much of a racket as it was 2:30 a.m. in the morning and all noises were exaggerated somewhat given the deathly silence.

Eric then had a brainwave and reaching for his mobile, he tried phoning Terry. The call went straight to his answerphone, which was not a very practical outcome for Eric it had to be said. Eric moved to the front window of the house and began banging on that instead of the door, but it was evident that all three of them were in deep sleep and weren't going to be awoken no matter how hard he banged.

So Eric came up with another idea and called directory enquiries. He had the full address and so it was worth a shout he thought.
'What's the address?' the woman asked him after he got through to the switchboard. Eric confirmed the address from the napkin.
'And what's the name?'
'Erm… Martin' Eric replied realising that he was unaware of his surname.
'Sorry, I'm going to need the full name'
'I don't know his surname… look it's about minus three here and I'm only

wearing a shirt… if you don't give me the number then I'm likely to die of hypothermia and it'll be on your head' Eric retorted now frustrated that he couldn't get into the house as try as he might. 'There was a woman who died I seem to remember in a very similar situation' Eric continued, 'You must have heard about it?'
'I'm sorry, but without the full name then I can't give out the number' she replied realising that Eric sounded slightly in a pickle.
'Is it Jones? How about Smith, Taylor, Davies, Roberts?' Eric now rattling off the more common names he could think of.
'I'm sorry, I can't help you' she exclaimed.
'I'm sorry too' came Eric's immediate response and with that he hung up.

A minute or so later Eric heard the sound of a woman's stiletto shoes clip-clopping along the pavement out front and walked out to the entrance of the drive, although conscious that he didn't want to alarm her at that late hour. Eric explained his predicament to her and despite empathising with him confirmed that he couldn't stay at hers. As one of Martin's neighbours, Eric asked her if she knew his surname but wasn't surprised when she didn't as knew it was unusual that you would remember such detail unless you happened to live right next door. Eric was no further finding a solution to his problem, now wishing he'd gone back with his mate and not stayed out in the first place.

After exhausting his options, Eric realised that he'd have to stay at a local Travelodge or the like and so-called the taxi firm that had dropped him off, pointing this out to them. The one lucky break he had that evening was his phone battery not having died on him, which would have left him in a much bigger hole. Eric spoke too soon though as after the taxi picked him up, his phone died. 'Great', Eric thought as he was now unable to ring ahead to hotels and check their availability for the night. Instead, the taxi would have to take him to the hotel and find out when he arrived.

Eric was at least glad of the warm environment inside the taxi, having spent half-an-hour in the elements. On arriving at the nearest hotel, Eric asked the driver to wait outside until he was sure that they had a vacancy. With no room in the inn so to speak Eric got back in the cab and the driver set off to try another, slightly further afield. Again, the hotel was fully booked and Eric had to go in search of yet another. Eric couldn't believe how busy the hotels were and then it suddenly dawned on him; it was Valentine's night. 'Bollocks' he thought, the realisation washing over him like a bad dream and adding to his frustration.

He couldn't believe how things had seemingly conspired against him. It was laughable and if it had happened in a situation comedy then not many would have believed it. Even the taxi driver could see Eric's plight, confirming that he would have let him stay at his for the night had he not got a young daughter. Eric felt like saying 'What, you suggesting I'm going to hurt her?' but realised that his intentions had been sincere. Having tried a further two hotels and with no luck, Eric was left with two options; one, travel even further afield and chance his arm that a hotel there had a spare room or bite the bullet and travel back home down the M6, which to repeat was a 50-mile journey, having started out from Martin's house.

Eric made the realistic assumption that the chance of finding a spare room for the night on Valentine's Day was as remote as finding out he was related to Barrack Obama and so asked the taxi driver if he was able to take him back. The driver was happy to do so; of course he was, the fare worth a pretty penny to him and with the roads empty, then he could be there and back in around an hour-and-a-half maximum. Before agreeing to take him though, the driver asked to see the cash upfront. As Eric had run dry following his extended night out on his own, he asked the driver to find a hole in the wall and took out 100 notes, which he showed to the driver on his return.

Just as they had set off for the motorway, Eric suddenly had a brainwave. His mate, Reg and fiancé had recently moved into a house some 20 miles nearer than his home. However, there were only a couple of slight problems. It was now after 4:00 a.m. in the morning and Eric didn't have a phone.

It was at this stage that Eric had started to think about his relationship with Emma, cursing himself that had he not split up with her then he wouldn't have been in this predicament in the first place.

Eric asked to borrow the driver's mobile in order to phone his mate, which he was happy to do given the situation. However, it meant Eric had to phone directory enquiries (again) first to obtain his mate's landline number, not having memorised it and aware that he'd probably switched off his mobile in any case. This time, Eric knew the address and his mate's surname and was therefore put straight through.

Now, if you were in bed at 4:00 a.m. in the morning fast asleep and you received a phone call then you'd probably be rather reluctant to answer it, fearing the worst. So, on picking up the receiver, Eric quickly apologised for waking him and confirmed that everything was okay, he was en route towards his in a taxi and could he bed down at his for the night. A tired Reg agreed he could stay but given the time suggested he would let him in but that they should wait till they all woke up later on before explaining what had happened. Eric agreed, grateful for a place to kip for the night.

On finally making it to Reg's house, Eric was staggered by the tariff; he'd kept his eye on the taximeter for most of the journey, the running total reminding him of what a complete numpty he'd been. The final readout said £97 and Eric begrudgingly paid the money over to the driver, tipping him three pounds for some inextricable reason. Perhaps he was just relieved it was all over.

As Eric approached the house, Reg opened the front door, having been expecting his arrival. Eric could see both he and his fiancé were up and both majorly squinting as you do when you've been rudely awoken at an ungodly hour and turn on the lights. Eric apologised to them both and was shown to his room, where at now 4:30 a.m. in the morning he was finally able to crash out.

Chapter Twenty-Four

I Just Need to Use the Bathroom

Having split up with Emma, Eric had also gone back to thinking of Di, who now lived only a ten-minute walk away (again) and to fitting back into the social scene with his mates and going out at weekends, including back to their old stomping ground of Randy's. It was there that Eric found his next lady friend.

Eric hadn't seen Gail inside the club and it was only when waiting in the queue for a taxi afterwards that he first came across her. It was late and it was bloody freezing. Given that most girls went out in a handkerchief-sized dress and heels and little else no matter the weather, Gail was a smidge cold so had purposely bunched up with Eric and his mates in the hope of shielding her from the elements. After exchanging pleasantries, it transpired that Gail lived not too far from Eric so she jumped in a cab with him and his mates, escaping the weather and being vocal in wanting to share the cab fare home.

It was a little frustrating for Eric in the taxi as although he liked the cut of Gail's jib (despite her broad Liverpudlian accent) he didn't feel he could chat her up with his friends sat in the same cab and with conversation flowing freely between them all. Gail was the first to disembark and so Eric decided to bail out too, knowing this was his chance to speak to her 'mano a mano' and besides, he only lived a matter of a ten-minute walk away in any case.

Eric had noticed that Gail lived just around the corner from Di and it was this fact which would spark one of his future escapades. Realising he could kill two birds with one stone, Eric had picked up two bottles of vino one afternoon when finding himself with little to do (probably only FA Cup matches that weekend). He'd then hid one of the bottles in some bushes in betwixt the two girl's houses and popped round to see them one at a time as per his arranged plan, presenting them each with an alcoholic gift. His efforts did not go unnoticed and he managed to get a blowjob from each of them in the same afternoon. It was textbook stuff. He couldn't quite believe what was happening to him now as he seemed a million miles from the Eric that had once been as popular with women as a dose of thrush. This was certainly the pinnacle of his female relations to that point, like Timmy Lea from the 'Confessions of a Window Cleaner' doing his door to door visits. (4.2/10 IMDb)

Back to the story and Eric and Gail were chatting after exiting the taxi outside her house. As it was cold and Gail was notably interested, she invited Eric in, although quick to point out that her mum was asleep upstairs babysitting for her. The pair were still a little inebriated from their nights out and it didn't take long before Eric and Gail were kissing, the main lights off, Gail having plumped for the ambience of a small lamp in the corner of the room.

As the two were both hornier than a pair of rutting elk, things progressed onto the lounge floor and Eric couldn't believe his luck, the knowledge that her mum was upstairs elevating the whole experience somewhat, the jeopardy providing that little more excitement.

Just as things were beginning to get more interesting for Eric with Gail's handkerchief dress making way, the light in the adjoining hallway suddenly came on. 'Bollocks!' Eric thought as Gail leapt up quicker than Usain Bolt on anabolic steroids, before fixing herself and rushing to cut her mum off at the pass or in this case the lounge doorway.

By this time Eric had sat back on the couch and smartened his appearance up also, now playing the role of 'perfect boyfriend' material complete with halo and a block of Lurpak in his mouth.
'I heard a noise and didn't know if you were back so came down to check' Eric heard her mum say to Gail. After confirming to her mum that she was fine and also had a guest, her mum retreated back upstairs.

Both Eric and Gail were visibly relieved, knowing that a couple of minutes later and they would literally have been caught with their pants down. Eric hadn't been bowled over by the experience, feeling rather embarrassed and like a naughty schoolboy so was quite keen to leave at that point. His exit was so swift that he hadn't even given any thought to seeing Gail again or at least swapping phone numbers to make the possibility an option.

The next morning, Eric reflected on the previous night's antics, both with cringeworthy embarrassment and laughter. Perhaps he would see Gail again as long as there weren't any further unwanted surprises. Without her telephone number though, the only real practical way to contact her was to write her a letter (snail mail) as he knew where she lived. Coincidentally, Gail lived just a couple of houses away from where Eric had spent the first six months of his life, although his memories of that time were a little sketchy to be fair. So he wrote to her, ensuring to confirm his mobile number if she wanted to get in touch.

A week or so later and after Eric had already accepted defeat and that his idea had been futile, he received a text message from Gail. Everyone loves a bit of mystery it seemed and receiving a letter like that out of the blue had been a pleasant surprise for her. The pair decided to meet up again.

Gail invited Eric round to hers, this time without her mother or child in attendance, which gave them a chance to get to know one another better and whilst stone-cold sober. Eric soon realised that Gail was going through a divorce and was contesting custody (custardy) of her son, who was around three-years-old. Straight away, Eric had decided that he could do without this kind of baggage but as Gail was an attractive girl, lived less than a ten-minute walk away and he was still playing catch-up, then he felt it wouldn't hurt to hang around for a bit and see what developed.

One of the first things Gail did was to ask Eric to cast his eyes over her handwritten letter to her solicitor regarding the amount of time she felt her ex should be permitted access to their son. It was immediately obvious to Eric from reading her letter that Gail was again not someone who was blessed with brains (like Becky) and another reason why this was never going to work out.

Despite this revelation, Eric made like the Littlest Hobo once again and went about rewriting her letter for her. He did not just ensure it was grammatically correct and there were no spelling mistakes but added some salient points that would definitely show her in a much better light in front of a judge and give her a better chance of getting what she wanted. Of course, Eric ran everything past Gail before making any additions. The crux of the matter, Eric believed, was that in order to sound fair and of sound mind, Gail needed to convey in her letter how she appreciated the importance of a father-figure in the life of her son and it was this that Eric used to open with in her letter.

Gail was a confident girl in general terms; certainly when it came to bedroom activities and liked to be in control. This wasn't the best news as far as Eric was concerned, not exactly an expert in these matters. Once he started receiving any instructions in bed (apart from perhaps turn the light out) the commands would usually have the rather disappointing effect of turning him completely off and rendering him useless, although with his mind also occupied on shrouding his big leg, then he was certainly up against it. Fortunately, he managed to get through it okay but he knew things would have to change dramatically for him to start to enjoy the idea of sex (in general) and not be put off due to other extenuating circumstances.

Eric only saw Gail a handful of times before the nail in her coffin came in the shape of a family party. Eric's older brother having married in the States at the end of the summer had been keen to mark the occasion back in Blighty for all those who couldn't attend the wedding across the pond. Therefore, they hired the big room at a local social club in town and put on a spread of vol-au-vents, cheesecake and of course garlic bread (Peter Kay).

Eric had mentioned the party to Gail and given they'd only seen each other briefly, he'd assumed she wouldn't want to attend, a bit too early to be meeting Eric's family and just a little daunting he thought. However, as Gail was quite a confident woman, the idea of the party didn't faze her one iota and she was keen to partner Eric at the event. 'OK', Eric thought slightly startled and it appeared he would be tasked with chaperoning her all evening.

Gail scrubbed up very well indeed and it was only her broad scouse accent that Eric was a little wary of, knowing his family were likely to have all kinds of trouble interpreting her. The room was a decent size, with a separate area to the side of the dancefloor, which had been designated for close family; two large tables pushed together where Eric's mum and dad, brothers and nan and granddad were seated. The newlyweds were doing the rounds and meeting as many friends and family members as they could, knowing they would soon be back living over 3,000 miles away.

Everything seemed to be going pretty well with Gail sat next to Eric at the table and having been introduced to everyone present. An hour or so into proceedings though and Gail, picking up her handbag and standing up from her seat then went and ruined all her previous good work by announcing 'I'm just going for a slash', her voice travelling across the whole table and audible by all of Eric's family, their faces telling their own story.

Eric turned a shade of crimson; he knew that Gail was down to earth but this was just a little too common for him and he made a mental note; he would not be seeing her again after that night.

Chapter Twenty-Five

Emma Mark I – Part II

Gail had again highlighted to Eric how difficult it could or would be to find someone on his own wavelength and free from any baggage. It made him realise how much Emma and he had been good for each other and how he had perhaps not considered this fully before the split.

Eric was finding it tougher than he'd thought to try and put her completely behind him. He still had feelings for her and as everyone knows, a few drinks down the hatch and things not seemingly going as well as planned and it was easy to get back in touch, especially with mobile phones making it effortless to make contact.

So he did. It seemed Emma was of a similar opinion and following some slowly-slowly-catchy-monkeyness in the shape of another first date at a local Holiday Inn, it wasn't long before Eric was back in the fold. As part of their repatriation and future plans together, there had been some home truths discussed and one of these was the very real need for them to set up nearer to everyone else in the land of the living especially as Eric had felt so isolated, not being able to drive (legally) even with Emma's car at his disposal. Eric, therefore, agreed to make inroads into passing his test as part of the deal.

Emma sold her house and made a pretty penny on it too, turning a profit of around 140% over a relatively short space of time. Emma had then returned to living with her parents as Eric had already done (his parents and not hers) but then he'd decided to regain some independence and moved into rented accommodation with his mate Terry. The first day of their tenancy came less than 24 hours after Eric passed his driving test, in April 2004.

The terraced row where Eric and Terry now dwelt had been part of ye-olde drinking tavern hundreds of years previous and meant that each had a sizeable cellar. Eric called it the Alice in Wonderland house as the front door was only around 5'9" at most and meant Eric and anyone above this height had to stoop as they entered. The good news was that there was also a pub literally a hop, skip and a jump from the rabbit hole.

Chapter Twenty-Six

Be Careful What You Wish For

Both saving money as they lived separately, the plan was for Eric and Emma to ultimately find their own place together. There was no rush though and Eric's tenancy agreement ran till the end of the year in any case. In the run-up to Christmas, Emma was visiting Eric in his warren and Eric was completely devoid of ideas for what to get his girlfriend for the big day. He prided himself with being able to select a decent gift for someone, himself not overly keen to receive anything due to embarrassment and the awkwardness that came with it.

He'd realised that he wasn't going to buy her any clothes this time following the lingerie fiasco and also the purchase of a kimono-style dress the following Christmas, when it only became apparent that the split down the side went right the way up to Emma's waist and left little to the imagination as her arse hung out of it every time she sat down. This was especially inappropriate as they'd spent the festivities at Eric's parents' house.

As luck would have it, Eric's prayers were answered as whilst watching some TV together, an advert came on to showcase a radio-controlled helicopter. 'I've always wanted to have a go with one of them… or a plane or boat' Emma announced in front of the gathered assortment, some of Eric's other friends present at the time. 'Ta-da!' Eric thought to himself and the next day he went checking out all the model-kit shops in the city, not a stone's throw from his house.

Given the complexity, practicality and cost of radio-controlled aircraft, Eric instead plumped for a state-of-the-art speedboat; the 'Ripmax Intercepter Ultra' no less and costing the lion's share of £200; not some cheap toy by any stretch. Eric felt pleased as punch and after wrapping it was looking forward to seeing Emma's face when she opened it.

In the run-up to the big day, the pair were staying over at his parents' on Christmas Eve and opened their gifts for one another in Eric's old bedroom the following morning (by now the bunk bed having been dismantled and the two single beds pushed together to form a plentiful double). Eric liked spoiling his girlfriends and enjoyed drawing out the gift presentation process to lengthen the excitement.

Therefore, after Emma had assumed she'd opened everything, there was still one very big surprise left. Eric left the room momentarily and came back in smiling, clutching a rather large gift-wrapped oblong in both hands. The box was approximately one-metre in length and Emma's face was a picture, both at receiving another gift and thinking what the dickens it could be. Tearing into the gift wrapping, she was still completely at a loss as to what it might contain and then on finally revealing the almost 1:1 scale photo of the boat along its entire length, she didn't hold back with her reaction.

Eric was smiling like a Cheshire Cat, his eyes transfixed on Emma's face as he waited for the excitement to transcend her facial features. Instead, Emma began to cry; not tears of joy by any means but the tears of a girlfriend thinking 'what the fuck have you bought me?' It was a rather awkward moment for both of them, especially Eric whose family were downstairs full of Christmas cheer and here were Eric and Emma looking like they'd both been handed some really bad news.

Talk of Emma having mentioned she'd 'always wanted to have a go at playing with one' seemed futile now as it appeared that Emma's real desire was in reality not up there on her list of priorities and it appeared she'd just been making friendly chit-chat.

The speedboat ('take it back' and 'look at what you could have won'… Bullseye) became a running joke in the family, even after Emma and Eric split, Emma herself able to see the funny side further down the line. It wasn't for almost a decade until the 'Intercepter Ultra' experienced its maiden voyage but that was when Eric was with a new partner and one who was genuinely thrilled at the idea of putting it together, sticking on its decals and finding a suitable boating lake to test it out on.

Yes, Megan or Meg was a proper tomboy and there were times when Eric would joke that she had a bigger dick than him; but we'll meet Meg later in around eight years' time following Speedboat-gate or around five years after Eric and Emma separated for good.

Early in the New Year (2005) Eric and Emma moved into a small but perfectly formed semi-detached, a modern house with a Tudor-esque frontage, tucked away in the corner of a cul-de-sac. Yes, it was in one of the town's cheaper districts but the estate was aesthetically pleasing and was only 50-yards from the peace and tranquillity of the countryside, spoilt only slightly by the local donkey sanctuary and the railway line that ran directly behind their garden at the rear.

Buying a new home and moving in was just the tonic for their relationship at the time and both were excited to be planning and experiencing their new life together. It helped massively that they were now much closer to everyone and even work was only a short three-mile commute.

Despite being content, Eric had not really felt an urge to think about engagement rings and taking their relationship to another level and it was Emma who became rather vocal on the subject. Feeling pretty much cajoled into it, the two went ring-shopping and Emma picked out the one that she liked. With the ring purchased, it was only really a matter of time and the thought of any real surprise had been scuppered.

So one night Eric proposed, having traded a well-planned-out balloon ride over the country plains (err, right) for a more quiet proposal affair at home, placing the ring on one of Emma's cat's collars and hoping it jumped on her lap later that evening as per usual, instead of running off out the back and losing it. Who says romance is dead? Emma said yes and Eric was engaged for the first time; Emma for a second.

Chapter Twenty-Seven

Mosquito Coast

One thing that hadn't changed was that Emma was still very quiet, tediously so Eric thought. She was still not confident enough to really put her own opinions forward or come up with any plans, seemingly everything being left to him. After having spent holidays with Emma in Boston (Massachusetts not Lincolnshire) Tunisia and then a curtailed trip to the Dominican Republic, Eric had realised that holidays with Emma were about as fun as contracting diarrhoea. He knew he would have to think of a plan for the next one to overcome this hurdle.

The reason they'd had to forgo their holiday in the Caribbean was due to the time of year coupled with Emma's blood type, apparently irresistible to mosquitoes during the wet season. They'd only been there a matter of a few days of the scheduled two-week break before Emma had quite literally become a moveable feast for the malaria spreading insects. The problem was not helped by the fact that the door to their apartment was similar to Bridgette Bardot's smile, having sizeable gaps all around.

The evening rainfall was both frequent and torrential, the vista from their ground-floor dwelling like a scene from Jurassic Park (8.1/10 IMDb), the sparse outdoor lighting reflecting off the drenched tropical flora surrounding them and Eric expecting to see a small jeep come crashing through the undergrowth being pursued by an ink-spraying Dilophosaurus at any moment.

Emma had type-B blood, which must have been quite a delicacy amongst the local mosquitoes, Eric cataloguing at least 85 separate bites over her body on his video camera for the sake of holiday insurance. The couple were left with no other choice but to return much earlier than planned. In fact, it was lucky that Eric had his big leg (he never thought he'd say that at any stage in his life) as had been advised to keep a constant supply of Penicillin following his proneness to cellulitis.

Eric believed that these meds were the only thing that prevented any infection taking over her body and winding her up in a far worse situation.

The £2,700 holiday had been a complete waste and their insurers rejected their claim based on the fact that they hadn't contacted them whilst in the Dominican. This was rather frustrating given that Eric had attempted to contact the UK but the line was so bad that he may as well have tried using a paper-cup on the end of a 4,000-mile piece of string.

As Eric's video camera was relatively new, having been bought by Emma for a Christmas present, Eric was still at the stage where he enjoyed filming almost everything. On arrival home to the safer climes of the UK, Eric was therefore keen to show his family the scenes he had captured whilst on holiday and so after the pleasantries were out of the way, Eric connected his camera up to his mum and dad's TV and pressed play. Eric's mum and dad and elder brother were in attendance together with Eric and Emma.

They sat there watching as Eric narrated scene by scene; first some video of onboard their flight and of the resort and surroundings. Then the video moved on to show Emma lying on the bed in the apartment, wearing only her two-piece swimsuit as Eric was obtaining evidence of her mosquito bites and the reason for their holiday curtailment. Eric conceded that it was slightly embarrassing, although with the very serious nature of the bites, then it seemed like a valid reason for his girlfriend to be shown. However, things were about to get a lot more embarrassing for everyone.

Eric had completely forgotten about the conversation he'd had with Emma whilst she lay on the bed, the sound coming through as clear as day through the TV speakers. Just as Eric had zoomed away from some close-ups of the bites on Emma's legs, he was now greeted with the whole of his girlfriend in the shot, lying back on the bed. Before switching off the camera, the sight of Emma in her bikini had notably turned Eric on a smidge and without a clue as to what everyone in the room was about to hear, it was too late… Eric (on the video) had already said it. 'Show us yer flange'.

It is fair to say that everyone felt exactly the same, the levels of embarrassment so high that Eric's dad instantly disappeared from the room, the atmosphere so awkward you could cut it with a cricket stump. It was only after returning home that Eric and Emma laughed their tits off, the occurrence still making Eric laugh to this very day, although surprisingly never mentioning it ever again to his mum or dad.

Chapter Twenty-Eight

Four Heads are Better than Two

Following on from their lacklustre holidays together, Eric needed to come up with a plan for future breaks (as mentioned) as was aware that he couldn't enjoy himself fully on his own with Emma. Then bingo bango bongo, he came up with a brainwave; he'd ask his best mate and wife if they fancied going on holiday together.

It was a brilliant plan, one that Eric couldn't believe he hadn't thought of sooner. He could knock about with his mate playing pool, drinking, and talking male pursuits (not dissimilar to Pinocchio and his friend Lampwick on Pleasure Island... although not including the smoking fat ceegars or turning into a donkey perhaps) whilst Emma and his mate's wife could sunbathe together and talk babbling crap. It was a win-win siduation.

So it was that the foursome flew off to the Canaries and to the island of Tenerife, staying at an all-inclusive hotel resort and Eric's plan had worked a treat. Not only did Eric not have to lie by the pool all day and get bored shitless but mealtimes were more interesting too, conversation freer flowing and a lot more entertaining.

The fellas even found time to develop Anglo-Dutch relations by allowing an older guy from the low-lying country to play a few games of billiards with them. Eric and Reg tried their best not to laugh at his extremely serious-looking fizzog and demeanour throughout (they assumed he was a bit radio-rental in fairness) but more so the fact he looked the spit of (Eugene) Tackleberry from Police Academy (6.7/10 IMDb).

One of the highlights of the holiday had been Eric's mate, Reg, trying his hand at rifle shooting. The pair had been cajoled into trying the activity by a glamorous-looking holiday rep whose job it was to drum up interest (it worked) and both Eric and Reg were up for something a little different that day. Despite Eric having the eyesight of Clarence the removal man in comparison to Reg's RAF pilot beating 20-20 vision, Eric fared much better than his friendly counterpart.

However, given Reg's relatively poor showing, he wasn't too keen to wait around for a downs lad, they'd nicknamed Rooney (on account of his likeness to the famous footballer, who had not that long moved to Man United) in case he also bettered his score.

Chapter Twenty-Nine

Wedding Day Nerves

Looking back at his relationship with Emma, Eric knew that his heart was never in it; the build-up to and manner of their engagement having been a massive indicator of his lack of desire for commitment. Was it just with Emma that he'd feel like this or did he have commitment-phobia in general? It took a bit of time for Eric to pluck up the courage to break off the wedding, which was three-months prior to their holiday in Kos and six-months before the big day itself. By this time they were living in a much larger detached house over towards Eric's mum and dad's neck of the woods.

Despite Emma having flown the nest from the bank they'd first met, she now worked for a foreign bank only a few hundred yards away, which meant they could still car-share, saving on running costs and if anybody <u>was</u> interested, appearing more eco-friendly, which was more a happy coincidence than of any predetermined plan to lower their combined carbon footprint. In fact, Eric was of the opinion that if you imagined the world as a great big swimming pool and someone was pissing and defecating in it at one end, what difference did it make if you made an effort not to, down tother?

I seem to have digressed somewhat, where was I?… Yes, en route to their relatively new home some ten-miles from work and with Emma driving (which Eric found difficult plainly and simply because he wasn't in control of his own destiny… 'Luke; it is your destiny') Eric's pseudo-fear of Emma careering into another car or causing a crash due to her indecisiveness meant he was primed with the courage to utter the words… 'I don't think I'm ready to get married'… and that as they say was that.

Emma had spent the last six months planning for the big day, having her cantankerous mother bulldoze her way into proceedings and take over as she was prone to do. Emma was her only daughter and child however and so it was only natural for that to happen Eric conceded.

They had booked the reception venue at an old stately home in the countryside, the bridesmaids fitted and their dresses acquired, the deposit on the 1970's Rolls Royce limousines paid for and the table decorations sat pristinely wrapped in crêpe paper at the bottom of her wardrobe. It seemed her mother had been the proprietor of a Bridal shop back in the day and was therefore able to call in a few favours to help out with the dress, which they bought for a bargain by all accounts. This was the same dress that Eric was not supposed to see, let alone his bride-to-be fashioning it; bad luck apparently, if you believed in such superstitions, which Eric quite plainly and simply didn't.

It was the last Christmas before D-Day (2007) which was penned in for the following September (the pencil having been rubbed-out to make way for indelible ink by that point) and Eric was spending Christmas with Emma and her family. He was handed a digital camera with photos that his in-laws-to-be had taken on their recent trip to the Caribbean, nobody in the room realising that directly before the sunny shots stood Emma in her wedding dress, which suddenly appeared in full high-definition on the 2.7 inch backlit LCD screen, the slideshow returning to the beginning. Too late; Eric had seen it.

However, it wasn't until a couple of months later with Emma's father presenting Eric with his own father's (Emma's grandfather's) wedding band and suggesting he may wish to use it for the big day that it suddenly dawned on Eric that the wedding was <u>really</u> happening and it <u>did</u> involve him!! He suddenly felt claustrophobic and needed to get out of the situation, a situation that had manifested itself through years of contentment but not overwhelming happiness and certainly not love. I mean Emma had single-handedly forced Eric to the jewellers to buy the engagement ring in the first place so it was no real surprise when their relationship pulled up short. Yes, the wedding band <u>was</u> the catalyst that shook Eric by the short and curlies and he knew he had to tell Emma; the sooner the better.

Eric wasn't bitter or sad about having to sell the ring as it had been his decision to call the wedding off in the first place. In fact, everyone, including Eric was amazed Emma had given it back to him. Then again as she still had the engagement ring from her previous outing then maybe she didn't want it to appear that she was starting a collection.

Trying to sell the ring for anything like he paid for it was a different story altogether, which pissed Eric off no end; the best offer of £300 a joke when he'd initially forked out over six-times that. 'That's the going rate for second-hand jewellery' the shop assistant had told him, the same shop who had sold it to him in the first place. 'Second-hand?' Eric replied, 'It's not like it's done anything other than sit on somebody's finger; give it a clean with some fairy-liquid and Fanny's your aunt, it's as good as the day I bought it… second-hand?… please'.

It was notable that for a shop to buy it off him at £300 meant they were notably going to try and sell it for say £700-800 and make a further profit on the same item. It was the principle of the matter now and having been screwed over once, he was not about to relinquish the booty and be screwed over again. As he departed the shop he was keen to point this out to a browsing couple, hoping to prevent them from adding to the jeweller's coffers. Eric was starting to think he'd witnessed a robbery in a jeweller's, himself playing the role of the hapless victim and the jeweller donned in a balaclava demanding the money off him in the first place.

One good thing that had come of the intended wedding-plan as far as Emma was concerned was that she had a reason/target to start to get fit, conscious of wanting to look her very best for the big day. As a result of her increased exercise regime, she'd lost almost four-stone (that's 25kg to all you metric users out there) and although Eric conceded she looked amazing, it appeared she'd lost around three-stone (19kg) from her frontal orbs, which Eric was, of course, devastated about.

Eric's relationship with Emma would ultimately end in exactly the same way as it had with Di, the split coming after a very lacklustre holiday to the Greek island of Kos, turbulent at times but the weather remained glorious throughout. The trip had been booked months in advance and despite Eric having called their wedding off, both agreed to go and at least try to enjoy a bit of downtime. Before they flew to warmer climes, Eric was adamant that he did not want the relationship to rekindle for a second time, although he couldn't work out if Emma's intentions mirrored his completely. As the holiday confirmed that the relationship had run its course and there was no way back, they both began to live their own separate lives on their return.

It was a little awkward though as Emma and Eric remained living together under the same roof, neither wanting to move out as the house was in joint names. There were plenty of rooms, the only slight inconvenience that there was only one shower and that was in the en-suite annexed to the master bedroom, Eric having to avert his gaze when Emma was passing by in her towel.

Things were pretty amicable at that stage and so much so that they began actively dating, which seemed a little odd, although the pair agreed not to bring anyone back. Eric remembered meeting another girl in a pub approximately three miles away; the girl also called Emma coincidentally. It was one of the few occasions that Eric's date made her excuses after one drink, the chemistry sadly lacking between them. However, despite Eric realising that fact, he was keen to stay out as long as he could as was conscious that if he went straight home, then (the other) Emma would know that things had gone pear-shaped and he didn't want her to have the chance to feel inwardly smug. Eric, therefore, sat at the bar on his own and put out the vibe (although not wearing his tangerine suit or carrying his tangerine cane… Dumb and Dumber) and tried chatting-up the barmaid with zero success.

Chapter Thirty

Winning the Lottery

When Eric and Emma finally went their separate ways, things had regretfully turned a little sour as they tended to do when sorting out finances. They had to deal with the house moving forward, Eric keener than Emma to remain in-situ if possible due to the location. Things took quite a dramatic turn though when on visiting his parents one day, Eric learnt that Emma had secretly contacted his mum to suggest a roundtable discussion about their finances in order to make it more transparent and above board. This angered Eric greatly, the idea that not only was Emma undermining him but his parents not making him their priority.
'Is this situation not about me?' he exclaimed.

What his mum and dad didn't realise was that Emma's (and more likely her mother's intentions) were purely on account of believing that Eric's dad had won the lottery some several years prior to them getting together. They obviously held the opinion that Eric's family were sat on a fortune and would therefore be able to quote Emma very happy when discussing severance packages. You couldn't make it up I know.

It turned out that a man having the exact same name as Eric's dad (which wasn't a common name to be fair) had won the lottery, had four children (as did Eric's dad) and even had a link to the same place where Eric's dad had worked for most of his life. Eric had never seen any paper-cutting or local news story regarding it. If Emma's family had, then you could understand why they had come to their conclusions.

Confirming this news to his mum and dad, Eric's parents realised why Emma had been keen to include them as part of negotiations and his mum sent Emma a message to call off the plan, emphasising that the matter had nothing to do with them and was something she'd have to sort out with Eric.

Further bad news was to befall Emma after her dream of a big pay-out was dashed in the eleventh hour. Having invested more money into the house than Eric, using funds she'd acquired from the sale of her own house several years prior, she was naturally expecting a great deal more from a settlement. However, the timing could not have been worse for her (and conversely not have been better for Eric)

You see, given the collapse of the banks and the beginning of the recession at the tail end of 2008, the result had been to vastly reduce the value of the house. The bank, who they'd taken out their mortgage with, confirmed that the price had dropped by around 10%. Based on this, there was no way that Eric would be required to pay Emma anything like what the house had been worth when they bought it the previous year.

This good fortune allowed Eric to buy her out of the house and set up his brother as the joint mortgagee to get it across the line, despite his brother not living there or expected to make any contributions to it from that day forth. Emma still received a decent wedge though and after Eric's solicitor had crossed the t's and dotted all the lower case j's (Wayne's World 2 – 6.2/10 IMDb), he transferred the cash over to her.

Eric was now the sole occupant of his own pad, not even having to contend with any of God's furry creatures anymore, which had tested his OCD and patience levels to the absolute limit; Emma having had two cats. This was the first time Eric had lived on his own, rarely having been used to his own room before, let alone a whole house. It felt great. He could now do whatever the fuck he wanted for the first time; stay up till whenever it suited and of course now able to invite women over whenever he liked. This was a massive leap forward for Eric and it was a refreshing beginning to a new chapter in his life.

It wasn't the last time that Eric and Emma's paths would cross though as there would be another run-in almost nine-years later. It was quite a shock at the time for Eric as she was the last person he'd expected to see checking his profile out on Match.com. I say the last person; perhaps Debbie McGee, Benjamin Netanyahu or Meryl Streep would have been less likely in all fairness.

Yes, it seemed Emma's love-life had unfolded and appeared she was now a free agent also. Aware that she would know he'd seen her perusing his profile, Eric felt compelled to message her. It had almost been a decade since they last saw one another and absolutely no hard feelings (in both senses of the phrase) as far as Eric was concerned. Eric's message went something like this:

'AWKWARD!!… Look at us both washed up on here… hope everything okay with you and I'm sorry how things turned out between us. I certainly didn't mean to hurt you'

Emma sent Eric some laughing emojis in return and it seemed as though the time that had elapsed had meant she held no grudges either. They swapped a few messages but after Emma had asked him about what he'd been up to over the past nine-years, Eric was not really in the mood to type reams and reams and so suggested meeting up for a coffee instead. Eric was in no way looking to get back with her or even for shits and giggles but he had surprised himself with his own suggestion, the idea seeming rather mature and most unlike him when it came to dealing with his exes.

Although initially sounding keen to have a catch-up, Emma had obviously been advised against it by friends or more likely her parents and got back to Eric to say she didn't think it would be a good idea but was happy instead to continue messaging. However, Eric didn't need another pen-pal so wished her all the best for the future.

Even to this day, Eric's parents were of the opinion that Emma (mark I; there would be another) had been their favourite of all his girlfriends they'd met ('of all the girls he'd loved before' sang in my best Julio Iglesias impersonated voice) which I guess spoke volumes for her, Eric thought. He knew she was friendly, polite, well-mannered and considerate with a decent sense of humour, which were the reasons Eric had spent so long with her and why they'd been engaged to be married. It was a shame that she'd been a little on the quiet side and her lack of confidence, especially in the bedroom, had ultimately been deciding factors that Eric could not negotiate past.

Chapter Thirty-One

Facebollocks

After his split with Emma, Eric's first move was to get himself set up on Facebollocks (or Facebook as it was better known). He'd heard of social media more and more and it seemed like a great way to perhaps hook up with girls he used to know at school, Friends Reunited having seemingly been squeezed out by Zuckerberg's more popular creation. He knew which of the girls he had been keen on back then; his best mate Reg and him having rated the girls in their class/year on a home-made chart, the matrix (8.7/10 IMDb) used to mark each of them out of ten over a selection of what they deemed important criteria and characteristics still in a shoebox in his parents' loft (yes, boobs was one of them).

During school, as touched on previously, he'd had no luck with any of the girls, not having had a) the confidence or b) the looks to have even chanced his arm with any of them at the time. By the end of 2008 things were very different; Eric having aged relatively well and being slightly more confident having had a series of 'relationships' and certainly chalked up a few notches on bedposts.

In fact as evidence to support his rather meteoric rise from ugly duckling to that of a comparable bird of paradise (with one leg bigger than the other) one of the girls that had come near top of both his and Reg's chart had literally been taken aback after learning who he was in Randy's, not having seen him for years. Her levels of wowage were like sweet music to Eric's ears, her boyfriend at the time nowhere near as easy on the eye… or so Eric thought, perhaps on account of his jealousy and the fact that she was still a great piece of ass.

Eric realised after only a couple of weeks that the concept of Facebollocks was thee most pretentious and dull pastime he'd ever come across (I bet that last statement was popular) the site simply a vehicle for the insecure, needy or egotistical to chart their entire waking hours to their so-called friends and followers, at times only managing to keep their daily bowel movements to themselves.

Saying that, Eric once took a photo of his breakfast in the Dominican; several hours after having eaten it and his body having rejected the waste product. The reason for the photo had been due to Eric's amazement at the size of his single stool, like he'd just given birth to a brown snake. He was sure to place his hand next to the toilet pan for the purposes of size-comparison, which his mates would later appreciate when showing them his anal sculpture.

After only a few days of monitoring his Facebook account, Eric read how one girl he'd gone to school with had broken a nail hoovering. That in itself was tedious enough he thought but it was the spattering of sympathy from her followers as a result that saw Eric reach his tether end, the main theme being 'I feel for you hun'.
'Give me strength' Eric thought and his short dabble with the social media big-hitter was over almost as soon as it had begun.

That was apart from dipping in annually to check how many people still wished him happy birthday, the reminder sent to everyone somewhat increasing the odds on him receiving anything at all, especially from those wishing his infinitely more popular twin (who just happened to have the same birthday) their best wishes and feeling guilty not to bestow the same upon Eric also. Nope, his plan to meet girls via Facebook had come up short and so he needed to find something altogether more clinical and less cringeworthy.

The emergence and popularity of online dating was like a godsend to Eric, giving him the opportunity to use his talent of writing coupled with his sense of humour to communicate with a plethora of women all from the comfort of his own home (whilst sat in his string vest and eating Doritos). It helped address the imbalance he had when it came to his lack of confidence in and around the real deal when out in public. He'd always heard that women enjoyed a man who could make them laugh, and hopefully not just when removing his pants when things had progressed somewhat. Eric was about to find out if this was true.

Chapter Thirty-Two

Online Dating; Eric's Lifeline

Eric wasn't an ugly guy with his nose all over his face or the like and was relatively easy on the eye, some having even suggested he bore a slight resemblance to Tom Hardy in some of his latter profile photos. Eric hadn't known if that was a compliment at first, not having ever come across him; or if he had, not knowing who he actually was.

It turned out that Tom was born six-months after Eric and although he wasn't by any means spooky doppelganger material, he certainly passed as a more likely twin from certain angles than his actual twin brother. Then again, Eric looked more like Bungle from Rainbow than his twin brother, Ernie, so not really the best barometer to use when trying to portray Eric's likeness to Tom Hardy whatsoever.

Given the number of girls who had made reference to his similarity to Tom, Eric decided to test the theory further and having uploaded a particular photo of the famous heartthrob on his own profile, he awaited the moderators' decision with interest. The next day and Eric checked his profile; Tom was now officially part of his portfolio pics and that meant the moderators too had notably seen a likeness. I'm not suggesting Eric owed Tom a great deal of gratitude for his future dating triumphs thereafter but it was clear that around 60-70% had been taken by his photo more so than any of Eric's.

Online dating was a much cheaper and more practical option to meet women; Eric didn't have to get dressed up, spend a hundred notes or have to nurse a fuzzy head the next day to do it either. At least online it was less 'personal' and with less embarrassing elements to it, not having to feel the same levels of rejection than if you were stood there with them in person.

It also gave you a lot more insight into the girl (if she bothered to fill her profile in that was). Armed with this detail, it made ascertaining the likelihood of compatibility that more realistic than just being turned on by her in a cocktail dress across the dancefloor having consumed a few alcoholic beverages.

One of Eric's first dates came via Match Affinity (not as good as it's parent Match.com but supposed to be a more accurate way of determining compatibility through a more in-depth survey of likes and dislikes). After striking up an enjoyable conversation with a girl and as they seemed to be getting on well, then they discussed meeting up. She was due to go on holiday to Italy but was keen to lock horns before; given there would be a slight delay whilst she was away.

Eric invited her over to his and she was game. However, on arriving he soon realised that she was both a) taller than him (Eric was around six feet two and a half or 189cm) and b) not attractive in the slightest. This was rather an awkward one he thought as he watched the BFG (6.4/10 IMDb) literally ducking to walk through doors in his house, noticing that she was also wearing flat shoes. His evening plans now up the swanny, Eric was left to make a mental note for future dates; he would <u>have</u> to ensure that there were plentiful photographs in order to get a better impression of a girl's aesthetics. Fortunately for Eric, she picked up on his extreme lack of positive body-language, making her excuses about packing for her trip and she was gone.

Another of his dates hadn't even lasted half-an-hour at Eric's, despite having driven around 75 miles from Sheffield. In this particular case, it wasn't the aesthetics that were the problem, the girl actually looking better in real life than of her photos suggested. In fact, if it had just been a case of aesthetics then Eric would certainly not have kicked her out of bed for eating crumbly biscuits. No, the problem this time was chemistry and more precisely a distinct lack of it.

Eric had always placed a great deal of emphasis on intelligence in a girl as this would not only make for better conversation but meant that they were more likely to give as good as they got. On this occasion though, despite the girl appearing highly intelligent, her conversation gravitated towards politics and as she was an obvious capitalist, then Eric was turned off immediately, telling her what he thought of her opinions, whilst metaphorically showing her the door.

Another wasted night and back to the drawing board like Wile E. Coyote. Politics was a very good barometer to use when choosing a partner Eric thought, noticing that it hardly ever appeared as a question or topic to be filled in on the dating sites he'd come across. At least a couple of girls Eric had been in relationships with had voted Tory and Eric had no way of understanding why, other than to assume they felt it was some sort of status-symbol, believing that if they 'sided' with them then it made it seem as though they were well-to-do, had money and were a cut above. It was funny, therefore, that neither girl in question had any money whatsoever and both were in large amounts of debt.

Apart from Match and Match Affinity, Eric had also been on a couple of other dating sites, including eHarmony and Date the UK. Now Eric had relished the idea of joining eHarmony as it was pretty new on the scene and came across from adverts as a little more upmarket than the other offerings, Eric certainly not entertaining the likes of Plenty of Fish (POF) or Tinder, hearing nothing but bad things about them on the grapevine.

eHarmony's OSP had been built on its claim that it was thee most comprehensive and detailed compatibility site, a large amount of information required by the subscriber and a plethora of scenarios used to analyse personality. However, perhaps there was a flaw in the notion that more (information) was more (better results).

When Eric had finished completing the onerous array of detailed surveys and questionnaires and pressed search, the number of matches it actually arrived at after his details had been churned through the discombobulator was rather flimsy, to say the least. It was no lie that he was left with only three matches and of the two he actually liked the look of, the only one that didn't have kids was situated 75-miles away in Derbyshire.

Eric was enormously disappointed after all the effort on top of his initial outlay to subscribe. Perhaps he just had to accept that there was a shortage of stunning 35-year-old introverted Swedish nuns living within a ten-mile radius, with massive hooters, who enjoyed the beautiful game and had an allergy to all God's creatures. He surely wasn't asking for too much, was he?

'What a waste of money THAT was', he thought. It did, however, indicate to Eric (despite his increasing fussiness) that it wasn't realistic or even necessary to find someone who preferred the cold-side of the pillow or a walk on a crisp winter's day over a wet autumnal one and that some differences really weren't that important at all.

Chapter Thirty-Three

Nice Teeth, Shame About the Tits

Now if eHarmony could be described as the Roger Moore (RIP) of dating sites, sophisticated and with a splash of Dom Perignon '64, then Date the UK was Timmy Mallett drinking a bottle of WKD Blue. It was cheesier than eating a cheese toastie, whilst at a cheese-rolling festival in Cheeseville, Arizona. Still, there were the odd one or two that seemed normal enough and Eric managed to fish these out, one working not two-miles from him as a dental hygienist in town. As she was slightly older than Eric and notably having a few miles under the knickers, then she was happy to call in on Eric at his house and have a coffee.

She was a very attractive lady (lady you see… a bit too old to be referred to as a girl) and seemed pleasant enough but Eric began to get the feeling that she wasn't really there for the right reasons. Let me explain. Helen, as I will call her, was constantly looking at her phone, seemingly hung up on knowing what others were doing and not giving Eric the impression that she was paying him her full and undivided attention.

This was just a little off-putting to Eric, who didn't like being messed about. There was also her continual bragging about holidays, what car her ex drove, the fact she had horses and how her last home cost over a million pounds. This was possibly the last thing that impressed Eric, who was quite the traditionalist and keener to meet a down to earth type than one who was materialistic and fake.

As Eric excused himself and went off to the toilet, he had time to think about what Helen had said and came back with his agenda sorted and ready to be very open and honest with her. Sometimes politeness was just not an option especially when they were in his home. Eric rattled off quite an eloquent speech to her about how nothing she'd said was of interest to him regarding wealth and luxury items.

After finishing, he fully expected her to leave as although polite with how he had come across, it had certainly been a disapproving criticism of what she thought was important in life. However, to Eric's amazement, Helen wasn't offended in the slightest and asked if she could have another coffee. It was almost as if she agreed with Eric and could, therefore, stop pretending to be something she wasn't. After finishing her second coffee and having some more normal chat, Helen left.

Eric wasn't that bothered if he saw her again if truth was told due to the materialism factor on show and there were still plenty of options out there across the many dating sites. Helen, however, was notably still keen to see Eric and she came over again not long after. This time, it was later in the day and they'd decided to watch a film. Helen picked out the film Collateral starring Tom Cruise and Jamie Foxx (7.5/10 on IMDb) and the pair began to watch.

It was surprising how many unfinished films Eric would be party to over the years, the intentions all starting out the same with girls but more often than not ending with sex after some heavy petting just after the opening credits had finished. This was unless of course they were watching any of the original Star Wars films, when Eric wouldn't fidget <u>even</u> if Cindy Crawford was sitting naked next to him during her hay day and saying 'Take me now'. He remembered her famous artistic nude-shot lying on a beach whilst letting sand fall through her fingers seductively, which he'd had on a poster that hung from his wall at uni.

With the film around ten-minutes old, it had started innocently enough (the petting I mean and not the film); Eric massaging Helen's shoulders who sat on the floor with her back up against the sofa and between his legs. As she was enjoying the experience then one thing led to another and before you could say 'how the dickens did that happen?' then Helen was down to just her knickers. Eric didn't quite know what it was about him that caused women to shed their clothing so readily but he wasn't complaining whatsoever.

Unfortunately, on this occasion though, it appeared Helen hadn't fared as well as many others over time, especially when it came to Eric's favourite feminine parts. Eric couldn't believe his bad luck; each of Helen's boobs was like a conker at the bottom of a walking-sock and there was just no getting away from the fact that he was majorly disappointed. Eric still couldn't help but feel that she had an ulterior motive for being there with him but as he was pretty carefree at the time, then he was fine to play along.

Eric saw Helen a third and final time a couple of days later and on this occasion, it was later still. As it was so late then Eric surmised that she was planning to stay over and sure enough they ended up in bed together, Helen picking out Monsters Inc to watch before they visited the land of nod (8.1/10 IMDb). However, as mentioned previously, it was rare for Eric to watch a whole film with a girl at the best of times but with Helen looking rather resplendent in his Argentina replica-shirt from the 1998 World Cup (and nothing underneath) in bed next to him, then Mike and Sully played out to an empty auditorium, with more keenly anticipated pursuits having taken over proceedings.

It was the first and last time Eric had sex with Helen; not on the account of Eric's performance but it soon became notable that Helen had split up with her ex over some sort of cheating episode by him and she was on the rebound. Although having let Eric dip thy wick, Eric could tell it was causing her to feel bad about something and after coming to a premature end (the sex and not Eric) she made her excuses, got dressed and left.

Eric wasn't too offended cum disappointed as he knew she seemed a little weird from the start and besides, with boobs like an 80-year-old and later finding out she had a fanny like a clown's pocket too, then it wouldn't have lasted for too much longer anyway, especially with a veritable smorgasbord of females interested and waiting patiently in line.

Chapter Thirty-Four

The Camera Never Lies

Eric's main profile picture happened by accident. The photo had not been taken intentionally with online dating in mind, having instead been taken in a photo booth in the dark and dingy setting of a bus station some eight years previously, the smell of piss wafting through the manmade wind tunnel that connected it from the adjacent road, having provided many a party reveller the perfect spot to relieve themselves after hours. Eric had been out with his then-girlfriend, Isabelle, who was from Huddersfield and before catching her National Express coach back to t'Yorkshire, they'd decided to commemorate their togetherness with four passport-style photographs, retaining two each.

This was Eric's favourite photograph of himself ever and had certainly been chuffed with the outcome. It was in the year 2000, when Eric was 23 years young, although he continued to get his money's worth out of the same photo for a further nineteen years, still using it on his profile even to this day (only as a quirky addition and not trying to deceive anyone… I mean he looked closer to 16 than 42 in the photo so it was surely obvious to all those perusing it that it was indeed a younger incarnation).

This was at a time when mobile phones were still in their rudimentary early stages and nowhere near to having inbuilt 10 gigajigga pixel cameras front and back that we take for granted nowadays (if you're reading this story after 2030, then you're probably asking your parents what a mobile phone was). In fact, Eric remembered watching old cop shows in his youth when, in the absence of mobile phone technology, the detectives would dive out of their cars to rush to a phone box to make a call. Eric had a (bish bash) Bosch in garish orange, the colour not a coincidence and a result of the network provider's marketing/advertising strategy (the future didn't turn out as bright as Eric had hoped to be fair).

Thinking back, Eric could remember that it had a completely wank screen and looked like something you'd give a four-year-old to play with; think Fisher-Price. Text messages or texting was pretty novel back then too and meant having to press the corresponding keypad button up to four times in some cases just to select a single letter as part of the message (the antiquated method still used on Sky Remotes to this day when searching for stuff). It was surprising how people, including Eric, became so familiar with this method that they could type messages with one hand, whilst paying no attention whatsoever to the keypad. It seemed like thee most impractical way to message someone; a bit like calling the emergency services on an old rotary-dial telephone (hurry hurry… we're losing him).

Anyways, I digress. Despite the black and white Boyzone-esque photo having been taken of him in a loving clench with Isabelle who sat on his knee, Eric was obviously not too hung up on retaining memories as he had no qualms with picking up a pair of scissors and dissecting the pair of lovebirds, carefully ensuring that none of Isabelle's head was in the shot (although if you did look closely enough, you could make out some of her wispy hairs resting against his).

Well, that episode in his life had been a/nother brief encounter, lasting only a couple of months and Eric was not the most sentimental type about relationships that didn't work out. The coming together of Eric and Isabelle had though been responsible for a much more important turn of events and that was the marriage of his best friend and the creation of their children, Eric's godchildren.

Chapter Thirty-Five

A Momentous Occasion

It was in the year 2000, which seemed like a massive symbolism of the future to Eric, looking forward to it as a ten-year-old boy (not in the excitement stakes but more considering something that would be happening at some point) and working out how old he'd be when the new Millennia began.

Eric and a larger-than-usual assortment of his friends had decided on a night out in town. Given their knowledge and experience of the city haunts, they'd pretty much move from place to place in an already predetermined route and as per usual to the first floor of a semi-classy bar, which tended to be quieter and had the added bonus of serving cocktails. Given the cost of a cocktail was markedly more than a pint of Castlemaine XXXX ('I think we overdid it with the Sherry') then it was notable that nobody was rushing to get a round in. On that occasion, it was Terry who took out a small loan and was able to furnish everyone with a Slow Comfortable Screw (against the wall) or a Screaming Orgasm (Eric's personal favourite).

As the half-dozen or so group of lads stood in a circle chatting and sucking alcoholic concoctions through a straw, little did they know (especially Eric) that there was a trio of slightly younger girls sat a few yards away and keeping their eye on the talent that was on offer. As mentioned; Eric wasn't the type to do a purposeful recce of any establishment for pussy as he knew he would gulp and look shy if he and a girl with potential became locked in eye-contact.

As it was nearing time to head off to the final venue of the evening; a nightclub down the road, the group began disbanding, some to use the toilets, whilst the others stood finishing the last dregs of their cocktails. A girl approached the three who were still in position and asked them where they were headed next. She mentioned that her friend was interested in Eric and so she was hoping to catch up with him later. Confirming their plan to the girl, Eric and friends repatriated outside and moved on to the club.

Eric was slightly buoyed on hearing the news that a girl was interested in him but as she and her two mates had sat on the periphery and the ambient light wasn't great, then he wasn't sure if the interest was what he would deem flattery or not. In fact, Eric was now feeling rather nervous that he appeared to be in the sights of a girl, which was not something he was used to at all.

They pitched up in their usual position on the top floor of the nightclub, where it was usual to hear predominantly Craig David (said in the stylee of Bo-Selecta) tracks interspersed with the pre-release version of Sophie Ellis-Bextor's Murder on the Dancefloor at least 400 times. Eric had sat at his usual speck on a barstool overlooking the majority of the congregation, the dim light making it somewhat difficult to discern the diamonds from the ruffians. Then, Eric noticed a kafuffle behind him and it seemed the triumvirate of girls from the cocktail bar had landed.

Despite having drunk a fair bit by now, this did not mean Eric was lacking in nerves but it had helped dull his anxiety somewhat. Eric was sat on his own as his mates were carrying out a meet and greet behind him. It wasn't long before Eric was joined by someone and it wasn't someone he recognised.

Isabelle was a cracking looking girl and not just on account of Eric's beer-goggleage at the time. He was pretty chuffed that a decent looking feline like her had been attracted by his chiselled and rugged looks (cough cough) from afar. The two began to chat and Eric felt immediately awkward. I mean this wasn't something Eric was used to. Fortunately, he didn't make a complete dick of himself to Isabelle and the pair were both equally interested in each other.

Meanwhile, it seemed that Eric's mate Reg had been getting along with one of Isabelle's mates extremely well too. As for the other girl who appeared to be sucking a lemon all evening; well Jim had come over to Eric during an intermission in proceedings and exclaimed 'Christ! Talking to her is like walking through wet tar'.

It turned out that Isabelle had come down from Huddersfield with the sour puss to visit her friend Angela (who Reg was now getting on famously with). Given that excitement levels were running dangerously high, Eric and Reg managed to wangle their way back to Angela's for the night, who was studying at uni and where she had shared living quarters. Despite Eric and Isabelle spending the night on a makeshift bed in the communal lounge made up of sofa cushions, Eric thought it was great to be getting accustomed to one another so soon.

The next morning, it seemed Reg had a prior engagement, which meant he had to be up and out pretty early. Having woken just before Reg's exit (as it later transpired) Eric had discovered he was in 'bed' with a naked Isabelle and therefore it felt rude not to slip her his length once again. However, proceedings were interrupted somewhat when, after Angela's bedroom door opened, Reg now had to negotiate his way through the lounge, where Eric and Isabelle lay. It was quite comical; Eric and Isabelle acting all innocent and receptive to Reg when underneath the duvet cover, Eric was balls-deep inside her. Eric didn't let on to his mate but he would be sure to confirm this to him by text not long after to both their amusements.

It soon became evident to Eric that Isabelle wasn't going to get a job at Hooters anytime soon, her frontal orbs not big enough to really have Eric doing somersaults and wanting to marry her. For Reg though, having met Angela that night, it was the beginning of a beautiful relationship. Reg and Angela had moved in together three-years later and were married two years after that. Two beautiful children followed; a daughter and then a son and Eric was honoured to be given the custodial title of godfather to them both. Eric was chuffed to bits for his mate who it seemed had got lucky with his first roll of the dice and would be spared the requirement for any future dating and failed relationships like him.

Eric saw Isabelle on a few more occasions, even meeting her mum and dad at one stage, having caught a National Express coach up to her hometown. The distance between them, coupled with Eric not driving, however, was impractical, to say the least, but there was also the likelihood that Isabelle's rack was not doing it for him either; Eric and Isabelle would go their separate ways after a brief liaison.

Chapter Thirty-Six

Eric's Online Filtering (50-Point) Plan

Although Eric was moderately intelligent, he knew you didn't have to be a brainiac anthropology Ph.D. student to work out that the advent of mobile phones, coupled with social media and online dating sites, must have caused an increase in divorces, adultery/cheating and realistically the birth-rate of the nation. It was a no-brainer he felt as mobile phones were personal and with seemingly everyone being caught up in the self-perpetuating FOMO scene and the majority hell-bent on obtaining as many followers or friends as they could to satisfy their own insecurities and levels of self-importance, then everyone and anyone could become another notch in their popularity column (breathe).

Eric found it laughable how the youth of today had been brainwashed, like zombies drawn to their smartphones and not able to apparently operate without incessantly keeping in touch with everything happening on various sites. Out one evening on a date down his local (but of course) he'd noticed a group of youngsters on an adjacent table, the art of conversation dead it appeared as they were as quiet as the Etihad Stadium during a big match.

All they were doing was showing each other things they'd found on their phones and swapping places in a choreographed routine to have group selfies taken of them out together. They were then obviously uploading their photos to the same sites they were looking at in a bid to make out that they were apparently having lots of fun. Eric questioned the latter and it was indeed a sad state of affairs.

'I can resist everything but temptation' was very apt, Eric felt, in respect of the new era of multi-communication channels, giving rise to an almost limitless number of conversations, especially for those in relationships who imagined the grass to be more spectacular down the road. Before the advent of mobile phones and online dating sites, he could be pretty confident that if he met a girl in a social setting and asked her out the following weekend, then there was a good chance that it would take place. However, post the social media flirting proliferation, then the intervening period could provide each person with a swathe of other opportunities and therefore a much greater chance to have their head turned prior to any previously agreed meet-up.

Eric had seen it for himself firsthand and anyone subscribed to dating sites could not resist checking their messages and list of winkers to satisfy their own curiosities and to be on the lookout for an even better catch. Eric knew that's exactly why they were on there in the first place and this was normal anthropological behaviour but it was a worrying trend he believed and one that would jeopardise the integrity of relationships at a more alarming rate than before.

Online dating was pure and simply based on aesthetics and brought about an increase in shallowness, most girls Eric noticed not even bothering to fill in any written description whatsoever ('I'll fill this in later') and simply making do with a couple of pics at best. Anyone who disagreed was talking absolute bobbins Eric thought and those championing the phrase 'it's what's inside that counts' were usually the type that were certainly not going to win any beauty pageants anytime soon. As harsh as it sounded, it was the truth.

The online dating sphere seemed laughable to Eric when stepping back from it all; the concept akin to him chatting up a girl in a pub (let's pretend) and then when a new guy walked in, the girl saying 'just hang on a second… I need to go and speak with him and work out if I like him better… I may be back'. Eric was not against online dating; how could he be? He had benefitted hugely from it and it had provided him with years of enjoyment.

Eric learnt quickly that he had to develop even thicker skin if he was to enjoy the dating sites for what they were and could not afford to let any negative comments or rejections put him off his continual stride in the pursuit of fun and his main aim; to find the Holy Grail. The longer Eric spent on the sites, it was obvious the more experience he gleaned from using them and after countless dates, his tack would continually evolve into an unwritten list of prerequisites (but more accurately a list of negatives to look out for and to avoid at all costs).

Eric's search criteria methodology:

1. Never converse with a girl who doesn't have a photo.
2. Never converse with a girl who doesn't have a full-length photo or at least a top-half shot (in other words not just of her face).
3. Never converse with a girl who uses (Instagram/Snapchat) filters on her photos. How old is she? Usually added to convey youthfulness and modernity but in nine out of ten cases, it's the woman trying to conceal her rather questionable aesthetics. Never have the words 'you can put lipstick (in this case tiger ears and a nose) on a pig but it's still a pig' most famously quoted by Barrack Obama and interpreted by some quarters to be directed at Sarah Palin.
4. Never converse with a girl who has a dog/s, especially those that have sharp pointy teeth and that shit bigger than me.
5. If a girl has a dog that shits smaller than me but she has photos of her kissing it on her photos then do not converse with her; they lick other dog's arses and eat their own shit… enough said.
6. Ignore girls who have photos of tropical island vistas or Machu Picchu (and not them). This is a dating site and I don't want to see their holiday snaps.
7. Never converse with a girl whose photographs are mainly with her socialising with fellas. Too much of a tart.
8. If the girl makes it to the conversation stage following a split-decision on her photos then she must be happy to send me a full-length real-life photo of herself.
9. If the girl has several photographs of herself ranging from chubby to less chubby, then you can bet your bottom dollar that her most current photo is the chubbiest one.
10. Automatic disqualification for any girl who has spelling mistakes in her write-up (especially your/you're) If she hasn't checked for errors before pressing 'submit' then either she is haphazard or can't spell… either way it's a no.
11. Be sure to look out for photos taken from above looking down at their face. This is a widely used trick which can take pounds/kilos off.

12. Never converse with a girl who has tattoos on her hands.
13. Never converse with a girl who has tattoos on her neck.
14. Never converse with a girl who has visible tattoos.
15. Never converse with any girl that has piercings all over the shop, especially a security door chain on her face.
16. Never entertain a girl who describes herself as a 'free spirit' – this basically means she's a bit of a slag.
17. Never converse with a girl who has blue, pink, green or some other ridiculously unnatural coloured hair (almost always contravening points 4, 5, 7, 12, 13, 14, 15 & 16 also).
18. Never converse with a girl whose write-up is explicitly stating what she doesn't like about men (too negative). (Remember, this isn't Eric's profile write-up; it's the evolution of his prerequisites following his online dating journey).
19. Never converse with a girl who says she is very busy but would love to have a man in her life. Do you think I'm going to fit in around you then?
20. Never converse with a woman who states that they have three or more children and that she gets on well with all their dads.
21. Never converse with a girl who says she likes going to music festivals. She's obviously pretty untidy and there's also a good chance that she's a 'free spirit' (see point 16).
22. Never converse with a girl who is vegetarian or who mentions campaigning for animal welfare (despite not having anything against this, they're likely to be too flowery and oversensitive and nag me for eating meat).
23. Never reply to messages from women who look like Dennis Taylor or Sloth from The Goonies (7.8/10 IMDb) (believe me they do exist).
24. Never reply to an initial message from a girl which says 'Hi', 'How are you?' or 'How you finding it on here?' (lacking in any originality whatsoever).
25. Never reply to an initial message which is obviously a copy and paste job and makes no effort to mention anything specific about my profile.

26. Once trading messages with a girl, discontinue messaging if it's obvious she can't spell or use grammar correctly.
27. Once trading messages with a girl, if she hasn't made me laugh by at least message three then discontinue messaging.
28. Once trading messages, if a girl hasn't asked any questions about me by her third message, then she's almost certainly too far up her own arse and should discontinue messaging.
29. Never feel tempted to thank a girl for her message no matter how complimentary it may be if there is obviously no chance of romance. In my experience making conversation only makes women think they're in and further messages are almost certainly forthcoming.
30. Don't bother conversing with a girl if they haven't written anything about themselves.
31. Don't bother conversing with a girl if she has put 'My friends would describe me as…' or 'this part was so difficult that I decided to ask my friends'. Anyone who can't describe themselves must be retarded.
32. Don't bother conversing with a girl if they've stated the bleeding obvious, such as 'I love to laugh', 'My family and friends mean the world to me', 'I enjoy nights out and nights in', 'I'm a glass half full type of girl' No shit?
33. Do not under any circumstances converse with any girl who says 'I work hard and I play hard/er'
34. Do not converse with women who say something along the lines of 'I enjoy the finer things in life' Waaaay too uppity. This includes describing themselves as a foodie (Pretentious; Moi?)
35. Do not converse with any girl who has stated that they are searching for a guy who is between the ages of 18-99 or something similarly ridiculous (gold-digger)
36. Do not converse with a woman whose only photo is of her wearing a burka (this did happen I swear).
37. Do not continue conversing with a girl if she disappears from the conversation for more than an hour and is definitely still online. Safe to say she has had her head turned by someone else as difficult

as that may be to comprehend.

38. Do not reply to a girl who lives more than 50-miles away (just not practical).
39. Do not reply to a woman or discontinue messaging if they put 'so tell me about yourself' Have you not read my profile?
40. Do not reply to a girl or invoke conversation if the girl's photographs are all with friends and it's almost impossible to ascertain which of them is actually her.
41. Do not reply or invoke conversation if their profile is a jibbering mish-mash of baloney that is evidently written by a foreigner whose sole purpose is to try to steal your bank details… usually twinned with 'too good to be true' photographs of a really hot girl, which tend to be very random model-esque shots stood in the park by a tree or lying on top of a wall etc. Just ask yourself why? (Usually paired with point 35).
42. Do not reply or invoke conversation with a girl who has more than a dozen photos. Any more than that and she is far too vain.
43. Do not reply to a woman who only has one photo. (We all have a bobby-dazzler fluke of a shot that we're happiest with (see earlier chapter regarding Eric's Boyzone pic).
44. Never get back to a girl who replies to you weeks or months after she read your message. You obviously weren't top of her priority list <u>then</u> so she can get fucked.
45. Never message or reply to a girl who says she runs her own salon or is in the 'beauty' industry. Far too high maintenance. Can usually tell by their photos as heavily made-up.
46. Ignore women who stipulate that their favourite parts of a man's body are his legs. Probably not going to work out well.
47. Do not converse with a girl or reply if she uses abbreviations for everything and/or uses text speak. (eg. YOLO so wud u like 2 meet up?) Just lazy tbh.
48. Do not converse or reply to a girl if her main profile pic is of her pulling a tongue. She's obviously not that serious or is mentally challenged.
49. Do not converse with a girl if she describes herself as a social butterfly. This means she has waaay more friends than me and will

have an increased opportunity to have her head turned and sleep with someone else.

50. Do not converse with a girl if she uses the phrase 'what you see is what you get'. Fucking obvious alert! That's unless of course they are like the T-1000 in Terminator 2: Judgement Day (8.5/10 IMDb) and can metamorphosise into other people or random objects.

(Well it had to be a 50-point plan given his OCD now didn't it?)

Chapter Thirty-Seven

Eric's Dating Profiles

Eric liked to mix it up a bit in regards to his own profile, trying different angles of attack to see if he could appeal to more or different femme fatales. Here are a couple of actual profiles he used (to great effect) during his online dating journey:

- 1 -

Is it hot in here or is it just me?

Having suffered from a serious heart defect for many years and recently inheriting millions of pounds from a distant aunt, I thought I'd give this online dating a go… If only there was someone out there for me.

I'm like the gift that keeps on giving, a veritable PlayStation 5 if you will, where the entertainment envelope has literally been pushed back to its extremities (so to be clear no more pushing of said envelope can be done… so there's unlikely to be a PlayStation 6 is what I'm saying).

What you get with me is everything you could ever dream of… except perhaps modesty although this is me selling myself so no time for a lack of assertiveness, confidence or dampening down of my cornucopia of award-winning attributes.

I am polite, considerate, thoughtful (slight difference to considerate I've always thought) reliable, moderately funny (may need to rethink aforementioned modesty gag), you've probably noticed my rugged/chiselled and youthful looks already (on second thoughts best leaving it in) I have a modicum of intelligence and can hold a decent conversation… although do swear occasionally when the mood takes.

Now for the potential banana skins…

I am very competitive and will pull your pants down at most things… you have to ask yourself can you live with this?!

I'm not a great cook either and so if you're after a budding Gordon Ramsey then I'm not for you.

Some have said I look like Tom Hardy but judging by my work colleagues' reaction to that I think it's fair to say I don't.

If you believe the news, then the polar ice caps will soon melt away and the soaring temperatures will cause deforestation on a global scale, there will be a nuclear war with Russia but worst of all, the BBC will continue to make episodes of The One Show… so what are you waiting for? The clock is ticking so you're best getting in touch ASAP and making the most of me whilst we're still here.

I know I'm not perfect by any means but hopefully, I'm perfect for you.

I'm reliably informed that there is someone for everyone so let's see if that's the case.

'Like all young men I set out to be a genius but mercifully laughter intervened.' (William Golding)

- 2 -

Are you sitting comfortably?… Then I shall begin…

Once upon a time, there was a young prince called Eric who lived in the Kingdom of Cheshire. He had everything he could ever wish for; chiselled and rugged-looks, a fine crop of hair and all of his own teeth (at time of writing).

He had also been gifted with intelligence, coming near to the top of his peerage as he progressed from Medieval Page to Squire and finally graduating from Knight School with a Desmond.

Prince Eric found it second nature adapting his communication style to suit all the weird and wonderful townsfolk he came across during his lifetime and those who chose to share in his company had always been certain of a good-time had, his regaling of hilarious anecdotes and of previous japery whilst usually sat in a homely tavern and washing down a flagon of ale for good measure.

As his upbringing had been one of both love and strictness (being disciplined from time to time for his over-exuberance in his pursuit of jousting and for not sheathing his sword at all times) Prince Eric had all the attributes which were the desire of princesses, ladies and comely serving wenches alike… although he hadn't quite grasped modesty to be fair. You could say in summing him up 'he is a right good catch'.

After spending several years rehearsing for life in matrimony with a fire-breathing dragon, Prince Eric was very unhappy at the prospect. So one night, just as day turned to dusk, he collected all his most treasured possessions together (Playstation 4, I-Pad, Hearsay CDs, teddy bear and toothbrush) wrapped them in a bindle and rode off (in his BMW… but don't worry ladies he still has a sizeable member) into the sunset in search of a new life for himself.

After resettling and making what he could of his talents and rich skillset as a shop assistant at Sayers the Bakers, Prince Eric then went about trying to hunt for his future plus-one, someone with whom he could grow old, raise little prince and princesses with but above all enjoy a great deal of happiness, fun and excitement along the way.

As his tireless endeavour of putting up 'wanted' notices on trees and fence posts across the village bore no fruit, he instead elected to try his hand at online dating… To be continued…

Care to join the fray and help finish off the tale?… If so grab your ink and quill and write me!!

Chapter Thirty-Eight

Likes and Dislikes

Eric was just a little bemused at how and why a lot of girls didn't even bother writing anything about themselves on their profiles and quite a few dodged answering the basic questions by electing to choose 'I'd rather not say'. Choosing this option to answer simple yes/no questions meant it was always extremely apparent what the actual answer was anyway, making their attempt to hide certain aspects about themselves seem ridiculous and if nothing else confirming their intellect or complete lack of it. For example, the very popular 'Do you have any children?' Well if they said 'I'd rather not say' then it didn't take Albert Einstein's cleverer (and seemingly less famous) brother to work out that she was the 'old woman who lived in a shoe'.

Eric couldn't help feeling that writing nothing was sheer laziness. I mean if they were trying to sell their house would they not want a description within the sales particulars? Slightly less lazy and a popular method of making it look like they'd made an effort in filling in their profile spiel was to simply list their likes and dislikes. If done with a lot of wit and originality then it could work well, especially if the other person could relate to those daily gripes or overlooked hidden gems.

It also meant that those scrolling through profiles were less likely to be put-off when confronted by numerous paragraphs, more likely to peruse a quick list, easier and somewhat more reader-friendly. You didn't need to be a wordsmith either as such and yet it could be just as successful, gaining the interest of others through nostalgia and humour and build-up an immediate connection to that person. Eric preferred to write in the true sense as he felt he could put his humour across better that way as well as including a description of himself.

Chapter Thirty-Nine

First Date (D1)

If a girl/woman had managed to successfully bypass Eric's lengthy and rigorous prerequisites, then it wasn't long before he was considering locking horns and organising a first date or D1 as he called it. Eric didn't see the point in continuing to chat for days or weeks as his experience had shown him that it didn't matter how well this went; there was no substitute for meeting in person and ascertaining if there was any chemistry or the elusive spark, which was the much sought after elixir of dating. Chemistry was 97.2% of the whole shooting match as far as Eric was concerned and the basis for everything else to trampoline off. The other 2.8% (if you were interested) was aesthetics and boobs (of course).

Eric couldn't believe how many times there had been no spark after meeting a girl over the years. Without it, then the date and potential relationship was dead in the water no matter her aesthetic qualities and how much he would have given to bone her. Eric had always maintained that he'd much prefer an average-looking girl with a cracking personality over a girl who was drop-dead but as dull as a wet weekend in Grimsby (sorry Grimsby). Yes, despite Eric revelling in written communication, he'd learnt that it was certainly better to lock horns sooner rather than later, whilst the metal was still relatively warm.

After doing his damndest to ignore the girl's attempts at setting up a telephone call pre-D1, then it was then just down to agreeing on a rendezvous. Eric's preference was visiting the girl's house, not something that you'd suggest was the safest option on their part, given they hadn't met him before. However, there was, of course, good reason for the choice for Eric, especially if the distance between them was not conducive to finding somewhere equidistant and therefore preventing the sinking of a few alcoholic beverages (don't drink and drive!).

If the girl was happy to accommodate Eric at her gaff then the first thing to note was that she was obviously confident and it was odds on that she would be happy to get past first base if the chemistry was there. Of course, there was a great advantage for the girl too as she didn't have to make an effort to get somewhere on her own and usually at night, able to relax with a few home measured G&Ts and wait for Eric to arrive.

There was also no awkwardness to be had when meeting at their house; as there could potentially be when meeting in a pub or coffee shop, which was alien (8.4/10 IMDb) to both. Eric remembered ditching a rendezvous site once when it soon became apparent that a great number of other dating duos had elected to meet there also. It was quite funny when he noticed a dozen other people standing around, dressed to the nines, clearing their dry throats and looking anxious. 'Hmm' Eric thought, 'that one looks better than mine… I wonder if…'

It was also a much cheaper evening too for Eric (even cheaper for the girl) if he received the okay to spend the evening at hers, the cost of a couple of bottles of vino or Prosecco a lot less than the equivalent prices at a swanky pub or wine bar.

Despite what you might be thinking or what the girls thought of Eric from his profile and subsequent messages, Eric did have a few dating rules and this included no nakedness until at least D3. Eric wasn't a slag. He'd be lying if he said this rule had never been broken before but it was a rule he liked to uphold wherever possible, especially if he met a girl who had definite potential and the chance for a long-term romantic episode.

Chapter Forty

Red Sparrow

One example of meeting a girl at her place on D1 turned out to be one of the largest disappointments in Eric's back catalogue of dates, despite having been built as one of his most keenly anticipated. It was very rare for Eric to meet for any date in Manchester, due to his complete lack of knowledge of the city and the impracticality of getting there. Still, a couple of times, he'd thrown caution to the wind and gone balls-out on account of his enthusiasm.

On this particular occasion, he'd got chatting to a Russian girl (via Tinder… yes, it had become more popular and less seedy so Eric had jumped aboard). She was your archetypal blonde female tennis-player-looking Russian girl and Eric was salivating at the prospect of meeting her.

Unfortunately, the timing of their initial contact could not have been worse as she was about to embark on a trip home to Kazakhstan to see her family ('Kazakhstan is number one exporter of potassium; other Central Asian countries have inferior potassium'… Borat) That meant that D1 would need to be put on hold and also meant plenty of messages traded between the pair. Given the length of time, they had been communicating prior to her returning from Astana (the capital city of Kazakhstan at the time and very recently renamed Nur-Sultan) the good news for Eric was that as the two were getting on amazingly well over WhatsApp, then she was happy for Eric to meet her at her apartment.

'Back of the net', Eric thought, who found the concept of meeting her there infinitely easier and more practical (also remembering the aforementioned benefits of being invited over to the girl's place on D1).

Eric was rubbing his hands with liquid testosterone and after picking up some Prosecco, he jumped a train into the centre of Mancunia. It was a Sunday just after lunchtime. As luck would have it, Anna, as I will call her, lived only a short walk from the station entrance and before he knew it, Eric was pressing the keypad at the entrance of her apartment block.

Without saying a word, Anna buzzed through and Eric was able to gain access.

Anna was housed on the seventh floor and Eric was now at the height of his anxiety. It was always the same on any first date, no matter how many had come before. In order to give him more time to compose himself and given he had a slight phobia of lifts that he hadn't used before; he decided to take the stairs. Yes, to repeat she was on the seventh floor and as Eric was quite possibly in the worst physical condition he'd ever been in, then he was beginning to think that was a big mistake. Spending a few minutes catching his breath on reaching Anna's level, he circumnavigated the corridors in search of her apartment.

He always went with the tried and tested 'knock ner knock knock… knock knock' routine as it came across as friendly and enthusiastic he felt. After a rather large delay, Eric assuming that Anna's apartment was so big it had taken her that long to answer the door, he realised that just wasn't the case on entering. Anna let him in and walking into the open-plan kitchen-diner, it allowed the dog to see the rabbit so to speak, Anna as beautiful in real life as her photographs had suggested and that Eric had hoped for. It was, however, clear that she hadn't gone to too much effort in the dressing-up stakes though and despite Eric having confirmed prior to the date he wanted it to be a sports casual affair, he hadn't expected her to have taken him quite so literally. Perhaps it was an Eastern European thing he thought.

Anna was dressed in a pair of skin-tight jeans and a T-shirt embossed with Vladimir Putin's face next to a large bear. Eric looked past this rather strange wardrobe choice for a first date with an Englishman and proceeded to hand Anna the bottle of Prosecco that he'd carried in his overnight travel bag. She was quick to open the alcohol and soon they were toasting their first meet. Anna was very confident, allowing Eric to kiss her almost immediately (as in pecks rather than anything too sexual) and to squeeze her arse as he did so. It was very clear from the get-go (hate that expression) that both were very turned on by the other.

As the date progressed, the pair had been kissing a fair bit and having a laugh getting to know one another, Eric fascinated by her story, having come from the old Soviet Union. Her accent was turning him on also and everything seemed too good to be true. After ordering a takeaway, Eric did the gentlemanly thing and took it upon himself to collect the food from reception and, yes, you've guessed it, took the stairs down and back up again. He was proper fucked this time and spent another couple of minutes taking a breather before returning to Anna with the food.

After finishing their burgers, Anna started to show Eric a number of YouTube videos (not that sort although he'd have preferred them) featuring her favourite man it seemed; Vladimir Putin. It felt a little surreal for Eric as he watched Anna taking great delight about the leader of her 'homeland'. It was like she was trying to brainwash Eric with propaganda but Eric wasn't really paying attention to the videos, more interested in Anna and her fit body.

Lying next to each other on the couch like a pair of well-established lovers, Anna then chose a film for them to watch together. The film was called Red Sparrow (6.6/10 IMDb), the title; the name given to (mostly) females being trained as assassins within the Russian Secret Intelligence Service. Eric was just a little 'Ruskied' out by now, realising that Anna couldn't have filled their first date with more pro-Russian symbolism had she tried. 'I mean what was wrong with Rocky IV (6.8/10 IMDb) or Red Heat (6.1/10 IMDb)?' he thought, putting his Smirnoff vodka down and straightening his bearskin ushanka-hat (the one with the tie-able ear flaps).

Anna spent the majority of the film staring at Eric as she sat next to him and repeatedly kissing him on the temple nearest to her. It was just a little off-putting for Eric who was trying to be polite and watch the film she'd been so keen for him to see. No sooner had the credits began rolling at the end than the two were on each other like two feral cats fighting over a chicken bone. Despite all the bizarre ingredients of the night, Eric was still majorly attracted to Anna and it was time to take it to the next level.

Chapter Forty-One

Putin on a (False) Front

Eric had now slipped his hands under the Putin T-shirt and was beginning to unfasten Anna's brazier whilst they were kissing. Things were about to turn rather sour for Eric though ('when dates with Russian girls go bad' which has probably already featured late night on Channel 5). Having unclipped her bra with one hand like the consummate professional he was, Eric's other hand was round the front and preparing itself for a treat.

Unfortunately for Eric, the treat was not forthcoming as it appeared Anna's excessively padded bra had been pulling the wool over his eyes for the entire date. To quote one of Eric's favourite films and the scene from Jaws 2 (when the kids were deciding which of the boats they were all going to ride in before being ultimately eaten by a great big plastic shark - 5.7/10 IMDb) Anna had 'tits like a sparrow' which was even apter given the film they'd just watched. Eric felt extremely short-changed, aware that he himself had larger boobs than her.

If realising that Anna was flatter than the Bonneville Salt Plains of Utah wasn't bad enough, Eric was about to get another unwanted surprise. No, she didn't have a penis. Eric had experienced a fair old amount of kissing in his lifetime, what with the numerous women he'd dated or met. He enjoyed kissing; it was sensual and he'd honed his skills in that department in order to tantalise and turn a woman on, a little bit of tongue-tip on tongue-tip action and some delicate touching of lips. However, on the very rare occasion, Eric found that the girl's kissing style had proved to be anything but. Anna was a case in point.

For some unknown reason to Eric, some girls (and Anna) believed sensual-kissing included thrusting their entire tongue into their partner's mouth and waggling it around at a rate of knots in a kind of pugilistic fashion. Eric almost choked having been unable to draw breath before Anna carried out her assault on his oral cavity. It felt like someone had put a live conger eel into his mouth and Eric was trying desperately not to swallow it. This was the apotheosis of schoolboy/girl kissing to Eric and it did absolutely nothing for him. However, as he didn't want to hurt her feelings, he allowed the nonsense to continue, giving up trying to fight back, the texture of her mouth organ rather unpleasant as it covered every square centimetre of his own. In the space of a few minutes, Anna had gone from a 9/10 to a 2/10 at best and Eric just wanted to leave.

As it was extremely late, then Eric had no other option but to stay the night with Anna, who had now cajoled him into her bedroom, the taste of her tongue still fresh in his mouth. She'd slipped into a fancy negligee by now and the pair got into bed, Eric managing to shield his big leg from her gaze as he got under the covers. After taking his top off, Anna was now inspecting his torso in some detail, akin to a monkey checking its troop for ticks or the like.

She seemed almost shocked to discover Eric's chest was hair-free, something that was very normal to Eric, having never had to shave that part of his body. Surprisingly, his twin brother was at the opposite end of the hairy spectrum; so hairy in fact that he gave Teddy Ruxpin a run for his money. Eric liked the fact that his body was smooth as a dolphin; apart from the cluster of uber-long hairs tufting out from his areola. It seemed that Anna's last romantic interlude had been with a Spanish fella and so reading between the lines Eric conjectured that he'd obviously needed to comb his back.

Things were going from bad to worse as now they both had major quibbles with each other in the physical sense and it did nothing for Eric's libido. He didn't know whether it was even worth carrying out 'the act' as he just wanted to get a good night's kip and head back first thing. Unfortunately, Anna was feeling horny still despite carrying on as though Eric was prepubescent and she continued with her infantile kissing technique. As Eric was fed up with that, he moved down the bed and between Anna's legs, helping her out of her knickers as he went.

Eric may have been as flaccid as a Beagle's ear but he knew he could depend on himself to quote her very happy in the cunnilingus department. Bringing Anna simmering to the boil nicely, she was then desperate for Eric and shouted 'Fuck me now' in her Russian accent. 'Swell' Eric thought to himself, fully aware that his flexible friend was not coming out to play. It was slightly embarrassing for both parties, Anna soon realising it was futile trying her snake charming routine (Like Mr. Chips on Catchphrase) and giving up the pair fell asleep.

Chapter Forty-Two

Delusions of Grandeur

There are questions that will always remain unanswered, discussed from one generation to the next; questions that not even the highest flyers of redbrick academia have come close to solving. Questions such as the reason for and the creation of the universe, the planets including Earth and the origins of life; about what happens to living creatures including Homo sapiens after they die and, most puzzling of all, why women who looked like Sloth from The Goonies winked or sent Eric messages on Match.com.

The longer Eric spent surfing online dating the more he'd get annoyed at those women who did; sometimes very angry indeed. It was obvious they had about as much chance of getting anywhere with him as <u>he</u> did setting up a ménage et trois with Holly Willoughby and Charlize Theron (If you're listening, ladies). Some of these women were like extras in a zombie apocalypse movie and it was questionable whether they were women at all.

The frequency became so ridiculous at one stage, that Eric worried he'd likely suffer a detached retina from his continual eye-rolling when discovering which delights of the female form had inextricably thrown their hat into his ring. Eric could only hypothesise that these were the same delusional types who would fancy their chances of winning X-factor despite sounding like a chimpanzee having been thrown on a bonfire.

There was then the phenomenon that Eric had got used to experiencing on dating sites, especially Match.com and which he felt deserved its own title and not simply bundled within the already popular saying of 'law of the sod'.

The dashboard on Match would indicate how many women (occasionally men) had perused his profile, how many had 'favourited him' and better still; how many had winked or sent an introductory message. Eric had coined the phrase 'full house' if one girl had selected/carried them all out, which was notably a rather big indication of their interest. Eric would never do that to a woman, even if he would have given his left arm (or maybe right leg) to bone her. He knew that the best approach was to take things slowly and calmly and not inadvertently put the willies up her by coming across as an overzealous teenager.

After logging in and seeing the corresponding data for each of the four options, it was almost always the case that the 'number of views' would usually be the greater figure. Eric would always check out those first and then systematically click on each of the other selections in order of importance; favourites, winks, messages. However, it was uncanny that after receiving four views (let's say) and one wink, then Eric knew instantly which of the four had winked; call it the sixth-sense (8.1/10 IMDb) but Eric just knew that the ugliest, oldest and most incompatible feline of the quartet would be the one that had batted her eyelids.

There were then instances where all four of the women who'd viewed his profile were all very shaggable in Eric's eyes and alas the one wink, although Eric poised enthusiastically at which of the beauties it could be, would turn out to be some Bella Emberg type who had winked straight out without having even the courtesy of checking his profile. Sometimes, it was just God damn unfair Eric thought but it did make it even more enjoyable when a fine specimen was genuinely interested and had made her feelings known.

Eric was not bigheaded or vain; he knew his limitations with the opposite sex but these women were pure and simply taking the absolute piss. He'd have sent them a message to confirm their lunacy but most of the time Eric was limited with the number of daily chats he could partake in as part of his subscription criteria and he wasn't about to waste any on the cast from The Munsters (Never made a film apparently).

Each morning at work he'd give the guys (including gals) an update on the 'rogues' gallery' as he called it, showing them photos of 'The Undateables' he'd screenshot after they'd winked at him the previous evening. This would certainly help to brighten up everyone's day and became so popular that one of the lads had gathered (electronically) all the photos together and set it up as a continual slideshow on his mobile, using the music from 'The Gallery' in (Tony Hart's) Hartbeat as a backing track (I preferred Chas to Morph and Sweep to Sooty, whilst we're on the subject of children's TV).

There were a lot of things that annoyed Eric in life and online dating was no different. We've already discovered that he was far from flattered to receive winks and messages from women who fell light-years of his standards but there were other issues that would seriously test his resolve also. One of these was regarding blocking profiles or 'black-listing'.

Given the complexity of online personalities looking for love or hookups, it was realistic to expect that not everyone would fancy you or share your sense of humour. It could also be said that someone could potentially misinterpret a message from that which the sender intended. Eric had a good idea about what kind of girl would appreciate his original and sometimes forward approach but as he learnt, his powers of judgement were not an exact science. As a result, Eric would now and again receive rather derogatory replies, which although made him feel slightly confused at first, would more than likely be substituted for annoyance and anger not long after.

As a safety feature and also a way of decreasing the search sample, subscribers could blacklist profiles, which meant that the profile in question would disappear from subsequent searches and not appear on any of the dashboard features from that day forth. However, that was not always the case as Eric noticed that if he or the blacklisted girl ever temporarily switched off their profile and reappeared sometime later, then those previously blacklisted profiles would suddenly reappear also.

The most annoying situation would arise when spiteful girls would respond to Eric in a defamatory fashion before instantaneously blacklisting him. This would mean Eric (or anyone in the same situation) would have no way of responding. On very rare occasions, Eric had done likewise but he was loathed to take this option, only doing so when he was extremely offended or felt the girl deserved to be brought down a peg or two. It was usually so much easier and less confrontational to simply blacklist the profile and move on.

Chapter Forty-Three

Tired of Rejection

Another extremely frustrating element of Match.com for Eric had been to endure the relatively new phenomenon of what he called historic decline responses. After re-subscribing once again and re-advertising himself online, it was obvious that Eric's reappearance had sparked curiosity from a number of felines, many of whom were perennial stalwarts like him. However, there was a process now in place it seemed that would resend Eric's archive messages to the girls he'd originally sent them to up to six, even eight-months earlier. It meant he received a swathe of default messages to his inbox from numerous girls (he'd obviously liked the look of previously) to confirm that they weren't interested.

This had to be the case as Eric couldn't believe that the same girls he'd messaged months before were all now (coincidentally) looking at their conversation threads with him, especially as this meant they would have had to each click on his profile and select the messaging icon, which weren't showing on his display. The old messages Eric had sent were now populating their inboxes and drawing their attention to him once again. It was extremely frustrating as Eric's lack of a response from them after sending the message initially, meant he <u>knew</u> they weren't interested and had already discounted them as possible options.

The fact that Eric was now receiving a plethora of decline messages so soon after re-subscribing was not really doing wonders for his confidence either. It was like a kick in the bollocks and a 'welcome back to Match; all these hotties you messaged ages ago still think you're a twat' and he couldn't believe Match.com would want returning customers like him to face such a negative reintroduction.

Eric was pissed off further because he couldn't vent his disappointment regarding the matter, the dating site's purposeful lack of transparency regarding contact information making it somewhat impossible to navigate. Tasked with trying to work their way through a myriad of 'FAQs', then they realised the majority, including Eric, would give up trying.

The worst thing about the unnecessary deluge of rejections that Eric received was it then meant he was unable to contact the girls who had sent them, his profile being blocked instantaneously as part of the process. Eric may only have wanted to tell them to get fucked but still, it was extremely frustrating not to have the opportunity.

Some evenings, all Eric wanted to do was to strike up a conversation with a girl from the dating site. He was the biggest night owl he knew and it gave him something to do whilst he lay there wide-awake. Finding someone to chat to wasn't as easy as it sounded for Eric. He wouldn't converse with just anyone; they had to pass as shaggable, even if that meant perhaps after a few drinks. He'd scan the profiles of women who were still online and select the maximum 500-mile radius in order to increase his chances. He wasn't necessarily after locking horns, just a bit of banter.

Constantly refreshing the search criteria and watching the numbers dwindle as the minutes ticked by, Eric would sometimes end up losing the will to live. It reminded him of when he used to visit the video shop near to his mum and dad's in his teens (a small privateer before the likes of Blockbuster came onto the scene). He'd go in full of enthusiasm and gleeful anticipation of picking out a film that would get his imagination whirring. However, more often than not, the time he'd spent pawing through the back covers of the assortment of titles would leave him almost brain-dead and walking out with nothing.

You could always tell how big a film was by the number of copies the shop would have perched in purposeful-sized alcoves on the walls; Eric remembering Jurassic Park must have been mahoosive at the time as the shop appeared to have its walls decorated with the dinosaur epic's motif.

Chapter Forty-Four

'We're Gonna Need a Bigger Bed'

Eric's initial foray into the world of online dating had been a real eye-opener. He was like the fat kid in the sweetshop after school and he wanted to sample all of it. There was enough pussy you could knit a sweater (Porky's 6.2/10 IMDb)). However, in his exuberance and given his relative inexperience, he learnt a very big lesson from one of his first outings and one that would definitely put him in good stead for the future.

It all began with such great potential; doesn't it always? The girl, who we shall call Sophie, was of a similar age to Eric, aesthetically easy on the eye given her profile photographs and her apparent intellect and sense of humour having been gleaned through countless messages exchanged between them. Eric was very enthusiastic about Sophie and as this was reciprocal, she invited Eric to stay with her for a weekend in the jewel in the crown of Lancashire; Burnley (did I mention she liked his sarcasm too?).

Having eagerly booked his train ticket and hot-footed it to the station after finishing work one Friday, Eric set off, arriving at his destination a little after 6:00 p.m. After disembarking and standing outside the station as per the plan, Eric waited and waited. It was deathly silent; no noise whatsoever; no trains at the platforms behind him and the dust having settled in the car park from all the commuters returning home for the weekend. Eric turned to his mobile phone and started to message Sophie to see if there was a problem.

It was whilst looking down at the screen of his phone that he noticed it. As it had been raining earlier that day, the small potholes and dips in the pathway still retained some muddy precipitation that had collected there and it was these little puddles of rainwater that began to ripple in unison, not dissimilar to the scene in Jurassic Park to signify the apparent close proximity of the Tyrannosaurus Rex.

It was then Eric looked up instinctively and was greeted by a sight that will live long in his memory… it was Sophie… and she was ORCA FAT!!…

not just slightly overweight with a bit of a muffin top… but gargantuan… it was like the Stay Puft Marshmallow Man in Ghostbusters bounding across the car park towards him (7.8/10 IMDb).
'You have got to be kidding me' Eric thought on working out that this was his date for the weekend, although you could probably add in an expletive or two if you want a closer account of his actual thoughts. Yes, Eric was trapped, his train long gone and his levels of politeness such that he could not bring himself to make his excuses and run for the hills. It was one of the only times Eric could remember when he wished it was Monday morning already.

Squeezing into the front of her small city runabout was like something from a cartoon (think Karate from Batfink); Eric a moderately big unit himself at six feet two and a half inches and a wide frame (no fat though… just a svelte and toned body… cough cough) sat shoulder to shoulder with Sophie, the pair barely managing to close their doors; like two gobstoppers lodged in the mouth of an adolescent… what do you mean as if that would happen? It was a little scary for a time as Eric remembered before his mum managed to pry one of them out.

Later that evening, Eric's heart sank into his shoe as Sophie cajoled him into her bedroom, his wish not to upset her too powerful to say anything. He gulped à la Jerry mouse from the Tom and Jerry cartoons when having been cornered by his adversary, there appeared no obvious means of escape. He undressed whilst Sophie was in the bathroom, wishing he'd brought his Star Wars-themed pyjamas to act as a shield between them.

As the bed was only a standard double, Eric spent the entire night balancing his body at the furthest point from her, one buttock hanging precariously over the edge and devoid of duvet cover. He did not wish to feel Sophie's nakedness against his, especially after accidentally coming into contact with her initially, her folds of fat like giant layers of pizza dough ready to be whirled into the air by a moustachioed Italian baker. Eric was majorly unhappy and the weekend was proving to be the longest one on record already.

Next morning and Eric was up and dressed earlier than usual for a Saturday, slipping out of bed quietly so as not to wake Sophie and to avoid being caught out if she rolled over towards him like a walrus with an itch. Sophie had planned to take Eric out and show him the sights of Burnley

(Eric remembered thinking it shouldn't take too long) and drove them to an idyllic park. It was a nice day and the two took a walk around the lake at its centre.

After a hundred yards or so, something even more excruciatingly awkward and sickening happened; Sophie held out her hand towards Eric's. 'Marvellous' Eric thought not believing things could have got any worse but holding hands with Sophie whilst walking in public was indeed a new record low. Eric felt physically unwell and was praying to the powers above that he did not come into contact with anyone he knew as that would be something he could never live down. Fortunately, he was spared further ignominy.

Eric's problem was that he was just far too polite but he was adamant that he would never get himself into such a predicament as that ever again. Sophie's profile photos had been all of her face and she'd been rather uneconomical with the truth when plumping for the 'about average' option in regards to her body description.

From that day forth, Eric made it one of his chief prerequisites that he would never engage with a girl on dating sites who didn't have a full-length pic unless it was abundantly obvious that she wasn't the size of a sumo wrestler. He also made a pact with himself to drive to the girl's house; giving him means of escape should lightning ever strike twice in the future.

Chapter Forty-Five

Eric's Dating Questionnaire

Whenever Eric was traversing Single Street and had dipped back into online dating over the years, he would always notice some familiar runners and riders still knocking about on the merry-go-round; in fact it got to the point where it was like flicking through his mate's Panini sticker swaps… ' had… had… not had…' These women were either as pernickety as Eric and having the same luck finding a plus-one or they weren't actually after a long-term relationship at all.

Eric grew tired of seeing the same handful of women on his searches, adamant that he would never lower his horizon and start chatting to them as there was obviously a reason why he hadn't chatted to them in the first place. After all his escapades, he'd learnt there was no way he was going to amend his prerequisites.

The older Eric got, the more realistic he was to accept that women his own age were likely to come with baggage but his ethos had always been the same; it depended on whether their baggage was small enough to fit in the locker above his head or would need to be stowed in the cargo hold. Over the earlier years, Eric had dated a variety of women, from those with children and therefore ex or exes in the background, women with a menagerie of pets, those who had the mental capacity of a Cadbury's crème egg, those with boobs smaller than his and worst of all; those who didn't know the difference between 'your' and 'you're'.

He already knew that he had to find one who was tidy, bordering on OCD but without being far too OCD that she spent ten-minutes checking she'd locked the front door (perhaps just the twice would suffice). If she enjoyed watching football and rated Star Wars (8.6/10 IMDb) higher than Grease 2 (4.3/10 IMDb) then that was a Brucie bonus as far as Eric was concerned.

Having had his fill of abject disappointment with the opposite sex, Eric had automatically begun formulating a picture of the perfect specimen of womanliness in his eyes. In order to aid the process of locating her, Eric turned his attentions to compiling his own set of quiz questions, the option now available within his profile on the dating site. It was ideal for Eric as not only could he gauge whether the girl had a sense of humour but also whether she was compatible (as long as she answered honestly of course). The fact that he had a quiz also meant slightly more chance of interaction from the prying ladies or so he thought. His questions were as follows:

1. We're watching a film together and there comes a part where an animal is going to be killed. Do you a) accept it's a film and the animal more likely than not wasn't harmed during the making of it and carry on watching unperturbed (Yes) or b) shout 'turn it off… turn it off, I'm not watching this'? (No)
2. We're driving back home one night; it's late and there's hardly any traffic on the motorway so I decide to kill some time by putting my foot down a bit. Do you a) think great, we'll be home sooner and therefore have more time to relax together when we get back (Yes) or b) shout 'slow down, this is too quick and I don't like it'? (No)
3. We're getting on like the proverbial house on fire and it comes to the stage when it seems right for you to meet my parents. Does the idea of meeting them a) make you want to run the other way and hide as you're very nervous in such situations (Yes) or b) make you think 'great, I agree it's time to meet them and I'm looking forward to it'? (No)
4. There's a Champions League match on telly which I'm keen to watch live but it clashes with a Springwatch episode you'd pencilled in as part of your evening's entertainment. Do you a) let me watch the football whilst I massage your back and neck in a very tender and sensitive fashion (Yes) or b) tell me to sod off to the pub whilst yanking the remote control out of my hand because you need your fix of Chris Packham? (No)
5. We've had friends over for a meal and a catch up; the kitchen is wall to wall pots and pans and it's late… do you prefer to a) tidy it up right there and then and go to bed knowing everything is sorted (Yes) or b) say 'bollocks to that, let's get to bed and sort it all out in the morning'? (No)
6. It's coming up to your time of the month and you're feeling a bit

hormonal, do you a) tell me you're not feeling great and I'd be doing well to stay out of your way for a few days (Yes) or b) find anything and everything to have a go at me about including breathing? (No)

7. An urgent matter comes up and we have to drop everything and go. Do you a) say 'come on slow coach' as you make haste for the door (Yes) or b) suggest that you need at least ten minutes to fanny about applying make-up and to decide what to change into? (No)
8. The majority of our DVD collection mysteriously disappears (could happen) and we're only left with two films we can watch, would you prefer to watch a) Grease 2 (Yes) or b) Star Wars? (No)
9. You're in the local Co-op and have done a big shop. You're unloading the items at the till when you notice the woman behind you is only wishing to purchase a pineapple and some Cadburys mini-eggs (mmmm mini eggs) do you a) continue to unload the trolley thinking you got there first (Yes) or b) signal to the woman that she can nip in front of you and pay for her meagre haul before you? (No)
10. A friend of yours at work's cat has had kittens and they are desperately trying to find new homes for them all. She asks you if you would like one. Do you say a) 'Yes, of course, look how adorable they are and I know they would make a perfect addition to our home' (Yes) or b) 'No thank you, I prefer my house not smelling of piss and shit and my furniture not being torn to shreds'? (No)

Chapter Forty-Six

'I Work Hard and I Play Hard'

One thing that Eric couldn't abide above all other things when searching for a suitable partner online, were women who had no originality whatsoever. I mean, it was their personal write-up which was the biggest indicator to him if they had something a little bit different about them and whether they had a sense of humour he could appreciate and which perhaps complemented his own; something he believed was paramount for a partnership to work.

The number of women who put the same things down in their profile spiel was ludicrous (you know who you are) and the worst offences were as follows:

> My family and friends mean the world to me
> I'm a glass-half-full person
> I love to laugh
> I enjoy nights out and nights in.

These were immensely obvious statements that surely didn't need saying and it grated enormously with Eric. Interestingly, after over ten years of online dating, he was still yet to find a girl who confessed to being a pessimistic social misfit recluse who had found an alternative to staying in or going out and was a complete fun-sponge to boot… but there was still time he thought… plenty of girls lurking across the border in deepest dankest Wales. To be fair, as long as she had a decent set of jubblies then they'd still be fair game to Eric and probably a lot more interesting than all the other sheep bleating out the same banality.

There was no way Eric would strike up a conversation with anyone who was master of the art of saying the bleeding obvious, no matter how succulent she appeared. However, there was one statement that blew the rest out of the water as far as he was concerned and so much so that he made it his number one most stringent rule; never converse with a girl who says 'I work hard and I play hard/er'. There was no negotiating on this front and was considered thee most heinous of crimes in Eric's eyes.

Girls lacking originality in their profiles served as a warning to Eric as he didn't want to end up like a lot of couples he saw sitting silently in pubs on a Sunday afternoon hardly saying a word to one another as they ate their two meals for a tenner. He'd be in there watching the football and after noticing their apparent vow of silence in progress; the situation would both sadden him and make him feel awkward, especially if he was sat at close quarters to them. He almost felt like walking over and starting up conversation at times.

Perhaps this was normal and Eric was the only one who was never short of something to say on account of his very fertile imagination and overactive brain. If there was one thing that Eric was guilty of, it was overthinking things. It was this quirk which Eric knew had been the root cause of expediting the curtailment of many of his relationships, always finding a different angle, an inconsistency or a nonsensical occurrence to mull over in his cranial member and unable to just accept that sometimes things just happen without needing a qualitative and logical reason. Perhaps this was why he enjoyed Columbo so much; the dishevelled raincoat wearing one-eyed detective's famous line 'Just one more thing' resonating with Eric quite a bit.

Chapter Forty-Seven

Off-the-Shelf Sperm

After experiencing nigh on a decade of dating escapades from online sources; Eric happened upon a potentially life-changing or certainly life-defining event. In order to set the scene and tell the whole story, however, I need to take you back a few years and to the twelve days of Christmas beginning in 2008.

It was during this time that Eric was contacted by a woman from Peterborough on Match, who was extremely keen to meet him after perusing his profile on more than one occasion. Despite the 250-mile round trip, the girl, who we shall call Sally, did not think twice about visiting Eric at his home, which as some of you will be thinking, was extremely dangerous and stupid on her part and against all good advice and common-sense practise.

As they got on reasonably well and given it was not uncommon at that stage of his life to travel the length and breadth of the UK in pursuit of good times, Eric reciprocated and a week or so later he made the trip to the East of the country to see Sally, his trusty shagnav (as he called it) being an invaluable asset to him and making his life immeasurably easier.

Although Sally was a nice enough girl, Eric, however, was not overly keen on an extended relationship with her following further meet-ups, especially as she had obvious false boobs and was just a little too scatty and high maintenance for his liking; although he could possibly have lived with the scattiness and high maintenance to a point.

Fake boobs, however, were sacrilegious as far as Eric was concerned and Sally's were terrible; it was as if she'd just stolen two small Christmas puddings and stashed them willy-nilly up her top (think Les Dawson and Roy Barraclough as Cissie and Ada). The Yuletide desserts appeared to be positioned rather erroneously Eric thought and could only speculate that the shoddy workmanship was down to the surgeon being very much at the experimental stage of his career. With the lights out and the pair in bed together, Eric struggled to even locate her modified mammary glands and the enjoyment derived after finally tracking them down was just not the same as a real pair of knockers. Eric had joked with his mates that he perhaps should have painted her nipples with piccalilli so he could use its fluorescence as a method of tracking their position under extreme low-level light.

Eric said adios to Sally after returning back to Moonbase Alpha; it was always easier and much less awkward to end a relationship from afar. Thankfully, the split seemed pretty mutual and another short interlude had borne no fruit. Eric could afford to be fussy at that stage in his life, having only very recently come out of his six-year relationship with Emma mark I and only three-months after they'd been due to get married. He was even more reluctant to stay in an average relationship with a girl living so far away; especially as he knew there was a veritable murmuration of fillies much closer to home. He would just need to have some patience and see who would turn up next.

A few weeks passed after Eric had sent his John Deere letter to Sally and he was already conversing with other potential suitors on the dating site. Then, Eric received a text out of the blue from her, which was just a short message to confirm that she was pregnant and that it was possibly his child she bore. 'YOU WHAAAAATTTTT!!!???' Eric reacted, the news of course coming as an ENORMOUS shock to him.

Having spent a bit of time trying to compute the whole situation, it was then that he realised he'd been duped into providing Sally with off-the-shelf sperm and there were no two ways about it. Her search on the internet had been specifically geared at finding a suitable donor than concerning herself with a long-term relationship and had selected Eric given he was a tall, good-looking, witty and dare I say it, an intelligent specimen of the male form with an IQ of 146 (or so an online test had confirmed anyway). It appeared Eric ticked all of Sally's boxes and there was only one left that she needed filling in so to speak.

When considering his mental aptitude, it was a little ironic therefore that Eric had stupidly assumed Sally had been on the pill as why else would she have partaken in unprotected sex with him he thought? (Always wear a nodder guys and get checked out regularly).

Given the rather serious consequences of Eric's short relationship with

Sally, Eric felt compelled to see her once more in order to sit down and discuss the very important issue face to face. He felt angry that Sally had completely disregarded his rights to only create life when he had found the right partner and it was something that both parties were serious about. Instead, Eric felt like he had somehow been raped and there was no way for him to reverse what had happened.

Eric's only solace came from the fact that Sally mentioned she'd been with a couple of other guys around the same time (nice wholesome girl it appeared) and therefore she couldn't be 100% certain that she was pregnant with his child. As Sally was intent on having a baby, then Eric left thinking that if there was only a 33% chance of it being his, then that was something he could live with as he was certainly not ready to be forced into a change in lifestyle due to a girl's conniving plan to fall pregnant. Eric did not hear from Sally again.

Chapter Forty-Eight

A Shock to the System

That was until September. I'm sure the sharp ones amongst you will have worked out why. Eric could remember the date vividly because he was sat at the dining table at his parents' house celebrating his dad's birthday when he received a text from her to say she had given birth that morning and confirmed the weight, time of birth and the name she had chosen. You could say that Eric felt a smidge uncomfortable but as he had spent the last nine-months not considering the situation once, his stance remained unaltered, the information doing little to change his mindset.

What happened two-days later though was something that, still to this day, remained unquestionably eerie for Eric. Let me just confirm wholeheartedly that he was in no way a believer in spirits, ghosts, premonitions or the like and felt it was mere hocus-pocus nonsense and akin to the medium, Clinton Baptiste in Phoenix Nights: 'I'm getting the name John… is there a John in the audience?'

Eric had popped round to see his parents again and noticing his mother outside in the back garden hanging out some washing on the line, had walked out to greet her. It's a massive cliché I know, but Eric's mum then came out with something that literally made the hairs on his body stand to attention.

'I had a vivid dream last night that you had a daughter and called her Ava' she exclaimed.

Just like that, his mother had not only dreamt that he'd had a child, the child being born around 48-hours (6.9/10 IMDb) previous, that it was a girl and (if Eric was the father) the first girl in the family but most startling and incomprehensible was that Sally had given her newborn daughter the middle name Ava after her grandmother. Eric had not told ANYBODY about the situation with Sally, not even his closest friends as was worried it might cause a problem between them or lead to them convincing him to do something about it.

Eric had a scientific brain, a logical and methodical approach to problem-solving and was certainly more the Scully type who would find rational and factual theories to account for strange goings-on than consider supernatural forces at play. However, on this occasion, Eric had no choice but to admit that his mum had a gift and that gift was a little disconcerting, to say the least.

Fast forward to March 2018 and Eric noticed Facebook Messenger on his phone. As someone who hardly ever used Facebollocks since his two-week trial-period a decade earlier, he was just about to consign the app to the cloud in the sky. However, he decided to click on it out of curiosity.

He noticed that there were a few of his contacts online and was a little perturbed to note that Sally was one of them. He clicked on Sally inquisitively and as his phone screen was populated with her profile, it showed her photo in much greater size and detail. Eric turned ashen immediately. He felt sick to the stomach. Her avatar (7.8/10 IMDb) was of Sally and her daughter, who was now around eight-years-old. Eric could see straight away that the girl bore an uncanny resemblance to his own mother when <u>she</u> was a girl and could also see himself in her eyes. There was no argument as far as Eric was concerned… he was looking at his daughter.

Eric felt compelled to make contact with Sally again after witnessing the unequivocal evidence, the situation having completely numbed him and made him feel rather unsteady on his legs. However, an hour or so later, the anger at being duped by Sally had come back to the fore and with such enormous consequences; it was difficult for him to feel any desire to fit into a life that Sally had engineered for her own gains.

A few messages were subsequently exchanged. However, the conversation soon turned a little sour regarding Sally's story about her not being able to take the pill on medical grounds ('but when I'm not at the doctor's I take them all the time' Duncan Thickett/ Steve Coogan) and that she had instead relied upon the calendar method, which angered Eric further, given that she had failed to mention this prior to having sex. This presented more evidence that it had been Sally's plan from the start.

Eric needed to consider his options and with that their communication ceased. It was not great timing, as without a job, money, his own home or an enriching and fulfilling life at that stage, he was certainly in no position to be introduced to his daughter. If Eric <u>was</u> to have a part to play, it was only going to happen when he was in a much better situation, when he could feel good about himself and feel more confident that his daughter would be proud of him as their relationship developed. He just hoped that if he did get around to seeing her then their first meet wouldn't include either Nicky Campbell or Davina McCall in tow.

Chapter Forty-Nine

Coincidence of Coincidences

One of the biggest coincidences in Eric's life had seen his first real girlfriend, Becky, begin work in the same office as him ten-years later; the odds arguably longer than Leicester winning the Premier League. However, there was a much bigger coincidence in Eric's life and one he coined the coincidence of coincidences; the odds on par with Maureen from Driving School taking fastest lap at Silverstone after being signed by the Toro Rosso team.

One of the many girls Eric got conversing with via online dating was Blodwen, a Welsh girl (who'd have thunked it?) who lived and worked approximately 20-miles from him in Warrington. They spoke on and off for some time, with other dates in betwixt but there was something putting Eric off from meeting her; possibly her photos but more likely given her location. However, experiencing a fallow period in his dating schedule and with Blodwen still very keen to meet up, Eric threw caution to the wind and after punching her co-ordinates into his shagnav one Saturday evening, he travelled to see her (well he had enjoyed her sense of humour enormously via the messages and felt she was worth a look-see).

After meeting Blodwen, who lived in a shared terraced house in one of the suburbs, Eric realised he'd committed the same schoolboy error that he had with Sophie from Burnley. Blodwen was rather more ample than he'd anticipated or hoped compared to her photos and any chance of physical attraction had immediately left the building and travelled back home. As Eric had made the effort and was far too polite to hurt her feelings, he thought he might as well enjoy a night out; besides, she was just as witty in real life.

The two therefore embarked on an evening out together and both had a genuinely good laugh, Blodwen's conversation and confidence quite refreshing compared to a number he'd met. Then it was back to hers; Eric staying over, which although had never been mentioned, had been assumed by both parties. The more Eric had drunk then it was a famous case of beer-goggles at midnight and as Blodwen had made him laugh and was fun to be with, then Eric had begun to fancy her a little more.

As Blodwen was a larger than average girl, she purposely hadn't put the lights on in her bedroom, a little conscious of her body perhaps as she began undressing and the pair got into bed together. Eric wasn't complaining about fumbling around in the dark as that meant he could be less surreptitious when removing his clothing, without her seeing his big leg.

A big plus factor at being a little chunky, Blodwen had a very fine set of boobs, which were of course a great selling point to Eric, like Play-Doh for grown-ups. As things steadily progressed and levels of nakedness had increased, Eric was aware that Blodwen was wearing a pair of Bridget Jones' (6.7/10 IMDb) big knickers; as he started to slip his hand under the elasticated waistband, Blodwen suddenly shot her hand down to cut him off at the pass and before he could roam any further towards the promised land.

'I wouldn't if I was you' she exclaimed, Eric recoiling his arm and sighing internally. Eric had two main rules when it came to sex:

1. Thou shall not dip thy quill in the devil's inkpot and
2. No brown love – 'why struggle with a tough brown when you can sink an easy pink?'

Despite having Aunt Flo visiting her for a few days, Blodwen was still keen to explore Eric and she was very accommodating. Eric felt somewhat guilty that he couldn't reciprocate, especially as he enjoyed that part of proceedings and if he said so himself, was rather a dab tongue at it.

The next morning and Eric and Blodwen said their goodbyes, Eric not interested in meeting-up again, his sobriety causing him to feel shocked with himself at his bedtime antics after seeing Blodwen in the cold light of day.

Eric found it easy to switch off and forget girls, especially when there wasn't scope for any follow-up dates and a plethora of other options waiting out there in cyberspace. He always ensured to have at least one conversation with a potential girl on the backburner, a fallback if you will in case D1 did not bear any fruit. In fact, it wasn't unheard of for him to secretively message another girl whilst on a date or stopover if things were going terribly, his mind already turning to his next victim.

A popular headache for Eric had been juggling with multiple girls on WhatsApp, having cajoled his favourite felines onto the more practical communication medium and away from the rather draconian online dating messaging portal as soon as he could. It also meant you could send photos, which Eric had been keen to receive from potential dates prior to D1 to satisfy himself that he <u>was</u> physically attracted to them before agreeing to lock horns.

It also meant that photographs of a more sexual nature could be shared; yes, the now infamous and renowned inclination of 'dick-pics'. The phrase was notably regarding a fella's primeval instincts to want to show off his baby-making equipment to the woman, something that was just impossible to do via the dating site due to all photos having to pass via moderators. Eric found it rather laughable at how a lot of women who started out as prim and proper at the beginning of their conversation with him (and some even specifically mentioning for Eric not to send them any such phallic photography despite having no reason for thinking he might) were sending him photos of their boobs an hour or so later and on the odd occasion even their most sacred area.

Eric found a large percentage of women he sexted on WhatsApp were just dying to see his thrombone, Eric's way with words able to turn even Sister Wendy into a quivering sex craved maniac. Before he revealed 'tonight's jackpot' to them he would always request to see them as God intended first, reminding them that in the movies, the woman always showed her tits and fanny before the actor's pork sword was ever likely to appear. It was only if Eric came across a girl with real potential in the future relationship stakes (otherwise known as the 2:50 at Kempton) where he would refrain from requesting pics or sending any himself.

Chapter Fifty

Some Would Call it Fate

Around six months after Eric's one-night episode with Blodwen, Eric had well and truly moved on and was now seeing a girl up in Lancashire. She was given the name Blackpool Em (not to her face but after their relationship finished) to distinguish her from his first fiancé of the same name, who Eric referred to as Em Mark I. Blackpool Em wasn't actually from Blackpool but obtained the name for two reasons; one, because it tripped off the tongue easier than Wrea Green Em and two; all main roads and junctions en route to hers were signposted Blackpool.

Seeing Blackpool Em meant a round trip of 150 miles for Eric, which wasn't very practical at all. In fact having spent a weekend with her, which he was prone to do, Eric did not always fancy the drive home on Sunday evening, deciding sometimes to set off very early on the Monday and make a quick pit stop at home before heading on to work. It was on one of these early starts that a rather peculiar set of circumstances began, like the aligning of the cogs of fate or was that planets?

It was around 5:30 a.m. when Eric set off, pitch black outside and the temperature a little parky to say the least. Eric was a little tired but with The Best of Keane resonating from the car speakers and the heaters blowing a gale then he was beginning to feel more awake. It wasn't long before he was speeding down the M6 towards home when he suddenly noticed that the illuminated readouts and button surrounds on the dashboard were flickering off and on. It was rather an eerie sight, Eric not having experienced it before since he'd had the car a couple of years. It was as if the electrics were being affected by a UFO, like in Close Encounters of the Third Kind (7.6/10 IMDb). Eric didn't have a clue what was causing it, the power to the car also becoming intermittent.

As the car's exterior lights were also affected, it was fortunate for Eric that around the same time, the sun had just begun to creep up above the horizon, his reliance on them somewhat less vital. However, the problems persisted. The car's power was now so erratic that it posed a danger to

Eric, not able to depress the accelerator pedal and expect the usual reaction. Eric did not want to stop on the hard shoulder miles from home and hoped that the problem would not prevent him from making it back to Moonbase Alpha. Suddenly, his nightmare was realised and all of the electrics switched off and stayed off, the dashboard completely blank and nothing made a sound; not even the engine.

Eric was now just free-wheeling given the car's previous momentum. Luckily, the motorway traffic was pretty light and Eric was able to glide the car over onto the hard shoulder from the fast lane and come to a stop without too much bother. At this stage, he'd realised that the battery must have died, the only possible cause for the way in which things had slowly degenerated. There was zero power and despite being reminded by a Highway Agency bod to put his hazard warning lights on after parking up behind him, Eric had already learnt that these wouldn't even work either. It was freezing outside and Eric didn't have a jacket but as the recommendation for someone in his position was to exit the vehicle and stand away from the road, then he braved the cold, whilst waiting for the breakdown recovery truck to appear.

One perk of having a job with the bank was that he automatically received the benefits that came with having an Advantage account, which included free breakdown cover from Green Flag. Despite the cover only being standard and not full, it was still peace of mind and included taking Eric and his defunct car (Hilfe Hilfe mein auto ist kaputt) to a garage within a ten-mile radius. As Eric was still approximately double that distance from making it back home, then the recovery driver gave Eric some options as to where he could tow him. Unaware of the standard of garages and given he wasn't really fussed; Eric left it with the driver to decide.

Having arrived at a garage and his car having been disconnected from the truck, it wasn't long before the bonnet was up and two numpties were peering over the engine, baring their teeth whilst taking sharp intakes of breath as though to suggest that the problem was both serious and expensive. Fortunately, the manager came across the garage forecourt soon after and after Eric described the problems and his own prognosis, he carried out a preliminary check and was able to conclude that a large bolt connected to the alternator (and allowing the battery to continually charge) was missing. It was as simple as that.

It was a little later that Eric remembered travelling home from work one evening around two-weeks prior when he'd heard a sizeable clang emanating from the engine bay as though something metallic had fallen through it. Although having been a rather strange occurrence at the time, he'd not felt the need to follow it up, assuming something had been kicked-up by one of his tyres.

As the bolt was a specific manufacturer's part, then the manager said he would have to order it and hoped to receive it the next day. Eric, therefore, had to abandon his jalopy and find alternative arrangements to get home and started walking towards the town centre, not having a clue of where anything was.

Rattling around on his own in a decent-sized house and finding it somewhat eerie, Eric had decided to take in a lodger when Emma Mark I had left, which was also a good way for him to subsidise the mortgage. Natalie or 'Fat-Nat' as Eric came to call her (not to her face obviously) was originally from that neck of the woods and as he knew she didn't work on a Monday, then he asked if she fancied picking him up. Natalie was happy to oblige and so Eric confirmed he was stood opposite a train station entrance.

Whilst waiting patiently for around half-an-hour for Nat to arrive, a VW Golf passed on the other side of the road and the girl behind the wheel stared over at Eric and raised her hand, waving and smiling at him enthusiastically. Eric waved back instinctively not really knowing who it was straight away, before realising that it was, in fact, Blodwen, the girl he'd shared an enjoyable evening with several months prior. Eric thought nothing more about her and returned home with Nat not long after.

Later that day, Eric was checking through his emails, when he came across one from Blodwen. Well, having seen her earlier that day, it wasn't the biggest surprise he thought, especially as the sighting would have triggered her memory. But wait. The message from Blodwen was sent prior to seeing each other that morning. It had been sent the previous evening, Sunday around 6 pm. Considering that some five/six months had passed since their date, then it appeared to be a rather big coincidence to have seen each other the very next morning after she'd sent her email, Eric having had no reason or compunction to visit Warrington again.

The coincidence was about to get even bigger as not only had she emailed

Eric the previous day but she'd specifically said she 'would love to see you again'. This was just a little mind-blowing for Eric (imagine him with his hands on his head and lifting them away simultaneously to his improvised sound of an incendiary device going off).

Chapter Fifty-One

A Weird Chain of Events

The massive coincidence reminded Eric of Air Crash Investigation, where the NTSB or whichever jurisdiction was involved, would eventually piece together a chronological run of occurrences that had come together to seal a plane's tragic fate. Although thankfully not life-threatening in Eric's case, Eric and Blodwen's coming(s) together had been just a little bizarre, to say the least. Let's run through the list of events that had to happen just to underline the massive probability against this situation having taken place:

1. Eric's alternator bolt had been slowly unscrewing (unbeknown to him) and finally came off, making a large clanging noise as it fell through the engine bay on his way home from work two-weeks earlier – Despite being weird Eric didn't follow it up, believing the noise was likely something on the road that was kicked-up.
2. Eric was seeing a girl near Blackpool and the easiest route from home was past Warrington. He could have been seeing a girl from anywhere else and not needed to pass Warrington at all.
3. Eric decided to travel back home on Monday morning, not Sunday night when Blodwen had emailed Eric to say she'd love to see him again (Email not seen by Eric until Monday afternoon).
4. The battery could have run flat at any stage after the bolt had come away but happened to be on his return from Blackpool.
5. The battery could have run flat at any stage along the 75-mile journey but did so adjacent to a Warrington motorway turn-off (appreciate there are a few but still).
6. Eric's bank account perks meant he received free breakdown recovery but the cover could only guarantee being towed within a 10-mile radius, which meant he couldn't get back home.
7. The recovery driver suggested a garage in Warrington and not another location.

8. The fact that the car could not be fixed without a specific manufacturer's part, leaving Eric having to find an alternative way home.
9. Eric decided to walk into town and ask Nat to pick him up from outside the station when he didn't have a clue where he was going.
10. The fact that Nat didn't work on a Monday meant he'd asked her to pick him up rather than catching a train and was, therefore, waiting outside the station.
11. The timing of Eric's trip back home, breaking down, reaching the garage, having the problem located by the mechanics and walking into town all coinciding with when Blodwen drove past.
12. Blodwen having chosen to email when she did after such a long time and said how she would love to see Eric again.
13. Blodwen's journey to work on Monday took her past the same train station that Eric stood outside of.
14. Blodwen gets her wish and sees Eric the very next morning, a little over 12-hours after sending her email.

Now, it would be a real Pulitzer prize-winning story if I said that following the freak occurrence, the two saw each other again, fell in love, got married, had little Erics and Ericas and lived happily ever after. However, reality away from the cinema and fictitious romance books doesn't tend to be quite so poignant. The bottom line was that Eric was still not interested in Blodwen and the tale only served to exemplify an amazing coincidence, where two people were brought within ten feet of each other after the strangest set of circumstances had played out.

Chapter Fifty-Two

Blackpool Em

As mentioned, in the intervening period between Eric's two sightings of Blodwen, he'd met another Emma online and despite the perceived distance issue at first, their rapport from the beginning was enjoyable enough for Eric to accept this somewhat impractical element.

Emma was slightly older than Eric, her birthday falling the day before his every year, although a couple prior to Eric's arrival on planet Earth. She did have two young children as well, which was also a first for Eric, having previously stayed at arm's length from any mothers even if they had been definite milfs. Eric held firm with the notion that if a woman had kids then it was more likely that she would have a fanny like Harry Potter's robe sleeve so prayed that Emma's were both caesareans.

Emma had split from her husband but he was still on the scene, in as much as the pair held joint custody and were fairly amicable to a point. There was obviously something very appealing to Eric about Emma for him to ignore two very sizeable prerequisites on his ever-expanding list.

The relationship lasted several months but there were at least three big issues (£7.50 please) why the relationship ran aground, a couple you may have already discerned. The first and perhaps main reason was the presence of her ex in her life and the continual arranging of tasks relating to the Perishers including fetching and carrying.

On one particular occasion, Emma had popped out to get her hair done, leaving Eric to fend for himself for a couple of hours. Whilst relaxing in her lounge, there was a commotion at the door and in came her ex looking stressed and on a mission. Eric felt rather awkward; I mean he was the fella now knobbing his ex-wife who'd left him and the whole scenario just seemed all kinds of wrong. He was trying to locate some of the kids' clothing for a specific activity and after finding what he was looking for he disappeared. This was the froth on the cake though and just underlined the bizarre love triangle set-up, which just didn't sit well with Eric. He wanted to feel like an important cog in the whole jigsaw and felt more like a bystander looking in from the outside and fitting in here and there.

The second reasons were the children. The kids, despite being great with Eric and vice versa (5.8/10 IMDb), weren't his though and he didn't feel comfortable playing the surrogate father figure whenever they were about. There was also the amount of time that was spent dedicated to them, leaving very little between him and Emma, apart from the evenings. Everything was about the kids and although Eric understood this would resonate as very normal goings-on for those who had them; Eric didn't and found the whole situation tiresome and restrictive. He naturally ensured that the kids were having fun and being looked after at all stages when he was with them but he didn't owe them anything really and life seemed so much more relaxed and unregimented on his own.

When the kids weren't about then Eric and Emma did have a 'normal' relationship, with trips to the cinema, seaside walks and even sampling the attractions of the Pleasure Beach. When they got home Emma would get to ride on the Big One again as Eric was always happy to oblige. Emma did have a healthy appetite in that department and they would often partake, even having spontaneous sex on the kitchen floor on occasions. In fact, Eric would be rudely awoken (in all senses of the word) some mornings to find Emma down the foot of the bed and already noshing on his cock having unfurled it from his briefs.

It wasn't all about sex though, having spent an enjoyable weekend up in the Lakes, their two birthdays having coincidentally fallen on each of the two days. Eric remembered going to watch Slum Dog Millionaire (8.0/10 IMDb) with her in a very small and antiquated picture house and as the set-up was a myriad of doors, narrow passages and steps, he'd managed to find himself on the next level up and stood in the projection room.

Turning around as fast he could, acknowledging his own mistake, he was mortified to note that a number of other cinema-goers had followed him, assuming he knew where he was going. Eric, now embarrassed, exclaimed 'So that's the projection room… fascinating' as though his disorientation had been purposeful all along. It was incredible how many times he would end up in such similar positions but at least he could see the funny side afterwards.

Chapter Fifty-Three

Whatever You Do... Don't Laugh

The funniest episode between the pair, however, had been at a school concert, Emma's daughter due to perform in the choir. Sitting amongst other mums and dads in the local civic hall was just a little bit strange for Eric, who felt his presence was tenuous at best and he was feeling way out of his comfort zone. As the lights dimmed and the curtains opened, the production began and the kids appeared on stage singing various ballads from musicals and all that jazz.

It was then the turn of one young girl, around seven years old, to sing a solo and she walked to the front of the stage and stood behind the assembled microphone perched on a stand. Eric assumed she was a rising star, the school's own front runner for a berth on Britain's Got Talent or some other such show. You could hear a church mouse in carpet slippers as the audience held its collective breath.

The piano introduction began and it was only a matter of time before the girl would begin her routine. She began; loudly and confidently and straight away it was a performance to behold. Not in a good way though; it wasn't so much an angelic voice (like Aled Jones circa 1985) but more the sound of a tone-deaf cat trying to pass barbed wire through its lower intestines. It was shocking and so much so that Emma had been unable to suppress her uncontrollable urge to laugh, which was now audible to those sitting all around them and beyond.

Eric was biting the inside of his mouth ferociously, desperately trying to keep it closed, Emma's failure to remain respectful having done nothing to help quash his similar urge. It was a highly embarrassing situation; for all Eric knew, the girl's mum and dad could be sat next to them. It was a very strange set of emotions; on the one hand literally snorting out mucus from his nose from restrained laughter and on the other, tinged with the stark reality of it being wholly inappropriate.

Eric was now digging his fingers into Emma's nearest thigh in a bid to inflict a little discomfort to assist her in refraining as the girl continued to murder the song. As two polite and supposedly educated adults, this wasn't exactly a mature example to set but it was just too piss-funny for words. For the rest of the evening, Eric and Emma would sporadically release a sudden guffaw which they would quickly mask with a cough, evidence that both continued to have flashbacks and again finding it impossible not to react.

Even if you'd taken the kids and ex-husband out of the equation, Eric still felt the distance between them was a right pain in the arse. It was 75-miles door to door and would usually take him around 80-minutes, although his record was a rather impressive 57 (mostly on private roads with no speed restrictions naturally). Long-distance (Clara) relationships were a very big factor for many people participating in online dating, the parameters for the catchment area being easily set to the user's preference. Eric knew that it was unrealistic and rather insular of him to be expecting to find the girl of his dreams (or even one he fancied) at the end of his street but it would make for a much easier life if that was the case.

Eric found it particularly difficult to confirm his feelings on the matter to Emma as he knew that she was extremely happy with him. It was probably not the best timing when he finally told her either, being a couple of miles from his at some local shops. Still, there was never a good time to break someone's heart and Eric did not extol any pleasure from it. The more he'd had dates and relationships, the more he felt it less of a biggie when parting the waves, although it helped enormously not to have too much of an emotional attachment.

Eric was now back on Single Street once more but as he had his own house, then at least he didn't have to return to his parents for the 46th time. As you will be staggered to learn, it wasn't long before Eric was back on the online dating sites and in search of a replacement, this time one within 20-miles and having no children. He'd given it a go and so at least he knew that a similar scenario would never work for him long-term.

The biggest factor for his decision had been a desire to spend time with a girl in a spontaneous fashion and not be told when and where it could happen. Eric would never get with a woman who had kids ever again, apart from a one-off no-strings bit of fun on occasions when Eric thought it'd be rude not to. As for whether the woman realised this at the time was another matter but Eric was not going to play father to someone else's kids.

Chapter Fifty-Four

Eric Continues Online Dating

As we have already learnt; having steadily become a seasoned pro in online dating etiquette, Eric had adapted his methods to ensure he wasn't wasting his time. He'd had too many situations where, after messaging a girl for weeks, they'd ultimately had zero chemistry after finally locking horns.

Eric began to conjecture that as his profile and initial messages to girls were quite witty and usually made them laugh, perhaps a lot of them were somehow expecting to meet the next Peter Kay and as humour through prose was much different to stand-up, then perhaps the girls were left slightly disappointed.

Eric was pretty funny in person, don't get me wrong but he wasn't about to sit there and reel off knock-knock jokes; that wasn't his style. Without really knowing the girl then his anecdotes in life could not readily be thrown in as part of the conversation, especially as most of his anecdotes revolved around other women (you noticed). So, in many first-date cases, it was pretty standard to end up reiterating the boring and cursory stuff that had already been discussed via messages previously.

Having come to the conclusion that it was best to meet with a girl sooner rather than later (if everything seemed to be panning out nicely over initial messages) it wasn't always the case that the girl was of the same opinion. Eric had become rather disgruntled with girls who were keener to take it more slowly and it was usually these same cautious types whose protocol would invariably include organising a phone call (or worse; FaceTime) with him prior to any meet-up (D1). This was something that Eric detested above everything else as he hated speaking on the phone period (full stop no erasies) especially with people he knew or in this case wanted to impress.

At least when meeting up, there was so much more to take in; the aesthetics of the other person, eye contact, body language, the potential for tactility and a smile could go a long way to working out whether the other person was interested or not. In contrast, a phone call could be so sterile, lacking in all of the above and with the added disadvantage of potentially and almost always speaking over one another and making the whole experience seem awkward.

Eric had a very professional telephone manner and having spent years of his career communicating with clients and customers over the phone, he'd received accolades for it. However, that was with people who didn't really matter to him in the whole scheme of things and there was usually a business reason or requirement for making the call.

There had been quite a few people over the years that told Eric his voice sounded like Ringo Starr, who narrated original episodes of Thomas the Tank Engine, was married to Eric's favourite Bond girl, Barbara Bach from The Spy Who Loved Me (7.1/10 IMDb) but probably best known as the drummer in a small-time Merseyside outfit known as The Beatles. This was a complete piss-take to Eric who knew he did not sound very scouse whatsoever, compared to a bona fide Liverpudlian (such as Jamie Carragher for example) for which subtitles were very much required.

Chapter Fifty-Five

You're Only Famous to Those Who Know You

Speaking of proper scouse-sounding people, Eric remembered the longest telephone call he'd ever had was with a Liverpudlian woman, at nearly five-hours in length and which began just after midnight. You won't be surprised to learn that it was with a potential date but the circumstances leading up to it were more mysterious and unusual than he was used to. It all began in late November/early December of 2009.

The first rule of online dating for Eric as you will have noted from his list was that he would never reply to a woman who didn't have a profile photo. This was obviously the first rule as it was the most noticeable aspect of the process.

Now it was sometimes the case where a girl had only just subscribed and therefore, keen to peruse the male talent, had started conversing with potentials prior to the moderators having given their photos the all-clear. This could sometimes take up to 24-hours. In this case, Eric would only reply to those girls once their photo had landed and they were aesthetically easy on his eyes.

There was then the other breed of women who blatantly weren't going to upload a profile photo at any stage. The reasons for this, Eric believed were four-fold:

1. They bore an uncanny resemblance to Grotbags from Rod Hull and Emu fame and realised they would find it almost impossible to catch anyone's eye (usually the same women who would tout the 'it's what's inside that counts' ethos)
2. They were fresh out of a relationship and were keen for their ex not to see them,
3. Worse, they were already in a relationship and were bored,

4. They had a certain job, such as a schoolteacher, where their anonymity was notably more important.

However, one day after Eric received a message from a woman who had no profile photos and very little other detail to work off, it soon became apparent that she didn't fall into any of the usual categories. At first, Eric had simply ignored her message, especially as she hadn't even given him her name. Eric could only assume that she had a hang-up about her appearance in some way. She messaged him again. Eric simply replied as he did in every such case and that was to say 'I don't talk to anybody who doesn't have a profile photo, sorry'.

However, Eric's curiosity was gained when she sent him a cryptic clue as to why she couldn't upload a photo. 'If I put a photo on the site then people will know who I am' she wrote.

'Hmm… Interesting' Eric thought, his overly fertile mind now running wild imagining who on earth it could be. 'Well, I'm still not having a conversation with you until I see a photograph' Eric replied, certainly not buying the potential scam for a second and not wishing to drop his online dating rules for anyone, no matter how famous they believed themselves to be. Instead of simply just telling Eric who she was, the woman had elicited Eric's email address from him and sent him a couple of photos. Eric was none the wiser, although he was not who you would call an authority on supposed famous people, certainly after the mid-nineties anyway.

Eric needed to know who she was and so asked her name and what she was famous for. Finally, after a long drawn out affair, she told him; she was a DJ from Radio Merseyside (we'll call her Debbie). Well, no wonder Eric didn't have a dickie bird who she was as the name meant absolutely nothing to him. Eric didn't really listen to the old crystal set whatsoever and even if he did he wouldn't be listening to Radio Merseyside out of choice.

Although not counting her as a famous person, Eric was pretty impressed with her photos, especially the one of her dressed in a Liverpool strip and appearing to be interviewing fans at an airport. If Eric was going to be uber critical and shallow, then her nose seemed quite a redeeming feature but then overall he'd definitely have dry bummed her given the chance.

After trying to do a little bit of research, Eric couldn't really find out very much about Debbie and the whole famous thing had done more to put him off in any case. Still, she seemed keen and after swapping telephone numbers they agreed to have a chat sometime soon.

One Friday evening around three weeks before Christmas, Eric had been on the phone to another girl, called Harriet, who was a teacher at a private girl's school. They had been messaging each other for a while and Eric had realised that she seemed to tick a great deal of his prerequisite boxes, especially as she was intelligent and could spell and use grammar correctly.

Whilst speaking to Harriet, Eric noticed that Debbie had tried calling him so after finishing a four-hour conversation with Harriet; he made time for a quick cigarette and piss-break before contacting the self-confessed celebrity disc jockey. It was now after midnight, so Eric didn't know whether she'd even be up for a chat at that hour but as he'd had a drink or two he was feeling buoyant and quite confident, especially after how successful the previous call had gone.

The first thing that Eric realised when she answered was how scouse Debbie sounded, Eric, making fun of her accent, suggesting he called her back once he'd found an interpreter. Heaven knows how the conversation lasted almost five-hours but five-hours it almost did last. They got on pretty well (obviously) and Eric enjoyed the conversation. He wasn't shy; he never was and probably had fewer filters than most if not everyone else he knew. Eric, therefore, admitted he'd never heard of her which helped to cement a certain genuineness about his interest, knowing that it wasn't about her perceived fame.

Sarcasm alert! It turned out that she must have been 'very famous' as her best friend was none other than Scouse Craig, the 'chippy' and pioneering winner of the inaugural Big Brother reality TV show. After Eric felt his brain frying from the mobile phone being stuck to his head for nigh on nine-hours that night and feeling his jaw physically ache, the two ended their call, with Debbie mentioning that she would soon be doing an OB (Outside Broadcast) Christmas special near his home. She even mentioned the possibility of dropping in on Eric at some point.

However, having had time to mull over the situation, Eric realised that getting potentially ensconced with someone like her was not really what he wanted and as Harriet was looking very promising, then he sent Debbie a John Deere message and his short but sweet interlude with her was no longer.

Chapter Fifty-Six

Hilfe Hilfe Mein Auto Ist Kaputt (Again)

Harriet was a very intelligent girl, having studied languages at Oxbridge and gone on to teach languages at a private girls' school. She was therefore just as good at spelling and with grammar as Eric and could, therefore, give him a half-decent game of strip Scrabble (you haven't played strip Scrabble?).

The first couple of dates had proved successful, Harriet having made the trip from Skelmersdale initially and with Eric reciprocating and visiting her at her rather small modern semi on an estate that had once housed a certain Paddy McGuiness according to her. It was during a trip up to see Harriet in his newly acquired Toyota Celica GT Liftback (after he'd managed to blow the engine of his Nissan Almera GTI on the motorway) that Eric would once again be faced with a farcical situation involving a car battery. You couldn't make it up.

It was a Sunday morning and a cold winter's day, although thankfully no snow or ice around (okay, probably around two degrees above freezing… still chilly). Harriet had a special meeting she had to attend at school and so left Eric in bed, trusting him to let himself out in his own time. All she had asked was that he posted her house keys through the letterbox after he'd locked the front door. Eric didn't like hanging around on his own in someone else's house so he was up early, just after Harriet had left. It was around 9:00 a.m. and early as far as Eric was concerned, especially for the Sabbath.

Making sure he had all of his gubbins with him, Eric locked the front door and posted the keys as per Harriet's instructions before unlocking his car and getting in. As it was brass monkeys outside and Eric not having a coat with him, he was planning to switch the heaters on full pelt as soon as he got the engine up to temperature.

Eric turned the key in the ignition and the engine gave the tiniest of whimpering attempts to start before all the dashboard lights went out and worse of all, the car's alarm began to sound. Eric had never heard anything quite like it. It was deafeningly loud and as it was early on a Sunday morning and surrounded by houses on the estate, then Eric felt almost sick with embarrassment and guilt. He hadn't even known that the car <u>had</u> an alarm and was certainly not given any indication by the fella who sold it to him. Eric didn't know what to do. Eric's first priority was to try to turn the alarm off but no matter what he did, he couldn't stop it, trying the key physically in the door and ignition once more.

Not only was the car making a quite stupendous noise but as the battery had died, there was no way he could start the car in order to heat it up for warmth. Having already posted the keys through Harriet's letterbox he had also technically shot himself in the face, unable to seek solace back inside and away from the deafening din.

Eric took advantage of his free breakdown recovery via his bank account once again and telephoned Green Flag. However, on hearing they wouldn't be there for an hour, Eric realised he'd have to put up with the ignominy of causing a(n) horrendous racket for the neighbours until the cavalry arrived.

As he continued to try different methods in an attempt to silence the alarm, Eric realised something. Whilst sat in the driving seat and locking the car from the inside and not moving at all, then the alarm ceased. The silence, as they say, was deafening and Eric was just happy to have some respite from the continual claxons, having endured them for what felt like half-an-hour already.

Eric had certainly got himself into yet another cracking situation and it seemed these things could only happen to him. Eric was now sat catatonic inside a broken-down car freezing his bollocks off in a T-shirt and jeans on a winter's morning and unable to break from his musical-statues routine until the recovery vehicle arrived <u>or</u> risk pissing-off the neighbours some more.

Just as Eric was enjoying the relative peace and tranquillity, his phone rang and knowing it could be the recovery firm, he knew he had to answer it. However, in moving his body to take the call then he knew that he would trigger the internal sensors and set off the alarm once more. 'Marvellous' Eric thought but after taking the call believed he could simply repeat what he'd done and get it to switch off again. Well, that was the idea anyway.

Try as he might though, Eric could not seemingly recreate his previous routine (whatever that was) and was left with no choice but to sit tight as the alarm continued to blare out.

Now Eric had assumed that once the breakdown driver had charged his battery up, the noise would be a thing of the past. He was again wrong. It seemed that without the code to the alarm system then there was no way of stopping it from sounding. To reiterate, Eric had not even been aware that there was one fitted on the car and mentioned this to the mechanic.

Things were about to get even more ridiculous. The breakdown guy confirmed that after-market alarms were not fitted in the same places in cars for obvious reasons; to prevent any potential car thief from knowing where to locate it and therefore disable it in quick time. In order for the alarm to be disconnected, the only option Eric and the mechanic (Mike and the Mechanics) had to silence it was to a) locate it and b) cut the wire thereby rendering it useless (although it would be a lot quieter for everyone).

Eric watched as the mechanic stripped the entire interior of his car, placing all the pieces on the driveway adjacent to it, which was starting to look like a giant Airfix model kit. By the time he finally located the alarm box (which if you're interested was under the passenger seat floor panel) it had been sounding intermittently for over an hour. The mechanic turned to Eric and asked him the question 'Are you sure you want me to cut the wire as your alarm will be useless after that?'

Eric replied quickly, 'Just cut the bastard'.

The only noise was now inside Eric's own head and he was relieved that there was no way it could return ever again. His only concern now was whether the mechanic could remember where all the parts he'd removed went and if he would fit them back properly.

Eric needn't have worried though and tipped him all the available cash he had on him (a tenner… yep, he'd wished he'd had more) for what was notably an example of him going above and beyond his remit.

Eric was now finally able to drive back home, cranking up the heaters as he went and laughing to think how Harriet would never believe what had ensued outside her house that morning after she'd departed.

Chapter Fifty-Seven

Drama Queen

Harriet was unlike most of Eric's previous girlfriends; diminutive and certainly more of a girly-girl hung-up about her appearance and certainly higher up the maintenance spectrum. She was also a tad immature and her relationship with animals was something that Eric found nauseating. Eric was a fessed up clean freak as we've learnt, bordering on OCD but certainly not the type to spend too long carrying out checks or superstitious routines. Harriet, on the other hand, was a perfectionist in that she spent so long attending to tasks that Eric felt constantly frustrated at her for dragging her heels and being late for everything. She was a complete nightmare.

Considering these facts, it was amazing how much time Eric ended up spending with her, although Harriet had been a great source of comfort when his brother had lost his life due to an aggressive brain tumour, following a relapse. This had been right at the beginning of their relationship and Eric knew that it couldn't have been easy for her being thrown in at the deep end so to speak.

Perhaps one of the reasons why they stuck together for as long as they did was due to their sexual chemistry, Harriet pretty similar to Eric on that front and both instigating carnal instincts readily and spontaneously.

The problems began mounting up when Harriet (after notably having agreed with Eric) sold her house and moved into his larger house around a year or so into their relationship, having been happy up to that point taking it in turns to visit one another at weekends. Given that the commute for Harriet to the school where she worked was extremely impractical following her move, then it soon became necessary for Harriet to find a teaching job closer to her new home.

This she did, which wasn't a surprise as schools were crying out for teachers and not many could boast a résumé like Harriet's. However, teaching a large mixed-class of comprehensive pupils was a big jump from only having had to worry about a handful of extremely well behaved and polite girls and Harriet found the transition very difficult. She would come home from school in floods of tears, stressed to the eyeballs at having to shout at the kids constantly, the headmaster having also had to come in at one point to regain control of her class. Harriet was just not cut out for this level of teaching and so Eric, who could see that she was unhappy, came up with a potential solution.

Eric suggested she should pack in the teaching and find something for her to concentrate on. With no kids terrorising her, not constantly having to mark books or plan lessons, then she would have more time to herself and take out the element of stress. In fact, the planning of lessons had taken Harriet so long at times that she had commandeered Eric to help her, the pair cut, stick and gluing into the early hours.

Harriet came around to Eric's thinking and began looking for another job. It wasn't too long before she found something suitable and handed her notice in at the school, her relief already palpable. Things were much better and Eric's suggestion had been proven a very good one and not for the first or last time.

It had not just been Harriet who had moved into Eric's home as she had to bring her menagerie of pets with her; namely three cats, two hamsters and a rabbit, although the rabbit was thankfully allowed to reside in a hutch in the back garden. As the hamsters dwelt in a smallish cage (perfectly big enough for hamsters but meaning in comparison to Eric) then they were pretty harmless too he thought. Until that was one day when Eric had for the first time shown a softer side towards the furry little critters, stopping off in the study where they were housed to give them a little stroke as he was making his way upstairs.

Opening the hatch at the top of the cage, Eric proceeded to place his hand carefully through the gap and down towards them as they moved about the wood shavings. He started to stroke one of them gently and was enjoying his little moment with his two new acquaintances. 'Arrggghhh!' Eric hollered; one of the hamsters suddenly took a chomp into his index finger and the pain shot through his body in a flash, his brain-synapses having gone into automatic pilot mode and signalled to Eric's arm muscles to retreat immediately. In a split second, Eric reacted, pulling his hand away and unwittingly with Harry the hamster still attached to it with his gnashers.

As Eric's hand in question reached the end of its retreat arc and came to a sudden stop, the G-force experienced by the hamster must have been comparable to that of a jet fighter pilot going through a steep rapid climb and then suddenly applying the brakes. As such he was unable to hang on anymore and was jettisoned across the study and out through the open door into the hallway. The hamster's size and weight were such that it appeared to Eric as though it had unfurled a small invisible parachute whilst airborne, seemingly floating down to earth, touching down on the carpet with very little force. It was a big relief to Eric that it had landed safely and was uninjured during the incident (no hamsters were hurt during the making of this book). Eric quickly and carefully scooped the hamster up and placed it back in the cage and made a mental note; leave the hamsters well alone in the future.

No, the main culprits that caused Eric sleepless nights and a constant threat to his sanity were Harriet's three cats, two tortoise-shell female sisters and a black male runt. Despite setting up two cat scratching posts in the conservatory for them to use, it seemed that Jinx, the male, was having more fun lacerating Eric's new leather sofa than worrying about the posts. It really got on Eric's tits that these animals were destroying his house and there was little he could do about it.

Sadly, Jinx didn't last too long at the house; no, nothing to do with Eric but he was run over on the main road around 100-yards from the cul-de-sac. A neighbour had found him and had taken him to the vets but he was already dead ('Let me know if there is any change in his condition… he's dead' Top Secret!). Harriet was notably upset and so Eric, ever the considerate type, said he would collect Jinx from the vets and bring him home so he could be buried in the back garden. Eric took one of the cat-carriers with him and the vet placed Jinx, who was wrapped in a small blanket, inside. Eric then placed the carrier in the boot of his car and made the two-mile trip home.

It was only after arriving back and opening the boot that Eric realised he may have been driving a tad too hastily. As Harriet came out from the house and began walking up the drive towards the car, still teary-eyed and obviously upset, Eric was greeted by a rather unfortunate sight. It seemed that the cat-carrier had come apart during the journey, the blanket cocoon unravelled across the width of the boot and Jinx lay spread-eagled in full view of anyone who happened to be there. It was like something out of a situation comedy; Harriet on her way to the back of the car and Eric, shocked at his discovery having to quickly cover him up and try to put him back into the carrier before she did; his heart racing.

As their relationship continued, Eric had realised that Harriet was indeed the biggest cry baby he'd ever met in his entire life. She could cry at the drop of a pin and was a gold medallist drama queen, rushing off to Eric's mum and dad's anytime there had been an argument between them, which was usually linked to the animals or Harriet's inability to do anything in normal time. However, despite all her foibles, Eric was conscious that she'd made the efforts to move in with him, sacrificing her home (and making no money from its sale) and her previously cushy teaching job. Eric found himself in a position where he wasn't truly happy but felt he owed Harriet something and so the relationship continued in that vein.

Chapter Fifty-Eight

A 'Lucky' Escape

Life with Harriet was about to get a whole lot more complicated for Eric when something serious came to the fore and something that would change everything. Harriet fell pregnant. Eric remembered not really knowing how to feel about the news, the pregnancy not planned, although perhaps an air of natural progression within their relationship that hadn't really gone anywhere up to that point.

Any indecision regarding his relationship with Harriet had been put aside for now and the idea that his mum and dad would be overjoyed at the prospect of another grandchild (and one that lived within a mile and not over 3000-miles away across the pond). As Ernie was gay, his eldest brother having passed away and his other brother living over in the States, Eric was keenly aware that all hopes rested on him as far as further and more accessible grandchildren were concerned.

As expected, Eric's mum and dad were stoked at the news and his mum had even rushed out to buy a pram or more accurately a 3-in-1 travel system. Eric realised it was never a wise idea to get carried away and tempt fate over such matters due to the complex nature of embryonic development and sadly Harriet lost the baby at around the seven-week stage. Eric naturally felt empty at the news and was worried about Harriet, who was not the best at dealing with even trivial matters.

However, in a rather backward, some would say callous way, Eric was relieved that Harriet had lost the baby, having realised that he was still unsure about Harriet being the one he wanted to spend the rest of his life with. Although he would have ensured to make the best life for his child and with Harriet had the baby been born, the context had now changed and he no longer had to subscribe to the plan that had been previously mapped out for him. Instead, he now had the option of a rather big exit sign with letters six-feet high in flashing neon.

However, Eric wasn't a completely heartless bastard and it wasn't a case of him literally diving out of their relationship on hearing the sad news about the baby. There would be a period of convalescence for Harriet and that was after the rather grim reality that the foetal matter would need to be removed.

What Eric had expected to be a rather commonplace procedure, despite the complexities, turned out to be a nightmare for Harriet. Whether knowingly or not, the physician tasked with removing the foetus had taken away not just the foetal matter but with it far too much of Harriet's womb-lining, to which it had been attached. Unbeknown to everyone at that stage, Harriet's chances of getting pregnant were now extremely slim bordering on impossible.

Several weeks following the surgery, Harriet and Eric were told it was safe to restart trying for a baby and with Harriet keener than ever to get pregnant then her efforts appeared to have doubled. Eric felt obliged to partake, especially as the only other option was to tell her of his feelings and with his mum and dad in his thoughts too, the pram that his mum had bought still sat in his late brother's bedroom under a plastic dust cover.

Eric now found himself part of a weird adaptation of Russian roulette, where his life would be determined on the basis of Harriet falling pregnant following the discharge of his own love bullets. Weeks and months went by and yet nothing. It didn't seem logical, Harriet having fallen pregnant before without really trying.

As a standard procedure following the pregnancy loss (always thought miscarriage sounded far too vulgar) an appointment was made for Eric to have his semen tested in order that the medical staff could try to ascertain the potential reasons for what had happened. Despite the notable gravity of the subject, it had been almost impossible for Eric not to think of the scene from The Naked Gun 33 1/3 (6.5/10 IMDb), where Frank Drebin tasked with providing a sperm sample, emerges from a room carrying half-a-dozen full pots, his glasses hanging off his face, lipstick on and smoking a cigarette. Fortunately, Eric only had to provide one ejaculate's worth, which he was able to do in the confines of his own bathroom at home. After accomplishing the matter in hand (quite literally) Eric then peered through the transparent vial at his love juice, questioning whether a) it was a decent batch or b) whether he should try again.

Dropping his sample off at the hospital within minutes as per the instructions, Eric returned home and waited for the results. It was a strange feeling as there was no getting away from the fact that if he was told his swimmers weren't so much like Michael Phelps but fat holidaymakers floating around on inflatable doughnuts, then Eric would have to accept that he wasn't able to carry out one of the most basic functions that humans were built for; procreation.

What hadn't helped was seeing a girl he'd gone to school with sat in the waiting room of the fertility ward, the reason for Eric's presence an obvious one and not something he wanted to be made hearsay regardless of his test results. It was certainly no time for a convivial catch-up Eric thought, choosing to play the role of blissfully ignorant come rude.

A couple of days later and Eric's results were back. There was nothing wrong with his baby-making serum, which was of great relief to him. Eric was amazed, especially as his diet had been perhaps the worst known to man, his dislike for vegetables famous amongst his friends and family and fruit not high up on his list either.

The results meant that Harriet needed to undergo further tests, somewhat more obtrusive than Eric's part of the bargain. It was then that the gynaecologists noticed the problem stemming from the previous surgery Harriet had undergone. Ultimately, the hierarchy at the hospital put their hands up (probably better to have said raised there) and accepted that they had removed too much of Harriet's womb-lining and although not admitting blame as such, they offered Eric and Harriet free IVF treatment moving forwards. Despite being aware that they could potentially sue the hospital for damages to Harriet and preventing her/them from having a baby, Eric was not interested in the idea of pound signs as the chance of escape to a life back on Single Street was vastly more appealing.

All this had been going on for months if not years, with appointments for Harriet to see the gynaecologists and other related departments. Despite the seriousness of the matter, this all played out in tandem with Eric and Harriet's normal day-to-day work and home life. As mentioned, Harriet had found it a little tough teaching in a Comprehensive school and had therefore tendered her resignation after finding a new position for herself.

She hadn't entirely given up the teaching element though as realised she could still make some money by providing extra-curricular tutelage to those pupils she'd taught who either required or wanted additional help. A couple of evenings a week, they would come to the house, Harriet providing one-to-one tuition in the study and glad to be keeping her oar in.

Chapter Fifty-Nine

Love for Rent

Harriet's newfound happiness on a work front was short-lived as having only been in her new job for three months, she returned from her Christmas break to learn of some bad news. It seemed the company had grossly overestimated profit margins and in a bid to save on overheads, it was a case of her being the last in so first out. You could say it was not the best way to start off the New Year.

Harriet was now unemployed again and would not be bringing in any income until she could find alternative work. Having a logical brain, Eric came up with an idea, which he felt would help take the pressure off Harriet and her pursuit of finding employment. His plan would not only help to generate some additional income for them but was also achievable for very little effort.

The idea was to advertise a room for rent, very commonplace at the time following the 2008 recession causing austerity (still around today more than a decade later), existing homeowners feeling the squeeze and first-time buyers finding it almost impossible to get onto the property ladder.

The house was a decent size, designated as four bedrooms, although only two were used as such. It seemed the perfect solution and as Eric had taken in a lodger previously (Fat Nat) then it was also not one completely alien to him. Harriet agreed and the advert was up and running in no time as Eric's previous effort was still saved online, only requiring a few tweaks and more up-to-date photographs.

After a week or so and with little interest, Eric took a more proactive approach and began targeting potential lodgers instead of waiting for them to stumble over his ad. He began to email all those that seemed to fit the criteria, sending around half-a-dozen polite enquiries. A couple of days later, a girl called Megan responded. Eric had not even considered her previously as it was clear from her profile that she had a pet, and not any old pet but a degu. As Eric was not too enamoured with having to share his home with any of God's creatures (as you may have gleaned) already putting up with a mini Noah's Ark in the shape of two cats, two hamsters and a rabbit by this point, he was not overly keen to allow any more to enter the fray.

The animals had been the main cause of Eric and Harriet's arguments, Eric not a massive fan of watching the cats systematically destroy his home as mentioned; who would be? Conversely, Harriet had campaigned for them to have increased access to rooms in the house. However, a final verdict on the matter was reached by Eric after he caught the moggies dragging one of his leftover sausages from a pan on the cooker hob in the kitchen. Enough was enough.

To Eric, it had felt like the set of Born Free (7.2/10 IMDb) at times, especially when Jinx was alive, half expecting to see Rolf Harris walk into the kitchen one morning, whilst he ate his breakfast, complete with veterinary gown and stethoscope proclaiming that 'one of the little tykes wasn't feeling too clever today'. The cats were definitely high up on Eric's list of reasons why the relationship was on shaky ground and it was no coincidence that this started not long after Harriet had moved them in.

Back to the rental advert and after chatting further to Megan or Meg as she preferred to be called, Eric was pleasantly surprised to learn that degus were diurnal, which at least meant the rodent wouldn't be making a noise throughout the night. Backed up by the fact that it would be housed in its own cage, Eric came to the conclusion that it was worth giving her the option, especially as none of the other messages Eric had sent had resulted in a positive reply.

Eric let Harriet greet Meg at the door a couple of days later when she came round to meet both of them and to check out the room and shared living quarters. Eric was conscious that he didn't want to appear too enthusiastic given she was female and young enough to be his (much) younger sister. He was however very curious, having swapped a few friendly text messages yet never having seen a photograph of her. He heard her voice as she spoke to Harriet, sounding more mature than her twenty-three years and on opening the door to the study Eric clapped his eyes on her for the first time.

Her curly brown hair seemed to have a life of its own, strewn around her ashen face, her eyes wide and inviting but it was her smile that captivated

Eric the most. She spent what seemed like an effortless couple of hours chatting with both Eric and Harriet whilst slowly being shown around the house. Eric's first impressions were that Meg seemed a very pleasant and down-to-earth girl and he enjoyed her company from the start, trying purposefully not to maintain eye contact for too long, especially as Harriet was in tow. It was also clear that Meg had similar interests to him and this only made Eric more enthusiastic for her to move in.

Fortunately for Eric, Harriet also liked her and felt they had a lot in common too, Meg a vet and keen to talk about the menagerie already in situ at the house. It had also crossed Harriet's mind that Meg was the ideal person to look after the animals if she and Eric were ever away together, especially as one of the cats was diabetic and required insulin injections twice-a-day. Megan left the house and it all went very quiet, especially for Eric who wanted to see her again. However, he knew he shouldn't text her or force the issue regarding her decision. It was going to have to be her call.

Two weeks passed and Eric had accepted that Meg had seemingly found a more preferential home. So imagine his delight when she contacted him to ask for a second viewing, this time flanked by her dad. Despite having found a new job by this time, Harriet was still keen to have Meg move in if that's what she ultimately wanted. This was great news for Eric, who had become tired of his relationship with Harriet and had promised himself that he would do something about it later that year.

The penultimate straw for Eric, when he realised there was little chance of a continued relationship with Harriet, had come just prior to Christmas, when she attended her work's Christmas do at a hotel no more than five miles away. It was a Friday evening and as Eric was a night owl then he suggested Harriet left her house keys with him, especially as she was prone to forgetting things and misplacing them. The party was due to end around midnight and so there seemed no real problem at all with the plan or so Eric believed.

Midnight came and went and although Eric hadn't expected she'd be back on the dot, he did expect her to back before say 1:00 a.m. Having still not heard anything by 1:30 a.m., Eric texted her to make sure she was okay and asked how long she was likely to be, especially as she didn't have a key and he would have to let her in. No responses from Harriet were forthcoming. Eric wasn't so much concerned about Harriet now than thinking how inconsiderate she'd been not to contact him to let him know of her intended plan and ETA. Eric was pacing around by this time and not amused.

After the clock struck 3:00 a.m. and still no hide or hair of her, Eric tried phoning her mobile but there was no answer. 'What the dickens was she playing at?' he thought, although the dickens was more likely to have been a shorter word beginning with an 'f'.

It wasn't until another hour had past when Eric heard a commotion outside and looking out to see what it was, he saw Harriet flopping out of a taxi. She was absolutely paralytic; as drunk as Eric had seen anyone in his time and that included the perennially drunk homeless man asking for spare change in Hyde Park on his way to lectures at uni. Harriet was unable to stand up straight and Eric was angrier than he'd been in a long time and wasn't holding back from telling her what he thought of her actions. It was obvious she couldn't be trusted on her own and this was exhibit A. On asking her where she'd been till now, her response was enough to incense him even further.

Slurring her speech, Harriet confirmed that after the party had ended she'd been invited back to one of her male colleague's rooms, who was staying at the venue that evening. There were two fellas and her in the room (according to her) and witnessing Harriet's drunken state a few hours after, Eric knew she would have had no way of knowing what either or both of the fellas did to her once there. Eric was appalled that such an apparently educated woman had let herself get into such a state of inebriation and Eric lost any respect for her that he had left.

Despite trying to swear nothing had happened, whilst falling up the stairs, Eric now had major doubts. Harriet had also lost her iPhone, suggesting she must have left it in the taxi on her return home. She would never see it again, despite visiting the taxi headquarters the next day to ask if it had been handed in. Eric knew that Harriet would not have known what day of the week it was, let alone if she had her phone with her in the taxi; more evidence of how she couldn't be trusted to look after anything.

Chapter Sixty

The Last Straw

A couple of days after Meg's second-viewing and she got back to Eric to say she would be happy to move in and Eric was stoked at the news. Having someone like Meg in the house was great; she was a refreshing beacon of happiness, helping him to live in a more relaxed environment and enjoy interactions with her regarding their common interests.

However, things soon changed as not long after Meg had moved in, Harriet had come to the conclusion that she fancied Eric. It was not exactly the greatest start to Meg's tenure and Eric was left exasperated and frustrated, himself confirming that he wasn't interested in her. Harriet did not seem too worried about Eric having similar feelings towards Meg as she was 12-years younger and unlike her, Meg was clearly not too hung up on appearances, make-up and femininity in general.

Perhaps this was <u>why</u> Eric was interested as she was the complete opposite of what Harriet was about, which had caused Eric countless headaches and unhappiness for way too long. Fortunately for Eric, Harriet was not looking to boot her out of the house at that stage, despite her assumptions and instead gave Eric strict instructions not to sit with Meg and to keep his conversation to a minimum. It seemed like a pretty Nazi-esque way of going about things to Eric but as he preferred to have Meg living there, then whilst Harriet was about, he would follow her protocol.

It wasn't difficult to avoid Meg as the house had three lounges if you counted the large conservatory and Eric was happiest spending time in his man-cave on the second floor, in any case, his 120-inch screen supplied by his HD projector, which was linked to SKY, his Playstation and a stand-alone Blu-ray player. With a retro arcade-machine with 60-games also housed in the same room, then Eric was pretty much set. Things continued without any real cause for disharmony but unbeknown to Harriet, Eric and Meg's relationship was beginning to blossom, albeit very gradually.

You see, whilst Harriet was tutoring school pupils behind the door of the study, then this was an ideal opportunity for Meg to ascend the stairs to the top of the house and chill out with Eric, knowing she had around an hour before the lesson would finish, when she would then make herself scarce again. It was like an unwritten rule and it seemed to happen naturally, without Eric or Meg having spoken about it. Meg enjoyed gaming and so she would be content watching Eric play, whilst enjoying normal conversation with him. This three-way interaction under one roof continued for several months until that was when Eric finally received a reason to terminate his relationship with Harriet.

Given the three of them each had a car and given also the shape of the driveway, funnelling out from a single car-width at the garage to a two car-width drive at the end some 50-feet away, they would park in a way that meant that the first out in the morning was not blocked in. On this particular day, Eric had a rare day off and was parked around ten feet behind Harriet's car on the drive, Meg having already left for work as she had early starts at the veterinary clinic.

Eric remained in bed enjoying his lie in when Harriet, who was ready to leave for work and was (unsurprisingly) running late once again, bent down to kiss Eric and shot off down the stairs to the front door. Eric had considered shouting down to warn her of his car parked behind her, although only partially; more than enough room for her to make a slight adjustment and reverse past it as each of them had done from time-to-time.

Eric lay in bed looking up at the ceiling and heard Harriet's car engine switch on. Seconds later there was an almighty bang and without even having to look, he knew what had happened and could not believe how stupid Harriet could be. It was just another example of her scattiness, her complete disregard for things around her, too wrapped up in her own little world and what she needed to do.

Eric couldn't believe that not only was his pride and joy badly damaged in the front right quadrant but that his own girlfriend had done it on his own driveway and damaged the rear of her car as part of the process. In the whole scheme of things, this really was the most ridiculous thing someone could do and Eric was livid. It really wasn't the best start to Eric's day off and he made Harriet fully aware that their relationship was over. It had been the straw that broke the camel's back or more accurately the front of his car.

After a few more tumultuous weeks and some more arguing, Harriet agreed to move out. It hadn't been a pleasant time at all and Meg had been privy to their relationship finally unfolding, which Eric knew must have felt all kinds of awkward for her. Eric didn't want to hurt Harriet and was certainly not happy to see her upset, especially as it hadn't all been bad, just 80%. After Harriet had found herself somewhere to live, then she was gone, Eric even helping her (once his car had been fixed) with the process given that her two-seater sports car was as practical for carrying cargo as fishing nets were at retaining water.

Despite Harriet having a new job that she was enjoying, which had been the result of Eric suggesting she packed in the teaching, he couldn't help feeling bad about the way things had panned out. Here was a girl who had given up pretty much everything for him, been through the mill regarding her pregnancy and had been strong for Eric during the final weeks of his brother's life. Eric didn't want to think about it for too long; he had to see the reality behind his decision and ultimately he knew he'd made the right one.

After Harriet had left the building, Eric was left to reassess his situation, with Meg and him now the only ones living together. He was aghast and agog that she had put up with the last few weeks and not made her excuses and left but he was secretly pleased she hadn't. Eric liked her a lot and Meg had made it obvious by her staying power, that she too must have held feelings for Eric. This was borne out not long after; Eric having had a chat with her about the position they now found themselves in. 'I preferred you more than Harriet anyway' Meg exclaimed, leaving Eric feeling more than just a little pleased with her accolade.

Eric and Meg could now do what the hell they liked and instead of keeping their distance would now share lounges and occasionally watch films together. The pair were falling for one another in a big way, loving each other's humour and company. However, Eric was aware that she was still 12-years younger, he was her landlord and she had a boyfriend, despite him being a complete tool.

Eric was buoyed by the fact that Meg had been quite vocal in not wanting a future with her boyfriend due to him being a constant embarrassment to her. It made no sense to Eric why she was still with him and could only suggest she felt trapped or, like him, had been content to let things carry on for an easier life.

As the weeks went by, Eric decided to make the most of the emptier house and to try to create a healthier dynamic, away from a focus of just Meg and him. So Eric took in another lodger, a girl of similar age to Meg, purposely chosen as he felt that would give both girls someone to chat with and share common ground. In Eric's mind, he wanted to be with Meg but he wasn't about to jeopardise the whole set-up and risk losing her altogether. Not wishing to place all his eggs in one basket with Meg and to give him something to do, Eric decided to reacquaint himself with online dating.

Chapter Sixty-One

The Duck Pond Inn

Eric was on a roll; falling back into online dating after a four-year break and with a fresh batch of women to choose from meant he was like a dog with two dicks, making arrangements to meet up left, right and centre. However, after noticing that quite a few he was matching with were from the same area, then it dawned on him that he needed to find a convenient venue, somewhere relatively equidistant and somewhere with a bit of class and upmarket je ne sais quoi.

So it became that The Duck Pond Inn would be Eric's dating 'local'. It was 16-miles or around twenty minutes tops from door-to- bar and was literally two right turns heading out of town, another reason for its selection. Eric must have had 25-30 first dates at the 'Duck Pond' and it was definitely a big hit with the ladies, most of them having actually frequented the traditional country pub previously due to its aforementioned attributes.

The only thing Eric had to be wary of was letting it slip that he'd often go to that pub on dates and so felt the need to pretend to each of them that he wasn't au fait with the layout, 'I believe the toilets are upstairs' and walking around less confidently as though figuring out the place for the first time. Fortunately, as the place was rather big and catered mostly for dining guests, Eric never became too recognisable or familiar with the bar staff, which was handy as the last thing he wanted was for a barmaid to shout out 'same as usual Eric?' as his date was in earshot.

Eric definitely saw a rather rich and varied selection of women at The Duck Pond Inn, including a policewoman and doctor but neither of these lasted more than D1 and in the case of the policewoman, barely managing one drink. Eric wasn't too disheartened if meetups didn't go well this time around as he was more interested in Meg. He knew even if things went shockingly bad on a date, he would still continue to see her no matter what. He was also hoping that Meg would be a little jealous of him seeing other girls; perhaps enough for her to nail her colours to Eric's mast so to speak and make it more obvious that she wanted to be with him.

One of the intrinsic problems Eric found with viewing singles on Match.com was the unwillingness for a lot of felines to wink or at least make the first move and confirm an interest. Eric would fall into exactly the same pattern at times, especially if he was checking out girls who had already perused his profile. Despite being very interested, Eric was left feeling that it was perhaps futile for him to follow this up with an acknowledgement if she hadn't been buoyed to do likewise. Despite the rather well-documented equality bandwagon rolled out all over TV and social media, it seemed that some women still preferred the man to make the first move, which Eric couldn't help feeling smacked of simultaneous cake storage and cake consumption.

Realising that this scenario must have played out millions of times between other users then it seemed very plausible to Eric that there could be a plethora of missed opportunities out there; where both parties did indeed like the look of one another but were too scared to make the first move (a bit like a 'Gunfight at the O.K. Corral' – 7.2/10 IMDb).

There was one easy way to rectify this Eric felt and that was to make it compulsory for the viewer to decide one way or tother whether they were interested in someone's profile or not, similar to the daily-100 lists that Match provided. He knew that this would speed things up a lot and tasked with making a decision, any teeterers (as Eric labelled them) were more likely to opt for further interaction than to banish them to room 101 forever.

In fact, Eric believed that any profiles that the user wasn't taken by could be compartmentalised into a series of 'maybe' or 'no chance' piles and therefore not continually having their future search results clogged-up with the same unwanted faces or having to go through the laborious task of blacklisting them.

Chapter Sixty-Two

Wardrobe Malfunction

One of the most regrettable 'Duck Pond' dates Eric had been on during the time he lived with Meg was with a girl called Hannah. Regrettable due to the way the date had panned out and not that Eric hadn't enjoyed meeting her immensely. She was arguably the best-looking girl Eric had ever dated (still true to this day) even better-looking in person and I believe the term you would use was 'punching' (above his weight).

Hannah's level of attractiveness in the eyes of Eric was off the chart and that made him even more nervous in his attempts to impress her. In fact, if Eric had been given some blank paper and some Crayolas and asked to draw his ideal woman, then it would have turned out just like her; well more likely an identikit of some creature from the X-Files as Eric was rubbish at drawing but you get the idea.

Having greeted one another and bought the drinks (Eric having arrived early again to ensure he could have at least one cheeky pint) Eric and Hannah started to converse. Eric had perched himself in his usual position, ensuring that Hannah had to sit next to him, making it a lot more cosy and relaxed. However, the seating position would unwittingly prove to be a problem for Hannah as the date progressed.

Hannah was around five-years younger than Eric; medium height for a girl, around 5'6" not too short to cause Eric a crick in his neck when bending to kiss her and not too tall that he'd need to wear his platforms if she decided to don her killer heels. Her body shape was heavenly, not rakish thin suggesting she had an eating disorder or in need of a square meal but not bonny by any means. She was aesthetically perfect to Eric and her prize assets were like a gift from God, Eric adding to the creamy froth on his pint with deposits of his own saliva as he sat next to her (think Homer Simpson having found a jelly sweet down the back of his sofa).

Hannah's backstory was a very sad tale; she was a widow before her thirtieth birthday, her husband having died from a sudden heart defect and even more desperate was the fact that Hannah was pregnant and expecting their first child at the time. On hearing this, Eric felt slightly deflated. How could he laugh and joke with her now after hearing such terrible news? Her daughter was now three-years-old and Hannah had come to realise that life went on and it was time for her to live it and get out and meet someone new.

After only a few minutes into the date, however, it was soon apparent that Hannah seemed a little distracted and Eric realised that he was doing the majority of the talking. He'd noticed that Hannah appeared to have had a wardrobe malfunction, although he didn't think it too much of a biggie. A brooch that was holding the two sides of her top together at the neck had come away and it was gaping and flopping downwards, revealing Hannah's heaving bosoms in glorious Stereoscopic Panavision. Hannah tried intermittently to correct it but was having little or no luck.

Given their close proximity and Eric's height advantage, it was a slightly awkward situation; Eric not wishing to appear like he was staring at her bazookas (when all he wanted to do was stare at them) with Hannah (as he learnt later) mortified that she may have been giving Eric the wrong impression. The result left Eric feeling majorly disappointed as, despite the clothing mishap, Hannah had shown little interest in Eric; not listening intently to his conversation and appearing quite rude.

Believing Hannah would have preferred sticking a cactus in her knickers than to spend a second longer with him, Eric broke off the gathering; Eric had been on enough dates to know when it was going well and when it felt like he was just grinding metal so to speak. It was with a heavy heart he had to concede that this was an example of the latter, with Hannah seemingly underwhelmed and contributing little to proceedings, not even managing much in the way of eye-contact.

Once Eric realised a date had gone Pete Tong, then he would finish his drink, make his excuses and leave; he wasn't into wasting either his time or theirs, although predominantly his. He would exit the pub and have a smoke, something that he hid well from all his dates over the years. However, once aware that the girl wasn't interested or he wasn't interested in them, then any worries about making a good impression flew out of the window and it didn't matter if she found out he had genital herpes (not that he ever had).

Something strange happened with Hannah though as having followed him out towards the car park and noticing him smoking in the outdoor area, she walked over to him and pulled up a pew. Eric was now completely relaxed and no longer worried about being on 'best behaviour' as had made his mind up about her. However, they conversed more candidly now and at greater length than they had inside, despite the chilly conditions.

Eric learnt from Hannah that her late ex's family were very well-to-do and it was all polo matches, jolly hockey-sticks and in which of the fields to erect the marquee. 'More tea vicar?' Eric, although joking that her best friend must be called Taffeta (which Hannah found hilarious) made it apparent that pink champagne, caviar and hanging out with upper-crust types was just not his thing. He had already worked out that she would find it difficult to escape her current lifestyle as she was bound to them through her daughter and they would continue to look out for her and treat her as part of the family.

Despite her trying to convince Eric that she was a down to earth girl who'd been dragged into that lifestyle through her late husband, Hannah's frank outpouring did little to change his opinion; in fact, he now felt more content that he'd made the right decision and that the two were even less of a match than he first thought. At that stage, he decided it was time to leave and they walked to the car park together. As a true gentleman, Eric always asked the girl to let him know when they'd arrived home, even if the date had gone tits-up and there was more chance of Linford Christie making another comeback than of seeing each other again.

After arriving home, Eric sent her a text to say thank you and to wish her all the best in the future. However, Hannah's response was not what Eric had expected to read at all. In contrast, she had replied 'That sounds quite final' and 'I really liked you and thought you might like to meet up again'.

Eric was confused, especially as he'd not picked up on any real interest from her whilst in his company. It appeared that this was one of the only occasions out of a flotilla of dates he'd been on, where he had completely misread the signals and body language; although of course, the wardrobe malfunction hadn't helped.

Hannah explained that she was mortified when the brooch incident took place, which had put paid to her enjoyment of the evening until they moved outside. Despite Hannah's admission and Eric knowing that he had the opportunity to set up a rematch with her, Eric could not get his head around her situation, having her ex's family on the scene, having to potentially live-up to him in their eyes and of course a small child in the mix.

Eric made a very difficult decision that night as despite being highly attracted to Hannah, he knew he had to put his head in front of his cock for one of the only times in his adult life. They never saw each other again.

Chapter Sixty-Three

Real Life Soap Opera

The best result Eric had with his 'Duck Pond' dates was with a girl called Leanne. What I mean from 'best result' was that Eric got to frequently bone her and as they complemented one another's sense of humour well, then they saw each other for a couple of months (not quite long enough for Eric to divulge his elephantitus of the right leg). Leanne was from Warrington (another one) and as it would turn out, lived less than a mile if you were a bird and chose to take the shortest route from a future girl's house that Eric would end up living with temporarily.

Considering she was from the jewel in the crown of the North West, then it was surprising looking back at it why she agreed to meet at The Duck Pond, despite it being a fair old trek out of her way. However, Eric was now just wanting to make his meet-ups as convenient as possible and knowing the pub's ins and outs and finding it a doddle to get to, then he was keen to continue his association whenever possible.

Leanne wasn't the kind of woman Eric would go for in an ideal world but as his recent dates had proved as successful as the Sinclair C5 (If you've never heard of it then look it up and have a laugh… the thing couldn't even get over speed bumps) then he was becoming a little more desperate you could say. The bottom line was that he hadn't seen a grown woman naked for at least three months and was keen to end that run as soon as possible.

What Eric didn't like about Leanne was her obvious delusions of grandeur, harbouring an inflated opinion of herself and she was also guilty of wearing far too much make-up. Still, the pair were attracted to one another and therefore Eric was happy to see how things developed.

She was approximately five-years older than Eric, quite a tall girl, about 5'8", slim with candyfloss shoulder-length hair which was closer to white than blonde. From what he could make out, Leanne was also blessed with a half-decent set of threpennies; definitely a handful he thought. She was extremely tactile too (like Eric) and the two flirted with one another outrageously for the majority of D1.

Given how well their first meet had gone, they were both champing at their bits to see each other again and as she was a rather confident type, Leanne was non-plussed making the trip to see Eric at his home. Eric preferred girls coming to him after it was known that the two had chemistry as there was certainly a lot more to do entertainment-wise, his relatively new cinema room affording him with the ultimate venue for showing a girl a good time. Eric was also keenly aware that Meg would see him with a new woman, which again he hoped would persuade her into making her feelings known.

Having chatted for a bit in the conservatory and lubricated themselves with some alcoholic refreshments, Leanne suggested watching a film and so the pair ascended to the bat-cave on the second floor. Having chosen a relatively new film called Flight starring Denzel Washington (7.3/10 IMDb) the two sex-starved tigers lay down together on one of the black leather sofas, the lights extinguished and the projector whirred into life.

Having already mentioned how Eric had barely seen past the opening credits of films when 'entertaining', then here was yet another example. With sex pheromones in abundance and the pair continuing their tactility with one another, Denzel and co would only provide the backdrop to Eric's first experience of Leanne; which also acted to keep the wolf from the door, with Meg pottering around in the bowels of the house below.

Despite her age, Eric could see that Leanne looked after herself, her body in cracking shape and he was extremely impressed with what he could both see and feel. Things had progressed pretty quickly in the disrobing stakes as after releasing her puppies and getting his money's worth from them first, he then managed to remove both her jeans and knickers in the same move (to Leanne's pleasant surprise). He enjoyed Leanne's body enormously and given her reactions, then it was clear that she had also appreciated Eric's too. The pair were now even more enthused with one another.

As Eric had weeks of holiday entitlement still to take at work (given he rarely holidayed on his own and had been reluctant to plan any with Harriet) he therefore had plenty of time to spend with Leanne and would make the half-an-hour commute quite regularly. She lived in a modern apartment block on the banks of a canal and her pad was both pristine and spacious, which was a big thumbs-up from Eric. With no kids or furry pests, then Eric was now having to carefully reconsider his initial opinion of Leanne as things were working out very nicely indeed.

However, as things were seemingly going from strength-to-strength, Eric came across a fly in the ointment (yes, again). He was the type of person that once harbouring a doubt, he would let it overshadow everything else; more often than not allowing it to kill any chance of an extended relationship. Leanne was yet another example. Whether still not wanting to commit to another girl quite so soon after being single, his deep-rooted feelings for Meg or simply him just being realistic and not wanting to waste his time; Eric found out a couple of things that had made him reassess.

The first issue was that Leanne had apparently been seeing a Coronation Street 'star' before him ('you don't care about Tracey, do you Ken, do you Ken?… Noooo' said in my finest Mancunian accent). Leanne would mention it like a badge of honour as though she had been shagging Brad Pitt (or indeed Tom Hardy). Eric wasn't a big fan of the long-running soap opera, having spent a few years at pains to watch it with his exes for the sake of harmony but as far as he could remember there weren't any male characters (apart from perhaps Les Battersby and of course Ken Barlow) that would be much to write home about in any case.

It seemed this actor was already in a relationship (get me the chief editor of the Daily Mirror on the line for this scoop) and was infatuated with Leanne, sending her flowers and desperately wanting to see her. Having been happy to see him and sleep with him, then automatically this raised internal trust alarms within Eric's cranial recesses. Yes, you could argue that this was double-standards, what with his previous record but then this was Eric needing to have full and unequivocal trust in a woman if he was going to permit himself to drop his guard completely and 'commit'.

The other and more annoying issue Eric had with Leanne was her continual mentioning of a guy that she worked with. She just wouldn't shut up about him. All stories led back to him and his name was never far from her lips. Eric was just a little bit confused, to say the least. At first, he'd assumed she was trying the old 'keep them keen' technique by trying to make Eric feel jealous of her apparent great rapport with her work colleague. However, after several dates and having stayed over with her on a few occasions, it was becoming a little tiresome.

Eric had heard enough; it wasn't like she was mentioning any girlfriends during the same timeframe and therefore Eric could only hypothesise that she did indeed have slightly more than platonic feelings for him. One morning, as Eric remained in Leanne's bed and with her setting off for work, Eric was again tasked with letting himself out (Eric the latchkey date).

He was already thinking long and hard about seeing Leanne again, despite them getting along pretty well. Leanne stooped to give Eric a kiss as she made haste to leave and it was her final words to Eric before leaving that would prove her downfall. 'I better hurry; I promised I'd pick up McDonald's breakfast for…' You guessed it; it was him again.

Slipping out of bed no sooner had the sound of the front door closing disappeared, Eric was up and dressed. He carried out a complete recce of the flat and ensured he had everything of his packed in his overnight bag before he left; he didn't want the ignominy of having to return to pick up something he'd forgotten; but before he left, he had a couple of other things to attend to. Firstly, he carried out a complete tidy and clean-up overhaul, ensuring not to leave Leanne having to do a thing when she returned from work and it was like he'd never been there.

Finally, Eric took a piece of paper from a notepad Leanne had lying around and devised his John Deere letter, mentioning why he had taken the decision to walk away, even mentioning that she might want to start seeing the fella she seemed so hooked on.

Despite leaving various distraught telephone messages on his answerphone, Eric didn't deviate from his chosen path and it was back to Single Street for him, safe in the knowledge that Meg was still in his life and that there was always a chance with her perhaps.

Chapter Sixty-Four

Never in Doubt

With the other girl lodger having moved in by this stage, then Meg now had a choice to make. Would she gravitate towards her and make a new friend or still prefer spending time with Eric? It was pleasing for Eric to see Meg choose him and it wasn't long before he had chucked the other girl out on the grounds of being a kleptomaniac, things disappearing and later being found in her room.

In fact, it never crossed his mind that she may have been behind the theft of Eric's pride and joy the following year, the person having entered the house having a key to the conservatory door as there was no sign of a break-in and Eric never went to bed without checking everything was locked (he had mid-level OCD lest we forget).

At the time, Eric hadn't even considered her and was thinking it had to be the cowboy who fixed the lock on the conservatory less than four weeks prior. Either way, the car had been stolen. Eric remembered receiving a speeding ticket in the post around a week later, a further reminder of the hoons that had taken his car and of their obvious haste and recklessness after driving it away.

Well, that's what Eric's brain had found it reasonable to assume on opening the letter, although soon having to retract his angry tirade directed at the burglars on checking the date of the alleged offence. It had in fact been Eric travelling 50mph in a 40-zone two days prior to the theft taking place (Eric sends his apologies to the thieves that stole his car).

This was a big kick in the bollocks to Eric, compounding his misfortune with even more; done for speeding in a car that he didn't even have anymore and having never received a speeding ticket before or since that day. Again, Eric felt that these things could only happen to him.

Eric and Meg were getting on like a veritable fireworks factory on fire; Eric's attempt at teaching her how to juggle having ended in rather an awkward situation; Meg bending over and accidentally brushing his cock with her arse as she went to pick-up the multi-coloured balls that ended up strewn across the kitchen floor. There was also a toy-scrap that had ensued in the lounge when Eric had stood over her in a kind of jovial fashion when she happened to be knelt on the floor in front of him.

Things were definitely reaching eruption point and it was fair to say Eric's own juggling-balls were now akin to two dirigibles parked up for the night. Eric would traverse the steps up to his bedroom on the second floor every night and pass Meg's en route, each time majorly tempted to knock her up so to speak. His knuckles would be positioned centimetres from her door on occasions but he always managed to resist the temptation, instead the pair ending up texting each other for hours from their beds despite lying only eight-feet from each other through the floor/ceiling.

Then finally, it happened. It had just been a matter of time and their feelings for one another had been obvious from the minute she stepped over the hearth when checking out the house-share.

Eric was watching a Champions League match on his big-screen and Meg had come up and lain on the sofa adjacent to him, across the plane-aisle type arrangement. She was not interested in football whatsoever and so Eric knew she just wanted to chill out with him. The truth was he hadn't really been able to concentrate on the final knockings of the game, distracted by Meg's presence but doing his level best not to show it.

Not long after the match had finished and the highlights being discussed in the studio, Eric did something that, on reflection, he wished he'd never done. He reached out his right arm with his hand open towards Meg. She was very (pleasantly) surprised at the sight of Eric's offer; accepting it and allowing him to spool her towards him; ending up knelt in front of Eric on the leather footstools where he lay. Meg was definitely interested in Eric but with this sudden development came a great deal of awkwardness and nervousness for her and Eric could tell that this was the case.

He was a great deal more experienced than she and so having taken the lead, cajoled Meg into coming closer to him. Their lips got nearer and nearer to each other's and then finally they kissed. Eric had literally wanted to do that for months but had shown great resolve and a gargantuan helping of self-control up to that point to resist the temptation. However, it was <u>always</u> going to happen and it had been very much <u>when</u> and not if.

Chapter Sixty-Five

A Schoolboy Error in the Bedroom

The next morning and Eric bumped into Meg in the kitchen (not literally, it was a decent-sized kitchen) who was having her breakfast. There was a definite awkwardness in the air and although they'd only had a few kisses, it was still a massive change in their co-habiting circumstances. Eric was quick to break the ice. 'I really like you Meg and am glad what happened last night; I'd really like to get to know you better. However, I'm conscious that I'm a lot older than you and there may be others you'd prefer to see'.

With that the two went off to work, giving each of them time alone to think over the events of the previous evening. It wasn't long though until Meg confirmed she wanted to 'see him' and the two were officially a couple.

The problem Meg had faced was to come to terms with Eric actually liking her, having noticed a big difference in her own looks and type compared to Harriet and the girls Eric had dated after she'd flown the nest. However, it was because Meg was like she was that had led to Eric falling for her in the first place.

After Eric and Meg had finally got together after months of having to suppress their feelings for each other under the same roof, it was natural that they were keen to sleep with one another. However, given the length of time they'd known one another and living together as they had, Eric found making the next step with Meg the most difficult he'd ever experienced with any girl. Yes, he fancied her loads and yes, he'd thought about the moment for a long time but now faced with the reality of it being within actual touching distance, then he seemed more nervous, somewhat more desperate for it to work out.

As a consequence, Eric found himself putting it off or worse, when getting down to it, his thoughts would betray him ('Your thoughts betray you father; I feel the good in you' Return of the Jedi – 8.3/10 IMDb). Not able to relax properly, he was finding it hard to get hard. After this had happened a few more times, then it simply ramped up the pressure for the next attempt and Eric became trapped in a frustrating cycle of flaccidity. It had taken months to get to this point and he didn't want to waste all the effort and risk the relationship before it had even got off the ground through not being able to perform. He had never had this trouble before.

Then, one day, after both he and Meg were home together, things developed and they were once again in Meg's bedroom. Eric thought to himself 'It's now or never'. As Eric was conscious that he was struggling to provide 'proper' sex with Meg, he had instead been keen to pleasure her in other ways, knowing that he was a dab hand at it and had previously made her feel h'amazing. There was also the fact that if he gave her an orgasm by other methods, then there was less pressure on him to make her come via more traditional means; with his sword of dobber.

Placing his head between her legs, whilst simultaneously agitating her nipples with his fingertips, he began his choreographed tongue-routine once again. However, unwittingly, Eric had committed a rather rudimentary, somewhat schoolboy-error this time, which proved to be one of the most embarrassing situations he'd had with a girl in the bedroom.

As Eric smoked, he was conscious of his breath not smelling too great and although not affected by the scent himself, wanted to make kissing him a great deal more inviting for Meg. He'd therefore taken to chewing gum to help freshen it up. I know what you're thinking. Yes, when going down on Meg, he'd forgotten to get rid of the gum ('Unbelievable Jeff' Chris Kamara on Sky Sports Soccer Saturday).

Coming up for air after a couple of minutes, Eric was mortified to see that he hadn't been able to retain the chewing gum in a small ball pressed to the inside of his cheek; the sticky mess now clear to see in front of him, thin strands woven across Meg's sacred-V like an amateurish spider's web. It was just a little bit awkward to say the least.

At the same time; Meg was lying back enjoying the experience, oblivious to what was happening a couple of feet away to her undercarriage; Eric now beavering away trying to surreptitiously remove it, whilst also continuing his award-winning performance. As is usually the case with trying to remove chewing gum from any surface though, Eric was ending up with more and more strands of it thinning out, now stuck to his fingers as well.

Finally, Meg realised that something untoward was taking place and Eric had to come clean, his embarrassment clear to see, although trying to make light of the situation. Fortunately, they were able to remove the gum between them and Meg had seen the funny side, which of course came as a great relief to Eric.

Just as well they'd managed to clear it up, Eric thought afterwards, as the only effective way <u>he</u> knew to remove gum from something was to place it in the freezer and wait for it to harden. Perhaps on this occasion, that method would have been just a little tricky to carry out. 'Can you just put your fanny in the freezer for ten minutes please Meg?'

In an ironic aside to proceedings, chewing-gum-gate had relaxed Eric enough to remove all previous nerves regarding sex and the pair enjoyed the full gamut of options… no, not that, I told you Eric never dropped anchor in poo-bay.

Chapter Sixty-Six

Friends Will be Friends

As is usually the norm after getting together with a new partner, both Meg and Eric would get to know one another's friends. However, in this particular case, it was slightly different, in that they had both already met each other's friends by virtue of sharing living-quarters for almost seven months.

Eric's friends weren't shocked at learning of his new relationship as he'd been pretty vocal as far as wishing to be with her and Meg also conceded that her friends had been able to guess who her new love-interest was also.

Whether it was the difference in age or purely young girls being jealous or unhappy at their friend being caught up with someone else and not them, the difference in behaviour from both sets of friends was telling. Eric's work colleagues would ask questions about Meg and ask when they were going to meet her, whereas, conversely, Meg's would try to organise things without giving any regard to her new boyfriend.

Eric just had to accept that this is how it was but he was a little put out by the imbalance. Meg was notably caught in the middle and unable to control how her friends acted. Looking back at it, Eric confessed that he should not have let the situation bother him quite as much as it had.

Chapter Sixty-Seven

'Fawlty Towers'

Eric and Meg had great fun spending time with one another and seemingly making up for lost ground. This culminated in their engagement during a whistle-stop tour of France on a nine-day driving-holiday in which they circumnavigated approximately two-thirds of the beautiful country (C'est Magnifique!).

However, their engagement had served to cause unease with Meg's parents, especially dad, who was now very vocal in wishing his daughter to return to help him with the family business, concerned that she may instead be tempted to now settle with her new man some 200-miles away.

Eric's feelings for Meg were such that he was willing to give up everything and move; noting the importance of her family in her life. With Eric's forced redundancy at the bank some six-months later (yes, the same bank he'd met Emma mark I at over a decade before and which Becky Blackbeard had also joined the fray) the pair devised a plan to move next-door to Meg's parents and to set up a B&B, which Eric would then manage singlehandedly, whilst she worked for her mum and dad and helped them with the family business.

It was a massive leap of faith; Eric placing his house on the market for sale, packing all his worldly possessions into a bindle (in the shape of a large Pickfords' lorry) and moving with Meg to begin a new life together.

After a couple of months following the move and having set-up the B&B, the doors opened to the public and Eric began his new career as Basil Fawlty. The bed and breakfast was in an antiquated Victorian farmhouse nestled on its own in the 'arse-end of nowhere' (as I believe he called it… or an idyllic and secluded country location as he felt best to describe it on his corresponding website and various booking channels). However, that episode of Eric's life and the veritable soap-operatic crossovers and storylines is perhaps a story for another day.

The bottom line was that their new life did not afford them the work-life balance that they'd hoped for, Eric felt bored and isolated and the two slowly drifted apart. The split turned pretty unsavoury in the end, Eric having stupidly trusted Meg and her family; having signed a joint tenancy agreement for the farmhouse, not realising that the contract stipulated he would not have the option of selling his business at any point in the future. When the relationship crashed onto the rocks, the hospitality venture, despite having been a surprising success, had not been running long enough to repay the credit that had funded his outgoings during the setting-up process, let alone provide him with a pot of money on which to rely.

After inviting two independent business agents to the premises, both suggested Eric could realistically look to make a 400-500% profit on the monies he had invested, which was based on the lease still having some 14-years left to run and the goodwill of the business (picking up a very creditable average feedback rating on Booking.com of 9.3/10 from over 150 reviews).

Although having invested nothing financially, Meg would not accept a very generous offer of 25% of the net profit from any subsequent sale to sever the joint tenancy, giving Eric no other option than to leave everything behind following his final six-months of facilitating the prearranged bookings and return home.

Chapter Sixty-Eight

Homeward Bound

Having had no other choice but to leave the majority of furniture and belongings he had accumulated throughout his lifetime, Eric arrived back to his old roots. He could not afford to have everything shipped back and besides, there was nowhere he could store any of the items without incurring further costs.

Moving in with his parents (for the 83rd time) and having sold his car to make ends meet, he now sought work, trying to reintegrate into the system for the first time since leaving university, which was proving to be more difficult than he'd anticipated. He really needed a break, someone to give him an opportunity to showcase what he could achieve and to enable him to start the climb back out of the doldrums and make the most out of life again.

It was obvious to Eric that despite his experience, intellect and key attributes, his search for employment could not have come at a worse time; inclusion and diversity high on the agenda (as previously mentioned) whoever it was calling the shots. He knew he would not tick many boxes for potential employers; many of whom were keenly aware of the pressures to address the perceived demographic imbalance within company workforces. Policies had specifically been brought in to fast-track short-term quota fixes and Eric saw at firsthand the results of such initiatives with the company he finally received an opportunity with.

One of the drawbacks to Eric's situation, having pretty much lost everything he had ever owned and through no real fault of his own was his rather desperate position regarding the opposite sex. Who would want to go out with him now? He was a stone's throw from his 40th birthday, had little money to his name (and still owed money), lived with his parents and was unemployed. Eric had to agree that it was not how he'd planned it in the whole scheme of things and he was now probably the worst catch there was.

One thing (or person more accurately) that had crossed his mind at this juncture of his life was Harriet. Eric recalled how things had turned out for her and the comparisons with her situation were remarkable. Perhaps this was Eric's comeuppance, karma or the result of some sort of voodoo ritual that she'd carried out to avenge her similar fall from grace.

In fact, it was probably the case that Harriet had been left in a much better position than Eric, at least having a job and having retained a little more independence, moving in with a landlord and not back to her parents like him. Eric had never set out to hurt Harriet or cause her any harm but it was starting to seem that this had done little in persuading the higher beings to go easy on him.

Chapter Sixty-Nine

Down and Out (and Not in Beverly Hills)

Despite his predicament, Eric did return to the online dating sites; of course he did; it was his bread and butter and something to keep him sane whilst searching for work and having little money to entertain himself. In fact, Eric had started putting down some groundwork on the site after finding himself on his own at the B&B, with little else to do away from the necessary daily tasks. However, Eric had been sure to list his location back where his mum and dad lived as knew that would be where he'd pick up the baton once again after returning.

Eric may have had little going for him at that juncture but it wasn't quite time to remove his penis and store it in a pickle jar in his bathroom cabinet (like Jeff Goldblum in The Fly – 7.5/10 IMDb). Besides, meeting girls at a neutral venue or at their house would mean that they'd never really know about his predicament. A larger benefit of the online dating for Eric at that stage wasn't the meeting up but the communication and conversations with various females or the chatting-up phase of the process.

At one point, Eric noted he had over 180 conversations with girls from dating sites saved to his WhatsApp archive and there were countless more he'd previously deleted. These contacts were also great options for Eric to revisit and ascertain if any of the 'teeterers' could be persuaded or had changed their mind in the intervening period. Everyone liked a pleasant surprise and sometimes just receiving a message from him was enough for them to throw caution to the wind, especially if they'd had a bad time of it along their own dating journeys.

Eric was used to seeing the same runners and riders on the dating site that met his search criteria but would also trawl through the historic winkers to ensure he hadn't missed any diamonds amongst the horse-apples; the only drawback not knowing (immediately) which of them had been active recently and which had long-gone and just forgotten or not been arsed to remove their profile.

Then; one day; Eric spotted a new addition, a red-haired (yes another redhead) example with what appeared to be heavenly assets. Eric was already licking his lips. She was single, no kids and around five-years younger than him and appeared to have both high-intelligence and an original sense of humour (there was also no mention of 'work hard play hard' to be seen anywhere in her write-up either). The only negative (at that point) that he could see was the fact that she had a dog. However, as everything else was bob-on, Eric felt the need to investigate further.

Having sent her his usual opening gambit of 'Wowsers! You look hotter than a McDonald's apple pie' Eric jokingly mentioned travelling to see her for a drink that very evening. However, it appeared Vicky (as she was called) took his words quite literally and was very keen for that to happen. Eric was a little surprised to receive her enthusiastic response but as he wasn't <u>really</u> in the mood for a rendezvous that soon, he told her he'd love to but his car was in the garage being mended. It wasn't but it sounded like a viable excuse to Eric.

The pair began to trade further messages and it wasn't long before they'd taken it to the next level and swapped cellphone numbers (as Eric liked to refer to it) continuing their conflab on WhatsApp. Her messages were both refreshing and crude; the perfect combination as far as Eric was concerned. The only sticking point was how confident Vicky sounded and despite Eric's own veritable shagging experiences by now, then it almost always caused him to panic.

As both were enthusiastic to meet up, Vicky suggested a night later in the week and so D1 had been agreed. Vicky lived in Warrington (The centre of Eric's dating universe it seemed) although in one of the so-called nicer areas. Eric couldn't believe there was such a thing as a nice area of Warrington but kept that to himself for obvious reasons.

Cometh the evening and Eric was prepped; he'd made himself look presentable, knocked one out and sprayed Lynx Africa on all the key areas. He was ready to rock 'n' roll. However, just before he was about to leave his mum and dad's, he received a message from Vicky; she had to work late and wasn't going to be able to make their rendezvous after all.

Eric was slightly disappointed, especially given the late notice but these things happened from time-to-time or so he thought. Vicky instead suggested meeting at the weekend, selling it to Eric as a better option as they would get to spend more time together if all went according to plan. Vicky had a family wedding to attend on the Saturday but was confident that she'd be back in good time for an afternoon hook-up the following day.

Saturday evening came along and Eric sent Vicky a reminder and asked if she was still on for their date, conscious she may not be the most reliable person after cancelling their original appointment. She replied to say yes and that she would contact him the next day, although not specifying the likely time to lock horns.

Around 1:00 p.m. on Sunday afternoon and Eric had heard nothing from Vicky. He didn't know whether to stick or twist, meaning to make alternative arrangements so as not to completely waste his Sabbath. Frustratingly, all Eric could do was to await her next contact.

Vicky eventually messaged him around 6:00 p.m. and Eric was just a smidge pissed-off by then. Having been messed around again, there was no way he was going to give her the time of day ('to fuck me about once can be forgiven but to fuck me about again the very next time is taking the absolute piss you stupid cow' as I believe Oscar Wilde famously said).

Eric did respond to Vicky but only to confirm that he would be 'giving the other girls out there a chance instead'. Although realising himself how big-headed that sounded; Vicky was still upset at reading it, phoning Eric and leaving a very teary message on his answerphone. It seemed that she had been uber-keen to meet-up and began making excuses as to why she hadn't been able to contact him sooner. Eric wasn't interested in her excuses whatsoever.

Eric despised anyone messing him about and so his attention turned to other options. However, that wouldn't be the last time Eric would hear from her. Would it be third time lucky?

Chapter Seventy

Automatic Renewal

After filing Vicky under 'bin' Eric went back to the drawing board. Things were looking bleak though as it seemed that he had exhausted all the 'decent' options within his search criteria and was now left with only 'The Undateables' or those who had ignored his advances previously. Eric very rarely continued to chase after a girl on the site as he didn't want to appear like a desperado.

Conscious that his current subscription was coming to an end and having no job and a dwindling pot of money, he questioned whether he should continue with it. Yes, he was aware that he'd definitely had his money's worth from the £20 per-month in the past but now he was just bored of the same old faces. As luck would have it though, he received a message from a new face, which belonged to a girl called Donna.

Donna seemed like a ladette type from her profile pics but was an attractive girl with it and appeared to have a very similar sense of humour to Eric judging by her bio. He'd noticed her previously on the site but had been put off due to her contravening points 7 and 16 of his list of do's and mostly don'ts; namely the majority of her photos showing her socialising with predominantly fellas and describing herself as a 'free spirit'. This rang major alarm bells in his head and was the reason he'd avoided her like a box jellyfish when first coming across her.

Now Match.con had a rather underhand way of trying to retain subscribers, which would come into play when they had cancelled their current subscription and the automatic renewal date was drawing nearer. 'Automatic renewal' were two words that Eric detested with a passion, also used for things like his car insurance, where despite having had another year of no-claims and having shown loyalty to the insurance company, they would send him confirmation of their intention to automatically renew his cover and charge him a disproportionately higher tariff for the pleasure. Eric couldn't believe that insurance companies continued with such a practice and could only surmise that there must be a lot of people out there who didn't kick up a fuss and the insurance company could therefore continue to reap their premium increases unopposed.

The tactics that Match.con employed annoyed the shit out of Eric on many levels but mainly due to vastly insulting his (and most people's) intelligence and knowing that someone somewhere in their think-tank was having his or her back-slapped for coming up with such cowboy customer retention antics.

Below are actual methods that Match.con used and which Eric experienced during his online dating (this may have changed since but were in force at that time):

1. Unable to cancel subscriptions via the mobile phone app – Match.con confirmed that in order to cancel your subscription then the customer needed to do so via the website. As most people used their mobile, they were obviously aware that this would prevent or at least hinder subscribers in trying to cancel and thereby retaining a greater number of subscribers via automatic renewal.
2. When Eric tried to select 'Cancel subscription' then he received a message to say he could only cancel within 24 hours of the end date. Unable to cancel before then meant customers were likely to forget about this stipulation and in many cases, they would realise too late and after Match.con had already 'automatically renewed'.
3. They would use a mixture of unclear questions to try to retain you once managing to negotiate through the small print of the cancellation process. The questions were targeted at misleading you on purpose, of course, making clicking the correct button that little more difficult to interpret.
4. They would ask why you were cancelling in order to potentially target you with offers to stay. Like what's it got to fucking do with you?
5. Tempt you to stay with better value offers such as buy one month and get another free or on some occasions offering as much as 60% off a 6-month pass. Like a lot of things, this only annoyed Eric to think that he had been paying over the odds in the first place.
6. With around a week left on his subscription, Eric would see an

enormous increase in traffic from girls viewing, winking, favouriting or sending him messages. The increase was insane and obvious that in trying to retain Eric's custom, Match.con were going-big on promoting his profile, pushing it to the top of all searches and giving him unprecedented exposure (once Eric had re-subscribed, his profile would again drop down into the 'normal' category and go back to being relatively invisible and obtaining little interest in comparison).

7. Once the subscription had ended, then Match.con would continue to email him (unless he went back into his account and specifically unticked the corresponding boxes) telling him that a plethora of girls were interested, sending him messages and just 'dying to meet' him.

Chapter Seventy-One

The Falling Donna with the Big Boobies

It was towards the end of Eric's subscription that Donna had sent Eric a message, confirming that he was appearing at the top of her screen every time she logged into the site and as a result, she 'felt like she knew him'. This was proof if proof were indeed required, to back up Match.con's cowboy practices.

Eric and Donna moved onto WhatsApp pretty swiftly, especially as Eric had confirmed he would be disappearing off the site imminently.

Of all the girls Eric had conversed with via text messages, Donna was right up there at the top. She was genuinely funny for a female (not sexist but just Eric's opinion) and having also appreciated Eric's humour there was a great connection between the pair. As was usually the case when things were going great-guns, conversation would often turn to sex and Donna was no different.

It seemed that she had a rather big appetite for it. Having let the cat out of the bag and inferred he was a boob man, Donna had been sure to mention that she was the proud owner of a big set of knockers in order to whet his whistle. Now Eric had rather a fertile imagination but when someone said 'I have big boobs' then there was only really one way to follow that up; 'how big?' Eric began guessing as she kept her assets-size close to her chest (the irony I tell you). Donna finally came clean and quoted Eric extremely happy; she had 32GG's.

After Eric finished furling his tongue back into his mouth from the floor, he was now even more excited about the prospect of meeting Donna and he would have been lying if he said he was not just a wee bit interested to clap his ocular organs on her big-money-balls.

Donna wasn't a huge burly lass by any stretch or even guilty of carrying a few extra pounds. This was a perfect case of Eric having hit the jackpot; a relatively petite-bodied girl with enormous hooters; most men's dream and not unlike say Pamela Anderson during her heady days filming Baywatch (or Breastwatch as Eric preferred to call it). Eric conceded Donna may not have been as aesthetically pleasing as Pamela (who is?) but she was still an attractive girl as far as her profile photos went.

Naturally, the conversation turned to discussing D1 and despite Eric's previous reservations regarding her profile, there were now two very good reasons why Eric was happy to ignore his strict dating prerequisites. As Donna was not keen for Eric to meet her at her digs, then it was agreed that they would instead enjoy a day out near to Eric's, Donna catching a train.

It was a beautiful Saturday in early January, 2017 having been sworn in just a few days earlier. Eric was <u>very</u> nervous. He usually was before any date as you're now aware, no matter who the girl was but he was especially nervous about meeting Donna for two reasons. No, not them. One; they'd got on amazingly well over messages so Eric had higher hopes than usual and two; Eric had worked out that Donna was rather a confident girl.

As per Eric's usual plan pre-first-date, he'd gone for a quick pint or two beforehand to settle his nerves. He was sat in the bar of a hotel across the road from the station, where he was meeting Donna off the train. Funnily enough, it was the same hotel that Eric had been to four-weeks earlier for a job interview for the position as reception manager.

After proving he could set-up and run a successful B&B then he felt his newfound experience might enable him to make it in the hotel industry, preferring hospitality to the idea of returning to an office-based 9-5 job. The woman interviewing Eric was quick to point out that of the 16 candidates who had made it to that stage, Eric was the only male (and perhaps the reason why he ultimately didn't succeed). 'Would you be okay working with eight women and no other men?' she'd asked him. Eric smiled inwardly and replied 'When do I start?'

Donna's train was due into the station imminently so Eric downed the last dregs of his pint and made his way to the entrance to wait for her. He was now even more nervous than before despite his alcoholic libation.

There was a sudden flurry of activity as people began flooding out of the exit and Eric took a deep breath. A shortish girl, about 5'5" carrying a small rucksack ('… would you help me with my ruuuucksack?' Jamie Lee

Curtis in Trading Places 7.5/10 IMDb) over her shoulder and with earphones in came marching purposefully towards him, looking like she was about to carry on past at one point; Eric realising it was Donna and her confidence very clear to see.

She wasn't like Eric had expected, although it was impossible to know exactly how a date would turn out in person despite seeing photos and messages. She was an attractive girl but not as attractive as he'd hoped and she seemed just a smidge too sure of herself. Considering she'd said she had massive boobs, she'd done well to hide them he thought, her woolly-pully shielding them and Eric left wondering whether she had in fact tucked them under her armpits.

There was an obvious tension in the air at first, a flurry of nervous staccato volleys between them. It wasn't until they were back across the road in the hotel bar with a drink and Eric offering her his lips for a quick kiss, that both were able to relax. It was a textbook move, one that Eric had used quite a few times in the past, the majority working out well, with a few exceptions (it had to be said) to his forward approach (well, he couldn't win them all).

Now feeling the love so to speak, conversation became much easier and it wasn't long before they were enjoying each other's company a lot more and heading into town to sample some more drinking establishments. The more they consumed, the more loved-up they seemed to get with one another.

Agreeing it was perhaps wise for a pit-stop in the form of a sit-down meal (as opposed to standing up) Donna's apparent clumsiness, that she'd alluded to during previous conversation, was encapsulated on nearing the restaurant. She'd lost her footing on a cobbled path, only prevented from landing on her face by virtue of having linked arms with Eric en route and Eric having been able to react quickly.

After an enjoyable dinner, Eric took them to some further bars, knowing which ones would afford them a little more privacy and ambience. He was amazed at how Donna had managed to stick with him drink for drink and pints of lager just like him, although it was clear to see that the alcohol had affected Donna quite a bit more. She was drunk enough to exhibit another example of her clumsy repertoire, knocking over a full pint, the liquid being jettisoned towards an adjacent table and literally centimetres from ruining an evening out for the girl sat there with her partner.

Eric and Donna couldn't help but laugh at the occurrence, the two now sitting very close to one another and surreptitiously touching each other when nobody else was looking. Donna was getting rather hot under the knickers and Eric knew it, himself also very keen to see what she looked like without her clothes on. Although not quite getting to full-on gropage, their close proximity had meant Eric couldn't help but get a better understanding of how well endowed Donna was and like Scrappy-Doo, his mind repeating the phrase 'Le' me at 'em'.

Chapter Seventy-Two

A Free Spirit Indeed

It was now quite late in the evening, around 9:00 p.m.; the pair having been on the date since lunchtime. Eric was conscious that Donna still had to get home and so suggested it was best that she caught a train and walked her to the station. Despite her being very vocal in wanting to go back to Eric's and getting to know him a lot better, there was a zero-percent chance of being able to do that. Eric lived with his parents of course but had purposely not mentioned this slight drawback to Donna for obvious reasons.

Instead, Eric made out that he wasn't the type to sleep with someone on D1 (which was true for the vast majority of his dates) and that it was best if she went home and they could see each other again soon. Eric could hardly believe his bad luck; here was an attractive girl with the biggest tits he'd ever come across (no comment) and wanting to sleep with Eric and yet there was nothing he could do about it. With her train due imminently, Eric gave Donna a kiss and told her to let him know when she arrived home and with that, she disappeared through the ticket-barrier and across the bridge to her platform.

Eric jumped a taxi back to his mum and dad's feeling pretty upbeat at having had a very enjoyable day; his positivity slightly marred by the disappointment at not having had the chance to give Donna a full body cavity search. Expecting to hear from Donna whilst on her return leg, Eric was slightly surprised not to. After a couple of hours had passed and still not having heard from her; Eric texted to see if she was okay and had arrived home safely, conscious that she was on her own at night; Still nothing.

Eventually, some four hours after dropping her off at the station, Donna replied. It transpired that she'd 'bumped' into a friend she knew as she disembarked the train and had gone for a drink with them. Eric couldn't help feeling that Donna had hooked-up with a fella and the realisation was like a kick in the clinkers and one after pulling down his pants first for good measure. It was especially disappointing to hear this after their date had been so mutually enjoyable.

Eric was not impressed in the slightest that Donna hadn't even had the decency to let him know what was going on and despite her making out that it <u>had</u> been a girlfriend she'd met, Eric couldn't help having flashbacks to her 'free spirit' description and photos of her socialising with men on her profile.

Donna continued with a charm-offensive the next day but Eric had well and truly lost his mojo for her and it was back to the drawing board once again. It wasn't the last time they'd speak to one another though as it turned out.

Chapter Seventy-Three

Hitler is Alive and Living in Warrington

Just after the dust had settled following the date with Donna, Eric noticed Vicky was still active on Match. It appeared she had noticed him too as she chanced her arm and winked at him again. Eric was left in a quandary given she'd messed him about twice but had to concede her photos still looked mighty tempting. Given the bad luck he'd endured with Donna, Eric once again threw caution to the wind and placing his stubbornness aside for one minute, he sent her a message.

Having picked up where they left off, Eric was once again keen to meet up with Vicky despite what had happened seven-weeks previously. It appeared both had not had much luck finding a compatible plus-one during the intervening period, Vicky having even been asked by one guy to meet her at a motorway service station… as you do. Happy to forget what had gone before, the two arranged to actually meet up, although the arrangements, stipulated by Eric, were that he would be able to stay over at hers to enable him to have a drink. Vicky agreed.

Eric drove to Warrington and after locating her street, was now tasked with finding a parking space; the Victorians not having had the foresight to consider the need for driveways in the future and therefore it was a case of everyone for themselves.

Despite their two previous attempted first dates, Vicky was again proving to have the reliability of a Network Rail timetable and texted Eric to say she was running a little behind schedule due to work commitments. 'Great', Eric thought, after getting a further bad feeling about the girl and looking back at it, may well have been wiser to have headed home at that point.

However, given he'd gone to the trouble of purchasing some booze and driven over there; and the alternative a quiet night ensconced in his bedroom at his mum and dad's; he decided to wait it out. Eric made his frustrations known to Vicky via a text message and she later confessed that she was expecting him to be a little volatile when they finally met; Vicky primed with her guard up ready to retaliate.

Around 45-minutes later and receiving news that she was finally home, Eric knocked on her door, stood with the alcohol. On opening it, Eric could see that Vicky looked a little wary but realising he looked surprisingly normal, she beckoned him in and out of the chilly conditions outside.

Eric's first impressions of Vicky were indeed positive. She was a very attractive girl and despite not being quite as slim as her profile photos suggested, she had quite possibly the finest pair of boobs he'd seen in a long time (not having actually seen Donna's). They seemed to be saying 'look at me'. He felt like a kid in a sweetshop and conversation was going pretty well too. Another reason why Eric preferred meeting up with a girl in their house or his was it was a lot cosier, no chance of distractions and able to relax a lot more.

After drinking and chatting for an hour or so, Eric had picked up on Vicky's body language and flirting style and knew that she wanted a piece of his ass… or more accurately something around the other side of his body. He also knew she was interested as he was still there and hadn't been asked to leave.

Standing up and walking over to Vicky, who stood fixing herself another glass of wine in her open-plan kitchen, Eric slowly moved his lips towards hers and Vicky obliged, the pair kissing briefly. There was definitely going to be fireworks that night if he wanted them and it was obvious that the showstopper for her would be his Roman candle. However, Eric was fully aware that he liked Vicky enough not to jump straight into bed with her and besides; he was just a little nervous about her levels of confidence.

After the clock struck 1:00 a.m., the pair wrapped things up for the evening and made their way upstairs, no conversation regarding the move; more a natural understanding. On reaching the landing, Eric noticed the box room at the back of the house and made his way towards it, asking Vicky if that was his bed for the night. As Eric waited for a response, he noted that she'd temporarily vanished, reappearing seconds later from her room at the front and completely billy-bollocks.

Eric's eyes almost fell from their sockets. 'Heavens to Murgatroyd!' he thought to himself, rather taken aback by her presumptuous actions. Eric had been just a smidge correct about her levels of confidence and had rarely experienced such a quick turnaround, having only been in the house a matter of 3-4 hours. That said; it wasn't a career PB as he would go on to break that record with Svetlana and Zoë the following year (they didn't come as a pair sadly) when he saw them naked within an hour of meeting them.

As much as he was flattered that Vicky was now enticing him into her room, Eric couldn't help feeling that Vicky's strip was like having received his Christmas presents without any gift-wrapping, the anticipation completely shot and the excitement of removing the layers now impossible to recreate. Eric stood firm… quite literally… but he was not going to have sex with Vicky on D1; there would be another time for that and besides; he wanted to keep the excitement flowing for just a little longer.

Despite offering it to him on a gold-plated salver, Eric stuck to his guns. There would be no sex until D3 but he couldn't resist a little carnal pleasuring that night and teased Vicky with perhaps his greatest talent. Vicky was both impressed and grateful and was now even more desperate for the full nine yards.

Chapter Seventy-Four

Happy Birthday to You, Happy Birthday to Me

Despite Eric's search for work being more important to him at that stage than worrying about relationships, it did cross his mind that he could potentially incorporate vacancies in the Warrington area as part of his criteria. Eric and Vicky had been seeing quite a bit of each other and she had been vocal for him to move in, especially after he'd come clean to her about his current situation.

They had been en route to Nottingham for Eric's twin brother's 40th birthday bash (yes, Eric was also 40) when Eric had decided that it was a good time to tell her the truth, especially as it was a long walk home from Uttoxeter at that point in their journey. Vicky had her hand on his lap as he was driving when Eric came out with it.
'I've got something to tell you' he said slightly awkwardly and with a modicum of seriousness. Vicky recoiled her hand from Eric's lap immediately and braced herself for some disappointing news, the possibilities running through her head and now saying them out loud.
'You're married aren't you?' she exclaimed convincing herself that she'd been drawn in by a cheating scumbag and her happiness bubble would soon be burst.

On hearing that Eric's secret was actually him living at home with his parents, Vicky's relief was tangible and the admission coming as even better news, realising he could move into her hers with very little fuss. With her heart having returned to its normal position and her hand now back on Eric's knee, she had a smile on her face and was laughing at Eric for his deviousness. Eric was just glad she wasn't angry at him for having been rather less than transparent from the start. The fact of the matter was that Eric knew not many girls would be interested in dating a forty-year-old fella that lived with his parents and Vicky agreed that it would have certainly put her off.

Despite Vicky champing at the bit for Eric to move in, both on a relationship front and for monetary assistance, Eric confirmed he would not move in until he found employment, his priority not being swayed by her suggestions. It was unfair to his parents also as they had supported him through everything and he wasn't about to swan off and live with another girl without a job and after everything that had happened relatively recently with Meg. It may not have been the best set-up living with his parents but there was no way he was changing his mind on that one.

Ernie made friends at the drop of a pin and being gay, he was a likeable lad, offering no threat to heterosexual males and having more than the usual fella's common interests with girls. His life had centred around Nottingham since leaving uni there almost 20-years before and as a result, there were a lot of people keen to celebrate the landmark birthday with him. Eric's appearance was more akin to a guest celebrity (Tom Hardy) than anything else and having not met his brother's friends previously, many were drawn to him to settle their own curiosity as to what he actually looked like. It was possibly the only time in his life that Eric would feel genuinely famous.

Eric was glad that Vicky was with him as it meant he had someone with him for company, especially as she was in a similar boat, meeting most of the gathered assortment for the first time also. However, that's not exactly how things panned out in practice, with Eric having chosen to spend little time with Vicky following her somewhat ridiculous behaviour in ending up chatting to a doctor for most of the evening.

Eric couldn't quite believe she didn't have the social skills to break off from a conversation when it had run on long enough; especially as there were literally a hundred other people around including her boyfriend. Eric could only hypothesise that she actually liked him; would she really be so blatant about it? Eric knew she was the most attractive girl in the whole room and couldn't blame the man for his part in keeping Vicky talking.

At one point Eric had even taken to gesturing to her out of shot from her medical companion and Vicky made out that she was trapped. Eric rolled his eyes and gave up on her at that point, convinced that she was too much of an open flirt and decided to make the best of it on his own with his brother's obvious gay friends, picking them up and twirling them around Dirty Dancing-style to the cheesy 80s score.

At the end of the night and with most of the partygoers having departed, Eric was approached by the doctor, who was polite enough to shake hands and comment on how funny Eric had been on the dancefloor. Eric was close to having asked him if he'd had a good time with his girlfriend but decided against it.

Then came the turn of Eric and Vicky to leave and head back to his brother's flat where they were kipping for the night. However, Vicky had been drinking far too much all evening and began her over the top hugging of all men as they said their goodbyes; another indication of her flirty nature and something that Eric felt was rather uncouth. This was the first time he'd seen her in such an environment and he was beginning to think she was not someone he could trust.

An argument ensued outside the venue and Eric told Vicky that she wasn't the girl for him. It seemed pretty harsh at the time but Eric had been embarrassed and she had definitely come up short of his standards, knowing full well that he would never have carried on like that had the roles been reversed.

Vicky broke down into an absolute cacophony of tears and with it came a great deal of rage, notably having been fuelled by her levels of intoxication. Her reaction had been so theatrical that it had even caught the attentions of two nearby police officers, who felt the need to come over and determine if everything was okay. Having told them that he had just split up with her (in a very sober fashion) the police still took Eric's details for some reason and with that, they disappeared.

Back at his brother's flat, Vicky had gone straight to bed and things were just a little awkward when Eric finally retired for the night. He was angry with himself that he'd been the cause for a rather sour end to the evening for his brother and those still around to witness the events outside in the street. However, he couldn't help blaming Vicky for his actions.

Faced with the idea that they were splitting up, Vicky went on the charm-offensive with Eric and by morning it seemed that Eric was able to put the previous night's melodramatics behind him and they returned home in much better spirits.

Having opened up his employment search to include Warrington, it was somewhat apt therefore that Eric was invited to interview by a couple of firms not one-mile from Vicky's house and it was with one of them that Eric finally got a job. Given the practicality of allowing him to walk to work each day, then it made perfect sense for him to finally move in with her and he did so the weekend before his start-date. Eric and Vicky had been seeing each other for six-months by then but despite her enthusiasm for him moving in since around their third-week together, it proved to be the defining factor that would ultimately split them up.

Although Eric had sometimes spent up to half his week over at Vicky's prior to moving in, it was living with her 24-7 when Eric learnt how incredibly bossy and pedantic Vicky could be. Now lest we forget that Eric was slightly OCD but he had also received an average score of 97% for cleanliness at the B&B from over 150 reviews on Booking.com; so it was fair to say he was a clean and tidy person. However, it seemed in the eyes of Vicky that his efforts were just not good enough.

As Eric had learnt from his years of dating and relationships, the living together part was easily the most important as so much rested on how harmonious this turned out to be. Vicky, however, was about as accommodating and patient as one of the Stasi and Eric was regretting the whole move almost immediately.

She would tell him what to wear, even buying him clothes and although Eric appreciated her outgoings on him, it was all about turning him into something she wanted him to be. Eric's friends picked up on this straight away, having met Vicky initially at a friend's birthday, where she continually criticised him when he wasn't there to defend himself. She would also scrub his body in the shower like a mother would their child and woe betide Eric not spending at least four minutes brushing his teeth.

She was also uber-critical about how he washed her wine glasses, the majority of which Eric had bought her for her birthday when realising she was around five short of a half-dozen set. Eric didn't know whether he was allowed to scratch his arse at times and it was becoming clear that Vicky was the most difficult person to live with bar none.

Chapter Seventy-Five

Holiday from Hell

Perhaps the biggest example of how shockingly bossy and self-centred Vicky could be was when she planned a holiday to Madrid for them both; the flights, car hire and hotel having been booked a couple of months before and just so happened the trip came about only a fortnight into Eric's new job and therefore two-weeks after moving in with Vicky.

Despite having little money at that stage, Eric was keen to go halves with her as was not the type who found it easy to accept charity or someone paying for him. He therefore coughed up exactly half of the expected costs to Vicky; which included the hotel, which didn't have to be paid for until they checked out. Eric was also keen to ensure he took a decent wedge of spending money to add to the 'shared' kitty, which was only £100 less than Vicky's contribution, the difference; Vicky hadn't been out of work for eight months. Vicky was quick to point out to Eric that <u>she</u> would be holding onto all the money whilst away and this was non-negotiable. 'Heil Hitler' Eric thought to himself as he handed over his Euros.

The holiday to Madrid was not a random choice as the plan was purposefully made for Vicky to visit and stay with the family that she had previously been an au pair for some twenty-years previously. They were happy to put Vicky and Eric up for six-nights, which were the first six-nights of their trip, whereby the remainder of their stay in Madrid (four-nights) would be in a hotel in the centre and give them the opportunity to sample the city life and culture.

Staying with the family she knew meant that it was a cheaper holiday, not expected to pay for lodgings. However, Eric and Vicky took it upon themselves to buy the groceries and Vicky cooked some of the meals as a way to say thank you and to contribute something for their kind hospitality. There was also a large swimming pool they could use at the house and so all in all a rather good deal.

However, the one thing or more precisely three things that weren't so favourable as far as Eric was concerned was sharing the house and gardens with three dogs. These weren't your usual family pet dogs by any means and were in fact two humongous German Shepherds (I had a shepherd's pie last night… the shepherd wasn't too happy about it mind) weighing in at 50kg each and a smaller but more terrifying American Pit Bull Terrier, with a neck like Mike Tyson during his prime. Eric hated dogs and as per his dating do's and don'ts was particularly wary of those with massive pointy teeth and that shat bigger than him. Here there were three such exhibits on show.

The set up at the house was something not dissimilar to Guantanamo Bay, the only difference being that Eric didn't have to go around in a fluorescent orange jumpsuit and restraints. There were ten-foot black metal fences with spike strips along the top around the perimeter of the property and another separating the pool area from the rest of the house and gardens. Each entrance had a lock and the front gate was always locked, even when there were people at home.

One of the rules that the woman who lived there had been keen to pass on to Eric and Vicky was not to let the Pit Bull and dominant German Shepherd (both males) into the same area as in her words 'they would fight'. As a result, Eric and Vicky felt like they were on the set of 'The Others' (or 'Los Otros' as they were in E*spaña – 7.6/10 IMDb*) where before opening the door or gate ahead of them, they had to make sure that the one behind them was closed. At least they didn't have to keep the curtains continually drawn, Eric thought to himself.

Having arrived late on a Sunday evening, it was the next morning when Eric and Vicky got their first taste of relaxation, the temperature waay too hot for Eric and even a little too hot for the locals who were used to it. Taking full advantage of the pool, Eric was busy clocking-up some lengths and his senses somewhat diluted from what was going on around him. Then, stopping for a rest, he realised all hell had broken loose not 30-feet away.

It turned out that Vicky had gone back to the house to fetch some drinks for everyone but on her return to the poolside had stopped to open the gate, placing her tray of drinks down on the wall adjacent to it. However, in the time it took her to pick the tray back up and move to the opening in the fence, the German Shepherd had already made it through.

Before you could say 'don't let the dogs in the same area' then the Pit Bull had flown from its vantage point on the veranda next to the house and was on its nemesis like a tramp-on-chips, instantaneously locking its deadly jaws around its neck. It was pandemonium and Eric having put two and two together and realising that the dogs had inadvertently been brought together due to Vicky, was primed with ensuring that it didn't end badly, knowing that she would ultimately be blamed for the aftermath.

Despite Eric having a rather healthy fear of dangerous dogs, he ran to the scene and with no concern for his own safety had began trying to pry them apart, first pulling at the collar on the German Shepherd. However, the Pit Bull's immense clamp on its much larger foe meant it was nigh on impossible for Eric to get any grip on the collar which was tight against its neck.

As the situation developed, there was a continual screaming from the woman and owner of the German Shepherd and a lot of it was directed at Vicky. At one point, with Eric's hands getting waay too near to the business end of the fight, he'd even felt the Pit Bull's teeth glance his fingers. Stopping briefly to check his digits were all present and correct, it was then that another guest had run over with a hosepipe and began dowsing the dogs with a jet of water, ensuring to direct the water over the Pit Bull's nostrils, aware that if it couldn't breathe it would have to release its vice-like grip.

There was a mix of blood and water and people now slipping over on the wet paving and still a continual crying and screaming from the owner. Eventually, after a few minutes and what felt like hours, the plan worked and the dogs were separated. What hadn't helped was that after the fight had ensued, the other German Shepherd had been keen to lend a hand to its brother and just to add a little more fuel to the fire; the mother of the Pit Bull, who just happened to be there too, had been trying her hardest to help her son. It was like a WrestleMania tag-team event without the staged choreography and spandex.

Eric had later read that American Pit Bulls had a bite similar to that of a shark and could cut through bone and cartilage and once it got hold of its victim they had been known not to release even after having their back legs cut off. Eric couldn't believe that anyone with a brain larger than an amoeba would consider such dogs as pets, even if they felt they offered some level of security and deterrent to burglars.

After the dust had settled, it seemed that there had been a great deal of fortune as the blood present had only come from the Pit Bull's face, the German Shepherd having gnawed away at it whilst being pretty much starved of any other movement. The Pit Bull hadn't punctured the throat of the German Shepherd at all, instead having clasped onto its scruff and collar. It had been a rather lucky escape. As everyone was sat in silence, getting their collective breaths back sat near to the pool underneath a gazebo, Eric was walking to and fro, not dissimilar to Hercule Poirot at the end of a murder mystery, having arranged for all the suspects to gather together before his final summing up monologue.

Eric asked the woman and son how many times this had occurred, aware that the woman's warning the night before must have been as a result of them having learnt the hard way. Eric couldn't help thinking she would have been better using the words 'fight to the death' and thereby making it clearer as to the potential pandemonium that could and did result. 'This is the fourth time' she confirmed and this rather startling response was all Eric needed to know.

Eric suggested that Vicky could not be blamed for the occurrence if it had happened on three previous occasions, highlighting the rather unrealistic and impossible task to keep them apart and the rest of the congregation agreed. As a result of the latest episode between the dogs, the family made inroads to deal with the problem and a month or so later the woman's son had moved out and took his dog (the Pit Bull) with him.

The whole matter had only furthered Eric's dislike for dogs, unable to form any bond with the creatures no matter how small and cuddly they appeared to the layperson.

Chapter Seventy-Six

More Holiday Misery

Vicky's own dog was not a dangerous breed but it still proved to be a problem for Eric and also highlighted how such pets could affect the owner's relationship with their exes. Eric learnt this on only his second date with Vicky, which was after spending a weekend with her. As the pair lay naked next to each other in bed (underneath the covers naturally) on Sunday morning around 11:00 a.m., Eric was just a little startled when he heard the front door open and someone walk in downstairs. 'What the dickens?' Eric thought, feeling rather vulnerable and looking at Vicky inquisitively. 'Thanks Tom' she shouted down and the door slammed shut as they left.

Eric could not believe what had just happened. Vicky's ex-boyfriend had been looking after the dog and had dropped it back off at her house and let himself in with a spare key to her house. 'Wo Wo Wo Wo Wo and again Wo!' Eric thought. This was just far too ridiculous for him to compute.

It seemed that despite having split up months ago, the pair continued to share custody of the dog and it also meant Vicky remained good friends with her ex's mum and dad for the same reason. Looking back at it, Eric was surprised he hadn't called it a day at that stage but without other options available to him at the time and not having moved-in, then he wasn't going to shoot himself in the face.

After dogfight-gate and having to listen to Vicky explaining to the others why things hadn't worked out with her previous partners (yes, Eric was having a great time in Madrid) Eric was glad to get away from the 'at home with the Partridges' and to spend the next few days just with Vicky by himself. He'd been to the Spanish capital before with his brother and mates but that was some 17-years-ago and was more a football excursion than checking out the various museums and landmarks. However, Vicky's bossiness was about to be showcased like never before.

Firstly, she'd already planned her itinerary for the pair of them and this was one museum after another. Now Eric appreciated a bit of culture as much as the next man but to say he felt museumed out was an understatement. He was certainly of the opinion that once you'd seen one Paleolithic tool, then you'd pretty much seen them all. Despite this, Eric went along with her, before broaching the subject of a potential trip to the home of the current World Club Champions and arguably thee most famous team in the world; the Galacticos or Real Madrid to the North of the centre. Vicky's response had been quick and to the point: 'You can go if you like but I'll just have a look around the shops and get a drink outside'.

'Marvellous', Eric thought and so the Santiago Bernabeu stadium tour didn't happen.

The extremely hot days in Madrid at the beginning of July were sweltering and meant them taking regular pit-stops in cafés and bars for a cool drink and to make use of their air-conditioning systems. Vicky was up to her old tricks again though and whilst every other woman Eric saw walking about the busy metropolis was appropriately attired (even considering the mercury hitting 42-degrees in the shade) Eric appeared to be with the only girl whose breasts were literally hanging out and certainly causing a stir with the Madrilenian male and lesbian fraternity.

Eric felt pretty uncomfortable walking around with her and noticing her admirers with their eye-jerk reactions, her badongas seemingly rendering them all powerless not to gawp. It was pointless for Eric to mention this to Vicky though as she wouldn't change with her desire to attract attention.

Not content with deciding everything they did during the day, then evenings weren't much different either. Picking a restaurant seemed more hassle than it was worth; Vicky reminding Eric of the vast choice on offer within a practical catchment area of their hotel. Having narrowed it down to a choice of two or three each night and asking Eric what he thought, it was amazingly uncanny how ultimately Vicky would ignore Eric's choice and end up going to another. It was beginning to be just a little nauseating now and Eric was not amused.

The final straw on a holiday that Eric had felt pretty much like a bystander throughout was when it came to paying for the hotel when checking out.

Remembering that he'd already given Vicky half of the costs for the holiday (including their city-centre accommodation) it was rather surprising, therefore, when she mentioned not having enough to pay the bill and could Eric cover it. 'Unbelievable' Eric thought and he now knew he had to seriously consider his happiness and the relationship when they got back to Blighty.

Chapter Seventy-Seven

It's a Question of Trust

To a point, Eric could survive the day to day histrionics from Vicky; especially as sex was great and plentiful. Vicky had a voracious appetite for it and would frequently wait at the top of the stairs following her evening shower and shout down the romantic words; 'come up here and stick your willy in me'. Not exactly exuding class Eric realised but as long as there wasn't a football match on that he was watching, then he was happy to oblige most of the time.

The longer they were together, the more Eric would find things about Vicky that weren't conducive for a long-term relationship. The first of these was the amount of attention she was receiving from blokes, whether work colleagues, clients, ex-boyfriends, those she'd dated before and even friends of friends.

It was true to say that the reasons why Eric had fancied her initially were the same reasons why many other fellas were also keen. With the proliferation of social media and communication channels mentioned previously, it meant it was also piss-easy for any of them to contact her via her mobile phone.

Now spending more time with Vicky after moving in, Eric was privy to the rather frequent messages that she received; well he couldn't help but notice the notifications that would flash up on her mobile-screen as it sat on the arm of the sofa or on the bedside table. It was beginning to make Eric feel that perhaps not everything was quite right.

Eric knew that the receipt of such messages and phone calls from interested fellas went hand-in-hand with the way in which she carried herself, the way she dressed provocatively; always keen to showcase her tremendous cleavage and coupled with her flirtatious sense of humour. As a comparison, Eric's best friend's wife (who was also an attractive woman) was the kind who didn't lead anyone on and garnered respect; everyone knew that she was in a happy relationship and would not entertain or stand for any similar shenanigans.

I guess Eric couldn't have his cake and eat it; Vicky had appealed to him in the same way and yet now living with her, he was somehow expecting her to completely change her ways. However, it was one thing for her to say she couldn't stop fellas from messaging her but Eric knew it was an entirely different premise for her not to make a proactive decision to try to block any of their attempted advances.

For example, Vicky told Eric about a fella she'd seen prior to him and he'd fluctuated from sending her nasty bitter text messages one minute and apologetic heartfelt messages the next after they split. She mentioned how he had been a tool and how she was actually a little scared of him. However, despite this admission, she'd not done the one thing that would have brought an end to it all and blocked his number, preventing him from being able to contact her (at least using his mobile). 'Why hadn't she done this?' thought Eric. It was an extremely easy-fix and he wasn't buying the 'I didn't realise you could block numbers' tripe that she came back with.

No; Vicky loved the attention and she wanted to feel in demand. Eric could only conjecture that she wasn't about to delete or block numbers as she preferred to keep her options open and it was as simple as that. Moving forwards, Vicky's only reaction to Eric noticing her frequent messages from men trying it on with her was to cancel notifications on her phone. This only acted to confirm Eric's misgivings and he knew he couldn't trust her at all after that.

Apart from the messages Vicky was constantly receiving from fellas and her unarguable bossiness; there was also the unhealthy amount of time she spent at work. It was no joke that she would work late into the night and Eric would be lucky to see her for half-an-hour some evenings before it was time for bed.

Given her frequent absence from the house in the evenings; that meant she'd ask Eric to feed the dog and even take it for a walk, the latter something that Eric was loathed to do given his dislike for the creatures. Tasked with flying solo with the mutt out and about also meant a real possibility of having to carry out the most pathetic thing in Eric's eyes; picking up dog shit and even more incredulously; picking up dog shit whilst others could see you picking up dog shit.

Now, spending time in bed chatting with his previous girlfriends and partners had been part of the course with Eric and a good chance to catch-up and relax. However, Vicky, as you'll not be surprised to learn was a very different proposition.

She was so excruciatingly pedantic that it was a matter of days before Eric chose to sleep in the spare room; Vicky not happy to talk, only to read her book for a short time before lights out and never any kissing or cuddling. She would tut incessantly at Eric for daring to move and even commented on how loud his breathing was on occasions. At least Eric could relax in his own bed but as that became the norm, Eric realised that the only reason he was actually still under the same roof as Vicky was to make getting to work and back a lot more practical.

From moving into Vicky's house to living like a lodger had taken less than two-months and that included their trip to the Spanish capital. It had been a massive mistake but on the other hand, at least he'd realised that now and not wasted any more of his time. Eric was genuinely happy to see the back of Vicky and she was the first-ever girl he'd spent a decent chunk of time with and not given her a second thought after splitting up. That spoke volumes in itself and told Eric all he needed to know about his time with Vicky.

He couldn't quite believe her audacity at expecting a kiss as he left; being sure to tell her that unlike the millions of other fellas, he would not be contacting her ever again. With his final belongings in hand, he then walked off down the street like Bill Bixby at the end of an Incredible Hulk episode, satchel over his shoulder and hearing the harrowing melody of the TV series playing in his head.

Would he ever find someone to settle down with and be happy? Perhaps he wasn't destined to and his life was meant to be slightly more varied. Eric had no other option at that stage but to return like The Prodigal Son to his mum and dad for what must have been well into treble figures by now. It was indeed fortunate that he had a good relationship with them and they were always there for him when things didn't go according to his plans.

Having found himself experiencing another fallow spell in the female frolics department and feeling rather sorry for himself; Eric decided to contact Donna again, the thought of her pendulous globes that he'd never had a chance to play with now utmost in his cranial member. Maybe she was telling the truth that she'd bumped into a female friend on her return from their date and perhaps he had just been paranoid.

As luck would have it, Donna was glad to hear from Eric and they slipped back into conversation like nothing had happened. However, as there was quite a lot to catch up on, she suggested they spoke as opposed to typing to save themselves some time. Eric, as you're aware, wasn't a massive fan of speaking on the phone but on this occasion having already met her, he agreed. Eric soon realised that Donna had used the call to give him a bit of a tongue-lashing for the way in which things had ended last time out, Eric having labelled her an untrustworthy type (aka slag).

In quite a remarkable twist of irony; during the conversation, Donna had let it slip that it had actually been a fella that she'd met after returning home after their date. Well, that was all Eric needed to hear to confirm his initial theory and pointing this out to her in a follow-up message after their call, he wished her all the best for the future.

Eric was not going to get involved with a girl like her under any circumstances; not even for shits and giggles as he knew if he fell for her, then it would cause him headaches that he could simply do without. The chance of Donna bumping into a male-friend on arriving home at 10:00 p.m. at night and him being free to go for a drink with her seemed rather slim and Eric knew full-well that she would have contacted him whilst on her return journey from their date to arrange the rendezvous. This only served to reaffirm to Eric that he should definitely trust his own instincts in the future.

Chapter Seventy-Eight

If There's Grass on the Wicket

Although living with his parents again was not the best situation at his age, the relief at not having to abide by Vicky's rules was the biggest positive to take from the backward step. Having a job now, he was conscious that he could look to find somewhere to rent in a shared house and nearer to Warrington to make his commute a great deal more practical. In order to give him something to do of an evening, Eric had re-subscribed to Match; in fact, having revisited it whilst living as a paid-up lodger with Vicky after their relationship had crashed and burned.

After a few weeks, Eric found a suitable house-share in a quaint little village, a stone's throw from the hustle and bustle of Warrington and went along to check it out. It was a very olde-worlde small detached house, wooden floors throughout (upstairs and down) and the owner certainly a hoarder, the precious little space cluttered by knick-knacks and furniture.

She was a portrait artist in her late fifties and an archetypal mad-cat spinster type, effecting a rather posh and well-to-do aura, although Eric could tell this was painted on just like the canvasses she'd shown him. There was another person already in situ at the house and it appeared the pair had grown quite attached to each other given their repartee and mannerisms. He was around the same age as Eric, despite looking much older and was, in fact, an Iranian nuclear physicist, working out of the tech-labs near to the village.

The preface sounded too bizarre to be believed and there was definitely a situation comedy to be made out of it Eric thought (slightly different to 'Game On'). Keen to recapture some of his own independence, a lack of suitable accommodation outside of Warrington town centre and the people he would be sharing with appearing like good eggs, Eric agreed to move in. His bedroom even came with a four-poster bed, made from dark oak, which matched the floors almost perfectly. Unfortunately, there was little room left for anything else apart from a narrow walkway around three of its sides and Eric managed to twat his head continually on the wooden valance that sat atop it despite having good cause to remember it was there.

However, after only a couple of days, Eric realised that he'd made a big mistake; unable to relax and having little in the way of common ground with either of his new housemates. What was even stranger was the sound emanating from the bathroom adjacent to Eric's room, the Iranian seemingly banging a metal pan with a wooden spoon, which Eric could only assume was to keep the wolf from the door so to speak, masking his bodily functions and splash-down. It was all just a little bit odd he thought.

Despite confirming to the owner that he would be returning to his mum and dad's to pick up more of his belongings the weekend after moving in, she did not mention anything to Eric about her change of heart in respect of his introduction to the house. Instead, she waited for him to collect it and set it all out in his room and go to work on Monday before texting him some claptrap about how her daughters were both having terrible relationship problems.

As a result, they would need to come back home, which meant Eric was now surplus to requirements. Looking back at it, Eric was far too polite with the way in which he handled the situation but he'd been through a lot worse and therefore didn't let it bother him too much; especially as he'd worked out that the pair of them were two of the weirdest people he'd actually ever met.

Despite living at the house for less than a week, Eric had taken full advantage of the local pub, approximately 400-yards down from the house next to the canal. He'd received a message on Match from a young girl, who seemed quite interested to meet up and as she was a definite looker then Eric had given the idea some considerable thought. The only thing preventing him from jumping at the chance was her age; she was 22 years young, almost 20-years younger than Eric and easily young enough to pass as his own daughter. Eric pointed this out to her and suggested that she was probably better off dating fellas nearer her own age, aware that such a gap was very much pushing it for him.

However, explaining his dating escapades to his best mate at work (as he was prone to do) Bill, who was old enough to be Eric's dad, couldn't believe he'd dismissed the chance to go on a date with a girl due to her youthful age, joking if he could have her details instead. Having given him advice along the lines of 'I know what I'd be doing in your position' then Eric did a complete U-turn and contacted the girl to set up a rendezvous.

Happy to see him still, Beth drove out to the village and Eric sat in wait for her at the pub. The plan had been to watch the football that afternoon before she arrived, allowing him time to sink a couple of beers to help him relax and to make conversation flow more easily. Unfortunately, there was only one problem as it seemed the pub was the only one in a 50-mile radius that did not show live sports, a schoolboy error regarding his due diligence before moving into the house he thought and a rather rudimentary oversight.

Left to entertain himself, he was glad when Beth arrived just for something to do. She was a very good-looking girl, not wearing much make-up at all; she didn't need to and most definitely a tomboy type. Conversation was enjoyable for the most part and the pair got on pretty well. There was, however, something not quite right, something missing that Eric couldn't put his finger on. Perhaps it had been their seating arrangement, as Beth had sat opposite Eric across a very wide table, which as Eric had always tried to avoid on dates meant it was a little too officious with no potential for any tactility (go go Gadget arms).

After spending a few hours putting the world to rights, Eric walked Beth to her car but before she got in they said goodbye, Eric taking the opportunity to offer his lips to her and moving his towards hers. The kiss was great and he even had a feel of her cracking arse as a bonus point. 'You're quite a good kisser' she exclaimed, having been happy to extrapolate the experience. Although feeling her accolade was a little condescending given she was half his age, he didn't let it spoil the moment.

As there was no talk of a rematch or D2, then Eric had realised that she was ultimately not bowled over and he waved her off. Realistically, Eric knew that with such an age-gap there was no way there would be a possibility for a relationship, even before she'd turned up but that still didn't prevent his pride from feeling a smidge dented. He would have to find someone more his own age and so the search continued.

Chapter Seventy-Nine

It Could Only Happen to Eric

It was now nearing Christmas once more and Eric had to accept that he was going to be on his own again, something that hadn't been the case for the vast majority of them since the turn of the Millennia, which had in effect coincided with the beginning of his dating journey give or take a year. It was much cheaper though to be fair he thought; at least there was that. However, he'd have enjoyed having someone special to share it with nonetheless.

Eric had continued his online dating searches for something to keep him occupied and had come across a clutch of potential suitors. Having laid down some groundwork he gave himself some further lines to investigate once the Yuletide season had played out and everyone was back to normal in the New Year.

One of the potentials was a girl called Sharon who lived approximately 25-miles from Eric. She wasn't his typical go-to in the looks department (usually blonde with big tits and teeth… not big teeth; he wasn't into females with a mouthful of ivory or teeth like a policeman's horse) but he was still attracted to her and she seemed sassy and original via WhatsApp messages.

Having got on like the proverbial, the pair therefore decided to lock horns early in 2018 and it seemed Sharon was very keen and confident; happy to accept Eric's invitation to see him and meet at his local despite the distance. She caught a train and appeared in the pub as expected, Eric having got there a little earlier as usual to quench his pre-D1 thirst.

Sharon was younger than Eric; around six-years younger with cracking boobs (that she was showcasing quite liberally for Eric's and everyone else's pleasure). Not only was she a good-looking girl but she also had the personality to match, a very bubbly and chatty girl with a rich but comprehensible Brummie accent, which merely added to her charms.

The pair spent around four hours chatting and laughing at the pub and they enjoyed themselves so much that the time seemed to fly past like a Juan Martin del Potro tennis serve. Sharon's notable zest for life and youthfulness had been exemplified by her compunction to order tequila-slammers, which interspersed their normal round of drinks. Eric did feel a little too old for all that unnecessary messing about, especially as he was sat in his local and not out on the tiles around twenty-years previous. However, there was little Eric could do to dilute her enthusiasm and so partook in all the drinking she wanted so as not to come across too much like an old fart.

Everything was going amazingly well and Eric knew Sharon was gagging for it and would definitely be going back to his to check out the ceiling of his rented room, where he'd be helping her out of her wet things so to speak. Just as he was licking his lips in contemplation, something changed the lay-of-the-land for Eric; Sharon came out with something that was just a little too brazen for his liking. She exclaimed that she would pretty much sleep with anyone. Yes, exactly. Sharon no doubt believed herself to sound less shallow by her admission but the suggestion only served to ring alarm bells with Eric.

Her explanation for the liberal statement was that as she had been in a 15-year relationship from a relatively early age, she hadn't experienced much in the way of variety and was, therefore, less hung up about age or aesthetics, simply happy to receive some different cock (Eric's words not Sharon's). This was thee biggest turn-off for Eric since the time he slept with a girl with a pierced clit and the experience tantamount to shagging a cheese-grater.

Although he had previously been very keen, he couldn't help feeling that Sharon had now fallen headfirst into the 'free spirit' bracket that he had come across 12-months earlier with Donna (she with the extremely large breasticles) and basically admitting to being a bit of a slag.

Even Eric had standards (well there was one… coming up later in the story) but he wouldn't sleep with just <u>any</u> girl, despite his brother's advice when he was 17. No, Eric had gone off Sharon immediately and not least as her vocal appetite for sex could be suggesting it didn't matter what Eric looked like to her as long as he had a functioning penis. After initially feeling that Sharon was well worth a second-date, Eric's outlook was very different now and although he still wanted to bone her and play with her magnificent tits, there was no desire for anything more serious than that.

As Eric had alluded to one of his brothers having passed away; Sharon, having had a decent fill of alcohol and perhaps feeling a little more reflective by the end of the evening, asked him more about it. Eric would never openly discuss it as it wasn't the thing to talk about, certainly not on a first-date and the loss of his brother was very personal to him. However, as Sharon had specifically asked, Eric explained the sad and moving events that had seen his elder brother die from a brain tumour.

By the time Eric had finished, himself feeling rather emotional after reminding himself of the details; Sharon was in floods of tears. Eric was surprised to see her crying and assumed that this was a natural reaction to the sad story of his brother, especially as she had consumed quite a few double gin and tonics and was perhaps more susceptible to emotional outbursts. Or perhaps Sharon may have known someone close to her who had died from a brain tumour or the bad C, he thought, and could therefore relate to his own experience.

Eric asked politely if she was okay, passing her a serviette from the cutlery caddy on the table. Sharon composed herself before explaining why she'd reacted in that way. It turned out Eric was right; she did know someone who had suffered from a brain tumour… and that person was her.

Yes, she'd had one of the largest tumours removed from her brain and on her returns to the cancer hospital for check-ups was still revered by the surgeons as a walking miracle. She went on to explain that she had been told that she could lose the feeling in her right side at any point in the future, which would mean that side of her face would fall akin to a stroke-victim. She seemed to be very accepting of this potential likelihood and had a very positive attitude towards life as a result; hence not thinking twice about jumping on a train to visit Eric and knowing she would likely be staying over at his if they had the elusive chemistry.

Eric couldn't believe it. It wasn't funny in the true sense but he couldn't help feeling almost delirious with inner-amusement. It was like something out of a sitcom or black comedy and despite the gravity of her situation and Eric knowing at firsthand the enormous pain after seeing his brother slip away without being able to do a thing about it; here he was eight-years later laughing inwardly at the situation he now found himself in. It really could only happen to Eric.

On that bombshell, he could now appreciate why Sharon had said she would sleep with anyone and it was all about her having a good time and making the most out of life. Of course had she mentioned her life-threatening predicament on her dating profile then the stark reality was that Eric would not have touched her with a bargepole; not because he didn't believe she had the right to a normal and enjoyable life including dating but the idea of potentially immersing himself with someone who could potentially be dead within a few years. This was not something Eric would have signed-up for, especially had he fallen for her and his emotions had once again been up for some severe treatment thanks to cancer.

Eric was glad he'd already made his mind-up about Sharon in respect to any long-term prospects following her admission that she was just looking for fun and would sleep with almost anyone earlier in their conversation. He didn't feel quite so guilty now and had in effect saved himself from feeling like a grade A twat had he decided to walk away only on hearing her plight.

As it was now after midnight and the bar staff had begun shepherding people out of the pub, they walked back to Eric's. They did end up sleeping together in the end; seems Sharon was very persuasive and she did have an amazing body with the softest skin Eric had ever experienced. Eric didn't feel too bad about having great sex with her on D1 (despite contravening his own dating rules). Well, it would have felt wrong not to have granted Sharon her wish Eric thought and naturally had nothing to do with him deriving any pleasure from it of course (cough cough). He was nothing if not completely selfless and accommodating.

Next morning and as the two lay naked in bed together, Sharon received a phone call. It was her mum and she had some bad news; Sharon's nan had died. Eric couldn't believe it. Could anything else happen to make this date seem even stranger and more macabre?

Sharon's keenness to leave was palpable. She had to go home first before making her onward journey to be repatriated with her mum and family at such a difficult time. Eric did what most people in his position would have done and offered to drive her back, knowing it was both the quickest and most practical option given the circumstances. Eric never saw Sharon again.

Chapter Eighty

From Uzbekistan with Love

Eric soon realised that unless he increased the parameters of his search-radius, he would be looking at the usual suspects night after night after night… after night; and it would be both frustrating and tedious. Although not wishing to meet a girl who lived too far away (for practicality reasons) he felt he had no choice and so late one evening opened it up to the entire UK, especially as after the witching-hour, not many females were usually online. He came across a blonde girl from Glasgow, who he'd remembered having some interaction with the previous year so decided to cast his line and see if he could entice a bite from her once again.

By this stage, Eric had moved into another shared house, slightly further from his place of work but still much more practical than living with his parents and offering him more independence. The village was much bigger also and he had everything he required within walking distance, from pubs (showing live sports) to convenience stores, takeaways and even a veritable flock of hairdressers for when his eyebrow hairs were so long they were tripping him up.

His new landlady, who was actually three-years younger than Eric, was easy to get along with and despite her scattiness and complete disregard for basic hygiene and tidiness, was a million times better than the last pair of oddballs (if I've told you a million times, stop exaggerating). Eric now had a much bigger bedroom too and despite a mattress thinner than a camping mat, he knew that his landlady was also fine with him having girls over, although he was conscious not to overdo it too early on.

It seemed that the Glaswegian-blonde was indeed interested in Eric and replied immediately following receipt of his message. The two had a good laugh and despite Eric having not wanted to start seeing girls even 50-miles away let alone hundreds, it appeared she wasn't so hung up about distance; which when you considered her backstory you could understand why.

Svetlana was Russian, or at least she spoke Russian and was born in the area of the old Soviet Union now known as Uzbekistan. She'd moved to Portugal and lived there for a few years before she decided to migrate to the UK. So for her 250-miles wasn't such a biggie.

Eric was surprised, to say the least, when Svetlana suggested she caught the train down to meet Eric, not only the travelling-time and expenditure but the fact that she seemed non-plussed to be staying over with a fella she'd never even met before. She was not wet behind the ears it seemed and was roughly the same age as Eric, give or take a couple of years. This was certainly a result Eric thought, especially finding out that his landlady was away that particular weekend too and was enthusiastic for the games to begin (Eric and not his landlady).

Her train wasn't due to arrive at the station nearest to Eric till very late on the Friday. However, it meant Svetlana waiting almost 45-minutes at a station further afield for a connecting service. As Eric didn't like the idea of her waiting on a platform in the cold dead of night on her own, he suggested picking her up in his jalopy and thereby saving her the need.

The station was around ten-miles from Eric's and he arrived in good time for her arrival, waiting outside and feeling his usual nervousness prior to what was in effect D1. Had he not come over all chivalrous and offered to pick her up, then he would definitely have had a few cans of Shandy Bass in the comfort of his own home and helped take the edge off.

Like a number of girls before her, Svetlana had forced their interaction over the telephone a couple of nights prior to the weekend to ensure she liked the sound of him. Despite Eric having been the one to call her, the conversation hadn't got off the ground before he was thinking it had all been a terrible mistake, Svetlana only giving short sharp answers and seeming rather aloof and unfriendly. However, as Eric had questioned her apparent weirdness, then it seemed she relaxed a little more and they ended up having a much better chat than Eric had anticipated. Eric found her Russian accent very sexy, which was an even bigger plus-point in his mind.

With the train having arrived, Eric watched as the passengers all exited the station like a swarm of bees after their hive had been disturbed and was now scanning each of them quickly and methodically trying to ascertain which was his date for the weekend. Eric could only assume that she had been applying last-minute adjustments to her make-up or the like as she was the very last to emerge and walking up to Eric, it was clear that something was awry.

Chapter Eighty-One

Eric Finds His Perfect Partner

Even if Eric had not been feeling in the mood or 100% at the point of meeting a girl for the first time, he would always find an extra bit of enthusiasm or energy from somewhere and wing it. It was natural to want to make a good first impression after all. It seemed Svetlana, however, did not approach things in quite the same manner. For a start, there was not the expected gusto from her when Eric bent down to kiss her on the cheek and she seemed rather angry, not happy to be there.

Walking side-by-side, she never once turned to look at Eric as they made their way to his parked car a couple-of-hundred-yards away. He'd taken her bag from her and walked on the side nearest to the road as the true gentleman that he was (and of course if a car had careered into them then Eric's body would certainly have repelled it and prevented it from reaching Svetlana's). It was Eric doing all of the talking also. He was beginning to question the whole idea of the weekend and could only assume that she hadn't been as impressed with his aesthetics as perhaps she was hoping. Maybe Svetlana was going through an Eric moment when he met Sophie in Burnley.

Having got into the car and started the drive back to Eric's, he asked her if everything was okay, placing his hand on her knee in a bid to show his friendly tactile-side and to try to reassure her. She mentioned that she was a little tired but was fine. Eric was still not convinced and hoped getting back and able to fully relax would be just the (gin and) tonic she needed. Eric knew he fancied her as soon as he saw her, despite the only light coming from inside the station entrance and from the sporadic streetlamps en route to his car. She definitely looked better in real-life than of her photos, which was again another very pleasing result.

Arriving back and entering the house, Svetlana was steadily coming around and looking a lot happier. She confessed that when she'd seen Eric, she realised she fancied him more than she'd expected and this had made her feel much more nervous. It appeared that when Svetlana was nervous it affected her ability to speak, smile or function normally or so Eric conjectured. She was glad when he touched her knee in the car as it had indeed helped her to relax. 'Bingo bango bongo', Eric thought and it seemed any potential danger had been averted.

As it was pretty late by this time and Svetlana notably a little tired after her journey, Eric suggested that they should retire for the night. Eric had been keen to point out before she made the trip that there was a spare room at the house but it was noticeable that they both definitely wanted to share a bed together. At least that way they could continue to chat and get to know one another more and it was immaterial to Eric whether a sexy Russian girl just happened to be lying next to him in bed with very little on (cough cough).

Svetlana was mightily impressive and as she confirmed she had forgotten to bring her pyjamas (that old chestnut he thought) she asked to borrow one of Eric's T-shirts. This only helped to arouse Eric even further, the prospect of her wearing the shortest T-shirt he could possibly find in his wardrobe making him salivate as though contemplating devouring a packet of pickled onion Monster Munch (I bet you just did right?). Eric pretended to cover his eyes whilst Svetlana disrobed and put his shirt on before she slid into bed next to him. Eric was now officially in dreamland.

It was no surprise then when things got a little fruity between them. After some kissing and general petting, Eric moved his hands on to her boobs and was delighted to find that she was indeed a rather well-endowed young lady. Could things get any better he thought? After she got up to use the bathroom (not for a bath) Eric jokingly told Svetlana that when she returned, he wanted her to take her knickers off before getting back into bed.

As luck would have it Svetlana did not need asking twice. Eric was now pinching himself. She was indeed fitter than Steve Backley's dog and Eric wanted to explore her entire body, now naked under the duvet next to his (Eric having ensured that his big leg was undercover at all times of course). As Eric made his way down Svetlana's body, spending quite a time around her chest area for some reason, she suddenly held firmly onto his shoulder and began coaxing him back up towards her face; Eric didn't know if this was code for Aunt Flo being in town but then as he ignored her and continued south, she gave up trying.

Svetlana had enjoyed Eric's attentiveness very much judging by her reactions and she was now longing for things to proceed. Afterwards, following full intercourse and as the pair were relaxing together, Svetlana mentioned the reason she'd tried to prevent him from inspecting her lady garden was that she'd been so underwhelmed by previous men's attempts at satisfying her in that department. 'Those men weren't me' Eric thought, feeling rather pleased with himself as she had been blissfully happy at the result. Eric was also surprised to hear that the others she'd been with (and therefore assuming a number of the male population out there too) were sadly unaware of the finer workings of a woman's genitalia (still) and must have been simply mimicking a golden retriever licking cream off a doormat.

Having been laughing at each other's jokes and Eric asking some pertinent questions about her life back in the old Soviet Union, they were getting on better than Eric could remember having gotten on with any girl before (and that was some accolade). He was not only very attracted to Svetlana but she was also highly intelligent, spoke perfect English, shared a similar sense of humour, had never had children, no pets and the whole USSR/Uzbekistan backstory made her seem infinitely more interesting than most. He was mightily impressed with everything about her but hey, this was Eric remember and he reminded himself that he needed to reel his positive thoughts in and not get too carried away too soon. When something appeared too good to be true; he knew there was always a catch.

Still, this was the first time for as long as Eric could remember that a girl was seemingly ticking every conceivable box he could think of; and there were a few of them as you know. Eric had that feeling; the same feeling you got when looking for a new house when within seconds of entering the door, you realised almost immediately that it was the one for you.

Before Svetlana came down to see him, Eric had told himself that it would only be a one-off bit of fun as she lived too far away to even consider a long-term relationship. However, he'd now had to backtrack somewhat and was now confident that he wanted to see her again. If that meant risking his life with a trip north of the border then so be it (check out episode 5: Scotch Mist in Garth Marenghi's Darkplace).

Eric played the consummate host and had been sure to show Svetlana the sights, surprised that the historical landmarks in town had been superseded by the sighting of a squirrel. Surely they had bigger and better wildlife in her home country? he thought. However, glad to see she was having a good-time, Eric waited patiently as she felt the need to capture a hundred photographs of the common rodent and most bird lovers' nemesis.

Chapter Eighty-Two

A Douglas in the Ointment

Finishing their weekend with a meal in a swanky pub, Eric was rather disappointed that it would soon be over and Svetlana would no longer be on-tap so to speak. However, just as Eric had allowed himself to be drawn in by the Russian beauty, his enthusiasm would be dashed; well this was Eric and there was always something that would scupper his plans if they were going far too well after all.

Midway through her Hunter's Chicken (okay, well maybe not that swanky) the conversation had turned to friends and Svetlana mentioned her best friend… Douglas. Yes, Douglas. If there was one thing that Eric couldn't feel comfortable about, it was a girl with a male best friend. His twin brother's best friends were mostly female but Ernie was gay. However, Douglas, although Scottish, was not a jockey it seemed and in fact a much older married man; the news setting off alarm bells all over the shop.

Eric's built-up positivity about Svetlana suddenly seeped away like the air inside a balloon that had landed on a bed of nails and then been twatted with a mallet. He had now gone from liking everything about her to looking forward to dropping her off at the station so he could get on with searching for his next date. Eric thought it was simply unbelievable how these things always seemed to conspire against him and was left thinking 'what's the fucking point?'

It must be said that Eric did turn in an Oscar-winning performance for the final couple of hours with Svetlana, not wishing to make it obvious to her of his abject disappointment. It wasn't simply that she had a male best friend, which he thought a smidge odd but once Svetlana had started talking about Douglas, she wouldn't let-up.

It seemed that Dougie (as Eric would refer to him afterwards) had been responsible for Svetlana's last relationship break-up, having felt the need to have a run-in with him over his perceived treatment of her. Whether or not justified; with Eric not privy to all of the details; it seemed the fella had thought 'fuck this for a game of soldiers' and left Svetlana after three-years or so. No, Douglas had an ulterior motive and it was clear to Eric. Svetlana described how he spent a lot of time with her on days out and the like, had started learning Russian (as you do) and even accompanied her twice-a-week to quite possibly the least manly form of keep fit there was; Zumba.

Realising that Douglas was married with a kid, Eric couldn't help but ask whether Svetlana was also friends with his wife and her response had led to all 12-members of the jury in his cranial member passing the same verdict. 'No, she doesn't like me or the fact he spends his time with me… they're going through a rough time and Douglas thinks he will be leaving her once their son is a little bit older'. Case dismissed.

Eric was now laughing inwardly to himself about how Svetlana was apparently so naive not to see that Douglas obviously had plans for her and it wasn't something Eric was going to entertain whatsoever. There wouldn't be a second-leg away to Glasgow.

In fact, after some further thought, Eric realised it wasn't naivety at all but more Svetlana's clever manipulation, taking advantage of someone who would stop at nothing to help her out whenever she needed it; whether a lift to work or someone to help knock some shelves up for her at home. Yes, it was obvious that Svetlana wasn't romantically interested in Douglas but it was certainly not a normal arrangement as far as Eric was concerned.

Speaking of lifts, Svetlana let it slip that it was, in fact, good old Dougie who was picking her up late from Glasgow station when she arrived back on the train after midnight. 'So he knows you were coming down to see me then?' Eric asked hearing the unsurprising news.

'Nooo!' she announced in her Ruskie-Scotch accent. 'I told Douglas that I was going to see an old girlfriend as he wouldn't have let me come if I'd mentioned it was a fella I hadn't seen before… he is very protective of me you know' she continued.

'No shit' Eric thought, now smiling back at her with hollow eyes, computing how the situation was now sounding more and more ridiculous.

After Eric dropped her off at the station and watched as the train departed, he began typing his John Deere message out within the notes feature on his iPhone, in preparation for copying and pasting into WhatsApp and sending once Svetlana had confirmed her safe arrival home.

She was devastated to hear that Eric was no-longer interested and made even sadder to learn it was due to Douglas and nothing else whatsoever. It put her in a rather difficult position as she felt she was now caught between Eric and Douglas, although she'd tried her best to convince Eric that there was absolutely nothing going on between them.

As Eric was unwilling to change his mind about the situation, he'd joked to his mates that he'd probably get a call from Douglas next to have a go at him. In Eric's mind, this would prove him correct and that Dougie was indeed an unhealthy presence in Svetlana's life, with far too much importance and emphasis put on him.

Well, stone the crows, pick the stones back up and throw them once more at the crows; Eric received a voicemail from Douglas. The situation had now reached Def-Con 4, meaning Eric had quite simply had enough of the whole ridiculous carry-on, now delirious through bewilderment.

Eric didn't listen to the five-minute appeal from Dougie through embarrassment although did allow his mates to listen to it with him out of the room. They said it sounded like he was reading from a script as there was no umming and arring and the piece was far too long to be considered off the cuff. To this day, Eric has not listened to the message. Despite Svetlana's best efforts, Eric remained stoical about the whole matter and their communication petered out.

Chapter Eighty-Three

Winking Hedgehog

Although still rather disappointed at Douglas having scuppered what was quite possibly the most compatible match he'd ever found, Eric was soon back in the saddle and checking out the other runners and riders online. It wasn't long before he'd spied another feline showing promise, although this time it was definitely not a long-term relationship he was after.

Eric was a night owl; in fact, he was usually still up when the owls had set their alarms and hit the nest and could usually get by with as little as four or five hours kip. One particular night, after the clock had struck two; he noted from a select number of women still active on Match, that one was not too bad looking and lived less than ten miles away.

As she seemed to be pretty intelligent and had passed all Eric's initial-stage prerequisite checks, he decided to strike up conversation with her. Having also come through that with flying colours, Eric suggested they should meet up. As she was also keen, she asked where the best place to lock horns would be. After thinking long and hard, Eric came up with a rather spontaneous reply; 'have you ever heard of The Duck Pond Inn? I hear it's quite nice'.

One thing to mention at this juncture was her age. It seemed rather ironic that not only had the youngest date he'd had been called Beth but now at the other end of the spectrum, here was the oldest and her name was Beth also. Eric had jumped two generations in as many months. Young Beth had been 22 and now old/er Beth tipped the scales at 57 (quickly approaching 58) some 35 years between them.

Despite her being very much older, Eric was impressed with her natural beauty after meeting in the flesh, the smoothness of her skin nearer to that of a peach than a dried prune. She was extremely positive and smiley which Eric liked and he was getting a very good vibe indeed.

After a very pleasant evening together, Beth invited Eric to sit in her car outside and they enjoyed a bit of kissing, which led onto some heavy petting; Eric even sliding his hand into her knickers at one point to check out her punani, her dress having only just covered her crotch all night as she was keen to showcase her pins. As they were now both hot under the pantaloons, they thought it best to leave it there and arranged for a further meet-up; this time at Beth's given she had now satisfied herself that Eric was not a weirdo on the safe and neutral grounds of The Duck Pond.

Now it was obvious to Eric that you don't get to the lion's share of 60 years on planet earth, having been married for a sizeable chunk of that and sprouting out a number of (now) grown-up kids without having hit the ceiling in terms of confidence and experience. There was surely nothing else to worry about. This was very true of Beth after Eric rocked up to hers for D2.

It was strange that she didn't wear any make-up at her age but great if you could carry it off. Beth was just on the cusp in Eric's professional opinion, now having seen her during daylight hours. As she'd been expecting Eric over and given the plan was to spend an evening in, then she was dressed only in a nightie with absolutely not a stitch underneath; something that Eric would learn only ten-minutes in.

After fixing themselves a drink in the kitchen, they'd retreated into the lounge and got comfy on the sofa together, Beth electing to lie with her head resting against Eric's chest and her legs stretched out away from him like an old married couple. As a result of her lying down, however, part of her nightie had gathered further up her body and her hedgehog was now fully exposed and winking repeatedly at Eric. It was all a bit too familiar so soon he thought and it was obvious she wanted Eric's schlong sooner rather than later.

There was nothing wrong with Beth at all, especially for her age but Eric had a moment where the reality broke-through and he was left wondering what on earth had prompted him to think that dating a much older woman was a good idea, especially as he was a good-looking fella and could still easily attract someone far younger and less wrinkly (exhibit A: The other much younger Beth).

Having spent a couple of hours chilling out in the lounge, she hinted at taking matters upstairs and so after the usual use of the ablutions and with Beth already having turned out the lights, then the pair got into bed together. It was pitch-black and Eric couldn't see a thing. Yes, it was good that his leg would remain a mystery to her but he wasn't feeling the love whatsoever. I mean, one word of this leaked to his friends or colleagues and he would be the butt of Wayne Rooney granny jokes and other such banter.

Beth made her way down the bed and it was obvious she was making a bee-line for Eric's love truncheon, soon relieving Eric of his pants and getting to grips with his hallowed appendage (his penis not his big leg). Eric may not have been that enthused to want to slide it into her but there was nothing wrong with a blowjob he thought as he lay back waiting for the involuntary spasms to begin.

However, after twenty-seconds or so Eric realised that the experience was far from pleasurable and was even moderately uncomfortable bordering on a dull pain. 'What the fuck was she up to down there?' he thought, pictures entering his head of someone slicing a wafer-thin piece of doner off his block of meat. Eric was far too polite to pull her up (in both senses of the phrase) about it so did his best to pretend he was enjoying it.

Realising that Eric was still only packing a semi at best, Beth stopped with her mouth torture to Eric's relief and then, feeling around his chopper, she made a random but slightly surprising comment. 'You need to cut these pubes off… it's not good'. Eric was now rather embarrassed. He knew that Beth was probably looking for a comeback on noticing he'd not managed to raise a stiffler despite her best efforts but the observation did little to increase his chances of doing so after that.

The next day and after returning home from a disappointing sleep-over with Beth, he got right to it. Eric now felt obliged to give his thatch some much-needed attention following the encounter. To be fair, he did see where she was coming from and after having used the shared kitchen scissors as a cutting aid, he was left with enough hairs on the bathroom floor to fill a standard-size pillowcase.

The difference was enormous and it was great news for Eric. He now felt as sleek as a blue marlin cutting through the water, his coefficient drag like the nose of Concorde and after removing the foliage from around his fuselage; the sight was now a lot more impressive. Eric questioned why he hadn't done it years before but the answer was plain and simple; he wasn't big on self-groomery.

Both the Beths had made one thing abundantly clear to Eric. Coupled with his previous dates and relationships, he knew he needed to find someone around the same age as him (give or take at most three-years) if there was going to be any real chance of a successful long-term fix to his singledom. It made sense really as it was more likely that they'd have things in common for a start.

Chapter Eighty-Four

The Doctor Will See You Now

Having decided that online dating had become a little too tiresome, with the same old faces and none of the new ones doing very much for him at all; Eric had no real compunction to re-subscribe. Faced with less than 24-hours before being unable to view and communicate with girls on the site, Eric went on a final assault messaging all of the 'potentials' and dropping his cellphone number into their inboxes.

Eric had also learnt that even after losing his subscription services, he could still elicit girls' phone numbers as Match would show him the first few words of any message that he received to act as an enticement method for him to reach for his debit card. However, Eric found if he included a sentence within his profile to tell any admirers to simply start their messages to him with their number, then bingo bango bongo, he could contact them away from the site.

There were a couple of takers but only one that really came across as a goer to Eric. Her name was Zoë and he'd forgotten what she looked like by the time she'd got in touch. This was thanks to Match hazing over the photos of the ladies if you weren't a paid-up member (and her WhatsApp DP was of her dog; yes, Eric was desperate at this stage). The situation was therefore similar to purchasing an unlabeled can from the bargain-bucket at the supermarket, not knowing what you got till you opened it; could be macaroni and cheese or a can of Winalot Chum. However, Zoë's messages were positive, grammatically correct and with no sign of frequently misspelled words.

Eric was therefore agreeable to risk a meet-up and as luck would have it, she was happy to come to his for a coffee that very same day. 'Cashback!' Eric thought and he waited curiously to find out what she looked like in the flesh.

Whether Eric had let his standards drop somewhat or whether he was just desperate for a shag as mentioned, Zoë wasn't up there in the top echelon of Eric's historical conquests but then he had dated a lot worse. It seemed he'd opened the can to find sliced peaches in fruit juice; not his favourite but at least more edible than dog food. She was slightly older than Eric in years but in his opinion looked much older in body, although would never have said that to her of course.

She was a doctor and was a very confident type, slightly jolly-hockey-sticks posh-sounding and with a curly barnet. After getting on famously over a coffee in the back garden, Eric had even got away with a kiss on the lips after half-an-hour or so and it was evident that Zoë was wet for him.

Moving back into the house, Eric suggested they went upstairs, the house he rented with his landlady not conducive to sitting downstairs due to the dogs but there was an ulterior reason for the suggestion anyway. Despite her initial surprise, Zoë was happy to venture up and the two sat on Eric's bed chatting.

It wasn't long until they began to get on even better and Zoë seemed to have very little in the way of shyness. The two had lain down together by this point, still conversing but touching each other and kissing sporadically throughout. Eric then decided to try his luck, realising that Zoë seemed to be enjoying his attentions and was pleasantly surprised when after he started to undress her, she was happy to take up the mantle herself.

Considering they'd only met around an hour ago this was some development and Eric didn't know where it was going to end (although he had a very good idea). Zoë, now lying next to Eric in only her underwear was getting rather hot under the collar and a fully clothed Eric continued to test her resolve and see how far she was willing to go.

Eric mentioned to her how he'd like to see her boobs and it seemed Zoë was in a very accommodating mood that day as she moved her hands around her back to unfasten her bra with no hesitation whatsoever. Blimey, Eric thought as it slipped down her body to the floor next to the bed…' the doctor will see you now'. Having enjoyed himself with her medium-sized funbags, Eric was feeling pretty turned on himself and there was only one piece of clothing that was preventing him from seeing her as God intended. Surely she wouldn't allow Eric to see her naked so soon… would she?

It seemed Zoë was putty in Eric's hands and she was only too happy for him to relieve her of her final undergarment. However, what Eric was greeted with was not exactly what he'd been hoping for. No, it wasn't a penis (again). If ever the term 'a fanny like a dropped omelette' was apt then here was quite possibly the best example Eric had ever seen. To add insult to injury, she also mentioned that Aunt Flo was in the middle of a short staycation and therefore it remained just a heavy-petting session in any case.

There would be many other opportunities in the near future though as Eric had scarcely ever known a woman with such a sexual appetite. Perhaps it was her stressful job. She'd pop round a couple of times a week in and around her shift-pattern, predominantly turning up to the house first thing in the morning on her way home from work.

As Eric was, more often than not, still in bed, then it meant her slipping in next to him and Eric slipping into her. Eric had never experienced such animalistic sweaty sex before and it seemed that the two just seemed to bond extremely well. It would last quite a while as well (hence the sweat), Eric not as fit as he once was although Zoë was dripping too after a climax had been reached.

They'd then lay next to each other in a relaxed glistening state and watch a couple of episodes of Game of Thrones, which Eric was surprised to learn she'd never seen before, especially given how much sex there was in it. This routine took place for around two months, the pair of them soon realising that this was a relationship borne out of a sexual requirement and nothing else (or perhaps also a chance for Zoë to see the end of the very popular fantasy series) Eric already aware that he was certainly not interested in anything long-term.

Despite the majority of their time spent in the confines of Eric's bed, they did manage to get out and take in a couple of decent (long) walks in the countryside, which Eric felt would at least help stave off a likely skin disorder due to a lack of vitamin D.

Chapter Eighty-Five

Caught With His Pants Down

Eric had often heard and been a frequent user of the phrase 'caught with your pants down' but had not really given any thought to the saying in its truest form. That was until one hot summer's day when Zoë had returned with Eric to his house following one of their constitutionals.

On returning home it was evident that there was nobody else in; his landlady quite often out, attending to her horses, working or visiting family. Having spent a few hours getting hot and sweaty on their walk, the two were feeling just a little bit horny but it appeared Zoë was on a tight schedule and had to leave. Stood in the hallway near to the front door, they gave each other a kiss goodbye, one kiss leading to another and then on to other things.

Before you could say 'What's that you got in your pocket?' Zoë was knelt in front of Eric with his jeans and undercrackers pulled down slightly (Eric only too aware of his big leg) and reacquainting her tonsils with his flexible friend. It seemed rather animalistic and exciting all at the same time, the unusual backdrop providing more than a soupcon of jeopardy, the front door potentially swinging open and someone walking in.

As Zoë was getting into her rhythm and Eric maintaining eye-contact on the entrance, both were in for a shock. Eric's landlady suddenly appeared. Well, it was a potential hazard they'd considered after all. However, she hadn't appeared through the front door to which Eric had been giving his full attention. No; she had instead come in through the back entrance and from the garden terrace outside, where it appeared she'd fallen asleep sunbathing. Eric hadn't even considered checking there earlier when they'd arrived back.

The moment was like something out of a sitcom; Eric and Zoë hurriedly diving into the entrance of the nearest room to avoid detection, Eric pulling his pants up and doing his best to fasten them in world-record time (Norris McWhirter stood not six-feet away with a stopwatch and clipboard invigilating).

Turning his head instinctively when hearing the unexpected sound at the back door, Eric had seen her walk in but then move in the opposite direction towards the kitchen not ten-feet away and begin filling the kettle under the tap. 'Pherewww' he thought as had she been making her way to the toilet then she would certainly have come across the pair at close quarters.

Eric was almost certain that she must have seen his funstick (not bragging about his size but she was pretty close) and his girlfriend knelt rather conspicuously in front of him with a gob-full of bratwurst. Zoë made a timely escape at that point and Eric was left on his own, expecting to receive a tongue-lashing from his landlady; but nothing was ever said. To this day, she'd not mentioned anything about it and Eric was left wondering whether she'd purposely pretended not to have seen anything as it was far too embarrassing to have to deal with.

It was almost as embarrassing as the time that Eric had been seeing Emma Mark I again after their short sabbatical. Given that they'd missed each other and were feeling even more loved-up after a few drinks in town, Eric had instigated a sexual encounter in the disabled toilets on their way out of a pub; the handrails having proved quite practical as it happened.

However, on exiting the facilities, they were greeted by a man sat in his wheelchair and waiting patiently outside. Eric and Emma said nothing, passing him swiftly and appearing like the berry characters from the Ribena ads, their embarrassment obvious and the man somewhat shocked by the pair emerging. That was never how Eric had envisaged such liaisons turning out but then this was Eric and things rarely turned out as expected for him as you now know.

As Zoë had children, she'd planned a trip with them at the beginning of the summer holidays and that acted as a natural buffer, to bring their brief sex interlude to an end. She texted Eric to point out that she didn't feel the relationship was going anywhere and as Eric had felt the same for some time, he was happy that she'd been the one to confirm this. Well, it saved him a job and potentially breaking another filly's heart. What she went on to say after though was nothing short of ridiculous and piss-funny.

Eric could only hypothesise that given Zoë's profession, she had delusions of grandeur, imagining herself as some sort of God figure in regards to the sick and needy. This was perhaps why she felt it necessary to diagnose people that she came across, even when there was blatantly no diagnosis to diagnose.

Not content with just going their separate ways in a mature and adult manner, she told Eric that she thought he had Aspergers. 'Whhaaattttt?' Eric had never laughed so much in a long time but he believed that underneath the surprising and hysterical prognosis lay an altogether serious undercurrent of how she and doctors like her could be wrongly diagnosing people through some egotistical or superiority complex. Everyone Eric told, including his friends, found the concept hilarious too. Eric knew what Aspergers was; he'd seen enough episodes of The Undateables and was well aware of the social awkwardness attributed to the condition.

More annoyingly for Eric, after being labelled with Aspergers by Zoë, were her continual attempts at forcing the issue; trying to brainwash him into actually believing he had the condition by the use of subliminal messages. 'Do you have anybody to talk to about it with?', 'I know it's difficult to hear it and accept it' and things of that nature. Eric was 110% certain that he didn't have the condition and could backtrack 10% and still be 100% certain he didn't (Garth Marenghi's Darkplace).

It was only his parents who didn't react with the same laughter that his friends had, somewhat taken in by the doctor it seemed. This made Eric rather angry, that the people who knew him best wouldn't question the diagnosis, them suggesting that he looked into it further and that maybe she had been correct; she was a doctor after all.

Their reaction served only to confirm to Eric that people could be taken in by those holding positions of such responsibility as he'd previously thought. Still; it remained a running joke amongst his friends, whenever something of a social-interaction nature came up in conversation. They had also been keen to recommend that he went shopping at Morrisons on Saturday mornings as they had a two-hour window set-aside for the autistic; the lights dimmed and the till-noises switched off.

Chapter Eighty-Six

Cold Feet Kelly

Having run out of takers regarding the final contacts he'd made prior to his subscription ending, Eric had no other option than to take up Match.con's offer and reopen communication channels once again. His dating antics had been a popular pastime as you may have noticed and without it, Eric was struggling for other things to occupy himself with, especially after dusk and with no football on the tellybox.

Eric was straight back in the zone and like an air traffic controller queuing flights up for landing, he began placing girls that were worth further inspection into a holding pattern. Whilst carrying this out, Eric spotted a familiar face. It was a girl he'd first contacted whilst running the B&B some two-years before.

The girl had seemed absolutely perfect at the time when Eric first clapped eyes on her and after reading her profile. She was of a similar age to him, quite a tall girl at 5'11", slim, lived near his parents' house, no kids, no animals and was an attractive specimen of the female form to boot. So, you can understand how disappointed Eric felt when, despite his efforts, the girl had chosen to ignore him.

Despite the initial setback, he'd noticed her again a year later; just prior to Christmas 2017; deciding to try his Nigel Havers' routine a second time to see if he could win her over. Eric purposely mentioned he'd seen her on the dating merry-go-round for a while and asked if she needed rescuing ('my name's Luke Skywalker and I'm here to rescue you'). Whether it was the timing or something Eric had said, it appeared to work as Kelly, as she was called, responded. Eric was shocked given she'd ignored him previously. Perhaps his luck was about to change for the better.

After the first few messages though, Eric realised immediately that she was woeful at spelling, something he was vehemently against when it came to selecting females and it was the biggest culprit she was guilty of; your and you're. However, despite this heinous crime in the eyes of Eric, he was willing to overlook it just this once as everything else about her still seemed bob-on. Perhaps there was no such thing as perfect Eric conceded reflecting on the past twenty-years and all his trials and tribulations; as long as there was a decent spattering of his desired traits then surely that was the best he was going to achieve.

After a week or so of messaging each other in the build-up to the festivities, with conversation going great-guns, Kelly suddenly vanished off Eric's (air traffic control) radar and he was unable to re-establish contact with her again. He knew she had read his WhatsApp messages asking if she was okay (as the ticks turned blue) but for one reason or another she hadn't felt compelled to reply. It was very frustrating for Eric not to receive any further response from Kelly as the least he expected was an indication as to her sudden U-turn.

Eight months later in August of 2018 and after the sex doctor and he had parted company, he spied her for the third time. Still dumbfounded by her sudden incommunicado prior to Christmas, Eric made contact in a bid to ascertain what had caused her to go AWOL. Surprisingly, Kelly replied and confessed that she'd been very interested in Eric but had got cold feet when things seemed to be developing very nicely.

The pair fell back into conversing like they'd never had a break and Eric was still eager to meet up. Eric was living no more than ten miles from her by this stage and so everything seemed perfic. After getting on famously again, Eric put it to Kelly that he could pick up some alcohol and nibbles and come over to hers that very evening in order to get to know one another a lot better.

Surprisingly for Eric, Kelly accepted the offer and he was left strutting around his bedroom like the cock of the north, pulling out sporadic dance moves and announcing 'Sherrr-mon' (come on) a lot. This was a cracking result for Eric and he certainly hadn't expected the day to pan-out quite like it had.

This particular situation was not the norm though as despite never having met Kelly, Eric was completely devoid of nerves, which was most unusual for him prior to any D1. It seemed that with them having chatted previously and Eric having initially made contact with her over two-years before, he felt less pressure; more like visiting an old friend.

Chapter Eighty-Seven

We Meet at Last

Eric picked up some alcohol and drove to Kelly's, curious to find out what she was like in person. Arriving at her small but perfectly formed house tucked away in the corner of a cul-de-sac, Eric could see that she had a brand-new car, which compared to his jalopy was a further reminder of his fall from grace.

Eric knocked on the front door and after a slight pause it opened and Kelly was stood in front of him. 'Well it's about time really isn't it?' Eric announced laughing, always great at coming up with an icebreaker and to help the girl relax on first meeting. Kelly did look slightly different to her photos but she was still attractive and extremely tall; in fact, her legs appeared to go right the way up to her yayas as his old section head at the bank used to say.

As it was usual protocol for Eric to kiss his dates on the cheek when meeting (Just the once… he wasn't some new-age la-di-da type who went in for the two or even three-cheek technique) Eric was conscious that Kelly had turned to walk back into the living area from the small reception without properly honouring their initial coming together.

Eric, having followed on behind commented on the lack of a kiss and so Kelly came towards him. Without warning she proceeded to kiss him fully on the lips, the pair caught in a rather racy snog from the get-go and not something Eric had either meant or expected. He wasn't complaining though and it was testament to the fact that she was obviously attracted to him and absolutely 100% gagging for his purple-headed warrior.

Sitting down with their drinks, they continued to chat, regaling their previous interactions and finding out more about each other. As had often been a disappointing reality previously, initial conversation was an obvious indicator as to whether the girl was as good as she seemed on paper. Unfortunately, on this occasion, Eric learnt that Kelly was not the last bastion of society that he'd hoped for.

Discussing relationships and their backstories, Eric learnt that Kelly hadn't been in a proper relationship for over 18-years; the split, it appeared, having had a profound effect on Kelly and turning her off the idea of getting too close to a guy ever since. In fact, she was keen to point out that this had been the reason for her 'going dark' the last time Eric and she had been messaging. She basically got cold feet when things were seemingly progressing well with any fella.

Although Kelly was the most anti-relationship girl Eric had ever met, this didn't mean she was a timid, non-confident type (as the initial snog had proved) but it was more the notion that she preferred to do her own thing and have her own space. It wasn't something that Eric had expected to learn from Kelly but as they had literally only just met, then Eric didn't let it worry him too much.

What did worry him though was Kelly's disclosure regarding how she had worked around her unwillingness to entertain a relationship as a highly-sexed woman with needs. It turned out that Kelly had been seeing a married man for almost 18-months and on hearing the news, Eric's initial reaction was to think 'Christ, here we go again' and 'Are there no fucking normal girls left?'.

Eric could rationalise why she saw a married man as it was the perfect answer to her own situation; able to have a constant supply of no-strings sex, without the worry of emotional baggage or potential for a relationship to ensue. The fella in question being much older than Kelly was therefore in dreamland, able to have sex on tap with a much younger girl and yet still able to run home and play happy families for most of the week. 'I think that's what they call a win-win siduation' he thought to himself.

Eric was suddenly put off Kelly in a big way, what with her self-confessed moral inadequacies (I know; the cheek of Eric) and as she'd met the fella in question at work, it also raised doubts regarding the likelihood of her future interactions. Eric was rather quick to make his feelings known about her carry-on antics but instead of Kelly showing him the door, she stated that she was looking to move away from seeing the married man and towards considering a relationship. Eric made his position perfectly clear; continue to see the fella and she wouldn't be seeing him again. It was as simple as that.

There were definitely a lot of things Eric liked about Kelly and they got on really well, finding each other funny and having a very relaxed time together. Come bedtime and Eric realised he would be staying over; well he'd been drinking and there was obviously no way he could drive home.

This was no trouble at all to Kelly and despite having a spare room had assumed they would be spooning up together in her bed. It was again another occasion for Eric to feel self-conscious and run the gauntlet of keeping his big leg a secret from her and without any pyjama bottoms to mask his deformity, he would have to rely on his stealth-tactics once again.

Having disrobed whilst Kelly was in the bathroom, Eric had now gotten under the duvet and was confident that Kelly would not have the opportunity to notice, the ambient light from a bedside lamp not bright enough and Eric a dab hand at ensuring to keep his leg undercover at all times. Being semi-naked in bed together was notably not conducive to an early night and it wasn't long before the pair were at it like two wild otters.

Kelly had an incredible body and her legs were so long Eric worried he'd run out of spittle, although having ensured he'd got rid of his chewing-gum before getting underway this time. The sex had been right up there with the best he'd had, even better than with doctor Sex.

Eric put the magnificent intercourse with Kelly down to three reasons; one, he was attracted to her and she turned him on something rotten; two, they seemed to complement each other perfectly (think sword and scabbard) and three; Eric noticed some great results from having attended to his thatch, the increased sensitivity making him wish he'd trimmed it back a long time ago ('… in a galaxy far far away').

Chapter Eighty-Eight

You Can't Win Them All

Eric was now even more taken with Kelly and he definitely wanted to see her some more. However, having left at an ungodly hour on the Sunday morning, after being told her dad and brother were on their way around to carry out some home maintenance, Kelly reverted to type and messaged Eric to say she didn't think it would work between them and wished him luck in the future. Eric was once more flabbergasted (his 'gasts had never been so flabbered'… Frankie Howerd in Up Pompeii).

Everything about their evening together had been top-drawer and he couldn't believe that she wasn't interested anymore. After a carefully crafted response from Eric, it turned out that there were a few reasons for her admission, which stemmed from the claustrophobia she'd felt having spent the night with him; more accurately, the fact that she felt somewhat restricted and unable to relax properly.

Unbeknown to Eric, sleep for Kelly was already a difficult subject and something she'd struggled with for many a year. This was mainly as a result of her having type-1 diabetes. Having worked with someone with the same condition, Eric was aware of the continual need to self-regulate insulin levels via injections and monitor blood pH levels 24-7. It therefore seemed reasonable to Eric that Kelly would feel rather awkward with someone with her but confirmed that it didn't and wouldn't bother him as long as she was alright.

There was also another reason for Kelly to pull the plug and that reason was slightly less of a biggie in Eric's eyes. As she was a bit of a clean freak (which was a thumbs-up from Eric, himself a little anal when it came to house cleaning as you will have noted) it seemed she'd not taken too kindly to finding piss all over her bathroom floor. Eric assumed her actual words on discovering the urine puddles would have been along the lines of 'You're taking the piss!'

Eric was very apologetic on hearing her gripe but assured her that it was a well-known fact that men found it an impossibility to aim properly after sex, the urinary tract having been somewhat furred by remnants of love juice, an effect similar to sticking your finger in a tap and then turning it on. Eric assured Kelly he would sit down to piss from that day forth if it really was a deal-breaker.

Given he had a way with words and could sell shampoo to Telly Savalas, the two met up again and agreed to see how things went as it was obvious that there was definitely a great deal of scope. It soon became apparent that Kelly was just not used to a fella treating her well and she was pleasantly surprised at Eric's chivalry and caring gestures. In fact, Kelly repeatedly told Eric to stop being so nice to her, somewhat convinced she was not deserving of such actions. Eric ignored her and continued to be himself nevertheless and Kelly would just have to get used to it.

An example of Eric's chivalry took place after the pair had gone for a day out to the isle of Anglesey, having stopped off for breakfast at an American diner. It wasn't particularly warm inside as they ate their extremely unhealthy fodder and Eric could see that Kelly was shivering slightly.

Without a second thought (for his own personal safety) Eric unzipped his gilet and passed it to her, Kelly happy to accept the offering of an additional layer. Eric hadn't thought it was anything out of the ordinary whatsoever but a few days later, Kelly mentioned to him how it had been the nicest thing a fella had ever done for her. 'Blimey' Eric thought; 'this one is easily pleased', Kelly having reacted to the gesture as though he'd just saved a busload of schoolchildren from certain peril.

Eric had a fantastic time with Kelly on the Emerald Isle as he called it (sorry my Irish friends) despite the inclement weather and he could see Kelly felt the same way. Perhaps this relationship was going places after all. Unfortunately, though, Kelly was still finding it very difficult to adapt to a man in her life and it became easier for her not to have Eric stay the night; instead seeing him for a few hours and then ejecting him.

Eric recognised that Kelly did have a very responsible job and could see that he was causing her a distraction, especially as he'd spent their first night in bed together chatting till 7:00 a.m. It was imperative in her mind that she didn't allow the same to happen again and it was, therefore, easier for her to suggest that Eric returned home to his own bed.

Eric saw Kelly a few more times but just as it seemed they were making progress on one occasion, then the next it was back to Kelly being cold and unaccommodating. Eric could relate to how she was behaving as he'd been just like that when he first started on his journey with girls and relationships. She had notably had her fingers burnt by her first proper boyfriend (like Eric had with Becky) between her late teens and early twenties and the fallout from that had been telling.

Eric could also see that she had a very negative opinion of herself and that she preferred a life of stability and familiarity over one that would possibly risk her being hurt again. Eric found it a very sad situation but ultimately, it wasn't for him to try to change her and he would have to respect that she was just not cut-out for a long-term relationship.

The final nail in the coffin came when Eric came clean about his own situation, with no job, renting a room and having little in the way of money. By this time, Eric had lost his sexual mojo with Kelly and confirming this to her meant that she saw no reason whatsoever for staying in contact and wished Eric all the best in the future (once again).

Although no hard evidence to prove it, it was obvious to Eric from their final message exchanges that Kelly had gone back, cap in hand, to the married man to resume meet-ups. It was a little sad Eric thought, given that he felt she had a lot going for her and in his mind was better than that. It was another example of when Eric just had to accept that other people were different and although inextricable to him, it must have made perfect sense to her.

Chapter Eighty-Nine

The Also-Rans

Having met well over 100 felines over the years, not all of Eric's interactions made much of a splash in his life. That was the lottery of online dating. There were enough of them that had created lasting memories for good or bad reasons as you've read but this final section of the book is dedicated to those that only played small walk-on parts or minor cameo appearances that shaped Eric's dating path. One thing that he realised over the years was the old adage 'there's nowt so queer as folk' was indeed very true and probably the reason why the saying has survived the test of time.

One of Eric's first outings on the dating-front happened to take place in Warrington (Yes, little did he know that the town would become such a hotbed for him in the future) and was an invitation to the woman's house; we'll call her Christine. This gave Eric his first cause to use his newly purchased shagnav, his local geography second to everyone and the device's importance coming easily within Eric's top five inventions of all time (together with contact lenses, online dating, microwave oven and of course the flush toilet).

Christine was quite a bit older than Eric but judging by her profile photos, he was still very keen to meet up. On arrival, Eric didn't want to tempt fate so left his Pierre Cardin travel bag in the car, which he'd parked down the road to make it seem less obvious to the neighbours in case he was staying over. Christine was very easy on the eye, quite petite, with blonde hair and a very soft southern accent, which he liked.

Having literally stepped across the threshold and walked into her kitchen at the back of the house, she explained to Eric that she had three sons, aged 7, 8 and 9 and it was a dream of hers to one day take them to Disneyworld in Florida if she could ever afford it. Eric's initial thoughts were 'I'm not frickin' Noel Edmonds and this isn't an episode of Noel's Christmas Presents' feeling like she was expecting him to whip out his cheque-book and make Huey, Dewey and Louie the happiest kids in that part of Warrington. Instead, Eric elected for 'riiiigggggghhhhht' and a slow nod of his head as he hinted that the two sorted out some drinks.

It was amazing what a few alcoholic beverages could do to change someone's apparent shyness and respectability as Christine went from a veritable wallflower to dancing to Girls Aloud in her lounge and jumping all over Eric in a very tactile manner. It seemed Eric needn't have worried about whether she would fancy him and before it got too late, he was collecting his stuff from the car.

This was Eric's first online date where he actually fancied the girl and things were looking very positive from where he stood. The pair ascended the stairs to the bedroom at the end of the evening and Christine appeared in her pyjamas after vanishing momentarily. Naturally, Eric had already slipped under the duvet, masking both his large appendages.

Christine was a massive tease; confirming she didn't want to have sex at first but after they had enjoyed a bit of kissing and heavy petting and having slipped out of her overgarments, then she suddenly had no arguments whatsoever with Eric helping her out of her knickers. After having enjoyed classic intercourse and relaxing together, Eric remembered seeing Christine get up and walk naked out of the room to fetch some Orangina from downstairs (can you still buy that?) and thinking how easy the whole process had been from chatting online to now having sex with a beautiful girl.

He was certainly buoyed by the prospect of what lay ahead. 'Did things get any better than this?' he thought. There was no way he wanted to see Christine again though, given her disclosure of Tom, Dick and Harry and besides, he was aware that there were hundreds of girls out there to be discovered. Still, it had been a very enjoyable evening and a first real positive for Match.com.

Chapter Ninety

Bon Appétit

It was inevitable that not all (in fact most) dates would amount to very much. In some cases, they wouldn't last very long at all, especially as Eric knew that you could make your mind up almost instantaneously as to whether you fancied the other person and it didn't take too much longer to ascertain if they blatantly annoyed you. As we have already discovered, Eric realised early on in his dating career that there was no real point wasting time through online or WhatsApp messages as it was the meeting and talking in person that confirmed levels of chemistry.

If there was another thing Eric learnt early doors; it was not to allow himself to get too carried away with any prospective dates. Most of the time his imaginations just didn't materialise and he would be left in abject disappointment and in the knowledge that he would never regain the time or financial outlay he'd sacrificed to meet them.

One such example was a doctor from Manchester; the venue? The Duck Pond Inn of course. Claire was a very intelligent woman and messages between them had been fresh and playful. However, when meeting up, Eric soon realised that she was far too posh and living with her head right up her own arse. She was the type to refer to herself as a foodie and despite not saying it on her profile; she definitely contravened point 34 of his dating pre-requisites, preferring the 'finer things in life'.

Eric was a very down-to-earth guy and couldn't abide with anyone believing them self to be better than anyone else. He would soon learn another lesson that day and that was to avoid agreeing to a bite to eat on D1, which had been the plan before meeting Claire. Despite Eric wanting to leave immediately, she was still hungry and so after mentioning this, the couple were shown to a table and the menus distributed to each of them. Eric's levels of politeness prevented him from curtailing the date at that point, aware that it felt wrong to leave her eating by herself.

Eric, therefore, selected the smallest and cheapest starter he could find; garlic bread. Claire, on the other hand, had selected a somewhat more substantial meal involving Eric's pet hates; mushrooms, or work of the devil as he referred to them. Eric just had to be patient and after devouring his starter (for ten) in record time (spying Norris on the adjacent table with his stopwatch at the ready) he sat waiting for Claire to finish her entrée.

As soon as she had placed the last morsel into her mouth then Eric was, at last, a free man, making no bones about the lacklustre date to Claire. 'Well, I'm sure I'm not the only one who feels this hasn't gone quite as hoped' he announced getting up from his seat and blazing a path to the till to pay for their food.

Claire had been quick to follow, not particularly wanting to sit at the table on her own and caught-up with Eric as he completed his transaction. They chatted for a while in the car park, Eric having reverted to type and started smoking a cigarette. Claire was horrified to see him puffing away (she was a doctor after all so frowned upon it more than usual).

It was obvious that she thought a lot more about Eric than tother way around, Claire even bestowing upon Eric the title of 'best person I've ever met from round here' and with this accolade pinned to his chest like an imaginary rosette, she got into her car and drove off.

Eric knew that he would need to develop a tougher stance with any future dates that didn't pass muster as his time was important to him and he didn't want to waste it if there was obviously no chemistry between him and a girl.

Chapter Ninety-One

'Kissin' in the Back Row of the Movies'

Another very early dating foray came with a girl from Bolton (in fact the Lancashire town would become another popular dating location as it turned out although none of them had really amounted to much). Eric met Wendy at the Middlebrook retail park in Horwich (I know and some would prefer Paris or Rome) where the plan was to convene at Frankie and Benny's for some scran (I know, you'd have thought Eric would have learnt his lesson) and followed up with a movie at the Vue cinema if the date was going well. Wendy was just a little bit peculiar (well she had chosen to meet Eric you're right) bordering on insane and her levels of weirdness were just a little off-putting. Still, she was an attractive girl and so Eric was happy to see past her nerdy traits and concentrate on the aesthetics.

As they were both moderately happy with one another following their meal, then they made their way to the picture house and as it was only customary and polite to do so; Eric gave Wendy the choice of film. Given the weirdness issues regarding Wendy, then Eric wasn't completely surprised that she plumped for a horror film, which at 2:00 p.m. in the afternoon seemed like all kinds of wrong. With an auditorium almost exclusively to themselves, Wendy made haste for the very back row and Eric left thinking 'eye eye'.

Wendy had telescopic legs, her pins amazing to behold and making up about 80% of her height it seemed (think Mr. Tall from the Mr. Men series of books). She was obviously not a shy girl either as within minutes she'd unfurled them over Eric's lap and with the lights dimmed, then he just helped himself, stroking her silky smooth thighs, finding his hand climbing closer and closer to her love mound ('any higher Mr. Bond and my ears will pop'). It turned out that she wasn't that brazen after all and prevented Eric from ascertaining her levels of moisture but it was a pleasurable experience nevertheless and testament to how much he'd enjoyed himself, Eric couldn't remember much about the film afterwards.

Another thing Eric learnt that day was not to go to the cinema on a first date; in fact, perhaps leave it till at least date five he thought. With no chance for conversation, then all the good work he'd laid down prior to the film had evaporated and the pair seemed like complete strangers on exiting and into what felt like the aftermath of a nuclear closer; the bright sunshine difficult to adapt to after spending two-hours in a darkened room watching a predominantly dark screen together. It was another note to take down as far as his future dating escapades were concerned.

Chapter Ninety-Two

'Can I Have an 'O' Please Bob'

Fast forward a decade and during another spell of online dating, Eric had begun chatting with a woman from Southport. Mary was around seven-years older than Eric but her photos seemed pretty decent he thought and agreed she was definitely worth further inspection. The pair met at a swanky pub in Warrington (I'm getting the words mutually and exclusive).

Despite Eric having experienced a great number of dates by then, Mary had been the first to specify meeting in the car park. This was a little bit of a curveball to Eric as he would usually turn up early and lay in wait for his date to arrive whilst working on his Dutch courage. Still, on reflection, it made sense as it not only allowed the couple to check each other out before formalising the occasion with a drink but meant Mary, as the female, not having to wander into a pub on her own and potentially feel vulnerable. There was also avoiding the potentially embarrassing situation from not recognising each other once in the pub, which Eric had been guilty of on a couple of occasions in the past ('Hey!; you trying to chat up my wife?').

Sitting in his rusty banger and waiting for Mary, Eric noticed her arrive in her two-seater sports car and alighting with great dignity and class. She was the literal embodiment of the older woman with a high sex-drive, turned out in a long white fur coat (although she <u>was</u> wearing knickers as Eric would ascertain later that evening). With pre-flight checks carried out before push-back and a quick kiss on the lips, the pair entered the pub together. The chemistry was certainly there and but for Mary's broad scouse accent ('sorry, that was just noise') then everything was going tickety-boo. There was also a great deal of tactility on show and it was evident that despite Mary making out that she would never sleep with someone on a first date; she was now gagging for it.

Having finished his allotted one for the road followed by a soft drink, the pair then ventured back out to the car park, Mary trying her best to coax Eric back to hers. Eric was having none of it though as with work the next morning then he just knew it was a bad idea. Instead, the pair sat in Mary's car and things got a little steamy to say the least; Eric managing to familiarise himself with Mary's key areas shall we say (Yes, he probably smelt his fingers afterwards). It was as obvious as the toupee on Donald Trump's head that the pair wanted to see each other again and so Mary invited Eric to her house a few days later.

Eric arrived at Mary's, having traversed the Runcorn Bridge into the unknown lands that Eric had very little knowledge of. In fact, it may just as well have been Narnia as far as he was concerned as he usually just avoided it like the plague. At the beginning of the evening, Mary was putting out the usual spiel about Eric not being able to stay over but as in 99.37% of all previous cases, Eric wouldn't be returning home that night.

Despite Mary's continual questions and her apparent high anxiety levels, the pair ended up in bed together. Eric was happy to introduce her to his throbbing member but it seemed that Mary was just a little reticent about it.

With penetration off the evening menu, then Eric got to grips with pleasuring her in other ways, choosing to use his digits for a change on noticing she was packing pubes. If there was one thing Eric hated above all other things (and possibly even 'shrooms) it was getting hairs in his mouth and worse; down his throat. Eric's dexterity worked a charm and it wasn't long before Mary was coming to the boil nicely, quite a reserved and quiet approach compared to a lot of other women he'd strummed.

Well, Mary's veritable quiet groaning was soon to be replaced by an altogether disconcerting sound and one that would make Eric's libido book a one-way ticket to Ulaanbaatar. It appeared that when Mary orgasmed (which she childishly called an 'O') she would fall into the biggest coughing fit Eric had ever witnessed. The wheezing and coughing and gasping episode carried on for around a minute after climaxing and it was quite possibly the most off-putting occurrence in the bedroom that Eric had ever experienced. She sounded like an Octogenarian on 60-fags a day and any previous desire Eric had to try to bone her had completely evaporated.

It transpired that Mary had asthma so when Eric's magic fingers were propelling her into a frenzied sexual state of overload, her chest had become very tight and the orgasmic release had left her quite literally breathless.

Eric didn't like to criticise a girl if the date had gone tits-up or he wasn't wishing to see them again. On this occasion though, Mary had specifically asked to know why he was no longer interested in her. There was no real way of letting her down easily and so Eric was transparently honest, telling her that the way in which she'd orgasmed had made him feel like he'd just frigged off Thora Hird. Unsurprisingly, he never heard from Mary again.

Chapter Ninety-Three

A Couple of Welsh Birds

Another popular town for finding pussy was Wrexham. One of Eric's first-ever dates was with a red-haired girl (seems Eric must have had a penchant for them) from across the Welsh border and they agreed to meet in a wine bar in town. Beverley, as we'll call her, seemed attractive to Eric and although her communication style was somewhat short and to the point, he felt there was something about her, an original and refreshing frankness, which left him intrigued to discover more.

However, despite being sexually attracted to Beverley on seeing her in the flesh, Eric was about to get rather an unpleasant shock and something that he'd never considered would be a problem with a girl he chose to meet up with (no, this one didn't have a penis either).

After buying them both a drink and sitting down to chat, it wasn't long before Eric began to learn of Beverley's true colours. Thrown in randomly during their conversation, she came out with a barrage of racist jokes; it was like being sat with Bernard Manning or someone who had learnt all his lines and was able to reel them off. She found great delight in telling the jokes and it was she who was laughing at them, not Eric.

Eric was in deep shock, staring hollow-eyed at her, not appreciating her racist views whatsoever and feeling very uncomfortable. It was 2008 and he couldn't believe that there were still those who obviously harboured such views, especially coming from girls like Beverley.

What was most surprising to Eric was that she told her stories and jokes without a second thought as though believing Eric would find her funny, appreciate her humour and be a racist just like her. Beverley couldn't have been further from the truth and having realised how evil she was, then Eric quickly finished his drink, made his excuses and left.

Beverley texted Eric later that day to try to reopen communication with him and so Eric took his opportunity to tell her exactly what he thought about her. Eric was not shocked in the slightest when he received a torrent of abuse as a result but it only highlighted further how there were weirdos out there and something he'd have to keep an eye out for with any future hook-ups.

Speaking of weirdos, Eric saw another girl from the same Welsh town not long after, although this time Eric invited Catherine to come to his house. After agreeing, she turned up and straightaway Eric discovered that her online photos were not what he would describe as indicative of her or harbouring a good-likeness whatsoever. She looked like a serial killer to Eric, hardly an ounce of emotion or expression shown during conversation and slightly cross-eyed too (which just freaked Eric out when catching one or both of them across the lounge). It wasn't exactly how Eric had scripted it.

After noticing a weird lump at the top of her left arm just before it reached her shoulder, Eric had evidently been spotted by Catherine staring at it. Perhaps Eric had seen too many X-Files episodes but it just looked completely unnatural to him. Catherine explained it was her contraception that had been popped in under her skin and she found it infinitely more practical than having to take the pill by the traditional method. This was something that Eric had just never heard of before and the whole concept just blew his mind; girls walking around like micro-chipped animals. In fact, Eric's initial theory had been that she was a prisoner on day-release and it was a tracking-device; well she did seem like she wasn't all there.

Fathoming out that Catherine was also a little fucked-up in the talking stakes, Eric decided to ask her some normal, bog-standard questions to help her relax and to come out of her shell a bit. He started by asking her about her previous relationships. It soon became apparent, though, that Catherine's backstory also pointed towards weird goings-on and gave Eric even more reason to feel uncomfortable.

She explained that she had arrived home one evening to find that her ex-partner had hung himself from the furled loft-ladder jutting out from the hatch above the landing. Next to his body lay a handwritten message, together with a twenty-pound note. The message simply said 'Go and have a drink on me'. 'Righhhttttt' Eric thought now slightly concerned about having invited Catherine into his home in the first place and bizarrely finding himself working out how many pints you could purchase with twenty quid (five pints and just enough left for a packet of salt and vinegar McCoys was the answer <u>or</u> I daresay one bottle of Peroni and a pot of jellied eels if you lived in Londinium).

This particular date had been proof to Eric that the term 'never judge a book by its cover' could just as easily be used to suggest someone turning out a lot worse than they first appeared on their profile than of its more traditional usage to describe the opposite outcome.

Despite Catherine's idiosyncrasies and weird traits, Eric still slipped her his length though; well he hadn't had it in ages and just wanted to keep his oar in so to speak. However, he obviously didn't want to see Catherine again, making sure to let her down VERY gently by text message after she'd returned home. Eric was keener than usual to ensure that he locked all doors and windows to his house thereafter.

Chapter Ninety-Four

World Cup Willy

As mentioned previously, Eric was not the type to ever chat-up a girl whilst on a night out with friends. However, that hadn't stopped the softer sex from trying their luck with Eric on occasions. Another example of this was back in 2002, just before Eric and Emma mark I got together and during the World Cup 2002 in Japan and South Korea.

Eric and his friends were enjoying their evening, frequenting the usual drinking holes and ending up on the top floor of one of the only two popular clubs in town. The music wasn't Eric's cup of tea at all; mostly RnB but it was always much quieter (both in terms of sound and clientele) usually seats to be had and there would still be a spattering of pussy on show (not in the literal sense). At the time, Eric was still very much playing catch-up, not long having gotten over Di and always remained hopeful that a girl would see him and want a piece of his ass. It was a very rare occurrence but it appeared that on that particular night, there was a girl who was confident enough to approach him.

It was getting towards the end of the evening and so both she and Eric were pretty intoxicated. Her name was Cheryl and considering she'd been the one to chat him up, Eric was actually pleased to note that she was, in fact, a good-looking girl.

Eric was living with his parents at the time and so it seemed rather brash and indeed rash of him to invite Cheryl back to 'his'. Eric's blood-alcohol levels must really have been egging him on as despite his parents being very liberal and accommodating, that didn't usually stretch to taking random girls home with him after nights out.

Still, this is exactly what Eric did and Cheryl was obviously game. Getting into Eric's bed, which was now an oversized double (and no longer a bunk bed) Eric got to work with her under the duvet remembering that they both had to be quiet given Eric's mum, dad and brother were sleeping nearby. Eric managed penetration but it was very slow and almost robotic in style, worried that he was going to cause a squeak or bang from the bed's rhythmical movement.

Next morning and Eric knew he had to get Cheryl out of the house before the others awoke. It was a Sunday morning around 7:00 a.m. and despite being absolutely knackered, the pair of them had to pull themselves out of bed.

Another reason for their early rise was that Eric was very keen to catch England's first group match at the World Cup, which was against Sweden (finished 1-1 if you're interested). Japan was some eight-hours ahead (probably still is thinking about it) and so the kick-off times were slightly impractical for those in the West.

Despite the time of the year, it was still pretty cold at that early hour and as Cheryl was dressed only in a very revealing handkerchief-sized dress, with her boobs almost falling out; Eric did the honourable thing and lent her one of his jackets. The jacket also helped to make it less obvious to the general massif that she'd been sleeping around like a common tart, whilst navigating her way home.

Having spied Eric's DVD collection on her way out, she'd also managed to get away with his copy of the animated version of The Lord of the Rings (6.2/10 IMDb) the first Peter Jackson epic (The Fellowship of the Ring 8.8/10 IMDb) having recently been released to enormous acclaim and so Mr Tolkien was more popular than ever it seemed.

Well, when I say Eric lent the jacket and DVD, it soon appeared that he'd actually donated them to Cheryl as he never saw her or them again (so if you're reading this Cheryl, Eric wants his stuff back).

Chapter Ninety-Five

I Bet She Pisses Standing Up

It was fair to say that Eric had met a rather varied cross-section of women over the years, from all ages, shapes and sizes. There were, of course, those that were more attractive than others but Eric remembered a particular woman that had turned out to be so detached from her profile photos that Eric had been physically (sick) alarmed when she turned up.

We were back at The Duck Pond Inn (where else?) and Eric had gotten there early as usual to whet his whistle. It was a very busy evening, one of the busiest he could ever remember there and he'd been lucky to find a seat in the bar opposite the main dining area. It wasn't his usual speck but the beer-barrel style seats would suffice. Eric was keeping himself occupied with his mobile phone and looking up to see if she'd arrived, he was sure there must have been a gargantuan mistake.

Eric could have sworn that the Denise he'd seen photos of on the dating site depicted a woman that he was very much looking forward to playing naked leapfrog with. Instead, she looked like a 1970s male comedian in drag and walked towards him as butch as Butch Cassidy taking Butch (from Tom and Jerry) for a walk to Pat Butcher's house next door to the local butcher.

Eric had hit rock-bottom, conscious that the hoards of people around them would be (correctly) believing he had actually chosen to meet her; Eric could do so much better than this. I mean, she looked more manly than him. However, as he was far too polite and as it appeared she knew all the staff very well, then Eric couldn't bring himself to leave. You could say it was a rather uncomfortable situation he found himself in (again).

Despite driving, Eric suddenly had an insatiable desire to drink; it could only have been the embarrassment of being on a date with the she-man but either way, something was about to turn rather weird. Eric had heard of beer-goggles before but never on this level. He must have consumed more than he'd thought as come closing time, Eric was happy to go back with Denise to her neck of the woods (leaving his car) and continue revelling and drinking some more.

By the time they arrived at hers and got into bed (yes he got into bed with her) after some further alcoholic refreshments, Eric was feeling frisky and as the lights were already out, he can only conjecture that he may have slipped her his length.

The next morning and Eric felt ashamed of himself for letting his standards puncture through the barrel's bottom and to the ground underneath it, witnessing her looking even more unsightly without her make-up on. She now looked like someone called Dave.

However, despite the realisation, Eric would once more have to rely on his top-drawer acting skills; making out he was happy to see her again, which he needed to maintain until she gave him a lift back to his car some ten-miles away. There was, in reality, more chance of the moon falling to earth and people realising it was actually made of cheese than for a second meet-up (like in Wallace and Gromit's 'A Grand Day Out' (7.8/10 IMDb)).

To be fair she did have amazing boobs (once he'd got his hands on them) and gave a half-decent blowjob but that still didn't make up for the fact that she had all the femininity of Jonah Lomu at the peak of his rugby career. For some reason, Eric decided to remain stoically silent about this particular episode to his mates, telling them he'd had a quiet night in instead. Funny that.

Chapter Ninety-Six

To All the Girls Eric Loved Before

We're now pretty much bang up to date with Eric. It's now 2019 but not yet flying around in cars as portrayed in the 1982 film Blade Runner (8.1/10 IMDb). Eric actually turned 42 today although he isn't celebrating the fact; he rarely did with his birthdays. Things were still a little barren and there seemed no realistic way for Eric meeting someone new. After last seeing Kelly some five-months ago, it seems Eric had finally lost his enthusiasm for online dating; needing a break from it all and besides; his priority was now finding a new job and trying to reintegrate somewhere back in society.

Although he doesn't feel old at all, Eric couldn't help feeling like he'd missed the boat somehow and now, similar to his search for employment, knew it was rather unlikely that a girl would be knocking on his door anytime soon.

The truth was that nobody out there really knew Eric existed as he led quite a reclusive life, leaving his house rarely and the most social interaction (he still insists he doesn't have Aspergers) with those in his local 7-11 when popping in for fags or a 4-pint plastic receptacle of milk (usually a green-top semi-skimmed). Eric still felt he had a great deal to offer a girl from a personal perspective but for the moment at least, he knew his overall position was not conducive to attracting them.

During his love affair with online dating, Eric would frequently picture himself with a partner, like many of his friends, who met a girl, got married, had kids and were looking down the barrel of their crystal wedding anniversary (that's 15 years). Would Eric have traded in his last two-decades of dating escapades and relationships for one girl who he could actually get along with and feel a genuine and unconditional love for? Probably; but then perhaps he <u>had</u> found the one or ones and didn't realise it; too critical or fussy to see past what was really important.

How much had his suspicious mind prevented what could have been? Was he ultimately unwilling to commit to one girl and was marriage really something to aspire to? There were indeed a lot of questions buzzing around in his overactive brain. Whatever the plan had been twenty years ago, however, he now felt it was unrealistic to think there could be a Utopian life and a happy-ever-after ending like in a Disney cartoon.

One thing that Eric had been surprised at, before finding himself in the thick of it, was hearing how some couples had re-married their partners after a break-up and in some cases even following a rather acrimonious divorce. He became less surprised at such occurrences over time though after his countless dates and own relatively short to mid-term relationships. He understood how half the battle of finding a partner you could genuinely enjoy sharing your life with was ensuring that there was a natural connection.

It was certainly the case with Eric that he'd reconsidered his previous girlfriends after future opportunities had fallen way short of the mark. On those occasions, a date or a relationship had revealed more about his past romances than anything else.

The main part of the enjoyment Eric got from online dating was the mystery involved in meeting new girls. Meeting for a first date had always taken Eric out of his comfort zone despite his lengthy experience. Yes, he would only feel genuinely nervous around an hour before a date, en route to the rendezvous spot or sitting there in situ waiting for her to arrive. Being nervous and having his adrenaline pumping made him feel alive though. His nerves would always dissipate once having met the girl and so despite knowing this was the case, Eric had never fathomed out why he would be nervous the next time and the time after that.

It is impossible to know if, when and where Eric will find someone special enough to hang up his dating boots for good. He remembered seeing much older women on the dating merry-go-round over the years (some of the randy old sods having perused and even winked at Eric despite having a 35-year lead on him). It underlined that even in the twilight of their lives, some were still searching to fill a void, for as long as that would turn out to last.

To Eric, it was a stark reminder that we each only have a relatively short number of years on this rock and therefore choosing to share it with someone you could at least tolerate was imperative, although in the case of these olduns, it was likely that they'd simply outlived their previous partners.

Eric had a sudden thought of himself online at 70 still searching for a plus-one, his main profile pic of him donned in a flat cap and two-tone cardigan (well he surely couldn't get away with his Boyzone effort for another 30 years). He'd already seen a future incarnation of himself on FaceApp recently and the prospect really wasn't a good one for Eric.

There was no other option; he'd have to start redoubling his efforts now, whilst he still had his looks and some decent attributes left to help attract a half-decent specimen of the female form. Eric reached for his wallet and withdrew his debit card, deciding to give online-dating one last chance… like the very last chance… no more after this… full stop no erasies.

THE END

Answers to Eric's Dating Quiz

(although methinks you've probably worked out the answers already)

1. Yes – Carry on watching
2. Yes – Foot down
3. No – Confident meeting parents
4. Yes – Let him watch the football
5. Yes – Tidy up before bedtime
6. Yes – Tell him you're not feeling too great
7. Yes – Say come on slowcoach
8. No – Star Wars (obviously)
9. No – Allow someone else to pop in front at the till
10. No – Say Nooooooo! to a new kitten

If you're a heterosexual cisgender woman with cracking boobs, meet all of Eric's detailed criteria and prerequisites and score 10/10 in his quiz; then he's asked me to ask you to get in touch with him. After all; you could be the one he's been waiting for all his life… who knows; you might even like him… or more realistically find yourself within the pages of the next volume of his Love Chronicles… to be released in 2039.

REALLY THE END!

Available worldwide from

Amazon

---

www.mtp.agency

www.facebook.com/mtp.agency

@mtp_agency

Printed in Great Britain
by Amazon

42520926R00169